TOGETHER AGAIN

The first time they made love was in the front seat of a car. They were teenagers then, both knowing nothing of love except that they loved each other, both exploring the path of passion for the very first time.

They were older now, and so much wiser in the ways of the world. They knew all about the pleasures of the flesh, just as they knew the pain of betrayal. They knew how cruel the world was, and what it took to survive in it, just as they knew what damage they could do to each other's exquisitely arranged lives if they yielded to desire.

Then they were in each other's arms again, and it was just as it had been before . . . except that it wasn't . . . except that it was so dazzlingly and dangerously different. . . .

Only You

Only You

Cynthia Victor

AN ONYX BOOK

ONYX
Published by the Penguin Group
Penguin Books USA Inc., 375 Hudson Street,
New York, New York 10014, U.S.A.
Penguin Books Ltd, 27 Wrights Lane,
London W8 5TZ, England
Penguin Books Australia Ltd, Ringwood,
Victoria, Australia
Penguin Books Canada Ltd, 10 Alcorn Avenue,
Toronto, Ontario, Canada M4V 3B2
Penguin Books (N.Z.) Ltd, 182–190 Wairau Road,
Auckland 10, New Zealand

Penguin Books Ltd, Registered Offices:
Harmondsworth, Middlesex, England

Published by Onyx, an imprint of Dutton Signet,
a division of Penguin Books USA Inc.
Previously published in a Viking edition.

First Onyx Printing, August, 1995
10 9 8 7 6 5 4 3 2 1

PUBLISHER'S NOTE
This is a work of fiction. Names, characters, places, and incidents either are the product
of the author's imagination or are used fictitiously, and any resemblance to actual persons, living or dead, events, or locales is entirely coincidental.

BOOKS ARE AVAILABLE AT QUANTITY DISCOUNTS WHEN USED TO PROMOTE PRODUCTS OR SER-
VICES. FOR INFORMATION PLEASE WRITE TO PREMIUM MARKETING DIVISION, PENGUIN BOOKS
USA INC., 375 HUDSON STREET, NEW YORK, NY 10014.

If you purchased this book without a cover you should be aware that this book is stolen
property. It was reported as "unsold and destroyed" to the publisher and neither the author nor the publisher has received any payment for this "stripped book."

For
Carole and Richard Baron
and Mark Steckel

With love and appreciation

ACKNOWLEDGMENTS

For their invaluable help and encouragement, a heartfelt thank-you to the following people: Harriet Astor, Carolyn Clarke, Michael Connolly, M.D., Harry Fried, M.D., Stacy Higgins, Jean Katz, Dale Mandelman, Susanna Margolis, Susan Moldow, Harriet Rattner, Richard Reinstein, Diana Revson, David Richenthal, Robert Riger, Ellen Seely, Myra Shapiro, Joph Steckel, M.D., Tom Teicholz, and the members of the NYPD, who were so generous with their time.

As always, warm appreciation goes to Meg Ruley, Stephanie Laidman, and Jane Berkey for their efforts and advice, as well as to Pamela Dorman for her meticulous and insightful editing.

Special thanks go to Susan Ginsburg, whose extraordinary help continues to go well beyond the call of friendship.

Prologue

Only semiconscious, the young woman on the stretcher moaned slightly beneath her oxygen mask as the ambulance lurched to an abrupt halt in front of Mercy Hospital. Blood soaked her clothes, her face, her hair. The driver leapt out, racing around back to open the van's rear doors. Two other paramedics knelt inside, laboring over their patient. All three men reached together to slide her out, the stretcher's metal legs opening automatically to form a gurney.

Half a dozen police cars pulled up nearby, tires screeching, their wailing sirens piercing the night. Double doors leading to the emergency room swung open as the paramedics wheeled the gurney up the entrance ramp as fast as they dared. Police swarmed around them, calling out to one another, yelling into walkie-talkies.

Doctors and nurses came running as the ambulance driver started shouting: "We've got a thirty-six-year-old woman shot twice in the abdomen. Found her with blood pressure eighty palp, heart rate of one-ten. Got a large-bore IV in her, her blood pressure's now up to a hundred over sixty, heart rate's still one-ten."

They swung the gurney around into an area set up for incoming emergencies, as the residents on the trauma team went to work. One hastily cut off the woman's bloodied clothes, tearing the soaked garments away from her body. Another leaned over her, monitoring her labored breathing.

Jeffrey Hart, the chief resident, was already examining her, assessing the damage, making decisions.

"Let's get the blood cooking," he called out, his manner calm, but tension evident in his voice. "Let's send off a CBC, lytes, coags, type and cross, a profile. She's going to the OR, so we want to prep her."

The woman on the stretcher had been silently watching the controlled chaos surrounding her. Now, as if it were all too much, she closed her eyes.

"Nurse," Hart went on, "let's get a Foley in her, and we need another sixteen-gauge IV with lactated Ringer's."

"Right," one of the nurses responded.

"Is Dameroff out of surgery yet?"

Another nurse answered. "He's just finishing his last case. Lucy's calling upstairs."

Hart nodded grimly. "I hope he's ready. She's coming right now. Let's *move*, everybody!"

On the hospital's second floor, Dr. Benjamin Dameroff stood at the sink, following the procedure for scrubbing before surgery. Having just completed an operation, he had discarded his robe and gloves, but was still wearing a surgical cap and mask. Unwrapping a presoaped scrubbing brush, he stepped on the foot pedal to release a stream of water into the sink. He began scrubbing his hands with the harsh brush, soaping in between his fingers, under his nails, moving the brush along the backs and fronts of his hands for several minutes before going on to his arms.

As he washed, he took several deep breaths. This last operation had gone on for three hours and, coming at the end of a long day, had exhausted him. Now a multiple-gunshot wound was on the way up. But, actually, this was nothing; back during internship and residency, he'd regularly worked thirty-six hours straight, and he'd managed fine. Come on, Dameroff, he admonished himself wryly, don't get soft yet.

Finishing, he turned away from the sink, holding his forearms up so the water would drip down, away from his now-sterile hands. He strode quickly to Operating Room Four, where the scrub nurse handed him a towel. Drying his hands, he tossed the towel in a bin, then turned so she could slip a gown on him. As the nurse began helping him put rubber gloves on, he looked over and saw that the patient was already there. She was still awake. The anesthesiologist was leaning down over the operating table, talking.

". . . in the recovery room," he was saying as Ben came up behind him.

The other doctor moved out of the way, and Ben drew closer. Green sheets lay draped over the woman, but they were already stained red from her still-bleeding wounds. Someone had sponged off her face, and her skin was pale in the harsh glare of the operating room's lights. Eyes closed, she lay still as the anesthesiologist prepared to put her to sleep. Coming around, Ben looked directly at her face.

Oh, no. He took a sharp step back as if he'd been smacked. *No, not this, please, no.*

This couldn't be happening. She couldn't be here, bleeding to death right in front of him.

He couldn't operate on her. Someone else would have to do it.

He turned away, his hands clenched. But of course there was no time to get anyone else. He would have to be the one.

His breath was coming in short bursts. He'd never wanted to see her again, much less be responsible for her life. He turned back to look at her, momentarily paralyzed.

As if she felt his gaze, the woman's eyelids fluttered open. Weakened by loss of blood, beginning to receive the anesthesia that would render her unconscious, she nonetheless took one look at his face, half-hidden behind a mask, and a shock of recognition flashed in her eyes. There was something else, another expression, but he couldn't make out what it was.

Her voice was barely audible as her eyes began to close again, the anesthesia taking over.

"Oh, God," she whispered, *"it's you."*

1966

1

Brainqueer, Mr. and Mrs. Maxwell Smart.

Carlin heard the malicious whispers as she stood in front of the third-grade class. She knew they were directed at her and Ben Dameroff. As usual, she and Ben were two of the three finalists in the weekly spelling bee, and the rest of the kids hated them for it. Not that she cared. Her classmates had begun teasing them in first grade, when she and Ben both started devouring books while everyone else was still groping with the alphabet.

"Foreigner. F-O-R-E-I-G-N-E-R." Carlin stared straight ahead as she spelled out the word. She wasn't about to give the class the satisfaction of looking hurt.

She knew she was smart, although she paid as little attention to school as she possibly could. She never studied, never memorized a spelling list, never practiced her times tables out loud, as Miss Gordon had urged them all to do. None of this seemed to stop her from doing well in class, but it drove her teachers crazy. She has so much *potential*, they would say every parents' day. If only she'd *apply* herself. Ben was different—he practically memorized the encyclopedia.

She sneaked a look at him as he spelled out the word "chemistry." He looked straight at Miss Gordon, not seeming to notice anyone else was even there.

Ben Dameroff wasn't just a classmate. He was her best friend's brother. Natasha Dameroff, just a year younger than Ben and Carlin, had been Carlin's constant companion since, well, forever. The Dameroffs and the Squires lived down the hall from one another in the Riverview project, and Carlin spent almost as much time at Natasha's apartment as she did at home. But if she loved Natasha like a sister, Ben drove her crazy. Not that he was mean to her. In fact, he rarely paid any attention to her at all. Only when other kids ganged up on both of them did they admit they had a bond. But even then, he made Carlin furious. She wanted to lash back at them, to get even. Ben barely seemed to be bothered.

That was the part that drove her nuts. He was so sure of himself, so prepared for everything, so self-possessed. The teachers loved him, Natasha adored him, his mother lived for him. Carlin couldn't help herself; whenever she found the chance, she felt compelled to interfere with his perfection just a little bit.

Of course, in a way it was lucky Ben Dameroff was in her class. Otherwise she would be the only object of her classmates' scorn. And really, it wasn't fair, all their teasing. Carlin got by on pure instinct, and she knew it. Ben was the one who combined lucky brain cells with discipline. So, when it was just between the two of them, there was no contest. Ben was always the winner. Not that this bothered Carlin. Without Ben one step ahead of her, keeping the light of her accomplishments slightly dimmed, it was likely that no one in their class would talk to her at all.

"The word is 'counterfeit.'" Miss Gordon addressed herself to Steven Marks, the only other boy left in the spelling bee. Carlin felt some satisfaction as he tripped over the word. Steven had been bragging at lunchtime that he was going to win this week, had been giving Miss Gordon little gifts, as if she'd choose easier words for him if she wore his stupid ten-cent barrette in her hair. It serves him right, Carlin thought, as Steven slunk back to his seat.

She glanced over at Ben, but his attention seemed to be caught by the trees outside the window. As far as she could tell, he was unaware that anyone else was even in the room with him.

As Ben spelled "counterfeit" correctly, Carlin made a face at him. She could tell he noticed it, but his only reaction was one dismissively raised eyebrow.

"Ben, Carlin, it seems to be up to you."

Miss Gordon's cheerful voice took no account of Freddy Maurer's "As usual," sneeringly whispered from the back of the room.

"The word is 'pigeon.' " Miss Gordon turned her attention to Carlin.

Carlin hesitated. Was there a "d" in it? She could swear she remembered a "d" but she hadn't studied the word list, so there was no way to be sure.

"P-I-D-G-E-O-N," she finally spelled out loud.

"Sorry, dear," Miss Gordon said, turning to Ben with an expectant look.

"P-I-G-E-O-N," he spelled correctly, not lowering himself to gloat as Carlin watched Miss Gordon shake his hand in congratulations.

"Well, that was wonderful, you two," Miss Gordon complimented both Ben and Carlin as they returned to their seats.

"You'd think they were the smartest kids in the whole world instead of just the whole school," a boy in the third row jeered loudly.

"Now, class," Miss Gordon asserted brightly, "you should be pleased to have classmates who do such a fine job."

Ben and Carlin caught each other's eye at these words. For once their annoyance was mutual.

"How did you know 'pigeon'?" Carlin demanded as she and Ben stood with Natasha in front of the schoolyard at the end of the day. "You weren't even in school when we went over the spelling words."

"I bothered to study," Ben responded snidely. Carlin noticed his quick look at his sister to see if Natasha had caught the reference to his absence from school the previous Tuesday.

Natasha betrayed nothing, but Carlin was sure her friend must have caught on. Everyone in the neighborhood knew about how Kit Darneroff favored her son. It was *Ben this* and *Ben that* all the time. Carlin had never seen Natasha's mother be mean to her or anything, but when it came to stuff that was really fun, it was always Kit and her beloved Ben. Carlin's father had run into them on Tuesday as Kit and Ben were getting into the car, on the way to Albany—which was nearly an hour away, for goodness' sake—where movies played all afternoon. Carlin guessed that Natasha couldn't have cared less about sitting through *Alfie,* but she had no doubt that Natasha hadn't even been invited to go along.

Natasha never seemed to hold it against her mother, and she idolized her big brother, but Carlin knew it had to bother her. It was just so unfair. Well, she *should* mind, Carlin decided, unable to give up the opportunity to goad Ben.

"So how many cavities did you have?" she demanded, knowing that his mother had claimed a dentist appointment for Ben to get him out of class.

He aimed a furious look at Carlin, but he couldn't come up with any answer that would keep his little sister from getting hurt.

"I don't even know what you're talking about," he finally said, moving several steps ahead of the two girls.

Carlin knew she was being cruel, but she couldn't stop herself. "You know . . . Tuesday, when your mother took you to the dentist. What did he do to you that took all day long? It must have been something huge."

"The only thing huge is your ugly face," Ben retorted, getting into the spirit of things.

"It beats your big ugly feet," said Carlin, laughing.

Natasha covered her ears as her two favorite people in the world started fighting in earnest. She understood that both of them were trying in some silly way to protect her. Too bad she wasn't smart like Ben or brave like Carlin. Maybe if she were either one, her mother would like her better and she wouldn't need so much protecting.

But she couldn't stand it when the two of them screamed at each other as they did practically every minute of every day. "Please stop fighting," she begged, on the verge of tears.

Immediately, Carlin stopped taunting Ben. The last thing she wanted to do was to torture Natasha. But fighting with Ben was so much fun. Besides, she wasn't ready to let Ben off the hook quite this easily. She just needed some way to get to him that didn't also get to Natasha.

As the three of them passed the five-and-ten right near Riverview, Carlin thought of the perfect way to get under his skin.

"You know, Ben, there's a whole lot of new trucks at Dalrymple's," she said suggestively, knowing full well how much he loved the miniature foreign cars the store carried. They cost way too much for him to even imagine buying one.

"So what?" Ben tossed off. But he instantly sensed she had plans for him.

"You could just take one," she whispered in his ear, aware that he would never in a million years consider doing such a thing.

"You're crazy," he said, shrugging her off, as she was sure he would.

"At least I'm not chicken," she snapped.

"I'm not chicken," he replied, his voice adamant. "I'm just not an idiot like you!"

"If you're really not scared to do it, you'll prove it." Her voice was filled with mischief as she uttered the magic words. "Go on, I dare you."

Ben felt his face reddening. Carlin Squire infuriated him. There was no way he would do something so moronic. Stealing was dangerous and stupid and wrong. He knew he should just keep walking, go on home and ignore her for the rest of the day. No, for the rest of his life. But the words hung in the air. *I dare you.* In their lifelong struggle, those three words had always been their ultimate weapon.

"I'll do it because I *want* to, not because you *told* me to," he snapped as he walked into Dalrymple's.

His fury at Carlin was replaced by guilt as he stood in the doorway of the store, watching Jacob Dalrymple sweeping up the area behind the cash register. He felt as if he were moving in slow motion when he finally made his way toward the back, where the trucks and cars were assembled in a huge floor display. Peering one final time over his shoulder to see if Mr. Dalrymple were watching, Ben put out his hand and pulled one of the vehicles out of the pile, pushing it down into his pocket without even checking to see what it was.

It was only when he emerged a couple of minutes later and looked down at the bright red miniature Mercedes truck in his right hand that he acknowledged the wicked pleasure of what he had done. But it was wrong. I'll never do that again, he vowed to Mr. Dalrymple silently.

Still, his shame in no way interfered with the satisfaction of seeing Carlin work hard at looking unimpressed. Natasha observed them with dread. She knew that within seconds Carlin and Ben would start up with each other all over again.

"Come on, Carlin," she urged before her friend could find something mean to say in the face of Ben's triumph. "Come on over and play." Natasha pulled Carlin toward the walkway leading to the project's entrance, knowing that Ben would stay downstairs for an hour of basketball with some of the neighborhood kids.

"I can't today," Carlin answered, finally taking her eyes off Ben's victorious face. "My dad's taking me to the zoo. But I'll go upstairs with you."

Ben looked doubtful as the girls walked into the building. Carlin's father had been out of work for a few weeks, and it seemed as if he was supposed to take Carlin somewhere every day. So far, he hadn't come through even once.

Not that I care if Carlin feels bad, he thought as he headed toward the playground. It was just that J. T. Squire seemed like pretty much of a jerk. The Squires and the Dameroffs were big friends. Practically every weekend they went bowling or out to a Chinese restaurant. But Ben could never figure out why his parents bothered. J.T. was always telling long, braggy stories, sporting fancy multicolored ties and new wing-tip shoes. But, as far as Ben could tell, he never kept a job more than a few months. And he never kept his promises to his daughter.

Ben was certain that when he got home after basketball, Carlin would be in his living room playing Sorry or some other stupid game with Natasha. He felt sad for Carlin for a few seconds, before he remembered how much he hated her.

"I'm home," Carlin yelled as she walked through the door to her apartment. As usual, the pullout couch she slept on each night in the living room was folded up, the blankets put away, and everything was in perfect order. Lillian had to manage on very little money, but she worked hard to keep her apartment neat and attractive.

"Hi, baby," her mother's voice answered invitingly from the kitchen. "Come inside. I've got cocoa and chocolate cookies that are still warm."

Carlin walked into the kitchen without even taking off her coat.

"Goody," she said, taking a cookie from the cooling rack on the Formica table and blowing on it before biting in. "But I don't have much time. The zoo closes at five-thirty, so Daddy and I only have a couple of hours. There's this new baby zebra that was born two weeks ago, and they put it out every afternoon around four, so we have to hurry up." Carlin stopped her excited monologue long enough to take a sip of cocoa. As she put the cup down, she noticed her mother's expression.

"What's the matter?" Carlin asked, her voice muffled by the large piece of cookie she was in the process of biting off.

Before her mother had a chance to answer, her father stepped into the room. Carlin took in his outfit at a glance: his best gray wool pants and navy blazer, set off by a red and gray striped silk tie knotted carefully at his neck. She could tell he had just shaved, could smell Old Spice as he made his way toward her.

"I'll see you two fabulous girls when I get back," he said expansively as he put his arm through the sleeve of his camel hair coat.

"What do you mean, Daddy?" Carlin asked, putting the cookie down and pushing her cup of cocoa away from her. "We're going to the zoo, both of us. And Mommy can come, too, if she wants."

There was a hint of desperation in her voice as she kept going. Maybe if she said just the right words, she could keep him from doing whatever it was he was doing instead of what he had promised just that morning.

"Really, Mommy, you come with us. We'll have a great time. You'll see." She looked beseechingly at both her parents, but only her mother looked back at her. Her father was already on his way out the door.

"See you later, sweetheart," he said, blowing Carlin a kiss and waving to his wife.

Carlin sat quietly as the door slammed behind him. She saw the stricken look on Lillian's face, but she didn't say anything; she didn't want to make her mother feel any worse.

It was always Lillian Squire who was apologizing for her husband's imperfections.

Her mother sat down beside her and handed Carlin another cookie. "Daddy had to go somewhere with some other machinist friends. You know, Bob and Tim from his last shop. They may have a job lead for him."

Carlin didn't have to tell her mother how lame that sounded. She could tell Lillian already knew that. Her mother rose and walked back toward the sink, where she had been washing three large potatoes. She put one of them back into the refrigerator before placing the others in the oven.

"After all," she said as if she were having an angry conversation with herself, "we're so short of cash right now. It would be nice if he stayed home more often so we could save a little something."

Carlin felt unexpectedly irritated at her mother's words. I bet she didn't dare say that to Daddy, she thought to herself. In fact, I bet she spends the rest of the day working on the sweater she's making him for Christmas.

Carlin watched as her mother walked out to the living room, sitting down in the brown wing chair and reaching over to the basket at her feet. Sure enough, she picked up a mass of brightly colored yarn and began to knit. Every year her mother made something really special for J.T. This year's project was a wool turtleneck in shades of red and green and white, with reindeer and sleds knit right in. She had already been working on it for a month and a half.

Carlin couldn't stand it. "I'm going over to Natasha's," she said.

If Lillian noticed her daughter's annoyance, she wasn't letting on. "Make sure you leave time for homework" was her only comment as Carlin closed the door behind her.

1969

2

Lillian Squire finished lacing up her red and black bowling shoes. Leaning back in the bowling alley's hard plastic chair, she caught sight of her husband exchanging a laugh with Kit Dameroff, the two of them making selections from the rows of bowling balls in a far corner. The sound of their laughter carried across the harshly lit, noisy room. Lillian watched her husband suddenly grab Kit around the waist and waltz her in a large circle, the two of them grinning at their own silliness.

Kit's husband, Leonard Dameroff, still in the process of changing his shoes, was seated next to Lillian. He, too, had looked up just in time to see his wife dancing gaily amidst the local bowlers. As he straightened up in his chair, he gave a slight smile.

"Those two should be married to each other instead of to us," he said.

That night, as usual, it would be J.T. and Kit who were the fun ones, the life of the party. It had been that way ever since the Dameroffs and the Squires had begun going out together, soon after Leonard and Kit had moved to Westerfield.

With the two couples living down the hall from one another, the wives had quickly struck up a friendly acquaintance, and it wasn't long before they agreed to a night out with their husbands. Almost immediately, they had settled into a comfortable pattern of getting together every few Saturday nights. After Ben and Carlin were born, the couples valued their rare nights out even more, although Lillian and Leonard often wound up engrossed in a serious discussion, while J.T. and Kit traded silly jokes all evening long.

Lillian and Leonard were the solid, dependable ones, the ones who planned the evenings and made sure the reservations were arranged, the check paid. J.T. and Kit provided the excitement and the laughter, suggesting jaunts to different towns, even making their monthly bowling night a bit of a party with their teasing and sparkle. They all knew the flirting between Kit and J.T. was nothing more than harmless fun. But every now and then Lillian did feel a bit drab next to the beautiful Kit.

"Ready to beat their pants off, Lil?" J.T. Squire bounded up the two steps to the lanes where Lillian was readying the score sheet. He gave his wife a broad smile. "I'm feeling hot, baby. They can't win."

Lillian smiled back. J.T. looked especially handsome tonight, she thought, his neatly pressed turquoise bowling shirt contrasting with the shining black of his hair. She always worked extra hard at ironing that shirt so it was just right. She knew how important it was to J.T. that he look good when he bowled. He honestly believed his game suffered if he felt even a little sloppy. In fact, he believed that everything in his life was affected by the way he looked, and the truth was she worked extra hard on all his ironing and laundry. But that, she always told herself, was the price of having such an attractive husband.

Kit Dameroff came to stand next to her husband, cradling a bowling ball with both hands. "Come on, Leonard, we're not going to take that," she protested good-naturedly. "Let's show them how to do it."

She crossed over to take position and concentrated on the bowling pins at the far end of the lane, furrowing her brow as she prepared to release the ball. Tight pink pants and a bright floral patterned blouse knotted under her navel clearly displayed her slender figure. Her fiery red hair was gathered back in a high ponytail and she pursed her brightly lipsticked mouth in concentration. Lillian Squire looked down at her own gray skirt and white cotton blouse, neatly tucked in. She glanced over and saw that Leonard Dameroff was also watching Kit, his love for his wife evident in his eyes.

Kit took three quick steps forward and let the ball fly. She stood in rapt attention, hands clasped, as it hurtled along the lane, the loud rumbling culminating in the familiar crash of pins going down. As the last two pins teetered uncertainly and then went over, Kit flung her arms out in triumph, jumping up and down. Leonard stood, applauding. Disgustedly, J.T. smacked the table where he sat keeping score.

"Strike!" Kit grinned at her husband. "That's the way to start a game, right, honey?"

He smiled back. "Attagirl. Keep it up."

Kit bowled another frame, then returned to join the others. She put an arm around Leonard and ruffled his hair, giving him a bright smile. "Not bad, huh, for such an uncoordinated fumbler?"

Leonard looked at her and laughed. "Kit, the last thing you need is false modesty. Your game just keeps getting better and better."

Kit sat back, pleased that she had gotten even a mild laugh out of her husband. He did enjoy their bowling nights with the Squires, she knew that, and his mood seemed less heavy than usual when they were here.

J.T. rejoined them after taking his turn, obviously annoyed with himself for having knocked down just five pins. Leonard fared only slightly better.

"It's up to you, now, Lil," J.T. said to his wife. "Don't let the Squire name down."

Lillian was a surprisingly good bowler, but her nervousness showed as she got up. "I'll do my best, J.T."

They watched in silence as Lillian knocked over seven pins.

"Stay loose, and you'll take the rest down," J.T. called out to her. Frowning, she waited for the ball to be returned.

"Can I get you boys a beer?" Kit turned to the two men.

"Ah," said J.T. wistfully, "I've already got a wife who bowls like a champ and here's another woman to bring me a beer. If only a guy could have two wives, eh, Leonard? That's what every man needs."

Kit's eyes immediately went to her husband. She saw him stiffen slightly. Quickly, she spoke again, her tone playful. "A thousand wives wouldn't be enough for you, J.T. Now what about those beers? The offer isn't good for much longer."

"Okay, thanks, Kit." J.T. pulled his wallet and gave her a ten-dollar bill. "Bring something to eat, too, while you're at it. Pretzels or something."

"Be right back." She winked at Leonard. "Don't let them cheat while I'm gone, sweetie."

Kit made her way to the concession stand, a rueful smile on her face. Of all the things J.T. could have said . . . There was no way he could know about Leonard's family. She and Leonard had told no one in Westerfield.

No, no one in this town knew the truth about Leonard's father, Ed Dameroff. Of course, they knew about his stores; hundreds of thousands of people in this and twelve other states knew about Ed's, the chain of gourmet food stores. After emigrating from Russia to America in the 1920s, Yankel Dameroff had changed his name to Ed and opened a small local deli in Albany. In a little less than ten years, he had made enough money to move his business to one of the city's better neighborhoods. That store became known for its selection of unusual foods, a smattering of exotic and delicious taste treats that made it even more worthwhile for shoppers to stop off for a half pound of smoked salmon or pickled herring. The customers loved throwing in a jar of this or a box of that and Ed found the gourmet section of his store increasingly profitable.

When he finally decided the time was right to expand to a second store, he eliminated many of the food staples that he used to carry and concentrated on the high-end items, the jars of caviar, the imported biscuits and jams, the special mustards, along with his famous smoked whitefish and sable. Over the next decade, he continued his expansion, keeping the stores relatively small, but adding more and more locations. The idea behind each was the same, but they all had their idiosyncrasies, each one reflecting something of the individual store manager's personality. When Kit first met Leonard in 1955, there were over fifteen Ed's in the Northeast. By now, she supposed, there must be more than twice that. Things had changed, though; now all the stores were run in exactly the same way, huge spaces crammed with an astounding array of merchandise boasting sky-high price tags. The character seemed to be gone from the stores. But whatever the formula had become, it worked.

Not that Kit was privy to the operations of the Ed's empire

anymore. The name couldn't even be mentioned in their house.

How different from when Leonard had been working for his father. Kit remembered how Leonard had idolized Ed, a good-looking, heavyset man with a loud voice and a powerful temper. Leonard wanted so much to please him, had struggled so hard to do a good job at being indispensable in running the rapidly growing business. Leonard had skipped college so he could start learning the business right away, figuring the hands-on experience would be better than any college degree. He worked diligently—long, hard days—to find ways to make the stores better, cleaner, more inviting.

His dedication to the stores was the reason Kit had met Leonard in the first place. Although he spent most of his time in the Albany store, when a new Ed's opened in Rochester, he began traveling there regularly to help the manager get it up and running. Setting out on the drive at the end of the work-day, he would usually stop in Utica to eat dinner and spend the night at the Pinelake Motel—where Kit worked as a chambermaid.

At first, she barely noticed Leonard. She was far too absorbed in her own problems to pay any attention to the people passing through the motel. Her parents had died within six months of each other when she was seventeen, and with her sister dead as well, she'd been completely alone, struggling to support herself ever since. Lately, it seemed as if the jobs were getting more and more scarce, and she desperately needed this one; she was on the verge of being kicked out of the rooming house where she lived. But her boss, Mr. Hardy, alternated between telling her she was an incompetent fool who didn't deserve to work for him and fondling her when they passed in the dim hallways. His horrible grin and whispers were unforgettable to her. *"There'll be more to come later on."*

No matter how hard she worked, he found so much to criticize after she cleaned a room, she began to wonder if maybe she was just plain stupid like he said. In her efforts to appease him, she was always pleasant and polite, but she was afraid she was somehow encouraging his gropings at the same time. Frantic with fear over losing her job, she would toss restlessly at night and drag herself, exhausted, through the day. Her normally cheerful disposition was giving way to despair.

It was just at that moment Leonard Dameroff came along. The first time they talked had been when she accidentally walked in on him in his room, mistakenly thinking the room was vacant. She apologized, and he nodded, telling her it was perfectly all right. After that, they exchanged smiles when they saw one another, then greetings, and finally Leonard had asked her if she would like to join him for a cup of coffee when she was off duty. Right from the start, she could see he was a gentleman. She came to look forward to his visits every few weeks, to the quiet talks they shared and his kind concern for her. She was able to tell him about her life, the loneliness that ate away at her, and her fears about the future. Slowly, the relationship took on a different intimacy. They held hands and kissed good-night. Kit could see Leonard was coming to care for her and she felt as if she were gaining strength from him.

Secure in knowing Leonard was there for her, she found that Mr. Hardy's cruel words and passes lost their power. Amazingly, her indifference seemed to make him lose all interest in her; he merely nodded when he saw her, but said nothing. To her own surprise, Kit would find herself singing happily while she dusted and scrubbed.

She and Leonard had known each other for almost a year when he proposed, sitting across from her at the restaurant where they usually went for dessert and coffee after dinner.

"You're a jewel, Kit," he said quietly, "but you don't know it. And you can't shine here. I want to bring you home with me, give you a new life, the one you deserve."

Tears of gratitude welled up in her eyes. He was so *solid.* He would be an anchor for her, someone who would be a good husband and father, who would take care of her always.

"You're my prince," she whispered smiling, "complete with rescue. It's so corny, but it's true."

Leonard grinned as he took her hand. "I don't mind a bit if it's corny. I'm going to do my best to live up to it."

After they were married and settled in Albany, Kit asked Leonard if she could go to work at Ed's. Initially, he resisted.

"Honey," she protested, "I'm used to working and I want to be part of the family business, at least until we have a baby. Please let me."

Leonard frowned. "I don't see why my wife should have to work. My salary supports us."

In the end, though, he relented, and Kit happily joined him and her father-in-law at the store. Ed himself frightened her a little with his booming voice and quick tongue, but for whatever reason, Leonard's father seemed reasonably satisfied with her—to the extent he even noticed her. When he wasn't making her nervous, she loved being around him, listening, learning, in awe of his business expertise and the decisiveness with which he handled every problem. She came to share Leonard's worshipful view of him, and their desire to improve the store kept them up nights, happily debating merchandising or pricing plans. Leonard was the one who always put an end to their lively discussions, insisting that Kit needed her sleep.

"You treat me like a piece of crystal that might break at any minute," she scolded him.

He would put an arm around her and draw her close. "You're a delicate flower, and I have to take care of you."

"You're nuts," she laughed, secretly pleased. "But I love you anyway."

"I surely hope so," he answered solemnly. "Because you're the light of my life." Kit could feel her heart expanding with love and the knowledge that she would be loyal to this wonderful man until the day she died.

But those happy times were all a million years ago, or might as well have been. It wasn't very long after she'd settled in to work at the store that everything changed. Of course, she'd never forget the day the call came in. She'd been standing behind the bread counter, the delicious smell of warm bread enveloping her, talking to a local reporter who wanted to do a story on Ed Dameroff.

"Yes, there'll be three more Ed's opening up in the next year," she was saying, when the telephone on the wall behind her started to ring. "Excuse me."

She turned white at the news, dropping the phone and rushing to find Leonard. By the time she located him sitting at his desk in the store's back office, her face was streaked with tears.

"What is it?" He jumped up immediately to come to her.

"Oh, Leonard, it's Dad," she got out, "your dad. A heart attack . . ."

Leonard's grief over his father's death had broken Kit's heart; she would never forget the crushing sadness of his loss in those first few days. But it was what transpired soon after that turned out to be Ed's true legacy. Leonard had naturally assumed that his father would leave the business to him. And his father had indeed left the business to his son—but it wasn't Leonard. It was a son that Leonard had never even known existed.

It turned out that all the time Ed Dameroff was married to Leonard's mother, Rose, he had a second wife and family in Poughkeepsie. Neither family knew of the other's existence. Yes, Ed had traveled a lot—on business, he always said—but Leonard and his mother were at a loss to explain how Ed had managed this deception over the years, unable to comprehend the magnitude of such a lie. Ed Dameroff and his other wife, Betty, had a son who was a senior at Princeton, and he, not Leonard, inherited the stores. The rest of his estate went to Betty. Rose got only the ten thousand dollars still in the joint checking account and their house, which had always been in her name and' was fully paid off.

Leonard and Rose were left to face one another, incapable of making sense of anything in their lives. It seemed they'd known nothing at all about the man they'd lived with—every memory of the past was now colored with the sickening knowledge of the present. It wasn't enough to say they hadn't really known him, that he was a total stranger to them. For a reason they would never understand, he had chosen to betray them in the most callous way imaginable, and then abandon them utterly in the end. Kit ached for her husband as she watched him trying to console his mother.

Ed Dameroff's other son wanted no part of Leonard or his mother. In no uncertain terms, he made it clear in their one and only telephone conversation that they were not welcome on the premises of any Ed's.

Overnight, Kit's and Leonard's lives changed. Leonard had

been earning a healthy salary, and they had just bought a house, a sprawling colonial on two acres, in the Coleville area. Given free rein by her husband, Kit was having a ball decorating it. Suddenly, with Leonard's connection to Ed's severed and no other source of income, money became a serious problem. On top of everything else, their investment in a house was now a frightening liability. Kit could only stand by helplessly as Leonard sank deep into depression.

He tried to start over. Retailing was the only thing he knew, so he sold their house and they moved into a smaller one, using the profit from the sale and part of their savings to purchase a candy store in Westerfield. He stocked the store with a wide array of candies and better chocolates, along with newspapers, magazines, stationery supplies, and a large selection of pipes and cigars. In those first few months of owning his store, he was full of determination. He *would* make it on his own, would do it even better. Kit was so happy to see her husband coming alive again.

But somehow, it never worked. The store gobbled up as much money as Leonard poured into it. The bright hope that he had in the first months after its opening flickered and died as Leonard faced his financial situation. Where they once had more money than they knew what to do with, they now had nothing but a shaky business. It took every ounce of will he had to tell Kit they couldn't afford to stay in Coleville. They would have to move to Westerfield's Riverview housing project.

"Sweetheart, I don't care about things like that, you know I don't," Kit reassured him. "Will we have enough money to eat, do you think?"

"God, Kit, of course," Leonard replied, startled. "It's not *that* bad."

"Well, then," she said brightly, "what's the problem?"

But she saw the sense of failure in his eyes, and nothing she said could make it go away. She resolved that at least his life at home with her would be as happy as possible. Her mood was light and easy when he came in at night, and she did what she could to make their small apartment cheerful-looking. When their son, Ben, was born, she felt they had all anyone could ever dream of.

The birth of their son helped Leonard a little, bringing some of his old spark back. But then Kit accidentally became pregnant three months after Ben was born, only to go into labor in her seventh month and have a second son—stillborn.

Kit was hysterical with grief, although her pain eased over time, pushed aside by necessity when she became pregnant again almost immediately. But the premature death of their second child seemed to be the final blow for Leonard. He quietly retreated back into his shell, where he remained, grieving over his losses, the comedown in their life, the destruction of all his dreams. Even the birth of Natasha had no effect; it just seemed too late. For years, he lived under the heavy burden of his hurt, working hard, saying little. In the evenings, he barely spoke to Kit, coming home from the store to watch Westerns on television or just sit in the living room, staring into space. Kit could only do her best to show him she was there for him.

Over the years, his negativity had inevitably worn her down too. But she was still ready to live, to enjoy the world, to laugh when she could. If only she could get her husband to do those things along with her.

Thank God for my precious Ben, she thought now, as she approached the bowling alley's concession stand. And, of course, for my Natasha, she hastily amended.

There was a burly young man behind the counter. Automatically, Kit smiled.

"I'd like four beers, please," she said sweetly. "And what would you suggest to munch on?"

Eleven-year-old Benjamin Dameroff sat beside his mother in the car. He couldn't believe it. The radio station was playing "Raindrops Keep Falling on My Head" *again.* This must be the fiftieth time in two hours. He reached over to turn off the radio. They were almost home now anyway, and it was a good thing. At first he'd been pleased when his mother snuck him out of school this afternoon, claiming a family emergency. It turned out she wanted to take him for a drive to admire the fall foliage, and they'd been cruising around in the car until now, talking and laughing, stopping only once at a diner for some pie and a milk shake, which they'd shared. As always, it was a great treat to spend time with his mother. She was the most fun of anyone he knew.

But it was getting pretty late, and Ben felt anxious. They'd been studying the space program in school, and he'd chosen to do an extra-credit project on John Glenn. He'd completed his report on Glenn's life the week before, but he wanted to go over it one more time to make sure there were no errors when he handed it in tomorrow. There was also that math assignment to do, and he'd been hoping to get in some handball before dinner. He had a running game going with Jerry Wyckoff, who lived on the second floor of his building and was a pretty decent player. Ben didn't understand why Jerry wanted to keep playing, since Ben always won, but that was okay with him. Should he skip the game to go over his report? He frowned slightly.

"Darling, you're too serious." Kit tousled his dark hair affectionately as she observed the frown on his face. "What are you worrying about now?"

"Nothing, Mom," Ben answered. "I have some homework—I'm just thinking about that."

"Angel, you're so brilliant, you can do your homework in your sleep." Kit braked at a red light and turned to give her son a loving smile. "Take it easy, kiddo. Too much work and no play—do you know that expression?"

Ben gave his mother a small smile in return, but said nothing. He thought about the long hours his father spent at the candy store, trying to make life better for all of them. Talk about too much work. How could his mother say such a thing, knowing how hard her husband worked six days a week. Ben considered saying something to her, but decided against it. It wouldn't do any good. Nothing ever seemed to make his mom sad, and that was probably for the best.

His father was always so unhappy. Ben wasn't exactly sure where it came from, though he believed there was some connection to his dead grandfather Ed. Ben had heard the story, something about another family long ago and his parents losing a lot of money, but he didn't exactly understand it. It didn't make much sense. He was certain that in some way he himself played a part in his father's sadness; if not, why didn't Ben's straight A's and athletic abilities ever seem to have any effect on his dad? Ben would have done anything if he thought it would take away his dad's hurt. But all he could do now was try to make his father proud of him.

Kit turned the car at the next corner and Ben saw two girls sitting on a porch playing jacks. They reminded him of Natasha and Carlin. The thought of Natasha made him uneasy. As usual, his mother hadn't included his sister in their outing. Without ever admitting it to himself, Ben understood that his mother often preferred to be with him alone. He was reluctant to bring it up, but it was just so unfair.

"Mom," he said hesitantly, "how come Natasha never comes with us when we go out like this?"

Startled, Kit looked over at her son.

"Gee, honey," she replied, slightly flustered, "Tash had a big day at school today, and I know she was looking forward to it."

Ben knew she wanted him to let it drop, but he couldn't keep himself from pressing.

"But she *never* comes with us."

"Oh, that's not true." Kit's eyes were focused on the road but she gave a dismissive wave, clearly ending the discussion.

Ben was unaware how relieved his mother was when he finally let the subject pass. Uncomfortably, she shifted in her seat. Her son was right, of course. She *did* exclude Natasha from their trips. But she could never explain to him the feelings Natasha brought up in her, the horrible sense of reliving all those dreadful memories every time Kit looked at her.

It was no one's fault, really, Kit tried to reassure herself hollowly, as she had countless times before. There was no simple answer for the fact that every time Kit saw her daughter, she was reminded of her own younger sister, Natalie.

Everything about Natasha somehow brought back the memories for Kit. She shuddered now, remembering how frail and helpless her little sister had been, the way she wheezed, the awful sound of their parents pounding on Natalie's chest to help clear it. Their parents had devoted themselves to caring for Natalie; cystic fibrosis demanded that kind of endless attention. But Kit was torn between her anger at losing all but the most minimal of her parents' attention, and the guilt she felt for even daring to *be* angry. Day in and day out, it was *Natalie this, Natalie that, don't bother me, Kit, I'm preparing Natalie's special food, let's talk later, Kit, Natalie needs me right now.*

And then, the terrible end, when Natalie, virtually bedridden by that point, caught pneumonia at age twelve and died. Kit had shoved the confused mass of fury, sorrow, and guilt back into the darkest recesses of her mind, refusing to confront it. When Natasha was born, it was Leonard who had chosen her name in honor of Natalie.

"I know you'd want to name her after your sister, honey," he said to Kit in the hospital the morning their daughter was born. "I think it would be a nice thing to do."

Kit had been too embarrassed to tell her husband that she'd had no intention of doing any such thing. Instead, she'd nodded as if she appreciated his understanding.

Why does *my* second child have to pay the price for that other second child? she asked herself sadly. But something in her seemed to shut down when it came to Natasha. It had been that way from the second she was born. Kit had so looked forward to her birth, especially after the devastation of losing a baby; being pregnant with Natasha was like a fresh start, diminishing her grief the way nothing else could have. But it wasn't easy, her body strained by three pregnancies so close together. And Natasha had been such a difficult baby, suffering from colic, crying for hours on end, refusing to sleep more than twenty minutes at a time. The total opposite of Ben, who had been the happiest child in the world. Without realizing it, Kit sighed.

"What is it, Mom?" Ben asked.

Startled, she glanced over at him. "Nothing, baby. I'm just glad we're almost home." She gave him a dazzling smile.

The late afternoon's briskness was turning cold when she parked the car. Ben followed Kit as she retrieved their mail from a huge block of mailboxes in the lobby. Riding the small elevator to their apartment, she hummed brightly as she scanned the stack of envelopes, although Ben could tell they were mostly bills. She unlocked the door to their apartment, and the silence inside told them it was empty. Leonard normally worked until about ten o'clock at night but Natasha should have been home by now.

Kit dropped the mail on a table in the narrow entry hall. "Go and scare up your sister, honey," she called over her shoulder as she walked toward the refrigerator to check on what was around for dinner. "She's probably at Carlin's."

Ben set his book bag down on the floor with a sigh. He always tried to be obliging to his mother, but this was one job he hated. His sister and Carlin were always carrying on like such dopes, playing stupid games, whispering and giggling, acting like real *girls*. Whenever he tried to drag Natasha away to take her someplace, Carlin inevitably tagged along. And if Carlin went somewhere, Natasha absolutely *had* to go too. The two of them were stuck like glue. Carlin drove him nuts. She really knew how to get to him.

Resigned, he went down the hall to the Squires' apartment and knocked on the door. He heard a woman's voice call out, "Come on in."

Opening the door, he stuck his head in the apartment just far enough to see Carlin's mother frying chicken in the kitchen. It smelled delicious. "Is Natasha here, Mrs. Squire?" he yelled to her. "My mom's looking for her."

"Is that you, Ben?" Lillian Squire craned her neck to see him. "The girls are at the drugstore. Do me a favor and send Carlin on home, too, please."

"Yes, ma'am."

Impatiently, Ben went outside and ran the two blocks to the local drugstore, wanting to get this over with as fast as possible. He knew exactly what he'd find. Sure enough, there they were, putting makeup on each other like a pair of idiots, laughing and primping. But as he looked at his little sister, he smiled in spite of himself. Natasha was so cute, her ten-year-old face so silly and sweet beneath all those layers of rouge and eye stuff. He knew she loved to mess around with makeup any chance she got, claiming she was practicing for when she became a fashion model. The way people were always carrying on about how pretty she was, he was beginning to wonder if maybe the idea wasn't as ridiculous as it sounded.

Still, he didn't want to be caught dead with the two of

them looking like that. From the end of the aisle, he yelled out, "Let's go, Tash. Mom wants you."

His sister looked up, her face alight at the sight of Ben.

"Okay, okay, I'm coming." She grabbed a tissue from an open box on the counter and began wiping at her face, trying to erase the makeup.

"Come on, Carlin, we gotta go."

Adjusting her headband to keep her thick, dark red hair off her face, Natasha hurried toward her brother.

Ben glanced over at Carlin, whose face was still covered with makeup. Casually she reached for a tissue, and as she sauntered toward him, she blotted her lipstick, concentrating on her task. He shook his head in disgust as he spun on his heel and left the store. The two girls followed. All three turned in the direction of their building.

"What'd you want to put on all that goop for?" Ben asked, walking fast and not looking at either one of them.

"Well, hello and nice to see you too, Ben Dameroff," Carlin retorted from behind him, now wiping off the makeup in earnest. "Don't bother to be polite or anything."

Ben rolled his eyes. "Sorrrreeee. I forgot how important you are. We all need to bow down when we see you."

"Maybe I *am* important," Carlin answered tartly.

"Yeah, and maybe I'm the man on the moon." Ben laughed at his own joke.

"You're a real comedian," Carlin shot back. "But if you're such a big deal, look at what I have here."

Ben was immediately curious, but he made himself stop and give a long, bored sigh to show how put-upon he was before he permitted himself to turn around. "What?"

Carlin's hand was in her coat pocket. Smiling triumphantly, she pulled out a pack of Marlboros, already open and somewhat crushed from the time spent in her pocket.

Natasha let out a little gasp. "Where'd you get those?"

"A guy at school gave them to me. He needed some homework answers, and he thought I deserved a little reward for helping him."

Ben snorted derisively. "Some reward. Those'll kill you."

Carlin's eyes met his. "You are such a total and complete stick-in-the mud! One isn't going to hurt anybody."

"Are you going to try it?" Natasha asked, her eyes wide.

"Of course," Carlin replied nonchalantly. "And you're going to try one, too, Tash. I might even let Ben here try one, but he's way too much of a scaredy-cat, we all know that."

Anger surged through Ben. "I'm not scared of anything *you* could dream up, you can bet on that. Besides, smoking is just stupid and you're stupid for doing it."

"I don't know, Carlin," Natasha said doubtfully, staring at the pack of cigarettes. "My mom and dad would kill me."

"Look, let's go up on the roof, and you can just keep me company. If you don't want to have one, Tash, you don't have to. But we've *got* to find out what it's like. You have to try everything in life, or what's the point in being alive?"

"Tash, we have to get home," Ben said, trying to sound tough.

Natasha gratefully seized on his warning. "Yeah, I guess we do. Sorry, Carlin."

"Tash, I'll do it and I'll tell you what it's like," Carlin countered immediately. "Just come with me. You don't have to do anything, but it wouldn't be fun alone."

Natasha looked from one to the other. What should I do? she wondered frantically. No matter what choice she made, somebody would wind up mad at her. She hated these fights so much, and she was always in the middle this way. Why couldn't they just love one another as much as she loved them both? She bit her thumbnail.

"Ben, let's just go with her for a minute. She can tell us what it's like, and then we'll go home."

"Tash, no—"

Carlin interrupted Ben. "Great. It'll be cool."

They had reached the entrance to their building, and Carlin bounded inside and into the elevator. They got out on the top floor and ran up a small flight of stairs. Carlin leaned on the rusting door at the top and it opened easily, the three of them emerging onto the roof's hard and dirty black tar surface. It was windier up here than it had been on the street, and the sun had gone down, leaving a cold white sky at dusk.

Carlin walked toward the far edge of the roof, but since there was no protective railing, she stayed several feet away. Her dark hair blew across her face. With great ceremony, she extracted a crooked cigarette from the squashed pack. There was silence for a moment.

"Ha," laughed Ben, "I'll bet you don't have any matches."

His satisfied smile disappeared as he saw Carlin pull a book of matches from her other pocket.

"Shows you what you know," she said, putting the cigarette between her lips.

The wind kept blowing out every match Carlin struck, until Ben and Natasha helped shield the small flame by forming a circle around her with their arms. At last, she had it. She stood back from them and took the tiniest possible puff. A cough escaped along with the smoke she blew out, but she was encouraged. She inhaled a second time. Her face took on a look that said she was used to these more sophisticated forms of amusement, although her throat burned and she felt like gagging.

"It's no big thing," Carlin informed them, taking a deeper drag and forming her mouth into an O. She was just as surprised as the other two when she blew a nearly perfect smoke ring. Regaining her composure, she inhaled again and let the smoke out slowly as she melodramatically flicked the cigarette's ashes.

"Wow, you're really doing it," Natasha said in disbelief.

"Doing what?" Ben demanded. "Being a jerk?"

"You want to try one?" Carlin asked Natasha.

"No, she doesn't," Ben answered for her.

"Who asked you?" Carlin said to him. "You're afraid to, but maybe she's not."

"It's okay, come on, you two," Natasha said placatingly. "Besides, I can't. Models don't smoke."

Ben and Carlin both tried to hide a smile. They refrained from pointing out that she was still just a fifth grader.

"That's true, they don't," Ben said kindly. His gaze met Carlin's and he saw in her eyes that she realized he was trying to protect Natasha's feelings. Instantly, he was furious with himself for letting Carlin catch him acting so soft. His face reddened with embarrassment. Frantically, he looked around for some way to recover the situation. He got an idea.

"Athletes don't smoke, either," he said to Carlin.

Taking a few running steps, he jumped across to the next

roof, a tar surface indistinguishable from their building's roof, but separated by a five-foot gap. He heard Natasha and Carlin gasp. Turning back to them, he made sure to look bored, although he was momentarily frightened as he realized what he had done. Even from where he was, he could see that Carlin's expression had changed; he had clearly one-upped her.

"I've got better things to do with my lungs than ruin them with cigarettes," he called out to her in a condescending tone, relishing the moment.

"I could do that if I wanted to," she yelled to him.

Ben spoke soothingly, as if he were pacifying a small baby. "Sure you could, if you *wanted* to."

Carlin was getting angry. "I *could*. I just don't feel like it right now."

"Oh, please." Ben's tone said it all. He was enjoying himself thoroughly now. Tormenting her this way was fun, although he'd never really let her jump. It was more than six stories down to the ground, and he wasn't at all sure she could make the leap across.

"It doesn't matter." Natasha couldn't stand their fighting one more second. "Please, Carlin, forget it."

But Carlin had dropped the cigarette and clenched her fists at her sides. "Just because you're a boy doesn't mean you can do stuff better. I can too do it."

"There's no way," Ben yelled. "You can't."

"Yes, I can," she screamed back.

"Oh, yeah? Well, *I dare you*!"

As soon as the words were out, Ben regretted them. He had never intended to push her this far.

Carlin's eyes blazed. She strode to the edge of the roof and looked down, assessing the jump.

Natasha rushed over to her side. "Don't," she begged. "It's not worth it."

"Get back, Tash," Ben yelled in alarm. "Get away from the edge."

He wanted to yell out to Carlin, to tell her not to do it, that the whole thing was stupid anyway, and who cared if she could or couldn't. But she backed up, staring at the other ledge, assessing the distance. For a long moment, the three of them were frozen where they were, no one moving or saying a word.

Suddenly, Carlin sprang forward, going faster and faster, a final leap propelling her off the edge as she came flying across. Only one foot made contact with the rooftop; the other missed altogether. Ben lunged to grab her around the waist, barely getting to her in time. He pulled her back from the edge, his heart pounding.

"Are you okay?" he asked.

She pushed him away and straightened up. Her face was white.

I'm so sorry, he wanted to say. *I'm sorry I made you do something so dangerous. I shouldn't have. Please forgive me.* But he stood there in silence.

She took a deep breath. When she finally spoke, her tone was nonchalant once again. "I'm fine, of course. Why wouldn't I be? I said I could do it, and I did."

She called out to Natasha, who was staring at them from the other roof. "Meet me downstairs on the street. We'll ask your mom if you can have dinner at my house."

Carlin turned to leave, anxious to get away from Ben's gaze. She shoved her hands in her pockets so he wouldn't be able to see how badly they were shaking.

1975

3

There's a place for us ... the heartbreaking melody played through Carlin's mind as she walked down the path from Westerfield High. Somehow, in the late October afternoon, with darkness beginning to settle in, the song's lyrics seemed to take on a new significance. One month before, she and Natasha had stood in the back of the school auditorium, anxiously waiting to hear if they'd won roles in *West Side Story*. When Mr. Douglas had announced that Carlin would be playing Maria, it was Tash who jumped up and down with excitement for her friend. Carlin was so surprised to find she'd gotten the lead, she couldn't even take it in.

"Well, I guess it's the only fun I can imagine ever having in school," she'd said blithely, more amazed by her luck than impressed by what she was about to do. But the weeks of rehearsal had left her less cynical. The tragic romance, the wonderful music, it all made her feel as if she were visiting a magic place, where everything was grander and fuller than real life ever could be.

A sudden breeze blew through the large oak trees lining the walkway that passed the school gym, their brilliant red and yellow leaves a contrast to the graffiti-filled walls and rusted chain-link fences that marred the rest of the way from school to Riverview. Not so different from Maria and Tony's world, she thought, wishing that some genius would put music to Westerfield and make it into art instead of just a boring, impoverished town.

According to her mother, there had been a time not so many years before that Westerfield had been a nicer place. Not fancy, like Coleville, where all the kids wore Capezios and went to dancing schools and piano lessons, but at least

slightly less drab. But, one by one, the textile mills and the
shoe factories that had been the basis of the town's economy
went out of business, and more and more people found themselves out of work. The streets of tidy little row houses that
used to look like a real estate agent's version of "character"
now were covered in grime, with piles of old newspapers and
trash crowding most walkways. The only new buildings in
town were more housing projects, subsidized by the city, in-
habited by those who had lost whatever hope they'd had. The
Riverview project, originally advertised as "six floors of
Hudson Valley views with plenty of space for the kids to
play," now boasted an elevator that broke down at least twice
a month and athletic facilities consisting of two metal poles
holding the ends of a volleyball net, long ago reduced to a
sagging string.

Carlin stopped at the school's basketball court, gazing in
through the wire fence at the game in progress. Not surprisingly, she spotted Ben. He was usually out here playing in the
afternoons.

The game had clearly been under way for a while; most of
the boys' faces were streaked with perspiration, their expressions intent, wet shirts sticking to their backs. Several other
people had stopped to watch, but everyone both on and off
the court was oddly quiet.

Ben had the ball. Tilting her head, Carlin watched as he
dribbled furiously, dodging the opposing team members. As if
in a second, he had traveled across the court and taken his
shot, grim concentration on his face. The ball went in, but he
didn't slow down or even smile. He turned his head to yell
something to one of his teammates as he raced back to guard
his man. When the ball was back in play, Ben intercepted it
as the other team attempted to score, passing the ball, then
somehow reappearing in just the right spot when his team-
mate had to pass it again. His eyes narrowed, he quickly as-
sessed his chances and leaped to take a long shot, seeming to
hover in midair as the ball went in again. Carlin could see the
admiration in the eyes of his teammates, the annoyance on
the faces of their opponents.

Gee, she thought, he's really something. Acknowledging
this, even to herself, caused her cheeks to redden in embar-

rassment. What's the matter with me? she wondered as she forced herself to look away from the basketball court. Ben Dameroff had begun to confuse her. She used to fight with him all the time, often having more fun hurling insults than she would have had merely talking with Tash. But lately, she'd found herself almost wishing he would come into his sister's room when she was there. She studied him as he ran down the court, dribbling the basketball, palming it effortlessly before he jumped up and dunked it into the basket one more time.

He'd grown in the past year, his narrow body now capped by wide shoulders. With his unruly dark hair spilling down his neck and his worn blue jeans hugging his thighs, he looked grown-up somehow, handsome even. Sometimes, when Carlin would stay at the Dameroffs' for dinner, she'd find herself staring at the dark hairs now covering Ben's forearms as he'd reach for something in the middle of the table. She even found herself staring at the back of his head in classes, turning away suddenly if he happened to look back.

In the old days, everything was clear. She either avoided Ben or taunted him gleefully, occasionally succeeding in driving him out of his own house. Now she didn't know what she wanted from him.

She turned back toward the game, which was beginning to break up. Ben started talking with some of the other boys as he yanked off his damp T-shirt to put on the flannel shirt Carlin had seen him wearing in school earlier. She turned hurriedly and went on her way.

As she walked through the gray streets, she imagined what it would be like to walk home from school in Coleville across the river. Those kids went from fancy classrooms through lush green neighborhoods, with huge old houses and elegant lawns. She began to laugh. I'm getting like Natasha, she thought, conjuring up the thousand or so conversations they'd had over the years in which Natasha described her future life as a wealthy cover girl and penthouse occupant.

Carlin caught herself. I shouldn't be laughing at her, even secretly, she acknowledged. At least Natasha had a goal. Carlin couldn't imagine wanting anything enough to work really hard for it. She'd never had any idea where she was heading.

She'd lucked into the part of Maria as far as she was concerned, because of her long dark hair and passable soprano. And as for school, she barely worked at all. Not that she did badly—in fact, she was nearly at the top of her class—but that had more to do with the dearth of talent around her than with any conscientiousness on her part.

"What are you dreaming about?" Ben's voice nearly made her jump as he fell into step beside her, his right hand cradling the basketball.

"That's none of your business." Carlin's retort was quick and angry, as virtually all her conversations with Ben had been for as long as she could remember. But today she was also humiliated at nearly being caught watching his game and her discomfort made her lash out even more abruptly than usual.

Ben threw up his hand as if to ward off a blow and, laughing to himself, edged ahead of her.

Carlin immediately regretted her words. She would have liked his company on the long walk to Riverview. Not that they would have had some pleasant chat or anything, she admitted to herself, imagining just how short a time it would take for the two of them to get into a knockdown, drag-out. But it was an awfully long walk.

"Hey," she called ahead loudly. "Wait up."

Ben halted long enough for her to catch up.

"I didn't mean to sound so angry," she said. "You just took me by surprise."

"How're rehearsals going?" Ben asked, shifting his books to his right hand and starting to dribble the basketball with his left.

Carlin glanced at him suspiciously. To her surprise, he looked really interested.

"Well, actually, they're great. That is, the play is great. But Kenny Childs and I are not exactly Larry Kert and Carol Lawrence."

"Don't put yourself down." Ben smiled at her. "You have a pretty voice."

Carlin felt a flush rising in her cheeks. She could tell that he wasn't teasing her this time. In fact, he was being almost *nice*.

"You should do stuff in school," she said in return. "You know, join the basketball team or play baseball or something. The coach wanted you on junior varsity last year, Tash told me."

"I wish I had time for it, but I play often enough." Ben bounced the ball as he spoke. "You know, there's a pickup game around pretty much every afternoon."

"Maybe if you didn't have to ace every subject, you'd have time for some fun," Carlin heard herself saying sarcastically.

Now why did I do that? she wondered, realizing that the notion of fighting with him one more time made her feel more disappointed than excited. But it was so safe, being mean to him, rather than admitting this new feeling, which was infinitely more disconcerting.

Oh, well, she decided, unable to stop herself, in for a penny, in for a pound. "Like social studies this morning. God, I'll bet your paper covered the entire Renaissance on a daily basis."

As always, her term paper had been marked A– while his sported a big red A+.

Ben heard the usual challenge in her voice, but chose not to rise to the bait. Sometimes, he wanted to have an actual conversation with Carlin instead of a war. When he came right down to it, she was the only girl in school who even had a prayer of understanding the things on his mind. She might not work very hard, but she was smart as hell. Besides, she was so damn pretty, with those big green eyes and that long, dark brown hair. Even now and then, when he didn't want to murder her, he found himself longing to touch her, almost reaching over to smooth the hair back from around her face or brushing her shoulder as they walked alongside each other.

Besides, he needed someone to talk to. His father might have understood him, but he worked such long hours, Ben hated to bother him on his Sunday afternoons off. And all his mother ever said when something was bothering him was how great he was and how everything was bound to work out in the end. She even seemed to *believe* it, but all the faith in the world wasn't going to get him where he wanted to go.

As they approached Dalrymple's, Ben frowned. It used to seem like such an exciting store when he was a kid. Now everything looked dingy and disorganized. Even the discount signs in the window were gray at the edges, as if the same things had been on sale for a decade instead of a week. It was like everything else in Westerfield, hopeless.

I am not going to live a life that amounts to zero, he vowed silently, end up exhausted every night, not remembering a single thing that happened during the day. My father may have give up even *wanting* anything, let alone making something happen, but I haven't.

He thought about the photo taken just after his parents were married that sat on a book shelf in the living room. There was his mother, in a fancy evening dress with gold all over her belt and her shoes and the little bag she held in front of her. And his dad, resplendent in a black tuxedo, contentment all over his face.

Ben had never even seen that expression on his father's face. But he knew it was hidden there, somewhere. So many times Ben had thought, if I could just make something of myself, be successful, my father could hold his head up again. He knew he could make it happen. But it would take so much work to accomplish his goal, so many hours of studying to make sure his grades were good enough. So many times he had to put off what he'd like to do for the stuff he *had* to do.

"I'm going to be a doctor," he quietly confided in Carlin, slowing down as he said the words.

Carlin was surprised. Not that she didn't believe Ben was smart enough to do anything he wanted, but it was unlikely that anyone from Westerfield could hope to make it through college and medical school and what all else it took to become a doctor. She contemplated the things that Tash had confided to her over the years, Kit Dameroff's obvious efforts at careful budgeting, Leonard Dameroff's little candy store, without a single customer most of the times she'd visited it. But it was the hope in Ben's voice that really disturbed her. She found herself responding with scorn, as if by lowering his expectations she could make his eventual disappointment a little more bearable.

"Yeah ... and I'm going to be an astronaut."

Ben's response was gentle. "Well, you could, you know, if they let girls in."

Carlin couldn't decide which bothered her more, his unexpected sweetness or the truth behind his words. Girls really weren't allowed to do much, and even though Ben had been the one to bring it up, he still was the only available male around to take it out on.

"So just where do you plan to get the money for college, Dr. Dameroff?"

Ben managed to hold his tongue, caught confusedly between the urge to lash back at her and the unbidden longing to explore that mysterious hollow right where her head met her long, slender neck.

"Well, maybe, if I get lucky, I might win the Rutherford." He kept his voice even.

Exasperated, Carlin interrupted. "Shall we call a halt to the modesty number, *puleeze*."

Everyone in school knew that Ben Dameroff would be the recipient of the five thousand dollars the Rutherford Corporation gave the most deserving student at the end of senior year.

"Of course you'll get the Rutherford, but that's hardly enough for college."

Ben stopped walking as he explained his father's careful financial plans to Carlin. "You know Margaret Wahl, the math professor at Coleville Community College?"

Carlin shook her head no.

"Well, she's this financial whiz. She comes into Dad's store all the time for cigarettes, and a few years ago she agreed to invest money in a college fund for me and Tash. Actually, a lot of people use her." He walked slowly as he went into the details. "There's not that much money each month, but with her expertise, it should add up to enough for the two of us."

Ben wasn't at all sure this was so and it had been nagging at him for the past few months. In fact, he couldn't figure out how the small amount his father could spare each month could possibly cover even a couple of years for him, let alone for Natasha. And more than anything Ben longed to go to Harvard. A friend of his had been accepted two years before, and his description of the classes and the campus made Ben practically salivate.

But Carlin didn't take in the uncertainty. "If Margaret Wahl is so brilliant, what's she doing teaching in a lousy school like Coleville Community?"

You should be ashamed of yourself, she admitted silently, thinking she had scored a blow, albeit below the belt. Actually, she admired Ben's father for thinking ahead. Fleetingly, she thought about her own father. J. T. Squire would never have thought of such a thing, much less given up a new suit or an evening out to implement it.

"Besides," she found herself adding, her guilt making her even meaner, "how do you expect to cope with a patient's blood when you're scared of your own shadow?"

Finally, Ben allowed himself to feel annoyed. "I'm not afraid of anything."

"Oh, please," Carlin shot back, "you do everything your mommy and daddy tell you to."

This was so ludicrous that Ben wouldn't have bothered to respond if an idea hadn't suddenly popped into his head. He knew what he was about to suggest would be impossible for Carlin.

His voice grew quiet as he almost whispered into her ear. "My mommy and daddy aren't going to know about it tonight when I sneak out at midnight for *The Rocky Horror Picture Show*. If you're so brave, why don't you come, too?"

Her eyes told him how right he'd been. Good, he thought, thoroughly infuriated by now. Let her stew for a while. As he watched her wrestle with his challenge, he tried to enjoy his momentary victory, but his mind refused to cooperate. He couldn't keep himself from looking at her, taking in her slender curves and long legs. Carlin Squire had turned into a beautiful girl, even if she was a pain in the ass most of the time. He had to admit how good it would feel to have her beside him as he strode into the local theater. Embarrassed at this new thought, he made his voice especially tough.

"Show me how brave you really are," he said, knowing full well what her reaction would have to be. "I dare you."

Carlin thought hard. There was no way she was capitulating to Ben Dameroff, refusing to acknowledge the pleasurable thrill that accompanied her anger. Her curfew during the week was eleven o'clock. But her mother was usually asleep by ten. And her father usually went out after dinner and stayed out until eleven or so. Even if he got home after midnight, he would never think to check her room. At least almost never.

It was a risk, but well worth taking, she decided. Still, years of habit forced her to demand something in return, something just as hard for Ben as this would be for her.

"I'll tell you what," she finally answered, "if I go out tonight, you have to crash the Coleville dance with me on Saturday."

As the words came out of her mouth, she finally recognized the truth: the thought of spending a Saturday night alone with Ben Dameroff was exciting.

Ben turned away so she couldn't read the smile on his face.

"I can imagine nothing I'd like less than to go to a dance at that snooty country club populated by those spoiled brats from Coleville."

"You're just scared you won't get in," she retorted.

"I just don't have any reason to go," he answered, halfhoping she wouldn't take him at his word, but would talk him into it.

"I dare you."

As Carlin dressed for the country club dance early Saturday evening, she thought back to her night with Ben at *Rocky Horror*, all the kids dressed in outlandish costumes, just about everyone in the theater speaking the lines along with the actors.

It was amazing, she realized, as she recounted the details for Natasha the following day; she and Ben hadn't fought at all. In fact—this part she kept to herself—unless she'd been imagining things, it seemed as if Ben were going to put his arm around her once or twice, although it had never left the top of the seat behind her. But he *had* been sweet. That she certainly hadn't imagined. They'd talked and laughed all the way to the movie theater, still a little afraid they were going to get caught, but triumphant about having escaped their apartments unnoticed. And after the movie, they hadn't rushed right back, they'd almost dawdled, she realized in retrospect, thinking of the hour it had taken them to get back to

Riverview. Why, the theater wasn't even half as far as Westerfield High, and that trip usually took under twenty minutes.

Carlin pulled on a long black skirt spirited by Natasha from Kit Dameroff's closet. She smoothed the waistband under a black vest her mother had crocheted a few months before—originally intended to go over a blouse, it looked surprisingly snazzy, artfully covered with hunks of her mother's old jewelry. With pleasure, she remembered small snatches of conversation on their way to the movie. For the first time, Ben hadn't seemed like Carlin's nemesis or Natasha's brother. He'd seemed like a great-looking guy, she admitted to herself, as she thought of the way the freezing night air had caused his skin to glow, his dark brown eyes flashing with warmth as he listened to the things she had to say.

And Carlin herself hadn't felt the urge to be mean even once. Somehow the darkness made her speak more softly than usual, made Ben seem to listen more intently. There were no other kids around, no buses passing by, nothing to interfere with their intimate world in the pitch black night.

Carlin hugged these thoughts to herself as she checked her outfit in the full-length mirror nailed to the inside of her parents' closet door. Not exactly Coleville, she thought, her heart sinking.

God, why am I making him do this, she wondered, for the first time taking in the reality of a Coleville dance. The boys would all have those stupid blue blazers and the same dumb loafers. Those kids always looked as if they'd been handed uniforms at the door each morning. As far as she was concerned, the country club, in fact all of Coleville when you came right down to it, was a boring world she never wished to be a part of. Natasha was the one who dreamed of being surrounded by all that stuff, of being accepted by all those rich kids. I can't imagine why, Carlin thought, applying a final layer of mascara to her long eyelashes.

"I never should have talked Ben into this," she said out loud to her own reflection.

But when the bell rang and she grabbed her trench coat, she felt a shiver of excitement at the thought of going out with Ben.

"Does the damn doorbell mean I can finally get into my own room?" J. T. Squire's voice carried easily out to the hallway, as it was meant to.

"Sorry, Daddy," Carlin answered appeasingly, as she came out to the living room. "I didn't realize you needed it."

She kissed him on the cheek indulgently, but his only response was a shake of his head as he walked toward his bedroom.

"Didn't they look wonderful, both of them?" Lillian asked a moment later, taking his arm sentimentally when Carlin and Ben had left the apartment.

Her husband shook her off. He hadn't liked the sight of Ben Dameroff's athletic body suddenly set off by a sport jacket and close-fitting jeans any better than the amount of trouble his daughter had taken to be so beautiful for him.

"Why the hell shouldn't they look wonderful?" he answered disdainfully. "Carlin's *my* daughter, and that Dameroff kid's gotten everything on a silver platter."

Lillian frowned slightly, thinking about what he'd said. "But, darling, the Dameroffs aren't any better off than we are."

J.T. scowled at her. "Ben Dameroff is seventeen years old, his whole life in front of him, with a family that's been educated and rich for God knows how many generations. So his father hits one rough patch . . ." His voice conveyed barely concealed fury. "It doesn't come near wiping out the advantages people like that have."

Lillian sighed. She knew that any response at all would be a waste of breath.

How did I miss it all these years, Ben wondered, contemplating how beautiful Carlin looked as they boarded the bus that would take them to the country club. Finding manners he never would have dreamt of using in the past, he followed behind her, placed both their fares in the box, and waited for her to choose an empty row and sit down before joining her. The two of them had barely spoken since leaving Carlin's apartment. Ben felt unexpectedly nervous. In her long black dress and high pumps, Carlin seemed statuesque, like some movie star or something. Tonight, with a little makeup on her face and all that wonderful jewelry she had gathered from who knows where, she was breathtaking.

Ben felt flushed with nervousness, praying fervently that Carlin wouldn't notice. The scent of her perfume washed over him every few moments, and he had to force himself not to take her hand. Get a grip, Dameroff, he chided himself. This is Carlin. Natasha's Carlin. The girl you hate most of the time.

"Are you scared of crashing the dance?" he finally asked, knowing that crashing a dopey dance had nothing to do with his own nervousness.

"No," Carlin responded, slightly nonplussed at finally hearing him speak. She had practically forgotten they were going to a dance at all.

When the bus arrived in Coleville, she was startled when he put his arm around her to guide her toward the country club.

I know the way, stupid, she almost said before catching herself. What is going on here? she wondered as her stomach seemed to lurch to her throat. She unexpectedly felt a void when he removed his arm. They had arrived at the foot of the club's long driveway, and all around them were groups of teenagers. Sure enough, Carlin thought, they all look exactly the same. The girls wore floor-length pastel dresses in shiny fabrics, and nearly every boy had on the exact same navy blue blazer. She laughed to herself as she caught the one aberrant boy, obviously self-conscious in khaki chinos while everyone else around him was dressed in gray flannel slacks.

Ben noticed her expression and caught her eye. These kids were only sixteen, seventeen years old, and already they were big, stuffy blanks. The idea of suffering through an evening with these people bored him silly.

He looked over at Carlin. Now *she* didn't bore him at all. Dare or no dare, he had no intention of going to this awful dance. Suddenly, his nervousness disappeared. For the first time in his life, he felt like a man instead of a child. Taking Carlin's hand, he looked straight into her eyes.

"Listen, screw this party. Wouldn't you rather do just about anything else tonight?"

Carlin wasn't exactly sure of what he meant, but she per-

ceived the difference in his voice. Sometimes, that reckless
sound meant he was starting a fight with her, but that didn't
seem to be the case now. Carlin swallowed, not knowing how
to answer. As the moonlight reflected on the slight dip in
Ben's dark hair, all she found herself thinking about was how
incredibly handsome he was. Natasha was always talking
about her brother as if he were the best-looking boy in the
world, and for the first time, Carlin found herself agreeing.

Ben noted her hesitation, but he wasn't about to wait for a
response. Without a word, he took her hand and led her away
from the country club, striding down the road to the walkway
along the riverfront, Carlin practically running to keep up
with him. He stopped in front of a large oak tree, leaving her
breathless as she leaned back in the V where the branches
met. She felt almost frightened as he turned to her, looking
into her eyes for a long moment, then running his hand
through her long hair. Slowly he lowered his hand to her face,
tracing the outline of her cheekbone, then running his fingertips over her lips.

The intimacy of his gesture left Carlin breathless. Being
this close to him, having this boy—this man—she'd known
all her life, yet didn't know at all . . . Her thoughts were a
mass of confusion as Ben leaned down slowly, easily, as if
he'd done it a thousand times before, and kissed her. Softly
at first, his mouth gently teasing hers, she felt a sense of urgency, but she couldn't tell if it was coming from Ben or
from somewhere inside her. As if without any will of her
own, she felt herself responding, goaded by a longing somewhere deep down that was entirely new to her. Ben's tongue
eased its way past her lips and she was startled by how exciting it felt. She couldn't stop herself from meeting him,
openmouthed, her tongue exploring, savoring the taste of
him.

Without knowing how they got there, she felt his hands caressing her neck, taking in the length of her back, trailing
under her trench coat to the naked skin exposed by the little
vest she wore. She lifted her arms around him, taking in the
warmth of his neck, the muscular strength of his shoulders.
Nothing she had imagined up to this moment had come even

close to the extraordinary way he made her feel, the desire so intense, the satisfaction so deep.

When they finally pulled apart she felt empty, but the separation lasted only a few seconds. Keeping his arm around her waist, Ben looked at her questioningly. At the response in her eyes, he eased her down to the grassy earth, kissing her again as they lay on the ground, their arms around each other. His kiss probed even more deeply now, Carlin almost moaning in pleasure as his hands outlined her breasts, cradling them, stroking them through the fabric of the vest.

Why was he so good at this? she wondered half-consciously. Of course, she realized languidly, Ben was wonderful at everything he did. She felt awash in pleasure, breathless. Oh God, she thought, I wish we could stay like this for the rest of our lives—never move, never speak, never end this moment.

Ben felt as if he couldn't get enough of her. Her slender body seemed such a miraculous combination of strength and softness, her breasts rounding into his chest, her hip bones causing him pain that felt like pleasure. He wanted to taste all of her, his mouth abandoning her lips, slowly tracing down her neck. Magically, Carlin guided his hands under her vest, her nipples hardening in response.

She felt exposed as he fondled her breasts, his large hands accentuating the slenderness of her frame. She could only melt into him as she felt him harden through her skirt, heard him gasp with excitement.

Suddenly, Ben realized how out of control he was. A few more minutes and he would be past stopping. That's not how you treat someone you care about, his father had always taught him. And, God, he realized suddenly, how he cared about Carlin. Abruptly he sat up, deeply breathing in the chill air for a few moments, then smiling down at her. Reaching for her hand, he pulled her up beside him.

"We'd better get going," he said gently, kissing her quickly one last time.

They held each other's hands tightly as they waited for the bus back to Westerfield, conversation as fluid now as it had been impossible on the trip to Coleville.

"Which colleges are you applying to?" he asked casually as they boarded the bus.

"I haven't even thought about it," she answered, choosing two seats in the back.

Of course the truth was she *had* thought about it. In fact, she'd lain awake many nights wondering what to do. Her father's comments over the years had made it clear that college was "for saps and suckers . . . a waste of money that produced a worthless piece of paper." It was obvious that he expected his daughter to get a job when she finished high school and contribute to the household income. If she decided to go to college, she would have to take on her father in what undoubtedly would be a very ugly battle. She was still debating whether that was worth it.

Ben looked incredulous. "You haven't even *thought* about it? You must have gotten some applications," he insisted. "With your grades, you must have some ideas."

"I'm not even sure I want to go to college," she responded more sharply than she'd meant to.

"Jeez, you'll never get into college with that attitude." Ben laughed. "My father read to me from *Lovejoy's College Guide* instead of Dr. Seuss at bedtime from the time I was two years old."

Carlin pulled her hand away. She could hear her father's dismissive voice in her head. *That Leonard Dameroff would chop off his own arm if he thought it would get his kid into a fancy college.*

J. T. Squire wouldn't give up a single Saturday night out if that were all it took to get her a Ph.D.

Hurt at the thought, she lashed out angrily at Ben.

"That should make you the world's leading authority on colleges."

Ben was stung by her sarcasm. "Well, pardon me for living."

His derisive voice made Carlin furious. It was as if the person he'd been a few minutes ago had disappeared. Here was the old, familiar Ben, the one she couldn't get along with for two minutes.

"I can get into any school I want." She almost spat the words out, enraged at herself for letting her guard down earlier in the evening.

"In your dreams," he said as meanly as he could, humiliated at having made his attraction for her so obvious.

Carlin hadn't even signed up for the SATs, let alone bothered to put in five minutes studying since the beginning of the school year, but she wasn't about to let those things stop her.

"Wherever you apply, I'll get in, too."

Ben was infuriated by her arrogance. "Try Harvard," he snapped. "Let's see how you do."

The heat of his response caught Carlin up short. She willed herself to silence for a few seconds, slowly realizing she had hit a nerve she didn't begin to understand. She was tempted to back down, but his next words stopped her.

His mouth a thin angry line, Ben spoke without a hint of affection. "C'mon, Carlin. Apply to Harvard. I dare you."

4

Taking care not to smudge her freshly polished fingernails, Natasha adjusted the two pillows against the wall behind her to get into a more comfortable sitting position on the bed. She reached out gingerly to pick up the new *Glamour* from the night table and rested it against her propped-up knees. Relishing her own anticipation, she paused to blow on all ten pale pink fingernails. *Glamour* was her bible; each month she read every word, studied every picture between its covers. The November issue had arrived today, and she'd hardly been able to wait until dinner was over so she could finally sit down with it.

She settled in, gazing at the girl on the front cover. Her hair, her makeup—Natasha examined all that. But she also took careful note of the easy smile on her face, the angle of her head, the light in her eyes. This girl was exactly the way Natasha longed to be: carefree, happy, and, without a doubt, popular. And she was a model, which was just what Natasha dreamed of becoming. Any way she looked at it, she wanted what this girl had.

Experimenting, Natasha tilted her head to the exact angle of the model's. She opened her eyes wide and turned up her lips in a bright smile, coming as close as she could to achieving the same expression. But it wasn't quite right. For several minutes she practiced until she felt that she had it down. Reasonably satisfied, she opened up the magazine and flipped through until she found the fashion pages.

With great concentration, she reviewed the pictures. If she were going to pull off these looks, she had to copy them exactly, down to the last detail. Only then would she feel secure enough to go outside wearing something a little bit different.

Of course, her version of the clothes would be less expensive, the accessories cheaper copies of what was in the magazine; there was no way she could afford more than dime-store bangle bracelets and earrings, or bargain turtlenecks and scarves. But if she scoured the stores around Westerfield after school for what she needed, she could come up with a pretty close imitation.

She would be the first to admit that it was the same way when she cooked, a talent she had recently decided she should acquire. A recipe was a recipe, to be followed exactly. She couldn't understand experimenting with it; the whole dish might be ruined by a mistake. Every Tuesday afternoon, she cooked something new, standing alone in the apartment's small kitchen, clean and neat in her apron, *The Joy of Cooking* open on the narrow Formica counter. This week it had been beef stroganoff, the week before, meat loaf. She told her mother in advance what she would be trying out so the dish could be incorporated into their dinner that night. Kit always pronounced Natasha's cooking to be perfect, but Natasha wasn't fooled: she knew her mother was delighted just to have someone else help get their evening meal on the table.

Natasha frowned slightly at the thought of her mother. Kit, of course, never followed a recipe. She threw in a dash of this, a handful of that—it drove Natasha crazy the few times she'd tried to learn from Kit, standing beside her, asking how she knew the amounts to use. Kit had been happy to help, but her answers of "You just have a feeling" or "You get to know how much" were utterly useless. Still, whatever she cooked was delicious.

Kit had the same instinctive talent with clothes. She spent next to nothing on them, but it seemed like she could throw together a wonderful outfit for any occasion, rummaging around in closets and drawers, pulling on odd combinations of old skirts and jewelry and belts that always looked stunning. How she accomplished this was beyond Natasha's understanding—it might as well have been magic. Even without money, Kit could always compensate somehow through her own ingenuity and have everything come out all right in the end. That was just who her mother was. And we all know who I am, Natasha thought grimly. Nothing. No one. The fact that she had not an ounce of style or originality was really the least of it. The truth was that she wasn't even supposed to be alive.

Of course, she'd never told anyone about the time she'd overheard the conversation Kit had with Carlin's mother long ago about that other baby, the dead one. Natasha had been only five, playing alone in her room with her game of Candyland, when her mother's voice drifted in as she and Lillian Squire talked over coffee. Natasha had sat, not moving, not daring to breathe, as she listened to the story—how the baby was a boy, not even alive when it was born. There was a lot of what Kit said that Natasha didn't understand, but she knew enough to realize that it was that baby boy who was meant to be here, not her.

Even today, it was so obvious that Kit still wished she'd had that other baby instead. Kit barely noticed Natasha; in fact, she hardly even looked up when her daughter entered the room. When Natasha went to hug her, she could almost feel her mother holding back. All she cared about was Ben, Ben, Ben. Of course that was because Ben was completely great.

But even so ... Natasha thought about the day only last week when she'd come home to find the typically cheery Kit sitting at the kitchen table, looking glum.

"I'm sorry," Kit had apologized when Natasha asked if she was okay. "It's just that sometimes your father's being down gets me down too. I wish I knew what to do for him."

Surprised and pleased that Kit had chosen to confide in her, Natasha sat down and put her hand over her mother's. "You do everything you can. I know you do."

Kit shook her head. "It's not enough."

Natasha searched for the right thing to say. "Daddy's been this way for so long. Maybe it's just ... *him*."

Kit sighed. "But he used to be different. He was always kind of—I don't know—dignified. But he knew how to laugh and have some fun. It wasn't at all like now." Her eyes grew moist with tears. "If I could only find the right ..." She trailed off unhappily.

"Don't be sad, Mom," Natasha said comfortingly. "You're good to him and he loves you a lot, I'm sure of it."

Just then, Ben came in. Natasha watched in amazement as her mother seemed to spring back to life simply at the sight of him. "Hi, honey. How was your day?" she inquired brightly, immediately getting up to go to him, reaching out to brush his hair back off his forehead.

Smiling, he eased away from her motherly act of grooming. "Not bad. I was elected president of the United States, voted into the Baseball Hall of Fame, and I found a cure for the common cold. How was yours?"

Kit laughed, her sadness apparently forgotten. "I picked up a new sweater for you today. Come on and take a look."

As they left the room together, Natasha stared after them. Her efforts had done nothing to cheer up Kit. Yet Ben's silly jokes were all it took.

Natasha shrugged off the memory. It all made perfect sense, really. Why would Kit care about Natasha when she was taken up with Ben and her anguished longing for her dead second son, thinking about him every time she laid eyes on her unwanted daughter?

Besides, Kit had no doubt realized years before that Natasha had nothing inside worth loving. That was the rest of Natasha's terrible secret. She sometimes felt as if God had forgotten to give her whatever it was that made someone a human being. She had to pretend to be a person, pretend to be happy or excited, struggle to be interesting so the other kids would like her. Sometimes she imagined that it was the dead baby boy who'd gotten her—*soul* was really the only word she could think of. Maybe there wasn't anything left over for her. She was a void as far as she could tell, worthless and useless. Every day, she had to invent herself. It took every ounce of energy she had, but if the mask should slip and anyone should find out what she was really like—well, she couldn't permit that to happen.

The trouble was, the older she got, the more effort it took to hide the awful truth about herself. There were so many things to deal with now: the right clothes, getting invited to the right parties, joining the right clubs at school—the list was endless. At the same time, she had to keep her eye on the future. She would need money, and plenty of it, to keep up the charade. She'd have to live in the right kind of place, in the right kind of house. Let her brother Ben talk about restoring the glory of the family, worrying about their father's honor and all that nonsense. Natasha was going to get the hell out of Westerfield and get rich. Maybe once she had enough money, she actually could *become* somebody.

She continued reading for another half hour, then forced herself to put the magazine aside. Right now, she had to pick out her clothes for school and see if they needed ironing. She knew she would have a chance to see Tony Kellner tomorrow, and she had to look her best. Biting her lip in concentration, she selected two different outfits and spread them out on the bed. Tony would like the suede vest with the fringe, she was pretty sure of that. But it didn't look right with the very short black skirt, and she knew he'd like that, too.

It was time to pull out all the stops, go for the short skirt, let him get a good look at her legs when she casually passed by the school court where he'd mentioned he would be playing tennis after school. She almost had him, she could tell. A few more days and Tony Kellner would *definitely* ask her out. She just knew it. Smiling to herself, she hung the skirt on the closet's doorknob so it would be waiting there in the morning.

Senior class treasurer, captain of the tennis team, and *so* cute, Tony Kellner was, unbelievably, within her reach. It had taken her months of careful planning, but even she could see it had paid off. It had started with one piece of incredible good luck, when he'd come into a school assembly late and happened to slip into an empty seat next to hers; they'd started talking and she'd been able to tell him her name. After that, she'd arranged a few strategically spaced "accidental" meetings around school.

Things had progressed pretty quickly from there. Lots of girls wanted to go out with him, but it was Natasha he was having lunch with most days in the cafeteria, Natasha he casually offered to walk home after school no less than three times in the past two weeks. And she was only a *junior*. She wanted to jump up and down when she casually sauntered down the street at the end of the day, with students pouring out of the school's main entrance, heads turning as seniors and juniors alike saw Tony and Natasha heading off together.

The other girls must be *dying*. She grinned just thinking about it.

Another amazing thing about Tony, she reflected, was that he could be so easygoing, so laid back, and then, suddenly, so ... intense. She'd seen him horsing around with the guys, tossing a football, relaxed and laughing. But she'd also watched him in his tennis matches, ferocious at the net, his voice raised in indignation when a point was called against him. And she just melted at the sound of his soft drawl. His family had moved up from South Carolina when Tony was only five, but he still had the most adorable accent.

She knelt in her closet and pulled out her black heels. They'd be just right with the black skirt. Sexy, but not *too* sexy. She didn't want to look like she was trying too hard. Carefully, she inspected them. Then, with a frown, she turned and headed for the bathroom to get the black shoe polish.

His tennis ball and racquet poised above him, Tony Kellner held the moment, then, with a grunt, tossed the ball up in the air as he brought his racquet down behind him and up again to smash it over the net.

"Ace," he shouted, as the boy on the other side lunged toward the speeding ball.

Tony's opponent returned to his position, knees bent, both hands on his racquet. "Thank you, Tony," he called back sarcastically. "None of us would have known what that was if you hadn't announced it."

Tony smiled broadly. "My pleasure, Henry."

"Come on, let's get this over with," Henry yelled back. "It's too goddamned cold to be playing tennis anyway. I don't know how I let you talk me into this."

Tony got ready to serve again, but froze as he caught sight of Natasha Dameroff walking toward the court. He made certain his expression stayed relaxed, although he pretended not to see her. *She was here. She'd come.* As she paused momentarily to open her book bag to adjust something, he was able to study her unobserved. This was the first time he'd seen her in such a short skirt; her legs were just as great as he suspected. And in those high heels—he could almost feel himself getting hard, and turned away, busying himself by picking up a few tennis balls that lay nearby.

Finally, he looked over again, as if he'd suddenly noticed her just at that instant. She waved and smiled brightly. He gave her only a slight smile and brief nod in return, as if he had more important things on his mind, then turned back to the game. He resisted the urge to look at her again until the game was over nearly ten minutes later. With a combination of relief and smugness, he saw that she was still there. It was a damn good thing he'd won. But, of course, he'd asked Henry to play today because he knew he could cream him, and he'd been counting on Natasha's coming by.

"Hey, Henry, ah'll see you later," he shouted.

Henry, zipping his racquet into his case, looked up to see Tony toss his head slightly in Natasha's direction. Henry grinned, taking in the situation. "Right, Tony. Gotcha."

Pleased by Henry's reaction, Tony tossed down his racquet and sauntered over to Natasha, slinging a small white towel around his neck, and holding the ends with both hands.

"Well, helllooooo . . ." He drew out the word to let her know he liked the way she looked, and was rewarded by the sight of her cheeks flushing. Encouraged, he moved closer until their bodies were practically touching and looked directly into her eyes.

Obviously flustered, she took a step backward. "I remembered you mentioned something about playing today," she got out, "and I was just passing by."

Sure you were. He grinned. "That's great, dahlin'." Slowly, sensually, he slid his hand up and down her arm. He wanted to laugh out loud in triumph as he saw her actually catch her breath. "What do you say we walk back to the locker room, and after ah've changed, we'll get us a burger."

He left her waiting outside the locker room as he yanked off his clothes and grabbed a towel on his way to the shower. This was going even better than he'd planned. He especially enjoyed the fact that Natasha obviously believed she had made it all happen. It was clear she didn't have a clue that *he'd* selected *her* long before they talked the first time, that he'd waited for exactly the right minute to make his opening move. That empty seat next to hers in assembly had been so perfect, he thought, it was practically divine intervention.

Now why had he thought of an expression like that? He frowned as he hung the towel on a hook and stepped under the shower's water, scalding hot the way he liked it. Divine intervention was something his parents could still carry on about, but he knew better. Hell, all those years of praying, five, six hours a day sometimes since he was eight years old, that was when he believed in crap like that. His parents loved it, loved that he went to their meetings with them, thought his praying was a great thing. But it hadn't kept his mother from drinking herself into a stupor most afternoons, and it hadn't done a damn thing for him when he turned thirteen. That was when it really hit him that he'd been wasting his time all along.

He'd prayed endlessly that year that God would give him the strength to resist all the temptation in his path. The thoughts and feelings he'd begun to have were unacceptable to God, he knew that. But at night, alone under the covers, the pictures in his head drove him nearly crazy and he *had* to touch himself down there, moving in a silent frenzy until he exploded. Afterward, he would lie in bed consumed with shame, red-faced and afraid. Yet not ten minutes later, he would be doing it again, practically swooning with the pleasure his own fingers could give him. In school, all he'd have to do was *look* at a girl's bare arm, or the back of her neck, and he'd be frantically squirming in his seat, terrified he would come right there on the spot and wind up with the front of his pants all wet.

He doubled his efforts to talk to God, praying every night and all day on the weekends, kneeling out behind the house in the cold, reveling in the pain of the frigid winter air as he begged Jesus to forgive these disgusting sins, and to show him the right way. He did whatever seemed like penance at the time—skipping meals, not playing ball for an entire week, anything he could think of. But the feelings didn't go away. He began locking himself in the bathroom after school, unable to wait until he was in bed at night.

He knew perfectly well that decent people didn't feel what he felt. As his father had told him a thousand times since

Tony was eight or nine, people who gave in to their sexual weaknesses were on the road to hell. Yet, despite his tearful prayers, God refused to help. There was only one conclusion to draw. God wasn't interested in Tony, didn't give a damn what became of him. And that had to be because Tony *wasn't* a decent person. That was why his prayers about his mom had gone unanswered. That was why he was a slave to his animal lusts no matter how hard he tried to resist them. Tony wasn't going to heaven, and never had been.

Although they knew nothing of his other activities, his parents were shocked when they saw he'd turned his back on God. But their nagging brought only contempt from him, straining things between them to the breaking point. They finally gave up, telling Tony that they couldn't save him from the punishment that awaited him for forsaking the Lord.

Tony cared less and less. He began to formulate a plan. He knew there would be sex for him out there when he got a little older, that men could always get women to do what they wanted if they were willing to pay for it. But that wasn't enough. He was going to get himself the beautiful women, the kind who made other men wild with envy. Like those women in the *Playboy*s he snuck into his room every month, so classy when they were dressed, but wanting it all the time, pushing their luscious bodies at you, screaming for more when you fucked them. *That* was what he would have, and he set out to become what they wanted: successful, popular, acting as if it were all too easy for him. Maybe he was just poor Anthony Kellner from some dump in Westerfield, but he would have the best, the cream of the crop. In fact, the more he thought about it, the more the good life in general appealed to him. With money, he could enjoy anything and anybody he might desire.

Finally, he knew what he wanted, what he was destined for. The best of everything.

He'd thought he was on his way with Lisa Zorn last year. The delicate blonde who was in his class had all the qualifications he was looking for. Her translucent skin, her pale blue eyes, the slight swivel in her tiny hips when she walked—he watched her for weeks before deciding she was the one. Elegant, soft-spoken, but with a certain something that told him she would go crazy in bed.

As he observed her, it slowly became clear to him that this was more than just a choice of girlfriend; they were *supposed* to be together. Soon, she'd replaced all the other girls in his fantasies. For weeks, he had imagined the two of them naked together, in bed, on the floor, on the dining-room table, him caressing her while she moaned aloud her desire for him. Sometimes the images got a little rougher as she begged him to tie her up. He played the scene out in detail in his mind, her prone on the bed, arms and legs pinned to the bedposts, pleading with him to shove it in. He wouldn't even have to touch himself then, shuddering in a powerful climax just at the thought.

Tony turned off the shower and dried himself off. In the end, it turned out he had made a big mistake. She wasn't the one at all. How could he have been so blind? She was actually nothing but a stupid bitch. After all the attention he'd lavished on her, waiting for her in the hall after classes, asking her out constantly, even standing across the street from her house on the weekends . . . He'd done everything to prove his devotion to her, but she'd spurned him at every turn. She wouldn't go out with him, and began telling him she didn't want him around. It infuriated him, her inability to understand that they were meant to be together. *Of course* he'd yelled at her—he *had* to make her see how wrong she was. It didn't help. The next thing he knew, her father was threatening him with a restraining order if he ever came near Lisa again.

That was probably the best thing that could have happened, Tony reflected, as he slipped into his pants. It would never do to have a restraining order against him—the whole town would know, for Christ's sake. So he'd left Lisa in the dust, realizing he'd have to pick more carefully next time.

And he had. He smiled as he combed his hair. He thought of Natasha's red hair, the color of autumn leaves blazing in a bonfire, her delicious mouth that would kiss him all over, the full breasts beneath her sweater that he would touch and suck until he'd had his fill. There was no mistake this time. *She* was the one. But he was taking it real easy, bringing her in slowly, making it all look as if it was her idea in the first place. God, he wanted to go out there and throw her on the ground, tear off her clothes and ram into her until she screamed out with the ecstasy of him. He tucked his shirt in and paused for a final check in the mirror. "Be cool, man," he whispered to himself. "Be very cool."

"Got another hot date, Tash?" Ben stuck his head into the doorway of his sister's room, watching as she labored over her long hair with the curling iron.

"Maybe yes, maybe no," she answered mysteriously, her gaze still directed to the small mirror above her dresser. Damn, it was so hard to get her hair to lie straight; the natural curls refused to obey.

"The perfect Tony Kellner is making a return appearance, I suppose," her brother teased. "That makes it, what, four dates now?"

"Five." Natasha couldn't keep from grinning. "Each one better than the last, if I do say so myself."

"Can wedding bells be far behind?" Ben laughed.

Natasha gave him an exasperated look, but it was clear her annoyance wasn't genuine. "Get out of here, you jerk."

"I'll be in my room reading up on how to be the brother of the bride," Ben said solemnly as he closed the door. "Big responsibility, you know."

Natasha giggled. Unplugging the curling iron, she took off her robe and began to put on her clothes. It had taken her three days to decide on the rust-colored dress: a simple style, and the color complemented her auburn hair. Dinner with Tony Kellner's parents was about the most important thing she could imagine. She had to assume his invitation meant he was really taking her seriously as a girlfriend. It was overwhelming. She'd put her all into their dates, practicing everything she'd read in the magazines and books about how to get a guy to like you. They talked about every interest he'd ever had; she agreed to every suggestion he made about where to eat or what movie to see; she made sure to compliment him on his taste in clothes, the places he took her, everything she could find to praise.

It appeared to be working. Dreamily, she thought of last

Friday night when they walked home from the movies. He'd stopped in front of her building and fixed those dark eyes on her face.

"You're not *laaahk* other girls, Natasha," he said, his southern drawl somehow underscoring the urgency in his tone. "You're better. You're what I've been lookin' for."

He leaned over and kissed her, the first time since they'd started going out. His kiss was harsh, almost fierce. Then, he pushed his tongue into her mouth and moved it all around. It was the first time Natasha had ever been French-kissed, but she would rather have died than let him know it. She did her best to follow his lead, although she was relieved when he finished. It wasn't all that enjoyable, having somebody *in* your mouth that way, his tongue so big and thick. But much more important was that he'd done it. Tony Kellner had actually kissed her.

This was definitely a big night. Aside from meeting his parents, Tony might have some other idea beyond that first kiss. Natasha's hands grew clammy as she thought about it. The other kids in school were starting to talk about them as a couple, which was the greatest thrill of all. And Tony had dropped an offhand remark about the two of them possibly going to Artie Boyd's party in two weeks, the biggest, most important senior-class party of the year. Natasha had already started daydreaming about the entrance the two of them would make, she on Tony's arm, everyone looking at them. It was agonizing, wondering if he would actually take her or not.

As soon as she'd finished getting dressed, Natasha headed toward the kitchen for a glass of milk. She didn't know if there would be any alcohol around tonight—maybe his parents were very sophisticated and served wine, or maybe he'd take her someplace with liquor after dinner—but she'd read that milk coated your stomach and kept you from getting drunk. She had no intention of making a fool of herself; she'd drink two glasses.

Reaching for the milk carton in the refrigerator, she heard a knock at the door. It couldn't be Tony; he was meeting her in front of her building in forty-five minutes.

"Mom, where are you?" she yelled. "There's somebody at the door."

"I'm busy, Tash," Kit yelled back from the bedroom. "Can you get it?"

Natasha went to the entryway and opened the door. Carlin stood in the hall, dressed to go out in blue jeans and a pale blue peasant blouse, her jacket slung over one arm.

"Hey, Tash, you ready? What time is he coming?"

Of course, Carlin knew all about Tony and dinner with his parents. Natasha told her everything—well, almost everything. She'd omitted her mild distaste for the kiss; something told her it wouldn't look good for her to reveal that, even to her best friend.

Natasha stepped out into the hall to talk to Carlin instead of asking her to come in, pulling the door behind her. She had to, because of the trouble between Carlin and Ben. Not only wouldn't they speak, but they refused to be in the same room with one another. These days, instead of hanging around at the Dameroffs' apartment as they used to, Carlin would stop by and pick her up so they could go out. Of course, it wasn't actually necessary for Carlin to come by; she could always just telephone, or have Natasha come to *her* place. But that would have eliminated any chance of Carlin's seeing Ben. It was obvious to Natasha that Carlin secretly hoped she *would* run into him.

Ben was as bad as Carlin. He pretended not to listen, but Natasha could tell he was hanging on every word when she brought up her friend's name. One day, when she and Carlin were walking on the street in front of their building, she'd glanced up and caught her brother actually watching them from the window. Neither one would tell Natasha what the fighting was about this time. They'd always fought, so it wasn't anything new. But she'd never seen them this angry.

"Not for a while. Where are you off to?" Natasha asked.

"A bunch of us are going to Wagner's. There's a band there tonight that's supposed to be really good. But I wanted to borrow your lipstick. Okay?"

Natasha looked at her in mild surprise. Carlin almost never wore lipstick. Before she could answer, the door behind her swung open.

"Tash, did you see my copy of *The Broth*—" Ben broke off in mid-sentence when he saw who Natasha was talking to.

Carlin's face turned bright red, but she stared defiantly at Ben, who seemed rooted to the spot.

Natasha broke the silence, addressing her brother. "If you mean that huge book you're reading, no, of course not. Why would I know where your book is?"

Ben turned away. "Sorry," he mumbled, walking off.

Natasha shook her head. He had to have known she was out here talking to Carlin. Why else would she stand in the hall like a fool?

"Well, okay, bye." Carlin gave a quick wave and backed up, clearly anxious to leave. "Have a good time with Tony."

"What about the lipstick?"

"I changed my mind. It doesn't matter."

"Okay." Natasha shrugged and went back inside. What was wrong with the two of them? It was obvious they both desperately wanted to patch things up, but they were being too crazy to do it. Besides, she said to herself, I should be the one with the jitters tonight.

At the thought of her date, Natasha's nervousness returned in full force. Her stomach began to hurt, and she tried to ignore it. Ever since she was twelve or so, whenever she got tense or nervous, she got a stomachache. With a half hour left before Tony was due, she spent every minute of that going over her hair and makeup until she felt she'd done the best job she could.

Tony was already waiting downstairs when she got there, his coat collar turned up against the cold November night air. She saw him appraising her, and was vastly relieved when his look turned to approval.

"Darlin', you look good enough to eat," he said, taking her hand and bringing it to his mouth. He took a gentle bite.

She laughed nervously.

"My folks are waitin'. Let's go."

He put his arm around her and they began walking. Natasha relished the sensation of being held by him. She felt desirable and fragile, as if he were protecting her.

By the time they got to Tony's house nearly a mile away, her face was red with the cold and her legs in their sheer stockings were freezing. It was a relief to have Mrs. Kellner open the door and usher them inside.

Natasha shook hands with Tony's parents. She had expected them to be a bit exotic; she assumed Tony had gotten his passionate nature from them. But they were entirely average-looking—medium height, gray hair, and nondescript clothes. Natasha smiled and thanked them for inviting her to dinner.

Mrs. Kellner gave her a thin smile in return. Though she wasn't unfriendly, her tone was cool. "Y'all go on into the living room," she said to Natasha, her southern accent even stronger than her son's, "and I'll get the ham on the table."

"That sounds lovely," Natasha said stiffly. She wished she could relax, but she was only growing more tense.

Tony and his father led her into the living room. Wanting to distract herself from the stomachache that was back in full force, she looked around. The dimly lit room was cluttered with bric-a-brac, the furniture drab. The thermostat must have been turned way up, because the room was unbearably stuffy. Natasha thought briefly of her own home; her parents probably had less money than the Kellners, but their apartment didn't look anywhere near as run-down.

Sitting on the dark brown sofa, Natasha turned to the photograph of a man that hung over the fireplace. He looked about sixty, with a crew cut and black horn-rimmed glasses. Blown up to portrait size and hung in an ornate gold frame, the picture dominated the room.

Neither Tony nor his father was saying anything. Nervously rubbing her perspiring palms together in her lap, she finally broke the silence.

"Is that a relative of yours, Mr. Kellner?" She indicated the photograph.

"Oh, no, Natasha," he said, shaking his head, "that's Otto Mead. Our founder."

"Our founder?" she echoed uncertainly.

"Yes, the founder of our order. Mrs. Kellner and I belong to the Temple of the Lord. Have for twenty-five years."

"Oh." Natasha didn't know what to say. She'd never heard of the Temple of the Lord.

"It's a great group of people, little girl." Mr. Kellner was warming to his subject. "Our revival meetin's are some of the greatest sights you could hope to see. The laws are strict, a'course. No smokin', drinkin', dancin', stuff like that. But that's the way we like it."

So much for needing that milk, Natasha thought.

She was startled to hear Tony give a derisive snort. "Yeah, Mom wouldn't be caught dead taking a drink."

"Keeps our young people toein' the line," Mr. Kellner went on, ignoring his son's remark. "Keeps our sight on what's important, not all this garbage people are talkin' today." His voice rose in anger. "Human trash, that's all we got today, runnin' the world, walkin' the streets, just goddamned human trash."

Startled, Natasha sat back a bit. She glanced over at Tony on the chair nearby, but he was watching his father impassively.

"What religion are your mommy and daddy?" Mr. Kellner asked, leaning forward in his chair. "Natasha Dameroff's kind of a foreign name, not American, now is it?"

Natasha had a strange feeling. She couldn't explain why, but she somehow knew that it would be wiser not to tell this man that she was Jewish. She didn't like the feeling, but she heeded its warning.

"My mother liked the name Natasha, that's all."

"Just liked it, eh?"

With great relief, Natasha saw Tony's mother enter the room. She hoped the conversation would get sidetracked onto something else.

"Come to the table, everyone," Mrs. Kellner announced, wiping her hands on her apron. "Byrle, Anthony, please remember to wash your hands."

When they were assembled at the small table, Natasha smiled gaily as Mrs. Kellner brought out the food, but she could practically hear her own heart thumping frantically in her chest as they all silently helped themselves from the serving platters. The tension grew inside her until she realized she couldn't wait another second; she hastily excused herself and walked as quickly as she dared to the bathroom, where she turned on the water to cover the sound of her vomiting into the toilet.

"You're fine, you're *okay*," she whispered as she bent over the sink afterward, splashing cold water on her face. "It'll be all right."

She returned to the dining room with the brightest smile she could muster, hoping they wouldn't notice her flushed cheeks. Dinner was interminable. Natasha nodded and tried to appear interested by what little was said, eating the tasteless ham and mashed potatoes as if it were the best meal anyone had ever served her. She felt alone in the room with Mr. and Mrs. Kellner. Tony seemed to have withdrawn completely, his attitude one of utter indifference. Natasha wanted to weep with gratitude when he seemed to come back to life as they were finishing the dessert of canned peaches.

"We've got to take off now," he announced to his parents. "I promised Natasha's parents she'd be back by naahne."

"I understand," his mother said approvingly. She rose and began clearing the table, as if the evening were already over and forgotten. "Good-bye, Natasha."

"Good-bye, ma'am, and thank you so much for the delicious dinner," Natasha said.

Mrs. Kellner disappeared into the kitchen. Tony's father walked them to the door.

"Be good, you hear?" he directed Tony sternly as they put on their coats.

Tony gave him a nod as he escorted Natasha outside. The air was biting cold now, but it came as a delightful change from the stultifying atmosphere inside the Kellner house. When Natasha looked at Tony, she was taken aback to see that he appeared to have undergone another transformation. He looked happy, self-confident. He even looked taller. He grinned at her mischievously, his eyes sparkling.

"A thrill a minute, my folks, right, darlin'?" he asked her. "Well, we'll just have to try and make up for that."

Natasha had no idea what he was talking about, but he was hurrying her along the sidewalk and she tried to keep up.

"Tony, why did you tell them I had to be home by nine? My parents never said that."

He winked at her. This was different from his usual self, she thought. He was suddenly so lighthearted, not the intense Tony she'd been growing used to these past weeks.

"Ah've got a surprise for you. Just another couple of blocks."

They came to the corner and turned in. "This house," Tony said, pointing. "My buddy Curt lives here. He and his parents are away in New York City for the weekend, some convention deal for his dad or something."

"We're going there?" Natasha asked, the tension returning to her stomach.

Tony didn't answer. He raced the last few steps ahead of her and pulled a key out of his pocket, opening the front door to the darkened house. With a broad sweep of his arm, he gestured to her to come in. Hesitantly, she obeyed. She didn't know what else to do.

"Do you know where the light switch is, Tony?" she asked timidly, standing in the darkness.

His arms came around her from behind. Still standing in back of her, he unbuttoned the three buttons on her wool coat and pushed it open. Natasha was so nervous, she could barely breathe. Slowly, his hands moved up from her waist, coming to rest on her breasts.

"What are you doing?" she asked. It was the stupidest question in the world, but she didn't know what else to say.

Tony's voice was a seductive whisper. "We have this house to ourselves. A big bed. No one around." He paused for emphasis. "This is our night."

Natasha's mouth was dry. "But I don't know if this is the right thing. I don't know—"

He took a few quick steps, coming around to face her. There was anger in his voice.

"You're not a tease, are you, Natasha? I'd hate to think that."

"Come on, Tony," she said placatingly, "I only said—"

His tone was suddenly sad, as if she had wounded him. "And I brought you to meet my parents." He shook his head. "Can't you see how much you mean to me? Do you want me to beg? I will, you know."

He put his arms around her and moved in closer. She could feel the hardness beneath his pants pressing against her thigh. He rubbed it against her, back and forth, slowly. "I've been dreaming about you. I want you so bad . . . *so bad*, Natasha."

Natasha's heart was pounding in her chest. This was *Tony Kellner* begging her. The boy everyone wanted. And he was saying he dreamed about her, he wanted her, like a real man wants a real woman. The thrill swept across Natasha in a shiver. It was just like a movie. It was *better*.

She whispered her response. "I want to make you happy, Tony."

She felt herself being swept up in his arms. He carried her into a dark bedroom and put her on the bed, hurriedly pulling off his coat. Then he helped her remove hers. When he went to turn the light on, she stopped him.

"Let's leave it like this, okay?" she asked.

He didn't answer, but lay down next to her, beginning to kiss her deeply. His hands went again to her breasts, kneading them, rubbing them.

It was happening so fast. Natasha wanted to pull back, get some room to breathe. Why wasn't she feeling romantic if he was touching her like this, kissing and sucking on her neck now? He was like a dog, all over her. She was horrified at having such a thought. But she couldn't see to focus on what was happening.

Tony shoved her dress up and pulled her panty hose down partway, then slipped his hand inside her underpants. Natasha stiffened as his fingers began probing her, moving all around.

"Oh, yes, baby," he groaned. "Oh, yes."

Why couldn't she enjoy this? She willed herself to concentrate. Tony shoved her underpants down. Then he lay on top of her, pressing his groin into her thigh. She could hear his breathing grow heavier as he pumped up and down against her. This was *Tony Kellner*, she reminded herself. The other girls would give anything to be in her place. Should she give him her virginity right then and there? It didn't mean all that much to her, but if she were going to lose it, she wanted it to be in the right situation. Well, she thought, she wasn't going to do any better than this.

She wrapped her arms around him and thrust her pelvis against him in return, trying to appear passionate.

Her action seemed to make him lose control. Almost instantly, she heard his zipper being yanked down, felt his arm quickly moving around down there. Then, suddenly, the pressure of his bare penis, his fingers manipulating her, and a sharp, searing pain as he penetrated her. She shut her eyes at the pain and turned her head to the side, hearing his breath coming in gasps. Then she had a horrible thought.

"Tony," she whispered urgently, "do you have something? For birth control? I don't."

"Oh, Jesus . . . ," he gasped as he thrust in and out of her, "I'll p—I'll pull out. . . . Uunnnnhhh."

With a groan so loud it was almost a yell, he jerked away from her and shoved himself against her stomach, collapsing with a shudder. She felt a wetness spread across her stomach. Tony wasn't saying anything, just lying there trying to catch his breath, his face buried in her neck. She slid her hand to touch the liquid that had started to drip from her stomach down her side, and her fingers came away with something warm and tacky stuck to them. Disgusting. She was glad it was dark so he couldn't see her face at that moment.

So this was sex. It was hard to believe it would ever be something she'd really want, something she'd ever care about doing. But if this was what men needed, well, fine, she could handle it, no problem.

Tony's weight was making it difficult for her to breathe. When she couldn't stand it a second longer, she put a hand on his shoulder and gave him a gentle push.

"Could you maybe . . . ?" She didn't know how to put it. Tony made a noise, as if he'd been startled out of sleep.

"Sorry, baby, I was driftin' off there for a second," he said groggily, rolling off her. "You sure are somethin' in bed, you know that?"

Sliding an arm around her, he pulled her close and sat partway up to look at her. There was just enough light coming in through the window for her to make out his eyes staring into hers. "And you're my girl now, aren't you, Natasha, darlin'? We're a team, you and me."

Natasha nodded. As Tony lay back on the bed, she blurted out the question that had been on her mind for so long.

"So we're definitely going to Artie Boyd's party together?"

"A'course, a'course," Tony drawled, his slurred speech telling her he was falling asleep again. "You and me, whatever you want."

Natasha lay snuggled against him as his breathing became regular. She wasn't sleepy. Instead, she was envisioning a room full of high school seniors, with loud music, everyone dancing and having a great time. In her mind's eye, the door to the party room opened and there she stood with Tony, his arm around her. Every face turned in their direction and the whispers started. *There they are, Natasha and Tony. . . . Aren't they incredible-looking together. . . .*

Natasha smiled into the darkness.

5

The air in the car was so thick with tension, it seemed to crackle. Carlin hugged the front right-hand door, studiously averting her eyes from Ben, who was driving.

"Are we getting close?" Natasha asked from the backseat, as she checked her makeup for the fourth time since they'd left Westerfield a little over an hour before.

Carlin laughed at her gently, although there was genuine panic beginning to take hold in Tash's eyes. "Tash, Saratoga is another sixty miles, and the fashion show won't start for at least another hour after we get there."

Ben looked at his sister in the rearview mirror, unconsciously frowning as he caught her eye. Tash looked gorgeous, but her obsession with perfection was turning her into someone he barely recognized.

"You know, Sis, if you keep putting all that lipstick and junk on, your head might collapse from its own weight by the time we get to Shreyer's."

He regretted his words when he saw the wounded look on his sister's face. She was so damn sensitive, so insecure. Here it was, a day of bona fide triumph, and all she could do was worry that she wasn't somehow good enough.

"Listen, Tash," he added in a softer tone. "You'll be the most beautiful teenage model that stupid store has ever had."

Natasha smiled at him, although her eyes still betrayed her nervousness.

"You do look *naaaahce.*" Tony Kellner spoke up as he moved nearer to her in the backseat, stroking her hand sinuously and drawing her closer.

Listening to Tony made Carlin wince. It was bad enough having to sit next to Ben Dameroff during the two-hour drive to Saratoga, but listening to a southern drawl from a boy who'd lived in upstate New York since he was five years old was practically more than she could bear. Whatever the magic was for Natasha, Tony held zero charm for Carlin.

This is Natasha's day, Carlin chided herself, holding back the sarcastic comment she was about to make to Tony. Shreyer's was commonly known as "the Bloomingdale's of the North," and Natasha's having been selected as a model in its Christmas fashion show was a real coup. Carlin turned her head toward the pair in the backseat, carefully avoiding any eye contact with Ben.

"You look gorgeous, Natasha," she said, desperately trying to come up with things to talk about that would make the awkward silence between her and Ben seem less obvious. "How many girls were picked for the show?"

"Six, I think. The others were all seniors."

"You'll be better than any of them," Carlin said encouragingly. Carlin wished that, for once, her friend could just be pleased with herself. All that Natasha had talked about for ages was becoming a model and dating Tony Kellner, and now that both were happening, she seemed even less sure of herself than ever.

Carlin kept trying to ease her discomfort. "You know, that lady from Shreyer's public relations department, Miss Trager, said that people from New York might come tonight. Who knows, maybe even Eileen Ford herself will turn up."

She saw Ben almost smile at her efforts to help Natasha, then catch himself, his face tightening into the angry look he wore whenever she was around.

He turned to her. "What else could Eileen Ford possibly have to do on a Saturday afternoon?"

He had spoken so quietly, only Carlin could hear it. But that was just what he was aiming for, of course, she realized. He would never be that mean to his sister. Just to her.

She stole a look at him as he stared straight at the road ahead. He wasn't about to give an inch. Well, screw him, she thought. Neither am I.

She and Ben had barely exchanged a word since their fight on the way home from the Coleville country club dance a couple of months before. Carlin would never voluntarily have sat next to Ben for this long if Natasha hadn't gotten this great opportunity. Shreyer's had been sending scouts out to the hundred biggest high schools in the state for five years or so, and several of the girls previously selected for the Christmas show had become professional models after they graduated. Okay, maybe Eileen Ford wouldn't show up, but other fashion experts probably would. Natasha's fancies aside, this was the kind of exposure that could lead to something bigger, maybe even a break in New York after she graduated from high school.

Carlin and Ben had both been thrilled for Natasha, each determined to help her during what could be a rough day. There was nothing they wouldn't do for her. If only it didn't mean suffering through the day together. Carlin was still furious when she thought of that night in Coleville. As far as she was concerned, Ben had set her up, reduced her to Jell-O, and then moved in for the kill. She'd gone from fury during the fight to modification at the thought of what had come before, the uncontrollable heat she'd allowed him to ignite, the passion she couldn't stop herself from expressing. Well, that was over with. No more passion. And no more mortification either, she vowed to herself. She was back to rage, and it felt pretty good.

For just a moment, she thought about how grateful she should be to him. He had dared her to apply to Harvard, and she had actually sent for an application, spent countless hours filling it out, writing the stupid essay, working to earn the money for the check that had to be sent along with it. At first, she'd done it mostly to spite him, but since she'd mailed it in a few weeks before, she'd started to get really excited. Not that she thought she had a chance. But at least it was something to dream about. *My* dream, she thought angrily as she glared at Ben and hugged the car door even more tightly.

Her action was not lost on Ben. "If you fall out of the car, there isn't enough time to turn around and pick you up again. Sorry."

She wouldn't allow him the satisfaction of a response. She thought of continuing a conversation with Natasha, but the sight of her friend being fondled by Tony Kellner was too much to bear. It seemed as if everything and everyone was getting on her nerves. Forget it, she decided finally, closing her eyes and pretending to sleep as they rode toward Saratoga.

The mall in which Shreyer's was located was aglow in Christmas lights when they pulled into the parking lot an hour later.

"Everyone in New York State must be shopping today," Carlin said in amazement as Ben negotiated the parking lanes, all filled to capacity.

When he succeeded in finding a space that seemed miles from the store's entrance, all four passengers stayed put for a moment, overwhelmed by the swell of activity that surrounded them. Finally, Ben pulled on the door handle and broke the momentary spell.

"Come on, Sis, you're going to get famous today."

An hour later Natasha was draped in a diaphanous white gown, surrounded by bright lights and loud music, her entrance greeted by waves of applause from the audience. As she walked gracefully down the runway, turning every few seconds so all angles of the garment could be appreciated, Carlin could hear murmurings from the back of the room. Whatever insecurity Natasha had displayed in the car was completely gone now. Her hair swept up in a loose chignon, her expression now completely serene, she appeared composed and elegant, with a rhythm in her movements that suggested she'd been modeling her whole life.

The area press was out in force, and she could hear "What's her name?" "How old is she?" being whispered by several people with notebooks balanced on theirs laps. A local television crew's camera operator was following Natasha's path, trailing her up and down as she demonstrated the fluid lines of her dress. The soundman had stopped adjusting his controls and was staring frankly at Natasha.

Tony Kellner was clapping wildly for Natasha as she made her way offstage to change outfits. Carlin and Ben both stood as the models came out for a final bow when it was all over.

"It's not just us." Ben turned to Carlin, unable to restrain his excitement as the whole crowd cheered more loudly for Natasha than for any of the other high school models. "She was great."

Carlin grinned in agreement, too excited for Natasha to think about the person with whom she was agreeing.

When Natasha emerged in her own clothes twenty minutes later, she wasn't alone. Accompanying her were three women and two men, all dazzlingly turned out, obviously part of the store's fashion authority.

"Listen, Ben, Carlin"—Natasha was so excited, she could barely get the words out—"we're going out to celebrate, so tell Mom I'll be home as soon as I can. Well, no, that is, when I can get there. I mean, Mr. Carteret promised to get Tony and me back to Westerfield." She gestured toward the man in the blue pin-striped suit standing off to her left and whispered, "He knows agents in New York."

"Don't worry. We'll find our lonely way home just fine." Ben ruffled her hair playfully.

Natasha looked relieved as she carefully patted her hair back in place. Holding Tony's hand tightly, she followed the group as they swept out toward the exit.

Carlin and Ben walked back to the car under the already-darkening winter sky, unable to maintain their rigid silence in the wake of Natasha's success.

"God, she looked beautiful," Carlin exulted, thinking back to Natasha's first appearance in the long white gown.

"You know," Ben replied, looking quickly at her as he drove onto the well-lit road that led to the highway, "I wasn't sure she'd be up to it in front of all those people. But she was a knockout."

Carlin nodded, even managing to smile at him across the front seat.

"I could have lived without Rhett Butler," Ben continued conversationally.

Carlin laughed. "I remember Tony when he was six years old, and I could swear the accent wasn't half as thick. How has he managed to get more southern year after year living within a couple of hundred miles of the Canadian border?"

"Ahh don't know, Miss Cahhlin." Ben's imitation cracked them both up. By the time they reached the interstate, they were reliving Tash's appearance and talking as if they'd never stopped.

An hour or so later, Ben looked at the clock on the dashboard. Seven-thirty. "You must be starving," he said to Carlin, realizing how hungry he himself was. Neither of them had eaten anything since breakfast.

"I guess I am." Somehow in the excitement of the afternoon she had lost her appetite completely. No, she thought more honestly. In the warm presence of Ben, acting the way he'd acted once before, she found herself absolutely satisfied.

The realization made her self-conscious suddenly, and she could only nod when Ben suggested turning into a roadhouse a short way up the highway. The sounds of raucous music hit them the moment they opened their car doors, and as they walked through the front entrance, they found themselves in a dark, crowded room, young men and women three deep in a long wooden bar, a jukebox blaring rock and roll on the far side of the large room.

Even after they were seated, Carlin stayed quiet. Ben noticed her change of mood. He thought of asking her about it, but decided not to risk starting another argument. Matter-of-factly, he ordered hamburgers and Cokes for both of them, and Carlin nodded in approval.

He felt so confused, watching her as she sat looking at the couples on the dance floor. He'd been so mad at her ever since they'd had that fight. Carlin was so stubborn, so cold when she wanted to be. But, in the dim light of the round-house, she was so damned beautiful. And for a couple of hours in the car, she'd been, well, like *herself.*

Ben could hardly remember what it was they had fought about. In fact, it was all he could do not to run his hands over her long brown hair, its highlights gleaming in the spinning stage lights over the center of the room. In this strange, vibrant place, it was as if they could start all over.

The jukebox was playing "Born to Run," with everyone at the bar clapping in time to the gyrating pairs on the dance floor. The thick haze of smoke and the pungent smell of beer in the room made Ben feel almost drunk.

"Come on," he said, pushing his chair back and standing up. "Let's dance before the food comes." He held his hand out to her.

He could see the indecision in her eyes. She seemed to be

figuring out just how far apart they could remain if they
danced to the hard-driving music. Finally she took his hand.

But when they got to the dance floor, the record ended, immediately replaced by Barbra Streisand singing "The Way
We Were." Without hesitation, Ben took Carlin in his arms,
leading her in a slow circle around the floor. For a few moments she held herself stiffly, as far away from him as she
could while slow dancing. But as other couples crowded the
floor around them, they were pushed closer together, and Ben
took advantage of the narrowing distance, inhaling the scent
of her shampoo, raising his hand from her back to touch the
cool skin on her neck.

The lights in the bar abruptly dimmed and he felt Carlin
begin to relax into him, the warmth of her body against his
filling him with satisfaction. Hesitantly at first, he began to
caress her back through the thin fabric of her blouse. When
he felt her respond to his touch he was filled with an overwhelming mixture of relief and excitement. As the song
ended, they were completely hemmed in by the mass of couples around them, barely moving as they found themselves
locked in an embrace. It was as if their fight had never happened, as if they were discovering each other all over again.

The music changed once more, and most of the couples
left the floor. But Ben kept Carlin where they were for an extra moment, tipping her head up and surprising her with a
light kiss.

Carlin felt her heart pounding. Flushed, she broke away
and they returned to their table. They ate their dinner quickly
and went out to the car. In the cold darkness, she realized she
couldn't control the urge to touch him. She didn't want to. As
he was inserting the key into the ignition, she moved so that
her body pressed against him. Almost holding her breath, she
brought her face close to his.

"Oh, God," Ben breathed as she placed her slender hands
inside his jacket, studying his chest, inching beneath his shirt
buttons to find his skin. Closed in by the steering wheel in
front of him, surrounded by the frigid December air, he felt
impossibly aroused.

This time their mouths were ablaze, their kiss never-ending
as their tongues explored, their hands roaming.

Carlin urged him toward her, luring him on top of her on the wide front seat. She felt a thrill of unquenchable fire as he ground his body into hers. Impatiently, Ben tore open her wool jacket, pushing up her sweater and blouse, his fingers finding the softness of her breasts.

Overwhelmingly excited, she leaned forward for a moment, pulling her jacket off, yanking her sweater over her head, and urging his mouth to explore the secret place his hands had gone.

"Carlin . . ." Ben forced himself to stop, suddenly gaining control. "We can't do this."

Sitting up was an act of pure will. He couldn't take advantage of her. It wasn't fair. It was just the excitement of the day, of finding his way back to Carlin.

But Carlin knew better. "Ben, please." Her voice was just breath as she urged him down once more. She knew that what she wanted was right.

Slowly, Ben gave in. Heaving his own jacket and shirt off, he lowered himself to meet the swell of her breasts. Sighing with pleasure, he felt overcome with the textures of her, the softness of her skin, the rising tension of her nipples as they came to life in his hands. He and Carlin were wedged awkwardly in the ten-year-old Chevy, sprawled across the front seat, their heads almost slamming into the door handle as they kissed. But it didn't matter. Nothing did except the extraordinary feeling of being so close.

When her hands reached down to the front of his jeans, exploring with hesitant courage, he gasped with pleasure. Reaching down to unzip his fly, he stopped for a moment, terrified of hurting her.

"You're sure?" he asked, his voice trembling.

"Oh God, yes," she answered, stroking him, reaching beneath his underwear to touch his swollen penis for the first time, feeling him grow in her hands.

He responded to her with his hands, weaving surely under her skirt, trailing the insides of her thighs. His fingers slipped inside her panties, reaching down, finding her moistness with his fingertips, then moving in deeply as he felt her respond.

She seemed almost to ride his hand in pleasure as she answered his caresses, waves of ecstasy rocking her as his fingers went deeper and deeper.

"Ben, please."

He understood what she wanted, and eased off her underpants. Forcing himself to be gentle, he entered her, finding strength in her moan of pleasure as she received him. Slowly he pushed forward, cradling her head in his arms, smothering her mouth with his own as he felt himself break through.

But Carlin was too enraptured to feel any pain. She found herself moving with him, widening circles of pure ecstasy taking her to a place she'd never imagined. Within seconds her happiness was matched by his own thunder of joy.

As they lay in each other's arms, Ben finally began to feel the chill of the air around them. She must be freezing, he thought, guilty for a second. Yet he couldn't bring himself to leave her just yet. Finally he leaned down to pick up his jacket from the floor of the car, laughing out loud as he noticed the windows, thoroughly steamed over by the heat they had created.

For the briefest moment, their months of guerilla warfare flashed through his mind, but it seemed as if it had taken place years, decades before.

"Please, let's never do that again, okay?" he said tenderly, placing the coat so it covered both of them.

"Never make love again?" she asked, giving him a teasing kiss.

Grinning, he pulled away for a moment. "Not exactly. In fact, how would you feel about staying in the car for the rest of our lives?"

He smiled at her, then covered her mouth once again, this time hungrily, as if to seal their happiness for the rest of time.

6

"No, Tony, I swear it. Carlin's coming over to cut my hair. That's the truth." The telephone receiver cradled between her ear and shoulder, Natasha sat cross-legged on her bedroom floor, filing her nails as she spoke. She had dragged the telephone as far as it would go from its perch in the hall, but the wire barely stretched to the bedroom; she had to sit practically up against the door if she wanted to be in her own room and talk on the phone with any privacy.

"What time will you be done?" Tony demanded on the other end.

"I don't know." Although she kept her tone sweet, her irritation would have been evident to anyone observing how fast and hard she was dragging the emery board across her fingernails.

"Didn't you just see Carlin?" Tony asked in annoyance. "Can you really say you prefer seein' her today to seein' me?"

Natasha was growing more exasperated, but there was no trace of it in her voice. "We're spending the afternoon together. I'm really sorry, but I can't see you till tonight."

"But I miss you, baby," Tony said in a little boy's voice.

Natasha was relieved to hear the apartment door opening. "Tony, she's here. I'll call you later, okay?"

"But, baby—"

"Bye, Tony. You're the greatest." Natasha hung up before he could say anything else.

She frowned as she stood up. This constant questioning about where she was and why she couldn't be with him all the time was really getting on her nerves.

"Tash, Carlin's here," Kit called from the living room, "and I'm on my way out. I'll see you kids at dinner."

"I'm in here, Carlin," Natasha yelled.

Hurriedly, she spread a few sheets of newspaper on the floor and set a straight-backed chair in the center. Carlin appeared in her bedroom doorway. Natasha glanced over just long enough to give her friend a quick smile, then reached to pick up the scissors on the bureau.

"All ready for you," she said, turning back to hand the scissors to Carlin. "But, please, only take a half inch off. Last time you went a little crazy, and it was more like two inches."

Carlin nodded, not saying anything. Natasha took a closer look at her. Her friend seemed shaken.

"Are you all right?" Natasha asked in concern. "Listen, you don't have to cut my hair. We can do it another time. Or I can get somebody else."

Her thoughts obviously elsewhere, Carlin spoke distractedly: "No, no, Tash, I'm always happy to cut your hair."

"What's the matter?" Natasha persisted, coming closer.

Carlin brought her hand from behind her back, showing Natasha the white envelope she held, already opened. It bulged slightly with its contents.

Carlin's voice was barely a whisper. "Harvard. It's from Harvard."

Natasha's eyes opened wide.

"Tash." Carlin paused and gazed at her friend with a stricken expression. *"I got in."*

Natasha caught her breath. "You're kidding. You got in? *You got in!"*

She let out a yell and threw her arms around Carlin. "It's incredible, it's unbelievable."

Carlin pulled back. "But I never—it was just a stupid dare. Ben . . ."

"Of course!" Natasha froze, suddenly understanding. *"Everyone* gets acceptance letters today."

She rushed out of the bedroom to the table near the front door where her mother always deposited the mail. Sure enough, a pile of letters sat there. Natasha grabbed them, hurriedly sorting through. Carlin came to stand next to her, anxiously looking over her shoulder.

There it was, the crimson logo emblazoned on the envelope, addressed to Mr. Benjamin Dameroff. Natasha held it up.

"Oh, God," Carlin sounded anguished. "It's thin. There's only one piece of paper inside."

Natasha turned to her hopefully. "But does this *always* mean a rejection? Couldn't it be something else?"

"Maybe." Carlin tried to sound optimistic. "I'm not sure."

Natasha stared at the letter. If Ben were going to get rejected, she wanted time to find some way to fix it. She couldn't stand the idea of seeing him hurt. Not getting into Harvard would just about kill him.

Letter in hand, she raced into the kitchen and filled the tea-kettle with water, setting it on the stove.

"You're not really going to do that, are you?" Carlin asked as she entered the kitchen to see Natasha turning on the flame beneath the kettle. "You wouldn't steam it open . . ."

"Just watch me." Natasha frowned with impatience, waiting for the water to boil.

Carlin sank down onto one of the kitchen chairs. She'd never had any intention of going to Harvard. The truth was that this had always been Ben's dream, not hers. Every so often, he would talk about the things they would do together in Boston, or classes they might both take, but she always just laughed at him. Sure, she had fantasized about going, but as time passed, she'd realized how implausible the idea was. Even when she scored as high as Ben did on the SATs, she refused to take it seriously. Ben was the only one going to Harvard, everybody knew that.

Tears stung her eyes. She loved him so much. These past few months together had been the happiest of her entire life. She couldn't wait to get up every day, knowing she would see him. She daydreamed her way through classes, just waiting until she could meet him again in the hall and share a few minutes before the next class. The one horrible part was having to act as if she didn't mind that he still spent so much time playing ball after school or studying. But when he was done, he was all hers—to look at, to touch, to kiss. Then, the thrill of making love with him whenever they were lucky enough to find one of their apartments empty. Holding him, stroking his smooth skin, feeling the length of him against

her and the overwhelming sensation of having him inside her,
deeper, deeper, until they both exploded, Ben holding her so
tightly and calling out her name. She wanted to drown in
those moments, willing them to go on forever. But what
would happen to all that now?

The sharp whistle of the teakettle jolted her back to reality.
Natasha held the envelope over the steam, moving it back and
forth, waiting for the glue to release its grip. After what felt
like an eternity, she was able to open the envelope and pull
out the letter. She scanned it, then looked up at Carlin, who
sat tensely in her chair.

"The waiting list. They put him on the waiting list."
Natasha sat down, shaking her head.

Carlin felt sick. This was all her fault. She didn't really
give a damn about Harvard, and here she had stolen Ben's
place. If not for her, of course he would have gotten in. What
were the odds he'd get in now, that a spot would open up and
he'd be the one to get plucked from the waiting list and invited in? His dream for so long, and she had destroyed it for
him. She put her arms down on the kitchen table and buried
her head in them. Natasha sat down beside her, staring at the
letter in her hand dejectedly.

"What am I going to do?" Carlin asked woefully.

"About what?"

At the sound of Ben's voice, both girls jumped in their
seats. They hadn't heard him come in, but he was leaning
against the kitchen's doorjamb, holding several books beneath
one arm. His long, dark hair was disheveled, his cheeks still
flushed from the exertion of a basketball game. As she did
every time she saw him, Carlin felt a sharp flutter in her
stomach, and a strange twinge right behind her knees as if
they might not support her. Right now he looked so carefree
and relaxed. But wait till he heard . . .

Ben furrowed his brows slightly as he looked more closely
at the two of them. "What's going on? You look as if somebody died."

Natasha stood up, extending the letter. "Please don't be
mad that I opened it. I couldn't help myself."

"What's this?" Ben stepped forward and reached out to
take the piece of paper from his sister. He read it quickly.

Then, expressionless, he set his books down on the table and read it again, more slowly this time.

Crumpling the letter up into a ball, he turned away from Natasha and Carlin. There was silence in the room. For a split second, Ben's shoulders sagged with disappointment. But, almost immediately, he straightened up again, quickly taking a deep breath. When he turned back to them, his face was composed.

"Well," he said, "still a chance, I suppose, slim as it is."

Both girls nodded dumbly. Suddenly remembering, he looked directly at Carlin.

"Did you get a letter from them too?"

She nodded again.

"And?" he prodded.

She stared at him, unable to answer.

"Carlin?" he asked again.

She looked up at him in misery. "I . . ."

He spoke evenly: "You got in."

Her voice was barely a whisper. "Yes."

His pain was almost too much for her to bear. He nodded, seemingly as much to himself as to her.

"I shouldn't have, Ben," she said quietly. "I didn't deserve it."

"Yes, you did," he said slowly. "You had the grades, the great SATs."

It took some effort, but he was able to give her a smile. She wanted to cry, seeing the willpower it was taking for him to be gracious.

"And you did all that stuff," he went on, "singing in the chorus every year, planning the school carnival. All that made you more well-rounded or whatever they call it. I was always studying, just being a grind."

"That's not true," Natasha broke in. "You did sports and lots of other things too."

But Ben didn't answer.

What could he say? Carlin thought. His athletic pursuits were always played out in sandlot games and random courts; he'd never been able to commit the time to a real team, something that would have looked impressive on an application. Her activities just got in the way of her doing homework. Yet it was her indifference, not his determination, that was being rewarded.

"Besides," Ben went on, "Harvard's only going to take one person from a place like Westerfield. They want people from all over. And the one they picked was you. So you earned it."

Carlin could only guess what this speech was costing him. She'd never loved him more than right now.

"Ben." She stood up and went to him, slowing putting both arms around his neck. He held her around the waist in return.

"Now, listen," he said playfully, "if I hadn't dared you, you'd never be going, so you'd better do well—for my sake as much as your own."

Carlin buried her head against his chest. "I love you," she whispered.

Natasha jumped up from her chair, her voice determinedly cheerful. "Oh, Ben, it's not really a rejection. By next month they'll take you as well. July at the latest!"

He kissed the top of Carlin's head lightly, then looked at his sister with a smile. "There's always that chance, now, isn't there?"

Ben shoved his books inside his locker and slammed the door shut. He was late for the senior assembly. Hurrying down the corridor, he sighed briefly with relief that this day was almost over. Having to tell the other kids at school that he'd been wait-listed at Harvard had been just as difficult as he'd feared. It was no secret that Harvard had been his dream for years. The kids at school were shocked and sympathetic, which of course only made him feel worse. But at least it was out in the open now and the humiliation was over.

Besides, he thought, there still *was* a chance he'd get in. If not, he would just have to live with going to SUNY Binghamton, which was actually a very good school. In retrospect, he couldn't believe how foolish he'd been to apply only to Harvard and one backup college. He'd been so damned sure Harvard would take him. Maybe he just wanted it so much that he convinced himself it was inevitable. Applying to SUNY was actually a last-second decision, a concession to the fact that he should have a safety school and this one would be so much cheaper for him as a state resident. He'd never really considered that he might end up there. But there was always that chance of getting into Harvard from the waiting list. Or maybe he could transfer there, apply again after a year at Binghamton.

He nodded to himself as he approached the double doors to the school auditorium. Everything would be all right. There was even a somewhat bright side to not getting into Harvard. The tuition was a lot less at SUNY. The finances of Harvard had always been a problem looming on the horizon.

The auditorium was packed with students, and Mr. Vann, the principal, had already begun to speak, standing onstage behind a podium. Ben slipped into a seat in the back row. He'd wanted to sit with Carlin, who was somewhere in here, but he was too late.

". . . we go on to the rest of our program for today, we have a special announcement." There was scattered whispering in the audience, and with a frown Mr. Vann scanned the sea of faces before him, waiting for silence. When it was quiet in the room, he continued. "We are pleased to announce the winner of this year's Rutherford Award."

Ben straightened up in his chair. He hadn't known today was the day they'd announce the winner. A few students who'd seen his late entrance turned in their seats to look at him, knowing he was about to be named.

"It's our school's highest honor," Mr. Vann went on, "and we are so very pleased that one of our students is chosen to receive this privilege every year. It reflects so well on all of us."

Come on, Ben silently demanded, his entire body tense with waiting, *come on and get to it.* This award was his, everybody knew it. If he couldn't have Harvard, at least he could win this.

"So it gives me great pleasure to share the name of the winner with all of you today." The principal beamed. "This year's winner of the Rutherford Award is Carlin Squire."

Immediately, the room began to buzz, heads turning to a point in one of the middle rows where Carlin was sitting, shock on her face. Stunned, Ben stood up and, resisting the urge to run, strode out of the auditorium, curious eyes following him. Back in the corridor, he tore down the hall and outside as fast as he could, not stopping until he'd gone several blocks and was out of sight of the school.

He dropped down to sit on the curb. What had he done wrong? He'd planned and worked for so long, certain he was on the right path to getting what he wanted. But no one else seemed to think he deserved what he wanted. He couldn't have Harvard, he couldn't have the Rutherford.

Yet it wasn't enough that *he* couldn't have it. It all had to go to Carlin, the girl he loved more than anything in the world. It was as if he couldn't get enough of her. The power of his feelings frightened him, and he tried to maintain some control, forcing himself to spend a few hours away from her every day, playing ball or studying. But when he wasn't with her, she was all he could think about; his game wasn't as good, his studying suffered. His sweet, precious Carlin, the girl he'd hated so passionately all those years. That passion was transformed into something else altogether now, and it was far more intense.

Of course it was his own stupid fault. He'd dared her to apply to Harvard. But it never occurred to him that things might work out this way. He'd been truthful the day before when he said that she had the grades and the activities that made her a good applicant, but it was all a lark for her. She never took any of those activities seriously, and for as long as he'd known her, she'd never studied more than the absolute minimum. How many times had she made fun of him for working so hard, for the hours he spent in the library? Anger welled up inside him. It wasn't fair.

For a minute, he gave himself over to hating her. Something inside him screamed out that it was all supposed to be *his*, not hers. But the feeling died down quickly. He knew he had no right to be angry at her. She'd won it all fair and square. And if anybody was going to have a few strokes of good fortune, he would certainly want it to be Carlin.

He stood up and started walking. For a long time, he didn't think about anything at all, but just wandered the long, gray blocks of Westerfield, past the playing fields and run-down houses, past the seedy downtown and factories. The sun was getting low in the sky.

Finally, he began to consider his situation. Without the

Rutherford money, the family's savings alone wouldn't even come close to covering four years at SUNY. He knew his parents would do their best to scrape up whatever they could, but they were having a tough enough time right now. The price of tuition, books, a dorm room—he had to find some other ways to make money.

Okay, okay, he said to himself, just concentrate. There had to be ways. He wanted to keep his grades up in case Harvard was still willing to consider him later in the spring, but he'd have to get a job after school for the rest of the semester, that was all there was to it. His mother had always insisted he stick to his studying, not wanting him to be distracted by a job. It hadn't been much of an issue, given how few jobs there were for anybody—much less high school students—in this town. But now he'd have to do his best to find one. Then there was the whole summer ahead, when he could work two, maybe three jobs.

His jaw set, he felt his optimism returning. Maybe the people at SUNY could help him get a job in the library or something. If he worked nights . . . He wasn't so powerless. Finally somewhat cheered, he turned toward home. Back in his room, he'd try to make some concrete plans. And he had to call Carlin to congratulate her on the Rutherford Award. Looking at his watch, he saw it was already after six o'clock. He picked up his pace.

When Ben entered his apartment, he found his mother and sister together near the front door. Natasha had obviously heard about the Rutherford and already told Kit. Ben's mother gave him a warm hug as soon as he stepped inside.

"I can't believe it, sweetheart," she said sympathetically. "What a rotten break. But it was just those few thousand dollars. We can find some other way to make it up."

Ben broke away from her embrace. "Mom, I'm okay, I really am. Thanks."

Kit's face glowed with love as she smiled at him. "You can do anything, Ben, remember that."

"Hey, Ben, I'm sorry," Natasha said. "I wish you and Carlin could have tied for the Rutherford."

"Yup." Ben shrugged slightly. "But that's the way it went. If it wasn't me, I'm glad at least it was her."

The three of them turned at the sound of the key in the door. Leonard Dameroff rarely got home before ten, so they were all surprised to see him. But their surprise turned to concern when they saw how white his face was. His whole body was shaking.

"Leonard, what is it?" Worriedly, Kit rushed to him. "Are you sick?"

Leonard shook his head, looking down at the house keys in his hand as he turned them over and over.

Kit put a hand on his arm. "Look at me. What's the matter?"

He raised an anguished face to her. Then he looked at his children.

"I don't know how to tell you this," he said to them, his voice full of pain.

"Tell us what, Dad?" Natasha asked fearfully.

"I heard about the Rutherford Award—one of the teachers came by the store this afternoon and mentioned how surprised everyone was that it didn't go to you, Ben," Leonard said slowly.

"It's okay, Dad," Ben said comfortingly. "You don't have to get so upset."

"No, no, that's not it." Leonard shook his head. "Naturally, when I heard, I wanted to find out what that meant to us financially. I decided to call Margaret Wahl and get the total of our savings with her. But when I called her office at the college, they told me she'd left three weeks ago."

"Left?" Kit echoed. "Left for where?"

"They didn't know," he said, turning to his wife. "They said they only knew she'd left town. Quit her job and gone."

"What does that mean, Daddy?" Natasha asked tensely.

"I wasn't sure myself, so I got in my car and drove to her apartment building. Her name wasn't on the buzzer downstairs anymore. Finally, I found the super for the building and he told me she'd cleared out, just disappeared one day."

"And our money . . ." Kit waited breathlessly.

Leonard could barely get the words out. "The super said several other people had been around looking for her, yelling and screaming about how she'd run off with their money. He told me to call the police and add my complaint to the list."

Kit was ashen. "She ran off with our money? All of it?" He nodded.

Natasha cried out, "But, Daddy, Ben needs that money for college."

Leonard bit his lip. "I know, baby, I know."

"Oh, God," Kit moaned.

Ben stared at his father as if unable to comprehend his words.

"Mom." Natasha stepped forward, reaching out for her mother. "Mom, what are we going to do?"

Kit didn't seem to feel Natasha's hands on her. She rushed over to Ben, throwing her arms around him, tears in her eyes. "Ben, it'll be all right, everything will work out. I promise you, darling, I swear it."

Stung, Natasha stepped back. Ben didn't resist his mother, but just stood there, immobile.

It's all over, he thought. There was no way in the world he could go to college the following year. Without their savings, he couldn't afford tuition and books at the crummiest community college, let alone SUNY or Harvard. Admission from the waiting list to the Ivy League had become immaterial. Slowly, he let his head sink down onto his mother's shoulder.

I'll never be a doctor, he said to himself bitterly. Not unless I plan to finish medical school at fifty. That's about how long it would take for me to earn enough to get through school.

"Ben," Leonard said to him helplessly, taking a step forward, "I can't tell you how terrible I feel. Margaret Wahl always seemed so responsible, so respectable. So many people trusted her."

Kit motioned her husband away with a sharp wave of her arm, fiercely holding on to her son, her body tense with pain. Natasha and Leonard stood mute, watching the two of them locked into their own tight circle of grief.

7

"Goddamnit, move."

J. T. Squire honked his horn impatiently. If there was one thing that drove him crazy, it was some idiot behind the wheel stopping for a traffic light practically before it had turned yellow. The man in the Ford Mustang in front of him turned around briefly with a gesture that said, "Too bad, sucker." J.T. felt as if, one more time, the entire world had conspired to make his life miserable.

The thought of going home to the sight of Lillian knitting and cooking and clucking as if their stinking apartment was some important little world of its own made him sick. And Carlin, with her acceptance from her big, fancy school. Well, she was smart all right, just like her old man, but here she was falling into the kind of lucky break that had eluded him all his life.

Life hadn't been anywhere near that smooth for him. His parents had been big nobodies, and no university had mailed out any invitations to him when he was a kid. He was too busy working his butt off. Of course, he admitted to himself, finding work lately had been a little tough, but he did as much as he could.

As the light changed and the Mustang in front of him began to move, its motor coughed, and the car seemed to die. Serves you right, J.T. thought to himself before acknowledging that *he* wouldn't be able to move either until the Mustang managed to start up once again. My lucky star strikes again.

Realizing he could try to back out of the narrow one-way block, he turned his head around and checked for any cars behind him. Seeing nothing, he backed up quickly and came to a halt in front of Ben Dameroff's little candy store.

Now there was a man with luck he didn't begin to know what to do with, J.T. thought sourly as he stared through the dull glass window, DAMEROFF's painted on the front. Leonard, with his fancy educated family and his dynamite wife. If I had a woman like Kit Dameroff waiting for me in my bed, I swear I'd never leave the house.

J.T. backed the car up carefully, slowing down to gaze into the candy store's side window. Damn it, Kit was in there. Why would she be there at nine-thirty on a Friday night?

He pulled the car over to a parking space right next to the window. There was no sign of Leonard as far as he could tell. That seemed odd. J.T. had passed this dingy little place thousands of times, and regular as rain, Leonard would be in there alone, staring into space or straightening shelves. Bored, lonely, unhappy, whatever his problem was. It really galled J.T, a guy like Leonard, twenty years after one stroke of bad luck and he looked as if he were still in mourning.

He watched Kit move from behind the counter to a spinner rack of paperback novels. Listlessly, she paged through one of the books, the stillness unusual in a woman who always seemed to be on the go. Unlike her husband, Kit had certainly never let anything slow her down. J.T. let his eyes linger over the lines of her full-breasted body. Boy, could she fill out a dress, he thought for maybe the millionth time. Whenever the four of them went out together, he and Kit had always kidded around, but he'd never had the chance to stare at her as long as he liked until now.

He turned off the motor. Let Leonard Dameroff have something to really be depressed about, he thought as he got out and locked the door behind him.

Ten minutes later, Kit Dameroff looked up as the bell over the entryway of Dameroff's rang. In strode J. T. Squire, carrying a container of birthday candles in plastic holders, a package of frosted cupcakes, a bottle of red wine, a corkscrew, and two glasses.

"What in the world are you doing here?" she asked, laughing as he placed the wine and the glasses down.

"You looked as if you needed a celebration, so here it is." J.T. began putting the candles into the cupcakes, winking as he arranged them in the letters K-I-T and lit them with his Zippo lighter.

"You are the silliest man in the universe," Kit exclaimed as he unwrapped the wine bottle and removed the cork. She couldn't keep herself from giggling. In this setting, J.T.'s machinations were amusing.

"Leonard would die if a customer walked in right now," she said, still smiling.

"Where is Leonard, anyway?" J.T. asked.

"In bed with the flu. He's just miserable. You know, it's the first time he's missed work in all the years the store's been open."

"Why didn't Ben fill in?" J.T. couldn't entirely hide the resentment in his voice. Now there was a real pain in the ass, Ben Dameroff. Probably screwing his daughter every day, and didn't even have the grace to look happy about it.

"He's got a night job now." Kit's voice sounded uncharacteristically sad. "You know, with all that's happened, he's trying to save up as much as he can before he goes off to school next year."

"Well, this is not your natural habitat, I call tell you that much." J.T. poured a glass of wine and handed it to Kit as he looked at her admiringly. "You belong in Windsor Castle. No, in a sultan's palace in some sheikdom somewhere, dripping diamonds and snapping your fingers for service."

Kit laughed. It was flattering, all this ridiculous talk, even if it was nonsense. "I belong exactly where I am," she said, catching sight of a shelf of dusty children's games left over from Christmas two seasons before and wondering for a split second if she were telling the truth. In fact, things were a little depressing right now. Leonard, even more unhappy and withdrawn than usual, blaming himself morning and night for the Margaret Wahl catastrophe. And Ben, well, he might never get over this. Even Natasha. There was her daughter rushing around to model in various fancy stores, practically consumed by self-doubt, clearly unable to get any real pleasure out of any of it. Kit knew she could be unfair to Natasha, but she wished the girl could just kick up her heels. Maybe if one person in the family could enjoy life, the apartment wouldn't feel quite so bleak.

"A toast to the most beautiful woman in the world." J.T. raised his glass and took a big swallow of wine.

Kit was startled. She had practically forgotten J.T. was there. What in the world was he talking about!

"Oh, J.T., cut it out." She forced herself to sound mildly annoyed, but the truth was she felt tickled. For all his foolishness, J.T. was paying her a kind of attention she hadn't received in years. Guiltily she thought of Leonard, coughing his brains out this morning, refusing to call a doctor, turning away from her when she tried to cheer him up before she left for the store. Usually, J. T. Squire seemed faintly absurd, with his well-pressed suits and manicured nails. Kit appreciated Leonard's seriousness, his dedication to her and the children. But for right now, the sight of J.T.'s handsome face, eager and alive, his eyes filled with mischief . . . Well, she had to admit it felt pretty good. Finally she joined him, picked up the glass in front of her and took a long sip of wine, then another.

What is he after? she wondered, suddenly feeling the strangeness of the scene, the two of them celebrating God-knows-what in the middle of an empty candy store. Self-conscious for a moment, she found herself lifting the wineglass again, and draining it.

No question about it, she mused as the wine's delicious warmth took hold in her empty stomach, J. T. Squire was a very attractive man. It was fun to flirt with him when they all went out together. But he was so, well, irresponsible. She'd never taken their flirting seriously. For all the years of her marriage, the only man she'd thought about had been Leonard. He was solid, the perfect antidote to her own frivolity. Why, she asked herself as J.T. refilled her glass, was the thought of Leonard's seriousness suddenly stultifying?

J. T. Squire was silly and shallow, but for some reason, he looked almost dashing tonight. Idly, she wondered what had drawn him and his wife to each other in the first place. Kit was very fond of Lillian, but she seemed so wrong for J.T., so plain. It was hard to see any genuine affection between them. Most of the time Lillian would sit quietly, fully engaged in whatever project she was working on. As for J.T., he seemed to ignore his wife completely. Embarrassed even as the thought flitted through her mind, Kit found herself wondering if the Squires still made love. It seemed unimaginable somehow.

She frowned as she considered her own marriage. Who was she to make judgments? When she and Leonard were first married, they couldn't get enough of each other, but as their lives went from one crisis to another, they seemed to grow further apart in every way. If only Leonard would snap out of his melancholy, if only he could go back to being the man she'd married. He loved her as much as ever, she knew that, but his depression was draining all the joy out of their lives. She couldn't remember the last time they'd made love. If J.T. can look this good to me, she said to herself, it's your own fault, Leonard Dameroff.

Lost in her musing, she realized abruptly that J.T. had come around to her side of the counter. He was standing uncomfortably close to her, staring at her almost as if he'd been reading her mind. She felt herself blush.

Slowly he lowered his lips close to hers, hesitating for a long, tantalizing moment before covering her mouth with his own. Kit didn't resist. She stood there, her eyes closing as she gave herself over to the feeling of being desired, to the thrill of a man wanting her. The scent of his cologne, the feel of his hands as they roamed along her arms—it was all so strange, even vaguely unpleasant. Yet she didn't stop him.

What in hell am I doing? she thought in alarm, as her arms came up to encircle him and she began to return his kisses in earnest.

8

Natasha just knew the other passengers on the bus were staring at her. What's she doing out of school? she imagined them whispering as she buried her head in her history textbook. For several minutes she pretended to be engrossed in America's entry into World War II, then took a quick, furtive glance around her.

For the moment at least, no one seemed to be noticing her, she thought with some relief. All morning she had sat in class hearing nothing, knowing she was going to skip school that afternoon, certain that her parents, her brother, the school principal would be on her trail within minutes. She'd thought of asking Tony to drive her, but she'd quickly changed her mind. Weekends, lunches in the cafeteria, plus two or three school nights were enough. She couldn't believe how their relationship had changed over the past few months. In the beginning, he had always had the upper hand. She'd done anything he wanted to get him as her steady boyfriend. Now the situation had changed. All he talked about was how wonderful she was, how much he loved her and needed to be with her. She was beginning to feel trapped in a cage.

Better to make it to Klebann's by herself, even if it meant getting on a crowded bus in the middle of a school day. Ben would kill her if he knew what she was doing. As supportive as he was, driving her to local department stores whenever she had a fashion show, he just didn't understand the importance of preparation. Starting tomorrow night, Natasha would be one of only three models featured in an industrial show for new Chevrolets taking place half an hour from Westerfield, and she had to have the right wardrobe. This was big-time, professional. She would be making several hundred dollars for three nights' work.

Too bad they don't pay up front, she thought, huddling into her jacket. The only way she could afford the proper clothes for the show was to go to Klebann's, a large discount clothing store twenty minutes from her house. Her parents would never approve of her spending all the money she was about to earn on clothing she would probably never wear again. But Natasha knew it was a worthwhile expense—it would pay off in a career where a couple of hundred dollars more or less wouldn't matter. But nothing was going to happen if she didn't do every single thing exactly right.

And nothing is going to happen if I get grounded for the rest of my life, she thought, looking out the window of the bus one more time, still sure she was about to get caught. As she surveyed the empty lots and drab strips of housing around her, she felt a little frightened. This section of town was so dismal. Almost nobody lived here, and even the lone Seven-Eleven seemed to have no customers, judging by the empty parking lot. As the bus made its way to a red light, she saw only a boarded-up factory, closed years before, surrounded by desolate lots choked with weeds. She knew there were a couple of cheap-looking motels a few blocks up, right near the store, but she couldn't imagine anyone would be there in the middle of a Friday afternoon.

I guess that's how Klebann's can make their prices so low, she thought aimlessly. They must not pay very much in rent. She imagined the rows and rows of skirts and tops she would find once she got there. If she hit it just right, she could find a straight black skirt and a beaded or sequined top right away. Maybe even in time for her last class, she reflected, glancing at her watch. Then she could go home from school as usual. No one would have to know anything. Ever.

Suddenly the bus stopped. She watched the driver pick up his jacket and a bunch of papers, and walk down the steps of the bus. Standing on the curb, he entered into earnest conversation with another uniformed man.

For a few seconds, Natasha felt panicked, but quickly realized there was little chance the two men were talking about her. Calm down, she thought, reasoning that there must be a change in drivers right at this point. She forced herself to look casually out the bus window.

"Oh, no," she breathed out loud. Straight in front of her was a dilapidated building, the Starlight Motel, and right in the middle of the parking lot was her mother's car.

Quickly, Natasha slunk down in her seat, hoping not to be seen, but half-certain she'd already been caught. Yet as the two men stood chatting outside the bus, nothing happened. Guiltily, Natasha raised her eyes to the window once again. There was no sight of her mother, no sign of anyone. But it definitely was her mother's car. VHR707. That was her mother's license plate, all right. What in the world would Kit Dameroff be doing here?

She had no chance to find out as the driver picked that moment to reboard the bus, let out the brake, and move forward.

Finally, the bus stopped in front of Klebann's. Natasha took a furtive peek around as she stepped out onto the sidewalk. No one was even on the street. Sighing with relief, she made her way into the store, immediately spying a rack of black knitted skirts toward the back. Thank goodness, she said to herself, as she selected a size five and held it out in front of her. Maybe I can get back to school by seventh period. But the top proved more difficult to find. She'd gone through the entire store before she settled on a heavily embroidered gold sweater that almost passed for beaded if you didn't look too carefully.

A full hour after she'd arrived, she left Klebann's carrying a shopping bag with her new purchases. The bus stop was deserted. Anxiously checking her watch, she stepped out into the street and searched for signs of a bus coming, but she could see nothing. Settling in for a long wait, Natasha put the bags down on the sidewalk and leaned against a street sign. She couldn't help wondering about her mother again. What could she have been up to? Was there some store nearby? Light fixtures? Paint or wallpaper? It must be something like that, she figured.

But, as she waited, it began to gnaw at her. What could her mother have been doing? There were no stores for blocks except for Klebann's. Natasha stood impatiently, searching ahead for signs of a bus. Nothing.

Finally, she couldn't help herself. The motel was only about four or five blocks away. Without really thinking about it, Natasha picked up her bags and began walking. When she got around the corner from the Starlight Motel, she wondered what she thought she was doing. But curiosity overrode her anxiety. She hugged the side of the building. Yup, definitely her mother's old Chevy.

If the bus comes, I'll just get on it, she decided. Standing there, hiding from she didn't know what, she felt foolish. But five minutes later, as Kit Dameroff emerged from one of the motel's long string of rooms holding hands with J. T. Squire, Natasha felt as if she'd been punched in the stomach.

How can I have gotten myself into this? Kit couldn't stop the voice in her head as she looked out her bedroom window. The afternoon with J.T., the evenings with him that had come before. It all felt so sordid. And there seemed to be no way to end it. She'd tried to call it off, but every time she pulled back, J.T. tightened his grip.

She worried desperately that her husband would find out. She loved Leonard. So why are you sleeping with his next-door neighbor? she chided herself, agonizing guilt seeping through her chest. That first night had been such an accident. She'd been at a low point. One impulsive night. She'd never intended it to go this far.

I'll make it up to everyone, she thought, conjuring up thoughts of the Coleville symphony tickets she'd buy as a gift for her husband if she could save a few dollars from the household money. Leonard would love it. And she would spend more time with her daughter.

When Kit heard the front door slam, she almost jumped.

"Who is it?" she called out, looking at her watch. One forty-five. Much too early for Ben or Tash. And Leonard never came home in the middle of the day.

Natasha stood in the doorway to her parents' room, shopping bags in her hands, an unreadable expression on her face.

"What are you doing home, honey?" Kit hoped her voice sounded normal. She mustn't take out her own unhappiness on Tash. But her daughter just stared back at her.

Natasha took in the reddened cheeks, the high-heeled black

pumps usually reserved for Saturday nights. The signs of her mother's recent pleasure seemed obvious.

"What are *you* doing home, Mother?" Natasha's voice had an unusual note of insolence. "Isn't *that* the real question?"

Kit had no idea what Natasha was upset about, but the feeling of dread set in place by J. T. Squire just an hour before seemed to be growing, making her chest feel tight.

"What do you mean, sweetheart?" With great difficulty, she kept her tone as even as she could.

"I thought maybe the Starlight Motel had become home."

Natasha's words stung like tiny arrows of hatred, leaving Kit almost breathless with pain.

"Oh, God" was all she could say as she grabbed the window ledge for support.

"I don't think God's gonna make Daddy feel any better about this, Mother," Natasha replied bitterly, turning and beginning to walk out of the room.

"Tash, baby, wait." Kit ran across the room and took her daughter's elbow. "You can't tell Daddy. He just couldn't stand to find out."

Natasha stood stock-still, hating her mother for what she'd done, hating her for groveling, hating her for being alive.

"Baby"—her mother's voice was a sob—"there are things you don't understand, things I never intended . . ." Kit realized she was rambling. How could she hope to explain something to her daughter that she couldn't understand or excuse herself? "Darling, if you love your father, please forget whatever it was you saw. Please, Tash, you'll destroy him if you tell him."

"*I'll* destroy him!" Furious, Natasha strode out into the hallway, entering her own room and slamming the door shut behind her.

How could she have done it! Natasha screamed inside. And with Carlin's father, of all people. Too agitated to sit down, Natasha paced around the room. She would just bet that this wasn't the first time. Now that she thought about it, she remembered a number of times her mother had been out unexpectedly. In fact, she realized, Kit had gone out every Thursday night for the past three weeks. That must be their regular night.

Did they often meet in the afternoon as well, as they had today? Had Natasha just happened in on a bonus round?

It was all so disgusting. But Natasha couldn't figure out what to do. She couldn't tell her father. It really would kill him. And she couldn't possibly confide in Ben or Carlin. That's all Ben needed right now. No Harvard acceptance, no scholarship, no college-fund money. And by the way, Mom is a slut.

And Carlin, well, how do you tell your best friend her father is sleeping around?

Disconsolate, Natasha sat down on her bed. There had to be someone to share this with. The pain was too much to bear by herself. Besides, there had to be some way to make her mother pay for this.

No, she decided, her eyes glowing with anger, there were two people who should pay for this, a picture of J. T. Squire lying with her mother on a disheveled king-sized bed branding itself into her imagination.

There *was* someone she could talk to, she finally realized. Tony Kellner's handsome face replaced the ugly image in her mind. Would he hate her for having such a mother? Somehow it didn't matter. All she cared about was punishing those two. An idea began building in her mind. She could practically hear Tony's voice on the phone to the Starlight Motel next Thursday night. That was it, a phone call to their repulsive little love nest. That should scare both of them right out of their skulls.

She'd get Tony to do it. The way things were between them now, it wouldn't be a problem. Briefly, she considered how suffocating Tony had become. This might make it even worse.

She caught herself. The fact was Tony Kellner would do anything she asked. And right now that was all that mattered.

9

J. T. Squire filled a glass with water and drank it down thirstily. Replacing the glass on the sink's narrow ledge, he leaned forward to study his reflection in the medicine chest mirror. A few lines here and there, but overall pretty damn good for forty-three. He turned to the full-length mirror behind the bathroom door where he could see his entire body, covered only by one of the motel's skimpy white towels wrapped around his waist. Lean, good biceps, stomach still nearly flat. He smiled with satisfaction.

Sure, why wouldn't a woman like Kit find him attractive? He'd been a fool to wait so many years before making his move. But if he were going to be honest, he'd have to admit he hadn't expected it to be so easy; he'd figured that she wouldn't go for him or at the very least she'd get all crazy over the fact that his wife was such a good friend.

He gave his reflection a little smirk, combing his hair back with his hands. Turned out that, like most women, when she wanted something, she damn well took it. And she'd wanted him all right. She'd made that clear yet again not five minutes ago. He felt himself starting to get hard just thinking about the wild way she moved in bed.

Suddenly, a fleeting image appeared in his mind, a distant memory of Lillian back when they were first married. It was a hot August night and they'd been making love for hours. But they were still at it, drenched in their own perspiration, he lying on top of her, thrusting, grunting with exhaustion yet driven to go on. He'd heard her make a noise, a guttural groan that was barely human. It was the sound of a woman completely lost in sex, and it had been the biggest turn-on of his life, giving him a rush of power that made him lose control and climax. But, of course, that was long ago, long before she'd had Carlin and gained the forty pounds she was always swearing she would lose, long before she became like a little fat brown hen, clucking around the house, fussing over things nobody cared about, long before he'd lost interest in her.

He realized why that dim memory had come back to him now. Kit gave him that same sense of power in bed. He was in control here, and she needed what he could do for her. What was the story with that husband of hers? It was obvious Leonard didn't satisfy Kit anymore, maybe never had. Or probably, he thought smugly, she's just never had it as good as she has it with me. He bent over to touch his toes, feeling the comfortable stretch in his body. Always leave the ladies smiling, that was his motto.

On the other side of the bathroom door, Kit lay on the double bed, staring at the ceiling as she clutched the thin, graying sheet drawn up over her. This situation was bad, very bad. There wasn't even any point in reminding herself that it should never have gotten started in the first place.

She felt trapped in the affair and, what was worse, she was breaking under the weight of her guilt about Natasha finding out. No child should know such a thing about her mother, and then have to keep it to herself.

She shut her eyes at the memory of Natasha's confronting her, so full of anger and pain. How much more can I ask of the child? she thought, making her share this sordid little secret with me. Kit shifted uncomfortably. If only I could have been a better mother to her . . . but that was another matter altogether. The problem was what would happen right now. Destroying Leonard on top of everything else wasn't the answer. I had no choice, she decided miserably. I had to beg her to stay quiet.

She looked up as the bathroom door opened and J.T. emerged.

"Hey, doll," he greeted her with a grin.

Kit frowned. She had to try to extricate herself from this mess.

"J.T.," she began tentatively, "we have to talk."

He sat down on the edge of the bed, not listening to her as

he reached out to stroke her breast through the sheet. Still holding the sheet to her, she sat up against the wall, just beyond his reach.

"Please, J.T.," she went on, "pay attention."

He leaned forward, the grin still on his face. "C'mere. Let me touch that gorgeous body of yours."

She spoke more firmly. "We have to stop. We're going to hurt too many people."

Her words finally registering, J.T. sat back, an annoyed look on his face. "Nobody's going to get hurt. And you're nuts. We've got a great thing going here."

"No, J.T.," she said slowly, "we don't. We have a big mistake going here."

Impatiently, he stood up and faced her, his expression darkening. "The only mistake would be if you ended it," he said in a clipped tone. "You think you can drop me and I'll just fade into the background like a good little boy, show up for our homey double dates, pretend nothing happened? No, no, my Kit girl, Leonard is going to have to know about us in that case."

Kit stared at him for a moment before responding. "You wouldn't really tell Leonard, would you? What could possibly be accomplished by doing that?"

He turned away from her and walked to the dresser, picking up his watch and starting to put it on. "Do you really want to try me and find out?"

Kit started to protest, but the words died in her throat as the telephone on the night table suddenly rang. She turned to stare at it, horrified. There was no one who would call them. It rang again, the shrill noise loud and insistent. Kit sat, immobilized, her heart frantically pounding. Was it Leonard? Oh, God, what would happen now?

"Should we answer it?" Kit asked, panicked, seeing J.T. just standing there.

"Christ," he muttered, "who the hell could it be?"

The ringing persisted. Kit couldn't stand it anymore. Maybe it was just a wrong number, but she couldn't go on wondering. She grabbed the receiver.

"Hello."

"Mrs. Dameroff? Mrs. Kit Dameroff?" It was a male voice, clipped and authoritative.

"Uh . . . yes," Kit answered weakly, feeling the fear of discovery in the pit of her stomach. "Who is this?"

"This is Chief O'Brien from the Schenectady police. I'm sorry to inform you that your son has been involved in a bad car accident up here, along with a number of other kids. We're on our way to the hospital right now."

"What?" Kit turned to J.T. "Oh God, oh God." Her voice rose in hysteria. "Ben's been in a car accident, Ben and some other kids. In Schenectady."

J.T. grabbed the phone out of her hand.

"What other kids?" he demanded.

Kit was already out of the bed and halfway into her clothes, barely able to get on her skirt and blouse in her frenzy. Shoving her feet into her shoes, she saw J.T.'s face turn white.

"Not Carlin too?" she cried.

"Among the more badly injured," he repeated to Kit. "We're on our way," he said into the phone. "What hospital?"

J.T. slammed down the receiver and yanked on his trousers, grabbing his wallet and keys off the dresser. Then, even through his shock, something struck J.T. as odd. How on earth did the Schenectady police know to call the Starlight Motel to find them? Jesus, maybe someone knew about their affair and had directed the cops to call there. Maybe *everyone* knew about their affair. *Damn.* How were he and Kit going to explain their being here together today?

Kit was crying now. "Ben, oh Ben, my baby," she wept, still tucking her blouse into her skirt as she grabbed her coat and purse and tore open the door. J.T. was right behind her as they ran for his Valiant in the parking lot. He fumbled with the ignition key, hearing Kit sob beside him.

She turned a tearstained face to him when he started to back out of the parking spot.

"Hurry, please hurry," she cried.

With a screech of the tires, J.T. turned the car around and raced to the parking lot's exit. Neither he nor Kit even saw the twelve-wheel rig bearing down on them as they pulled out into the street. The last thing they heard was the terrible noise of metal on metal as the huge truck slammed into the passenger side of J.T.'s car.

10

Ben's headache was so intense, he felt as if the top of his head were going to blow off. He raised one hand and massaged his temples, trying to ease the pain. He would do anything for aspirin. The room was so crowded and hot, and the air so still. If only he could lie down and sleep. That would be the best thing, just to go into a dark room and sleep and sleep.

He glanced over at his sister. Natasha's face was pinched and white as she sat stiffly beside him, twisting the lacy white handkerchief she held. Her boyfriend Tony was next to her, watching her with an expression of deep concern. As Tony reached over to take Natasha's hand, Ben noticed that his sister seemed oblivious to Tony; she permitted him to stroke her hand without acknowledging him in any way.

Ben had barely known Tony at school, but he'd always assumed he was a pretty decent guy. Having gotten to know him since he'd been dating his sister, Ben had changed his opinion. From what he could see, Tony was little more than a self-important phony; he was full of stories about his endless accomplishments, but there was something about him that never quite rang true. Even now, his tragic demeanor struck Ben as an act. Why did his sister fall for a guy like Kellner? he thought, suddenly annoyed at her. All at once, he felt unbearably irritated. Why the hell was she wearing that big hat today? She looked ridiculous, like some heroine in a soap opera. It was all he could do to keep from slapping her.

The feeling passed as quickly as it had come. I'm losing my mind, he thought wildly. I've just got to get out of here. But he didn't move. Instead, he turned to gaze at his father, sitting on his other side. Leonard's head was down, his cheeks wet with tears. Every time Ben looked at him now, he could think of only one word: over. Leonard's life was now effectively over. He might go on, but he'd never recover.

The voice Ben had been successful at blocking from his hearing for the past few minutes suddenly broke through again.

". . . her loving devotion to her children and husband," the rabbi intoned, "her joy in being an active part of the community . . ."

Ben looked forward again to the front of the room. The plain casket was of dark brown wood, the Star of David carved on its cover. Only yesterday, Ben had picked it out by himself, realizing Leonard was too stricken to attend to the endless details involved, and wanting to spare him the anguish of it. At Ben's request, a single rose lay across the coffin.

This was intolerable, sitting here listening to some rabbi who'd never even known his mother talk about what a wonderful woman she was. What did he know about her laughter, the way she glowed when she was happy, the joy she could get out of something as simple as eating an ice-cream cone with her son? What did anyone know about all that? He wondered if his father had ever really understood what a dazzling jewel Kit had been, understood her the way Ben had. A pang shot through him at the disloyalty of such a thought; it was ugly to compare himself that way to the man who was his mother's husband.

Well, what difference did it all make now? he said to himself. She was gone forever, locked in that dark coffin, about to be buried in the pitch black coldness of the earth where she would rot away. Slowly, horribly. He clenched his hands, tormenting himself with visions of her grave, the grave they would soon lower her into, far away from them in the Westerfield cemetery.

The throbbing pain over his left temple was becoming intolerable. As he heard his father choke back another sob, Ben closed his eyes. Powerless to stop it, his mind replayed the moment when the call came in from the Westerfield police, the sight of his father's stricken face as Ben came to stand near him, waiting to hear what had happened, the halting way his father had explained. He saw the two of them standing in silence as they each took in the significance of where the accident occurred—and who was in the car with Kit.

No way to say good-bye, not a hint that morning that she would be gone forever by the evening. He couldn't seem to grasp it. Over and over he told himself that she was dead, but the words held no meaning for him. He couldn't cry, he couldn't even feel anything. I'll never see her again, he told himself once more, staring hard at her coffin, wanting to make it real. Never, for as long as I live. It just wouldn't sink in.

What *had* sunk in was that J. T. Squire was still alive. He'd killed Kit, but that son of a bitch was still alive. He'd always thought J.T. was a lowlife, unemployed half the time but always dressed to the teeth, running around like he had money to burn, full of his own hot-air ideas and opinions. He was always looking at himself in the mirror when he thought nobody else noticed. Sickening. Not that Ben would ever have told anyone how he felt about J.T. He wouldn't have wanted to hurt Carlin. Besides, it wasn't for him to judge his parents' friend, that's what he had always believed. At least, until now. But Ben couldn't remember a single time that J.T. had accompanied Lillian to any school event, whether it was open-school day back in first grade or the junior-year play in which Carlin had the lead. Birthday parties, holidays—J.T. only breezed in and out.

Then, of course, there was the way J.T. always came on to women. He flirted with everything in a skirt.

Ben twisted uncomfortably in his seat. It turned out his mother was one of those women, one who had responded to J.T.'s idiotic come-ons. *Shit.* Why couldn't J.T. have played his filthy little game elsewhere?

". . . in the Lord. Amen."

Leonard and Natasha were standing up, Tony holding Natasha's elbow as if she were an invalid. Hurriedly, Ben got to his feet and the four of them filed out of the room. He could hear the sniffling and sobs as they passed the other mourners, but he didn't look directly at anyone. There were so many people he didn't even recognize there. Where on earth did they come from? He'd had no idea his mother knew that many people, but at the same time it didn't surprise him; she was someone everyone enjoyed, wanted to be around.

The only person missing was Carlin. She was still at the hospital. J.T. was having the second operation in two days on his legs. Ben hadn't seen her since the accident, and had spoken with her for only a moment. Their conversation had been awkward. He longed to be with her, to bury his head in her warm, sweet neck and feel her arms around him. It was as if that could somehow make all this go away.

He followed Leonard out of the funeral parlor, into the black limousine that would take them to the cemetery. His father sat back in the seat, burying his face in his hands. Natasha joined them; Ben was relieved to see that Tony was riding in a different car. He watched his sister as she gazed out the window at the stream of people emerging from the service, many stopping to talk with each other for a few moments before going their separate ways, some to their homes, others to the cemetery for the burial. Ben saw the long black hearse parked in front of them, the casket already inside, just visible through the car's small back window.

Kit was up there in that hearse all alone. She should have been back here, alive, riding with them; she was the one who held them together as a family. It was never the three of them going somewhere together. Kit had to be with them, talking gaily about this or that. Oh, God, how he wanted to see his mother, oh please, just for a minute, just to say good-bye and hug her one more time, to smell her familiar perfume, tell her he loved her.

But there was only the heavy silence in the car, and the swirl of activity going on around them outside. He felt the limousine's engine start up, the driver smoothly pulling away from the curb behind the hearse. Their headlights on, the procession of cars got under way. It seemed as if this would never be over.

Ben envisioned Carlin again, desperately wanting to hold her against him. But at the same instant, he couldn't deny the thought he'd been trying to avoid ever since the accident. Carlin was the daughter of the man who killed his mother.

His shoulders sagged with the truth of it. No more, he begged silently. Please, no more.

* * *

Natasha shook her head. "No, thank you, Mrs. Arno," she said sweetly. "I'm not hungry."

"I understand, darling." Their neighbor from the apartment below nodded sympathetically and retreated back into the crowd with the tray of sandwiches, offering them to some of the others who'd returned to the house after the burial.

Natasha watched her go with mounting impatience. She had to get away from all these people. They were suffocating her with their concern. More importantly, she had to talk to Tony. It wasn't right to disappear in the middle of everything, but this couldn't wait any longer. Making up her mind, she walked quickly across the room to where Tony stood, talking to an elderly man and woman, appearing to be hanging on their every word.

Natasha grimaced. He was always doing stuff like this, trying to charm people, behaving as if he were building some kind of circle of influence that would serve him in the future. But he was always, well, *off* somehow. He invariably picked the wrong people, people who clearly couldn't help anybody accomplish anything, but who would be easily swayed by his particular brand of charm. Natasha thought his insincerity was obvious a mile away. Back when he first became her boyfriend she believed whatever he did was perfect. Now she knew better.

It was the way he tried to take over her entire life that was really driving her nuts. Sometimes she thought she'd scream, having to answer his endless questions about where she was or who she'd been with. It was as if he believed he *owned* her. She'd tried to ignore it, and certainly never shared her thoughts about it with anybody else. Seeing the envy of the other girls at school when she and Tony walked down the hall arm in arm still made it worth putting up with nearly anything.

But not anything like what had happened now. It had been a big mistake to ask Tony to make that phone call to the motel. Her stupid idea of a way to get back at her mother had killed her, and Natasha would have to live with that for the rest of her life. Just getting through the funeral service that morning was the most terrifying thing she'd ever experienced. Her stomach had hurt so badly, it had taken every ounce of will not to double over with the pain. And the service had gone on for an eternity. She shuddered. She was certain everyone knew what she'd done, that someone would jump up and point a finger at her, screaming that she was a murderer. At one point, the fear was so intense, her throat closed up entirely and she couldn't breathe. It was a miracle I didn't pass out, she thought. Standing at the graveside as they lowered the coffin, she'd been numb, hearing nothing of what was being said around her, burying her face in Tony's sleeve so no one could see how petrified she was as her father and then Ben tossed dirt onto the coffin. She was ashamed to admit to herself that she felt no grief or pain for her mother; her own terror at being discovered had crowded out everything else.

This would be her secret forever and ever; she knew she would take it to her own grave. But she wasn't sure she could count on Tony to do the same. She couldn't afford to have him around anymore, talking to her father or brother, letting slip who knew what. He might even decide to confess to them. Her stomach clenched painfully at the prospect.

"Excuse me," she said brightly to the couple talking with Tony, as she put her hand on his sleeve, "could I borrow him for a moment?"

Immediately, she realized her tone was much too cheerful for the occasion. Lowering her voice, she gazed sadly at Tony. "I need to talk to you."

"A 'course, darlin'." Tony put his arm around her.

Natasha spoke quietly so that only he could hear. "Could we take a little walk?"

"Sure thing."

He patted her cheek gently, and she resisted the urge to swat his hand away.

Outside, she led him several blocks away to a small playground. It was deserted, the rusted swings creaking as the breeze made them sway. Natasha leaned against the jungle gym, running her hands up and down the cool silver bars, not speaking.

"Are you okay, pumpkin?" Tony finally asked.

His words seemed to prompt her. She looked directly into his eyes. "I want to break up."

Startled, Tony took a step back. "What?"

"We're not good together anymore, Tony."

He stared at her. "There's no way I'm hearin' what I think I'm hearin'."

"Yes, there is," she said with a nod. "It's done with."

Tony was beginning to get angry. "Now, just a minute here. You got no reason to be sayin' this. I'm not gonna let you just dump me flat."

Natasha didn't reply.

"Hey," he said, his voice growing louder, "did you just ask me to do a little somethin' for you the other day, and did I not do it just like you asked? You see what happened because of that little somethin', now don't you, Natasha? Your mama was buried today, all on account of what you told me was going to be an itty-bitty practical joke." His eyes bore into her. "But I love you, and I'm willin' to do anythin' for you. Is this how you're gonna repay me?"

She drew herself up in defiance at his words. "That's not what this is about."

"Oh, it's not, huh?" He smacked one of the jungle gym's bars with such force, Natasha jumped. "Well, I think maybe it is. I think you don't want to have me around anymore because I know what you did."

His expression grew uglier. "You're a bad girl, you know that, Natasha? You do a thing like this and now you're trying to cover your tracks."

She turned to him angrily. "It's not about that, I've told you over and over. I don't love you, that's all. I thought I did, but I don't."

"*You don't love me?*" he yelled, his hands clenched into fists. "*You don't goddamn love me?*"

For a moment, she thought he would strike her. Then, suddenly, his demeanor changed entirely. He came closer to her, stroking her hair, taking her hand in his.

"Natasha, sweetie, you don't know what you're sayin'. You're upset, and you've got good reason to be. This is a sad, sad day for you. You're gonna go home and get some sleep tonight. Tomorrow you'll realize this was a mistake, and we'll pretend like it never happened. I love you, baby. I'm not gonna let you go this way."

She pulled away in annoyance. "Listen to me, Tony," she said sharply. "I'm not changing my mind. I don't want to see you again. Don't call me, don't come around anymore."

She started to walk away.

"You're some kind of special bitch, you know that, darlin'?" he said to her retreating back. She stopped at the menacing tone of his words. "You're like some kinda dead thing. You just put your own mother six feet under—and I do mean *you* put her under—but you can still do this to me."

She turned to face him.

"You think you're gonna get away with this?" he went on, a smile playing across his face. "You're wrong."

She stood there, transfixed.

His eyes took on a faraway expression. "We were a team, remember? Somethin' special. We could've done anythin' together."

Suddenly, he made a fist and punched one of the jungle gym's bars as hard as he could. Natasha stiffened as he winced in pain. Still, he punched it again, and again, his fury only mounting.

Fear finally made her take action. Hoping he couldn't tell how frightened she was, she spun on her heel and walked away.

Ben shut the door behind the last person to leave. He was exhausted but restless after so many hours of accepting condolences, politely thanking everyone for their sympathy, letting them hold his hand or take him by the shoulder to murmur their useless words of comfort.

He turned to survey the apartment, looking for something to do. But the women who had been there had pretty much cleaned up; he'd half-noticed them bustling about out of the corner of his eye. The glasses and dishes were gone from the living room, the dining-room table cleared of all the platters of food. His father had gone into his bedroom a few minutes before and shut the door; there wasn't a sound coming from the room. Ben walked into the kitchen, weighed down by the heavy silence. He saw that the drainboard was full of dripping, clean dishes and silverware, the sink empty, the counters wiped down. Nothing to do in here either.

He didn't feel like talking to anyone, but it was almost a relief when the telephone rang.

"Ben, it's me." Carlin's voice was tired. "Are you all right?"

Ben felt a flood of longing. He'd been wrong to have those thoughts about her earlier. She had nothing to do with what J.T. was.

"I'm fine," he reassured her.

"I feel so awful I couldn't be with you today," she went on sadly. "Please forgive me. But I just couldn't leave my mother alone at the hospital—"

Ben interrupted gently. "It's okay, really it is. Of course you couldn't leave her."

Her voice became thick with the effort of trying not to cry. "It's so terrible, Ben," she got out. "He's lost all feeling in his legs. The doctors are sure he'll never walk again." She began to cry in earnest. "He's just lying there so helplessly. He'll always have to be in a wheelchair."

At her last words, a fury swept over Ben with such startling force he had to grip the phone with all his might to keep control. He wanted to scream at the top of his lungs, to howl like an animal at her: *But that bastard's alive and my mother's dead. It should have been the other way around.* He trembled with rage. *If I could have my mother alive in a wheelchair, I'd thank God every minute of every day.*

He took several deep breaths, trying to calm down. Carlin, still sobbing, was unaware of his struggle.

"Oh, Ben," she said through her tears, "why did it have to happen?"

Ben forced himself to speak quietly, soothing her. "Everything will be okay, Carlin. You'll see."

She didn't answer, but he could hear her crying begin to subside.

"I have to go now," he said.

"I understand," she answered. There was a pause. "Ben, I love you."

Ben couldn't bring himself to say anything. He hung up the

telephone quickly. Maybe she would think he hadn't heard her.

He sank into a chair. The confusion of anger and pain was too much. His breath started coming in gasps and then, suddenly, he was crying at last. Alone in the small, brightly lit room, he rocked back and forth in the chair, the agony of his sobs piercing the kitchen's silence.

11

"Are you torturing me on purpose, or are you just an incompetent fool?" J. T. Squire screamed at the nurse's aide as she attempted to tuck in the bottom corners of his sheets.

The young woman looked helplessly at Carlin and her mother sitting beside the bed.

"Goddamnit, girlie," he went on, "I'm the patient here, I'm the one suffering. Not my wife and not my daughter. Maybe if you watched me instead of them, you'd manage to hurt me a little less."

Carlin was disgusted with her father's bullying, but the tears in his eyes stopped her from saying anything. However badly he was behaving, his pain was all too real. Three operations in six days had left him pitifully weak and vulnerable. And the fact that none of them had managed to restore any feeling in his legs was the worst possible news. Eventually the pain of most of his injuries would go away, but the chances of his moving again under his own steam were nearly zero. Carlin tried to calm him down as the nurse's aide smoothed out the top sheet.

"Daddy, she'll be finished in a minute. Do you want some juice, or an apple maybe?"

J.T.'s mouth contorted into a garish imitation of a smile. "Yeah, a glass of OJ is just the thing to stop this garbage from burning into my body." He lifted his left hand, which was connected to a thin intravenous tube leading to a fluid-filled sac suspended from a stand. Where the needle had been inserted into his skin was a swollen and discolored patch that indicated just how painful even the simplest part of his treatment was.

"And the broken ribs," he added, wincing as he tried to

move his upper body, "and the, what did they call it, multiple abrasions and contusions? Yeah, orange juice and an apple should fix everything right up."

J.T. shifted his attention momentarily from his daughter back to the nurse. "So have you learned that yet, how a piece of fruit can make a man walk again?" Now his voice had become a strangled cry. "Have they taught you that, girlie?"

Carlin saw the young woman wince, then avert her eyes from him as she tried to finish tucking the sheet in. It didn't matter how bad her father was feeling. He had no right to take it out on a stranger.

As if he could see the criticism behind her eyes, J.T. suddenly turned his attention back to his daughter. "If it weren't for you, none of this would have happened."

"What do you mean?" Carlin's voice betrayed utter bewilderment.

"If you and Ben hadn't gone to Schenectady and gotten yourselves in trouble with the police, I wouldn't have had to tear out of there in such a hurry."

Carlin looked at her mother, as if Lillian might clear up the confusion, but her mother looked bewildered as well.

"Daddy, I've never been to Schenectady in my life." She found herself wanting to yell back, to hurt him, but she forced herself to sound matter-of-fact. "What are you talking about?"

"The police called us. I don't know what the hell kind of mix-up there was, but they told us there was an accident, that you and Ben were both hurt." J.T. looked away as he spoke.

At least he seemed to understand that "us" was a concept he shouldn't feel proud of, Carlin thought, hating him for just a moment. But then she considered what he had said. Someone had actually called the Starlight Motel, had asked for J. T. Squire's room. And whoever it was had told them that she and Ben had been in an accident. What on earth for? Who would do that? The person had to know it would scare her father and Ben's mother. She paled. *That meant that someone had done it on purpose.*

It also meant that someone else knew they were there. They must have gone there regularly, she realized. Probably *everyone* knew about them. Dear God. Was she the only idiot in town too stupid to know what had been going on? It made her feel responsible somehow, as if by not knowing she had caused it all to happen.

It would probably make her feel even worse, but she couldn't help wanting to know more. Had they been involved for a very long time? Had they been in love with each other? "Daddy, did you . . ."

"Goddamnit!" J.T. screamed in pain as the nurse's aide accidentally bumped his arm as she was arranging the pillows.

"Why don't you finish up later, dear?" Lillian Squire's gentle voice freed the girl to leave the room.

Lillian turned toward Carlin. "Honey, why don't you go home now?" Her voice was soft as it always was, but there was an unusually determined glint in her eyes.

"Mom, I can't leave you here. I don't mind staying. Honest." She knew her mother was trying to forestall further questions, and in a way she was glad. Maybe neither of them really wanted to know the truth.

Lillian squeezed her daughter's hand appreciatively, but remained adamant. "We've been here all day every day. Someone needs to see to the apartment. You know, water the plants, check the mail. You'll be more help if you go on home." She urged Carlin to her feet. "One of us has to get some rest. Really, I'm just being selfish. This way, you can take over tomorrow."

Slowly Carlin agreed. "Daddy, I'll see you later this afternoon."

"You'll see him tomorrow, dear." Her mother's voice was firm.

J.T.'s only response was a weary shrug, as if to say it didn't matter whether she stayed or left.

Carlin trudged the ten blocks from the hospital to her home. It was as if she were trapped in a bad dream. For the past week, she'd been on an emotional roller coaster, only there seemed to be no highs. Just an endless series of downward spirals.

She was overwhelmed by her emotions. Her shock at J.T.'s affair with Ben's mother, her sadness watching her father suffer day after day in that awful hospital. But at least those feelings she was beginning to deal with. The fury was harder.

She felt so angry at everything and everyone. At her father for being such a jerk. At her mother for catering to him despite the humiliation he had caused her.

Worst of all was her hatred for Kit Dameroff. Even if her father had to have been equally to blame, it was the vision of Ben's mother that crowded her mind, dwarfing everything else. The very thought of beautiful, carefree Kit marching around the neighborhood every day, greeting everyone like a politician, was enough to make Carlin scream.

Kit was dead, she reminded herself quickly. She would never turn her glow on anyone ever again. Carlin had felt so bad about having to miss the funeral—not for Kit's sake, but for Ben's. She had also felt relieved. How would she have sat through half an hour on how fine a woman Kit Dameroff was?

She felt as if she didn't even know how to talk to Ben anymore. Even in the couple of phone calls Carlin had made from the hospital, their conversations had been stilted, like strangers making small talk. *I hate your mother. I'm glad she's dead.* These were the thoughts that flew around her brain as she uttered banalities to a Ben who seemed a thousand miles away.

And each time, genuine sadness would follow. She hadn't hated Ben's mother at all. She'd loved her. Everybody had loved her.

What a mess, Carlin thought dejectedly as she walked into her building. A thousand different feelings, and every one of them hideous.

As she puttered around the apartment, watering the plants and sorting the mail that had become a small mountain on the kitchen table, she felt a little calmer. The plants were bone dry, and the jumble of greenery in the living room soaked up the cool stream from the watering can. She divided the mail into piles, bills here, personal-looking stuff over there. Circulars went into the garbage.

Finally, Carlin sat down on the couch. Her eyes burned with exhaustion and she thought about taking a nap for a couple of hours. But her hand went as if of its own accord to the telephone. She needed to be near Ben, needed him to take her into his arms.

"Ben? I'm home."

"I'm on my way."

Within moments he was there, holding her. But as they broke apart, neither could find any words to say. Awkwardly, they found themselves sitting on chairs facing each other, instead of together on the couch as they usually did.

"I'm sorry I missed the service," Carlin said tentatively.

"It's all right. I understood." Ben knew he should ask how her father was, but he found he couldn't.

Carlin stayed quiet for a moment, hoping he would pick up the thread of conversation, but after a long pause she found herself telling him what she had just learned.

"Daddy said someone called the motel, claiming to be from the Schenectady police department, saying we'd been in an accident."

"*What?*"

She nodded, watching Ben take in the implications of her words, seeing his anger build.

"You mean somebody did this on purpose." Unable to sit still, Ben began pacing around the living room. "What kind of malicious bastard would do something like that?" he asked, as if Carlin could possibly have an answer.

"I don't know," she said softly.

"I swear to you," he went on, glaring at her as if she were somehow part of it, "if I ever find out who made that call, I'll kill him."

Carlin felt almost jealous of his rage. It was so pure. She couldn't shake off what she'd been feeling all afternoon: that if she had been smart enough to see what had been going on, none of this would have happened.

"Did you know about them?" She knew the question would hurt him, yet she had to ask it.

"Of course I didn't know. Are you crazy?" He stopped pacing and scowled at a picture of J.T. and Lillian in a silver frame centered on the coffee table. "Not that I should have been surprised."

Carlin took in his grimace at the photo of her father. She knew exactly what he was thinking, and it made her angry.

"And what does that mean?" she asked, a dangerous edge to her voice.

"It means nothing," he said, trying to hold back the words he wanted to say. But he couldn't stop himself entirely. "Let's just say your father has a penchant for trouble."

"Where do you get off making a crack like that?" It was almost a relief to feel so enraged.

Ben's face reddened. "Maybe if your father knew how to keep his highly pressed pants on, my mother would be alive."

Carlin knew they were going over the line, but there was no way to stop. "Who are you to talk about my father? Just because your father's been in a coma since forever doesn't give you the right to judge mine. Maybe if your mother hadn't flirted with everything that moved, none of this would have happened."

Ben raised his arm as if to strike her, but held himself back. He looked at Carlin as if he were seeing her for the first time. He'd never imagined he could hate anyone as much as he hated her at this moment.

His voice was pure ice. "I never want to see you again." He left the apartment, slamming the door behind him.

Enraged, Carlin stared at the door. They had passed the point of no return, she knew that. In the back of her mind she even grasped how painful this was all going to be sometime in the future. But for right now, she didn't care. She detested Kit Dameroff. And most of all, she detested Ben.

Just outside, Ben found himself holding on to the doorknob, unable to will himself down the hall to his own apartment. How could he have thought he loved Carlin? That was one mistake he would never make again.

He was on his own, no more attachments to people who would let him down. For a second, it made him feel strong. But suddenly the reality of the words sank in. *He was on his own.* There would be no Kit, no Carlin. The pain of it seared through him like a flame, but he pushed it aside, relieved to let his anger take over. Momentarily Carlin's face flashed through his mind. But he felt no sadness. Only the fury.

Fine, he declared to himself, finally letting go of the doorknob and beginning the short walk to his apartment. It's up to me. It's all up to me.

12

"Another bourbon, please." Ben shoved his empty glass across the bar, feeling the warmth of the drink he'd just finished spreading throughout his body.

The bartender looked at him skeptically. "You sure? That'll be your third."

"Of course I'm sure." Ben realized foggily that his voice didn't quite register the degree of indignation he wanted to convey. I must be getting drunk, he thought. Good.

With a shrug, the bartender took the glass and turned away, reaching for the bottle. From now on, this kid was on his own; if he wanted to drink until he passed out, fine. Of course, it was anybody's guess whether he was legal drinking age or not, but it didn't much matter. If the guy had been getting soused on cheap beer, that might have been another story, but springing for high-priced bourbon qualified him for service in this place anytime.

Rinsing out some dirty glasses in the sink, the bartender watched his customer's reflection in the mirror that lined the wall. The kid threw back his drink in one gulp, then slammed the glass down on the bar with a shudder.

"One more, if you don't mind." Ben's words were a bit slurred now.

His drink refilled, Ben set it down in front of him and looked into the glass, deciding to nurse this one for a while. Things were getting a bit hazy around the edges. Boy, it felt pretty good to get drunk. He could understand why people talked about drinking as a way of forgetting their troubles. Maybe if he did this night after night, he wouldn't have to think about the same stuff that pursued him every minute. Maybe he wouldn't lie awake in bed until two or three in the morning wondering what the hell he was going to do about coming up with the eleven hundred dollars he needed for his first semester at SUNY—and that didn't even include books and expenses, beyond room and board.

Frowning, he took a sip of his drink. If he was drunk, why was he still thinking about all of it, feeling just as rotten as he had when he walked in?

He wiped the perspiration off his forehead. The two ceiling fans rotating slowly overhead were doing nothing to cool the room, which was nearly as stifling as the unusually sticky June night outside. He glanced over at the four or five other men sitting at the bar beside him, hunched over their drinks, taken up with their own troubles. There were booths behind them, and Ben could hear people talking, their quiet conversations punctuated every now and then by a laugh or an angry outburst. A bright light shone through an open doorway to reveal a large pool table with a group of men standing around it, their silence broken only by the noise of their pool cues smacking the balls.

Ben had passed by this bar only once or twice, but he was glad he'd thought of it tonight. He'd *had* to get away from his family's apartment and his boring summer job at the supermarket, away from his father's sadness, from the painful emptiness of the place without his mother. Natasha had taken to ducking out any opportunity she got.

Wandering aimlessly, he was already four blocks away from his building when he'd remembered this bar. Dark, dingy, the kind of place you could be completely invisible. It suited his mood just right. Not the kind of place to be thinking of stupid things like college tuition or Carlin.

He caught himself sharply. Damn her, *damn her.* Thank God she'd gone away for the summer to work as a waitress in one of the big Catskills resorts; at least he was spared having to run into her all the time. But even so, no matter what he did or where he went, it was as if she were there. He heard her laugh tantalizing him, could feel her velvet skin, her naked body fitting so perfectly against his as he took her in his arms to make love to her.

In his dreams, in the few hours he finally slept at night, she smiled as she walked beside him, kissing him as if she couldn't get enough. Other nights, she was furiously attacking him, her face ugly with anger, once even savagely running him down with her father's car. The week before, he'd dreamt that he'd aimed a gun at her, and she had looked him dead in the eye, whispering, "I dare you." He had woken up from that one in a cold sweat. But last night, they'd lain naked together on a deserted beach under the day-bright light of a full moon.

He gripped his glass, wanting to hurl it against the wall with all his might.

He hated her guts.

He would kill for just one more night with her.

"Are you okay?"

Startled, Ben looked to his right. He hadn't noticed the man slide onto the stool next to his. Dark-haired and lanky, he was wearing a dirty blue T-shirt and jeans.

"You okay, bud?" the man repeated. "You're clenching your jaw so tight, I'm figuring you're about to break your teeth. Or, if not your teeth, at least that glass." He pointed, and Ben looked down to see that he was holding his glass so tightly, his knuckles were white. He immediately loosened his grip.

"I'm fine, thanks," he replied, nodding. "Really fine."

"Okay, good." The man signaled to the bartender. "Whiskey neat, Carl."

The bartender brought over his drink. "How's it going, Wayne?"

The man shrugged as he reached for the glass. "As good as you'd expect. Listen, anything happening tonight?"

The bartender nodded. "They've been at it about two hours now."

"Thanks."

Ben observed this interaction quietly. The man beside him appeared to be in his mid-twenties, obviously completely at home in this bar. Probably works in a factory, lived here all his life, Ben thought. He stared back down at his drink. That'll be me in a couple of years. I'm never getting to college, or anywhere out of this town.

The bartender had retreated to the far end of the bar, leaving the two of them alone again.

"Wayne Packard." The man extended his hand and Ben reached out to shake it. "How you doin'?"

"Ben Dameroff."

"So, Ben." Wayne took a long gulp of his drink. "Everybody's got a story in here, but they mostly boil down to two things." He smiled. "Women or money. Which one's yours?"

Taken aback by the directness of the question, Ben hesitated. Well, he wasn't about to discuss Carlin with some stranger, that was for sure.

He drank, letting the heat of the alcohol relax him again. "Money."

The man beside him nodded. "That's been my problem for years. Women I've got luck with."

Ben said nothing.

"So," Wayne went on easily, "you just *lose* some big money or *need* some big money right away?"

Ben gave a rucful smile. "Both of the above."

Wayne turned to look at Ben more directly, his gaze appraising. "Tell me. You got anything on you right now?"

"What?" Ben was wary.

"Hey, relax," Wayne said reassuringly. "I'm not hitting you up. I'm gonna do you a favor. Maybe." He polished off the rest of his whiskey. "See, I'm about to go into a poker game in back. The one Carl mentioned before. If you got enough on you to come in on it, I'll bring you along."

A poker game. Ben sat up straighter, thinking. His mother had taught him to play poker when he was twelve. Neither his father nor Tash had ever had any interest in it, so it was impossible to get up any kind of real game at home. But every so often, he and Kit would play, betting with pennies and ignoring the fact that it didn't quite work with only two people. They'd always had a great time anyway, cheating so blatantly that it became something of a contest to see who could be the most outrageous. Ben felt a pang of longing, recalling those games. It must have been two years since the last one.

"This isn't a small game, I gotta warn you," Wayne continued. "I usually lose my shirt right off the bat, but once in a while I get lucky, and, hey, we're talking about real good money."

Ben reached for a pretzel from a dish on the bar. Did he remember enough to play in a real game? More importantly, did he want to risk losing what little he had? He'd put in a backbreaking week working overtime, and he could bet away his entire salary in one hand.

Jesus, he thought, disgusted with himself. Why am I such a damned Boy Scout? This guy's offering me a chance to gamble a little. Maybe I could turn the few bucks I've got into something more. And if I lose—what the hell's the difference? I've got nothing now, and I'll still have nothing.

He fished his wallet out of his back pocket and looked inside it. Three twenties and a ten.

"Will seventy do it?" he asked. "I just cashed my paycheck yesterday."

Wayne shrugged. "It'll get you in."

Time to take a chance, Ben told himself. Resolutely, he slid off his stool, suddenly feeling completely sober. "Let's go."

Wayne led the way back to the poolroom. None of the men there looked up as the two of them passed through. There was another door at the far side of the room, and that was where Wayne headed.

Ben followed him into another dim room, which was even hotter and smokier than the bar. Inside, four men were seated at a round table, engrossed in their card game. Two men stood on the periphery, watching. The table was crowded with cards, money, open cans of Budweiser, a few bottles of Wild Turkey, and ashtrays overflowing with cigarette butts.

The cardplayers appeared to range in age from thirty to fifty. Ben took a closer look at them. They weren't an especially appealing lot. Two of them bore enough of a resemblance for Ben to assume they were brothers. They both sported long greasy ponytails, and easily weighed over three hundred pounds apiece, their fat bellies keeping them from pulling their chairs up close to the table. In contrast, a third player was painfully skinny; Ben took in the tattoos up and down both arms, the scraggly gray beard and yellowing teeth. The fourth man, chewing on a toothpick, had a pale round face and thinning brown hair. He was the only one who looked over as the door opened.

"Hey," he said in a disinterested tone by way of greeting. "You coming in, Wayne?"

"I thought maybe," Wayne replied, pulling out a pack of Camels from his T-shirt pocket and lighting up a cigarette.

The man with the tattoos threw down his cards in disgust and stood up. "I'm goin' out now anyway. That's it for me tonight." He spoke to the two men leaning against the wall. "Let's get out of here."

As Wayne moved to take his seat, he gestured toward Ben. "Mind if my friend here sits in too?" He grinned. "I believe he just got paid."

There was laughter around the table. Ben stiffened. It wasn't as if he'd thought Wayne was his new best friend, but it suddenly became clear that Wayne hadn't exactly been doing him a favor by inviting him to play. He saw me for exactly what I am, Ben thought. A stupid, naive kid. Taking my seventy bucks off me here will be as easy as swiping my wallet; in fact, easier.

Ben looked around the table. Four faces watched him in silence. I should get the hell out of here right now, he thought uncomfortably.

Finally, one of the brothers took a swig of beer from the open can beside him. "What's it goin' to be?" he said impatiently. "We don't have all night, kid."

The man who had spoken when they first entered the room began shuffling the cards. "Boys, I think we're scarin' our little guest here. I don't get the sense he has the *conjones* to play." His voice dripped with condescension. "It's okay, fella. You run along home now."

A strange sensation began to overtake Ben. The rage and powerlessness he'd felt ever since his mother died, ever since he'd found himself unable to come up with tuition money, ever since Carlin—all of it was swelling inside him, making him feel he was about to burst. Good little Ben, he thought furiously, always keeping the stiff upper lip. His eyes narrowed as he returned the gaze of the man who'd just spoken. *Screw you*, he told him silently. If you're going to take my money, okay, but you're not sending me out of here with my tail between my legs.

He grabbed an empty chair and slammed it down on the floor next to the table. "Deal."

"Well, fellas," one of the brothers put in, a nasty smirk on his face, "we got ourselves a new buddy."

The man who'd been shuffling finished abruptly. He began expertly flicking the cards face down in front of each player. "All right, *gentlemen.* The game is five-card stud. Jacks or better to open." His voice grew sarcastic as he directed his next words to Ben. "That okay with you?"

Ben sat down, concentrating on wiping any expression off his face. When he spoke, his voice was calm and without inflection. "That'll be fine."

The sun was just rising as Ben emerged from the bar. Shielding his eyes from the painful daylight, he turned left and hurried along, half-expecting to feel the blow of a crowbar or fists in his back. But no one appeared to be coming after him.

Still, he kept his pace brisk. He'd read enough books and seen enough movies to imagine that those guys weren't going to let him walk away with all their money. Of course, it wasn't just a few guys who'd lost so much. There must have been three or four others who'd rotated in over the course of the night. But it can't have made them happy to lose nearly six hundred bucks to some kid they'd never seen before, someone they'd expected to hand over his money in five minutes and be gone.

When he finally caught sight of his building, he slowed down. Apparently, they weren't going to rob or kill him to get their losings back. He rubbed his reddened eyes and ran his hand over the stubble on his cheeks, unable to remember the last time he'd felt so exhausted and dirty. That room had gotten only closer with every passing hour, the smell of beer and stale cigarette smoke even stronger. He desperately wanted to take a shower, to wash the whole disgusting night away, but he knew he wouldn't make it; the second he got inside, he was going to fall onto his bed. Luckily, it was Sunday, his one day off, and he could sleep the day away.

I suppose I should be thrilled, he thought. When I add this to what I'll make at work over the summer, there'll be enough money for SUNY. Hell, I beat the pants off those dumb bastards *and* got what I needed, first time out of the gate in a real all-night poker game. A lot of people would call that fun.

He felt the wad of money in his pants pocket. It *hadn't* been fun, not for him. Even if the game weren't illegal, and even if the men in that place hadn't repulsed and frightened him, the whole business of taking their money made him feel crummy. He shook his head ruefully. If he killed himself working all summer long, he'd barely walk away with this much money. Yet here he was, holding nearly six hundred dollars in his hand, won in only a few hours.

He grimaced, even as his eyes half-closed with fatigue. It had been as big a surprise to him as to the other players to discover he actually had a poker face that no one else seemed able to read. It also turned out that he had really learned something from his games with Kit. He knew when to stay in and when to fold. Obviously, he'd been lucky, he reflected. A couple of great hands got dealt his way on what turned into big pots. But still, he sensed that he was genuinely good at the game.

Of course, the men expected him to return next week for another game. Wayne had become his good buddy again when it became clear Ben was cleaning up, but as he was leaving, he did whisper in his ear that Ben had better show up next Saturday to let them all have a chance to win their money back. His tone had been friendly, but there was no mistaking his unspoken message.

Ben entered his apartment quietly, thinking only of the clean, cool sheets on his bed. Suddenly it occurred to him that, of course, this wasn't the only poker game in Wester-field. There had to be plenty of others.

He went into his bedroom, pausing just long enough to put the fat wad of rumpled, beer-stained bills into his bureau drawer before flopping down across his bed, too exhausted even to bother taking off his sneakers.

They must play poker in Binghamton, too. It was the last thought he had before falling into a dead sleep.

1978

13

Carlin felt as if she were flying above the Charles River instead of merely pedaling by it on her bicycle. Riding just in front of her, her friend Nancy Erickson dodged a Frisbee that was being tossed back and forth by two joggers on either side of the path, then turned her head and smiled back at Carlin. They'd been inseparable since they were freshmen the year before, and now the two were celebrating the end of finals.

"No more Veblen," Nancy yelled.

"No more Engels." Carlin pulled up alongside her.

Nancy looked across at her friend and smiled. "And no more Max Weber." She waited a beat. "Eber."

Carlin groaned in response, then began to laugh in spite of herself.

"You see," Nancy said smugly, "even my worst material is good."

"Well"—Carlin thought for a moment—"I wouldn't say that."

"And what would you say?" Nancy raised one eyebrow in mock seriousness.

"I would say your best material and your worst material are pretty much indistinguishable from each other." Carlin giggled as she began pedaling faster and pulled out in front.

The two girls raced along the narrow river, the tensions of their weeks of studying evaporating in the warm May air. After a couple of miles of sheer exertion, Nancy called out, "How about a rest stop?" and pulled over to the side.

Carlin joined her, extracting two plastic water bottles from the basket behind the seat.

"Jeez," Nancy said after laying her bike down and taking a gulp of water. "You never get tired, do you?"

Carlin stepped off her bike and carefully lowered it to the ground. "Not today I don't. I'd like this ride to last forever."

"Not much looking forward to tomorrow, huh?" Nancy asked.

"Well, I'd rather be on my way to Manhattan," she replied, sitting down and stretching her arms overhead. "Let's see, tomorrow night, you'll probably be sitting at Le Cirque, and the day after that you'll be prosecuting some Mafia chieftain. Oh, and then you'll stop in at Saks for a couple of hours and maybe you'll meet the mayor for cocktails."

Nancy's life as the daughter of the attorney general of the United States was so far removed from Carlin's world, she couldn't even feel envious. Thatcher Erickson's daughter had grown up in Manhattan, boarded in Massachusetts, and partied in official Washington every Christmas for the past few years. That Nancy had ended up her closest friend at Harvard seemed ridiculous on the face of it, yet the two girls had many more similarities than differences. They'd both been in Ec 10, the introductory economics course whose large lecture hall held at least eight hundred students. If they hadn't ended up in the small weekly section run by a teaching assistant, they'd probably never even have noticed each other at the freshman dormitory, Matthews Hall, and struck up a conversation. Second semester, they both became fascinated by constitutional law and wound up studying together most nights.

It was fun even when both were consistently professors' favorites in the four or five classes they'd taken together. Carlin was fascinated by Nancy's enormous range of knowledge, gleaned as much from the wealth of experiences that had been laid at her feet as from actual studying, while Nancy thought that Carlin was the smartest person she'd ever met. When Carlin had described herself as a "lazy slob" in high school, Nancy didn't believe her.

Carlin was pleased to think about how much she'd changed. Somehow, moving away from Westerfield, coming to a school with so many different people, seemed to open her brain up. It was as if a hundred miles from home, she had become the person her high school teachers had kept telling her she was supposed to be. No one had to talk about her *potential* anymore.

No, she admitted to herself, it wasn't only the move away from Westerfield. Her sudden seriousness had more to do with a competitiveness she'd never known she had. In the first couple of weeks after she arrived in Cambridge, all she heard from the others in her dorm were stories of Andover and Choate and Exeter and Boston Latin. After a month or so of complete insecurity, she realized she just had to buckle down. She figured that one underachiever from a poor school—especially one who didn't deserve to get in in the first place—could never measure up, but at least she could try not to humiliate herself. In the dim recesses of her mind, she could even hear Ben telling her how well she had to do, for both of them. Of course that was the day she got the letter telling her she'd gotten in. That was before . . .

So she'd forced herself to put in the hours studying, and lo and behold, when first semester was over, she'd gotten three As and a B, better than just about anyone else in her classes. She was amazed at first, but as she looked around at the perfectly groomed kids who'd talked so blithely about their years in boarding school, she felt triumphant.

Her newfound drive was based on more than mere competition. In the quiet green-shrubbed beauty of Harvard Yard, she found herself really and truly absorbed—by her classes, Boston politics, the architectural beauty of the narrow old houses along Beacon Street and the old wood Victorians on Brewster Street, the long lively conversations in the dark recesses of the Wursthaus.

It seemed everything in her life had finally come together. If anyone had asked, the only thing she could possibly think of as missing at this moment was a boyfriend. At that thought, the image of Ben Dameroff fluttered again at the edge of her consciousness. She willed it away, but all too quickly the image of Westerfield came back as well. She felt herself frown as she realized that the very next day, she'd be returning home for the summer.

"What's the matter?" Nancy asked, catching her friend's expression.

"Oh, nothing." Carlin hated to complain. Besides, how could she explain the nuances of another summer at home even to as good a friend as Nancy? Tash was the only one

who really understood. The summer after freshman year had
been a nightmare. Her father, pathetically enthroned in his
wheelchair, looking out the living-room window, issuing demands. *Not my brush, Lillian. I said my comb! Why can't you
ever listen the first time!* Her mother's meek responses. The
endless nine-to-five behind a counter at Dalrymple's and evenings tutoring summer-school students doing time at
Westerfield High.

Carlin didn't mind the two jobs. She certainly needed the
money. Between her four-year scholarship and the Rutherford
Award, the bulk of her tuition and board were covered, but
there were so many expenses, it was hard to keep up. Besides, at least working kept her out of the house. Away from
the J.T. and Lillian show.

And away from let's-see-how-many-ways-we-can-find-to-
avoid-Ben Dameroff-today, she silently admitted to herself.
She'd been panicked at the thought of running into him every
time she stepped into their building, every evening out she
shared with Natasha. Even Ben and Natasha's father was a
problem. Carlin felt so terrible for Leonard Dameroff, but
what could she say when she saw him? *I'm sorry my father
slept with your wife,* an evil gremlin inside her imagined
blurting out when he walked into Dalrymple's one day to
pick up some cough medicine.

"Yicchhh." She didn't realize she'd spoken out loud until
she heard her friend chuckling beside her.

"Well, at least nothing's wrong," Nancy said dryly.

Carlin smiled ruefully. "Home may be the place they have
to take you in, but that doesn't necessarily make it the place
you want to go."

Nancy might not understand everything, but Carlin knew
she would be sympathetic. Her friend had visited Westerfield
with Carlin last Thanksgiving. By the time the two girls had
left late Sunday afternoon, Carlin had practically had to gag
Nancy to stop her from saying something to Lillian. *Why
does your mother put up with that?* Nancy had demanded all
the way back to Cambridge. *That's a mystery to me too,* Carlin longed to agree, but there was no way she could say that
to Nancy without feeling she was betraying her mother.

Enough complaining, Carlin told herself firmly. "So when

are you starting at the district attorney's office?" she asked, purposefully changing the subject.

"Well . . ." Nancy sounded uncharacteristically coy.

"Well what?" Carlin eyed her suspiciously.

Nancy's summer internship with the New York district attorney's office in Manhattan had been arranged by her father months before. It was a plum job, one Carlin would have killed for. After freshman year, she'd made it her business to find out about every constitutional law and constitutional history class Harvard offered its undergraduates, knowing she wanted to go on to law school after college. Just the idea of getting hands-on experience prosecuting criminals . . . Hearing about the internship for the first time after Thatcher Erickson had set it up had been one of the only times Carlin had felt real jealousy. It was hard to imagine how her friend could hesitate.

Nancy stretched out on her stomach, her hand cupped under her chin. "What would you say if I told you I was thinking about *not* working in the DA's office this summer?"

"I'd say you were crazy" was Carlin's immediate response.

"How crazy would I be to spend the summer traveling through the continent of Asia, accompanied by Philip Mannhoff?"

Carlin whistled appreciatively. "All summer long? Every day and every night?"

"Correct, Professor Squire. Every day and every romantic Oriental night."

Carlin stared at Nancy as if to say, Are you making this whole thing up? After all, Philip Mannhoff had been the object of Nancy's desire ever since both girls had taken his class on Chinese history. Brilliant and charismatic, Dr. Mannhoff had the reputation of half-smart-ass, half-*wunderkind,* a combination Nancy found irresistible. But aside from lively class discussions, Nancy's obsession with him hadn't paid off.

At least until now, Carlin realized. "Is that why you've been in such a good mood all day?"

"That's right, *kemosabe.*" Nancy paused. "Last night," she began pompously, "at eight-twelve—as you will recall, that is precisely four hours after the Chinese history final exam ended—I received a phone call from the aforementioned Dr.

Mannhoff, inquiring as to whether one Nancy Erickson would care to join him on a two-month excursion to the Orient."

"Was this a social call or a business call?"

"Where is your spirit of romance?" Nancy asked playfully.

Carlin refused to be put off. No one's heart's desire called them for a two-month date out of the blue, not even Nancy's. "What *exactly* did he say?"

"Well," Nancy relented, "he did ask me to go along as a researcher, but if we're not sharing a futon by June sixth, I'll give you a hundred bucks."

Carlin shook her head. Knowing Nancy's determination, she wouldn't be surprised if it happened exactly as planned. Still, Dr. Mannhoff was not exactly a naive schoolkid, someone to be led astray by the manipulations of a college sophomore, even one as attractive as Nancy Erickson.

She wondered at her friend's confidence as Nancy just smiled at her indulgently. Suddenly Carlin started to laugh. Of course Nancy was right. He could have asked anyone to go along. He must have been interested in her all semester long and waited for their official relationship to end. "Congratulations. Try not to get married before junior year begins, okay?"

"Married!" Nancy sounded horrified. "I don't intend to get married until I'm fifty."

Carlin looked dubious.

"But I do intend to have a very good time every minute before I succumb."

"To your good time." Carlin raised her water bottle and took a long sip.

"*Au contraire,* my dear. To *your* good time." Nancy's eyes twinkled mischievously.

"I'll think of you when the thermometer hits a hundred, right around the first week of August," Carlin responded.

"You'll think of me all right, but you won't be bored to death in Westerfield. You'll be baking in the subways of Manhattan."

Carlin looked at her incredulously. "What are you talking about?"

"I'm talking about *your* internship with the Manhattan district attorney," Nancy answered triumphantly.

Suddenly Carlin understood what Nancy was offering her. She felt like bursting into tears, partly out of gratitude for such a generous friend, partly out of the impossibility of accepting. She could never afford an apartment in New York, never be able to raise enough from an intern's earnings to help pay for her third year at Harvard.

Nancy's eyes were glowing. She could tell what Carlin was thinking without having to hear a word, but she knew she had covered every base. Quickly she rushed ahead. "Between taking care of my aunt Maude's three German shepherds and working in the DA's office, you'll be earning over five thousand dollars."

"What!" Carlin couldn't believe what Nancy was saying.

"My aunt is being forced, poor dear, to summer in Geneva this year, thanks to Uncle Glendon and UNEP." Nancy's aunt's second husband had held various jobs in the United Nations practically since its founding. "It's easier to pay someone to live in their apartment and take care of Patty, LaVerne, and Maxine than it is to put all the doggie paperwork together. Besides, empty apartments on Sutton Place tend to get robbed."

Carlin could see that Nancy was serious. But there had to be a catch somewhere. It was all too perfect.

"Isn't the DA's office expecting Thatcher Erickson's daughter?" she asked.

"According to Thatcher Erickson, the Manhattan DA doesn't care who his college slave is, just so that slave intends to work her fingers to the bone."

A summer in New York City, an apartment, an exciting job, no parental disputes, no Ben Dameroff sightings, no Dalrymple's, no high school kids. Carlin couldn't believe her luck. Reaching across the grass, she grabbed Nancy in a fierce hug. "I'm going to have the best summer anyone's ever had."

Fluffing her hair suggestively, visions of Philip Mannhoff obviously in her head, Nancy grinned back. "No, sweetie. I believe the best-summer-anyone's-ever-had award will be coming to me."

14

"Winner pays, Harry. Come on. Fork it over."

From her table right next to theirs, Carlin couldn't help staring at the six police officers pushed into the semicircular cushioned booth at the coffee shop around the corner from One Police Plaza. It was clear they were all playing to the red-haired man seated in a chair pulled up to the head of the table, making the U into a circle. Although his uniform was the same as the others', he seemed to be the one in charge. She could sense the admiration from the group around him as he worked the table, chuckling to his left, whispering to his right.

"Yeah, Harry," she heard a balding young cop saying to him, "the only reason I ordered the extra fries was so your wallet wouldn't be too heavy to carry home."

The red-haired officer rose from his chair, his gaze turning to Carlin as he addressed the group as a whole. "I'll tell you what, guys. If the beautiful lady wants me to pay, I'll pay."

"Excuse me?" Carlin's face flushed as she realized that the cop had noticed her staring at them. She felt like a fool, sitting there unable to think of anything else to say. Two years at Harvard plus one month in the DA's office should have provided her with a better comeback than "Excuse me?"

The red-haired policeman walked the few steps to where she was sitting. "My friends and I have just completed our annual shooting practice around the corner. Now, the question is, Should I, the acknowledged master of this activity . . ."

His fellow officers hooted at the description.

"I repeat, shall I administer to the masses their expected spoils or shall I take you dancing instead—save my money for a dimly lit club where you won't have to sit alone at a Formica table?"

Carlin glanced from the wedding band adorning his left hand to the name on his shiny silver badge. "Mr. Floyd. As you appear to be asking me for a date, you can't possibly have a wife. So I assume that gold band is some form of friendship ring between you and your fellow officers." She waved briefly toward the other policemen. "I hope you make it to the club and you all have a fabulous time dancing with each other."

Grandly, she rose from her table and walked to the cash register, hearing, without deigning to turn around and look, the clapping and cheering from the table filled with cops.

Well, that was silly, she thought to herself as she walked back to the tall old building where she'd been given a tiny shoebox of an office. Silly but fun, she acknowledged, ringing for the elevator. She glanced at her watch as she waited. She'd begun to time how long it took for the elevator to arrive. A full ten minutes today, or maybe down to eight? It never failed to amaze her. However heroic these downtown skyscrapers looked from the outside, their ancient insides were barely functional. Her own space consisted of an alcove with a tiny desk. There she huddled ten or eleven hours a day, typing, filing, taking only an occasional break to go out for coffee. A summer in the district attorney's office had sounded exciting when Nancy had handed her the job, but it had turned out to be a lot less glamorous than she might have imagined.

Not that she felt entitled to whine. Nancy Erickson's gesture had been a dream come true. Nancy's aunt's apartment was spectacular, high above Sutton Place, overlooking the East River. The dogs were perfectly behaved. Better than many of the city's people, Carlin often mused as a stray hand would wander her way for an unwanted groping on the Lexington Avenue subway during the steaming 8 A.M. rush hour.

Carlin settled in at her desk. As usual, there was a stack of documents she was supposed to route to various city agencies. But for once, there was a brightly colored postcard as well, royal blue water lapping at the shore of an enormous white beach, one tiny shack barely visible in the background. She turned it over quickly, checking the postmark. Bali. Nancy's bold signature practically leapt from the bottom of the card. Carlin smiled as she read her friend's message.

> C. How does Mrs. Philip Mannhoff sound? Futon reached on day three. Let's see what another few weeks will bring. Hugs and Kisses. N.

It wasn't surprising to Carlin that Nancy and Philip Mannhoff had fallen into a relationship so quickly. Yet she felt slightly disconcerted, she realized, as she perused the message one more time. She'd teased her friend about marrying, but the notion that Nancy might actually *do* it was jarring. Nancy was all about brains and daring and independent spirit. Somehow marrying at twenty seemed like an artificial cutoff, the culmination of some other person's dream.

Carlin felt guilty for a moment. Am I concerned for Nancy, or am I jealous? There's the real question, she thought, forcing her attention back to the work in front of her.

Her eyes wandered over the first few pages in the stack of papers on her desk. Second-degree murder, plea-bargained to manslaughter. Grand theft-auto, marked down to a misdemeanor. She couldn't believe what she saw every day. It was as if no one got punished in this town. The aggressive first-year assistant district attorney she'd been assigned to had explained it to her one night over drinks. Between the overpopulation at Rikers Island, where prisoners were kept before trial, to the overcrowded court dockets, most criminals served sentences for more minor crimes than the ones they'd actually committed. A quick plea-bargaining session between a harried defense lawyer and a busy ADA made for swifter justice than the long, drawn-out jury trials that took months to prepare.

"Murderers don't go free," Steve Kaliff swore as Carlin looked dubious. "Honest, if it weren't for plea bargains, the system would sink of its own weight."

Carlin shook her head. So the system wasn't perfectly to her liking. Who was she to question it, one month in as a paid intern? She was lucky to be there, soaking it all up. Her political critiques could wait until she'd put in some real time.

"Hey, Carlin," Steve Kaliff called from the corridor, then he appeared in the doorway. "Come on. It's your red-letter day. You're going to court."

Carlin rose from her chair, feeling a rush of excitement. Steve had been promising her a day at an actual trial for weeks. She knew he'd been involved in prosecuting a man accused of holding up three electronics stores on the same night. For the past two weeks, Steve had been in his office by the time she arrived early in the morning, and, she'd been told, had stayed late every night. Even she had contributed to building his case, researching computer serial numbers. Most of the work the ADAs did was much less interesting in practice than it sounded in theory, but they worked unbelievably hard. Even here, where Steve had evidence that had been stored in the defendant's basement plus several eyewitnesses, the burden of proving a case was a long, tedious job.

"The judge is a dip," Steve murmured to Carlin as they walked toward the courtroom where the trial had begun the day before. "But even watching a dip judge and a new ADA will be more fun for you than pushing papers around all day long."

Carlin nodded happily, as another ADA stopped them at the door.

"Steve, give me a minute, okay?"

"I'll be at the water fountain." Carlin quickly stepped away. Knowing how long-winded most of the ADAs were, she expected to be standing alone for a good few minutes.

"You following me?"

Surprised by a voice behind her, Carlin turned around. Standing almost a foot above her, his red hair seeming to light up the long hall, was the policeman she'd sparred with in the coffee shop.

"Seriously, gorgeous, what are you doing hovering around my turf?"

"I wasn't aware that one man had bought up the criminal courts building. Or possibly you're referring to the entire Wall Street area." Carlin laughed, wishing she felt more seriously annoyed. Somehow this arrogant sexist cop had the capacity to ingratiate even as he was being a jerk.

"Let's go back to square one, okay?" The policeman took her right hand, shook it firmly, and released it. "I'm Police Officer Harry Floyd. Come five years from now or so and I'll be Sergeant Harry Floyd, and a few years after that Lieutenant Harry Floyd. And yes, I *am* married"——he looked at his wedding band almost ruefully——"and I am not, I repeat *not*, trying to pick you up. But you happen to be in my district, and as a good cop——on his way to being a great cop, that is——I want to know what a classy girl like you is doing in this dungeon of disgustos."

Carlin thought of affecting a blasé, silent act, but he was just too lively to ignore. "Well, Patrolman Floyd, I'm Carlin Squire, full-time college student and part-time intern at the district attorney's office. As far as I know, I haven't broken any laws in your district yet."

The policeman grimaced. "So you're working for the dealmakers in three-piece suits. Sorry to hear it."

"I think you might say I'm working for the people who convict the guys you go to so much trouble to arrest," Carlin answered defensively.

As she finished her sentence, Steve Kaliff walked up to them.

"We'll be returning to the office," he said woodenly. "If you're ready to leave, that is," he added, taking in Officer Floyd.

"Why?" Carlin asked, noting the look of dissatisfaction on Steve's face.

"Mr. Armed Burglary and his very expensive attorney have agreed to plead guilty in return for two years, suspended, of course, in that it's his first offense."

"You're kidding!" Carlin exclaimed. "But what about those other robberies uptown? What happens to that now?"

Steve's face was a study in frustration. "As my fellow ADA just said, 'You wanted guilty, you got guilty. Let that be enough.'"

He turned to look at the police officer standing alongside Carlin. Gazing at the name on his badge, he snapped his fingers. "You were one of the cops that was due to testify this afternoon, right? Well, you got yourself an afternoon off."

Carlin was crestfallen. She'd watched Steve spend hours each day preparing his case, saw those late nights reflected in the dark circles under his eyes.

"Listen"—Steve didn't wait for her to speak—"I'll meet you back at the office. You know the way." Abruptly he walked toward the elevator at the end of the corridor.

"God, those guys are gutless." Harry Floyd's explosion took Carlin by surprise. "We're the ones who put the bastards behind bars, then those morons with their advanced degrees send them right back on the street."

Without giving her a chance to respond, Harry took her elbow and motioned her toward the elevator. "C'mon, college girl. Let me show you what stopping crime really consists of."

"What do you mean?"

"I'm on night shift, you know, eleven to seven, all next week. Spend one night with me and my partner, and you'll learn more about criminal justice than you would in ten years in the DA's office. What d'ya say?"

"So then I went nights to Brooklyn College. I graduated last June. Now it's all up to me."

Sitting in the backseat, Carlin leaned forward, enthralled. She didn't even notice the steamy heat of the July night or the steady car exhaust rolling in the open windows of the squad car. Harry Floyd and his partner, Ned Tamerica, hadn't let her do any actual police work, but in the three evenings they'd allowed her to tag along, she'd gotten to witness any number of fights and friskings and even an armed break-in at a liquor wholesaler all the way downtown. Harry explained everything he was doing, how carefully he'd been taught to handle every aspect of his job in the six months he'd spent at the Police Academy.

"I'm planning on being top dog," he said to Carlin, taking advantage of an unusually uneventful Thursday evening. "I've got my degree, plus more smarts than anyone else in the squad room. Come the exam for sergeant, I'm gonna be first on line."

"How can you be so sure of yourself?" Carlin inquired.

"How can you not be?" Harry practically exploded. "Did you ever look around the DA's office? How smart are those guys? Any smarter than you?" He looked at her appraisingly. "I doubt it."

Carlin couldn't argue. Just as she'd been surprised to find out during her first year at Harvard, other people weren't really such geniuses when you played on the same field. No, in the past few weeks she'd been disappointed to learn that most of the ADAs she'd met didn't seem that smart at all.

Harry turned toward her in the backseat, his face displaying pure irritation. "Every day I sit through roll call, with those jerks on top of us checking to see if our shoes are shined and warning us about taking bribes and stealing dope."

From the driver's seat, Ned nodded. Carlin looked surprised.

"You thought roll call was case studies?" Harry answered her expression. "No such luck. Roll call mostly consists of your superior officers warning you of the impending appearance of your brethren who are paid to spy on you. You know, internal affairs. Anyway, I'm smarter than any of those guys, and that includes my illustrious captain."

"Well, you certainly won't be prosecuted for modesty." Carlin found his bragging less offensive than she might have if it had come from someone other than Harry Floyd. Everything about him was larger than life. And, she reminded herself, the officers he worked with really did seem to respect him.

The car stopped in front of a pizzeria on First Avenue and Eighteenth Street. Ned looked good-natured but serious as he turned to Carlin. "Listen, if I happen to score better than Harry on the sergeant's exam the next time it's given, and my body turns up in the Harlem River, this is the guy you should check out."

"C'mon, guys." Harry motioned to Carlin and his partner, starting to open the car door. "I'm thinking sausage and mushroom . . ."

His speech was interrupted by the sudden blaring of the police radio. "Sector C. Sector C. Disturbance reported on Ganesevoort and Washington."

Harry slammed the door as Ned started the engine and pulled out into traffic, heading crosstown. The car's flashing red light and screaming siren caused the cars in front of them to part like the Red Sea. It was less than five minutes later when the car abruptly halted near the corner of Washington Street.

"Over there," Harry indicated to Ned. "You stay in the car," he warned Carlin.

Carlin watched the two officers walk toward a darkened building. She realized she was in the meat-packing district, its large empty buildings and silent streets making it seem a scene from early in the century. She could hear the backup cars approaching, their sirens' pitch higher as they came closer.

But as she turned to watch the other police cars turn the corner, she noticed something to the left. Without thinking, she opened the car door.

"Carlin, what the hell are you doing?"

Harry's voice was angry as he saw her leave the car. But Carlin paid no attention. What she saw was too compelling. Sprawled behind the column of a building across the street was a pair of legs.

"Quick, over here," she called out loudly.

Harry and Ned came up behind her as she knelt beside the limp and battered body of a young woman with long brown hair.

She must be just about my age, Carlin thought, horrified, as Harry bent down beside her and raised his finger to the girl's neck.

"No pulse," he said curtly to Ned.

Carlin felt almost dizzy for a moment, standing up and taking a deep breath to calm herself.

"Drugs," she heard Harry note aloud as he picked up a small object near the woman's body.

"I bet that's not what killed her." Ned's voice was uncharacteristically quiet, as if respectful in the presence of death. "Look at this."

Ned was pointing to several large bruises on the girl's face. Fascinated in spite of herself, Carlin watched as he pulled the

hair back on one side. An ugly red gash covered her cheekbone, rising all the way up her forehead and into her hairline.

"What do you think she was hit with?" Carlin peered over
Ned's shoulder, her eyes wandering down the girl's body. She
moved in even closer.

"Hey, Carlin, whoa!" Harry stood up, blocking her inspec-
tion, and urged her back toward the squad car. "This is a
crime scene—not the place for a civilian." He looked nervously at the officers getting out of the backup vehicles and
moving toward them. "Come on. We could get in a ton of
trouble having you with us."

Carlin knew she should return to the squad car without arguing, but she felt she belonged right where she was. "It's as
if this girl could be someone I know," she tried to explain to
Harry and Ned.

"Listen, sugar," Harry said kindly as he took her hand and
moved her away from the body, "this girl is not anyone you
would know, not anything like you."

"How can you be so sure?" Carlin was allowing him to
move her back toward the squad car, but she wanted to find
out more before she let Harry go back to the body.

"For one thing, a young girl in a short, tight skirt, in
the middle of the meat-packing district in the middle of the
night . . . Well, how can I put this? I would guess you two
have certain professional differences."

"You mean she's a hooker. And an addict." Carlin wasn't
surprised.

Harry nodded, almost amused at the eagerness in her voice.
"Well, yeah. This is not a Harvard student in town for a summer job."

Carlin looked back toward the victim. Hooker or no
hooker, she couldn't help but identify with her. Under the
sexy clothes had been a young girl who must have awakened
every day certain that life could get better.

She turned back to Harry. "Okay, maybe she was no college student, but she *is* someone just about my own age and
I'd do anything to help you find the people who did this."

Her fierceness took Harry by surprise. He thought for a
second before answering. Carlin Squire worked in the DA's
office. She had access to files that might come in handy.

Shielding her in front of him so the policemen coming up the street wouldn't see her, he opened the car door and ushered her inside. Only when she was seated and well out of view did he answer her.

"Right now," he whispered in a low voice, "if you want Ned and me to keep our jobs, that is, what you can do is stay right here and keep your mouth shut. But maybe, just maybe, there will be something you can do."

Only two days later, Harry Floyd called Carlin at the DA's office. Instead of the glad-handing braggadocio his voice usually conveyed, this time he sounded relentlessly professional.

"Listen, Carlin, if you meant what you said, there may be something you can do for us."

"Name it."

"What probably killed that girl—her name was Jackie Franklin, by the way—was not someone but something, namely a Maserati."

"How do you know?" Carlin asked breathlessly.

"A combination of tire tracks and glass particles. I don't have time to go into the encyclopedia of forensics right now. But we think that was the instrument, and we're certain it was no accident."

Carlin could tell from the urgency in his tone that he hadn't called just to share his theories. "What do you want me to do?"

"Well, for the hell of it, as long as you're there in the DA's office, how about asking around? Like have any drug dealers who drive a Maserati been mentioned during depositions? It's not the kind of thing we can always get from computer files, but it *is* something an underpaid ADA might remember."

"I'm on it."

Harry laughed. "Go get 'em."

Carlin sat down with a complete list of assistant district attorneys, their business and home telephone numbers noted next to their names. If she worked up through midnight or so, she might be able to talk to all of them.

She grabbed the receiver. "What else, Harry?"

"Harry? Who's Harry?"

Carlin recognized Natasha Dameroff's voice immediately.

"Tash, where are you? You sound like you're around the corner."

"Well, I'm in a pay phone on Sixty-third Street and Madison Avenue, and I have no idea whether that's around the corner or not." Natasha laughed. "It's taken me three weeks to call your parents and get your number, which is two and a half weeks longer than it took me to find an apartment and my first modeling job."

"You mean you're here for good?" For a few seconds, Carlin felt transported to another lifetime.

"I mean I live here and I'm dying to see you," Natasha said excitedly. "You're coming to dinner tonight. My apartment's on Third and Eighty-fourth."

Carlin looked at the phone directory on her desk. "Tash, listen, I can't tonight. I'm in the middle of something. I'll explain it when I see you. How about tomorrow night?"

"I have a photo shoot for *Mademoiselle* that may run late tomorrow. Is Thursday all right?"

Carlin barely heard the last sentence. She found herself practically screaming. "You have a *what* for *what*?"

"I'll explain it on Thursday when I see you." Natasha taunted her sweetly as she hung up the phone.

Carlin laughed, then forced herself to put Natasha out of her mind. As eager as she was to catch up with Natasha, she had work to do. Let's see, she said to herself as her eyes ran down the first page of ADAs, what do you know, Mr. Lee Aaron at extension 2105?

Thursday evening brought two surprises. The first was the postcard from Nancy Erickson she retrieved from the mail when she stopped at home to shower before going to Natasha's for dinner. This time, the postmark read "Singapore."

C. Returning to Osaka in two days. Have been invited to horn in on minor economic summit between Japanese corporate council and American trade mission. Very polite fur should fly. Am planning to stay through first semester. You are instructed to miss me a little. By the way, Philip Mannhoff nice place to visit. Wouldn't want to live there. Much love, N.

* * *

Well, what do you know about that, Carlin thought, placing the card on the hallway table. She *would* miss her when school started up again, but she was relieved. Several fabulous months in Japan sounded far more exciting than marriage at twenty.

Natasha's apartment was surprise number two. The dining room chairs were Breuer, the wineglasses Baccarat, and the small blue and gold Oriental rug placed under the glass coffee table so spotless, it looked as if no one had ever walked on it. The whole place seemed to have been lifted, whole, out of Bloomingdale's fifth floor. Carlin couldn't imagine having an apartment like this, ever, or at least, she thought to herself, not until she was forty-five or something. But Natasha seemed thrilled by it.

"So which bank did you rob?" Carlin asked, accepting the glass of white wine Natasha handed her.

"The Bank of *Mademoiselle,* Sears Roebuck, and *Seventeen,*" Natasha said smugly.

"You've worked all those places in under a month?"

"Oh, Carlin, you wouldn't believe it. I got three of the go-sees I went to the very first week I was here." Natasha took a small sip of wine and her eyes sparkled with excitement. "When I first got to New York, I went over to the Lightman Agency. One of the people at Shreyer's had mentioned it when I first modeled in their show. Anyway, they fixed me up with this hair guy and this makeup person, they got my whole look together, and then took some pictures and showed them around. Then they sent me on these go-sees. The first one was to this huge advertising agency on Fifty-seventh Street."

Carlin saw Natasha's expression suddenly turn fearful.

"All these people were standing around, staring at me. I thought I'd die, I swear. I was absolutely petrified."

Carlin shook her head. How sad that even with her obvious success Tash could still be so deeply frightened.

Natasha saw her friend's concern, and willed herself to calm down. After all, she chided herself, this was a story with a happy ending. "The point isn't how scared I was, I swear," Natasha grinned. "They *hired* me. That's the point." There was pride in her voice now. "The money I earned on that shoot paid for *that*." She laughed as she pointed to the Oriental rug.

Carlin embraced her friend quickly, then looked her up and down. With her jade silk dress clinging to her angular body, Natasha looked like someone born for success. She wore her untamed red hair longer than she had in high school, yet somehow its wildness framed her face precisely. Idly, Carlin wondered exactly how much it cost to achieve such perfect spontaneity. "Tash, this is incredible."

"Well, I hope it keeps up, 'cause I've spent a lot more than I've earned, thanks to VISA. I just *had* to have this stuff," she said, running her hand over the back of an overstuffed armchair. "What with the first month's rent plus security, I don't actually have any cash left, but . . ."

Carlin laughed. "You better make it or some repo company's gonna have a field day in this apartment."

Natasha looked frightened. "Do you really think that's going to happen?"

"Honey, of course I don't." Carlin shook her head. It had been a whole year since she'd seen Natasha. Two, really, since they'd spent much time together. She'd almost forgotten Natasha's fearfulness, which always hovered so close to the surface. "Tash, you're going to be a famous model. You've known it since you were five years old. You were right then and you're right now."

Natasha's face brightened. "You and Ben always say that, but it's so hard to be sure. The two of you have no idea how many beautiful girls there are in this city, girls who've lived here for years, who know all the right people and go all the right places."

Carlin had to turn away. She hadn't heard Ben's name mentioned in so long. Suddenly the image of him flooded through her. She felt torn in half, longing to badger Natasha for every detail of his life, yet nearly compelled to turn tail and leave for fear of hearing a single word. It was all she could do to shift the conversation toward a subject that couldn't possibly involve him.

She avoided looking at Natasha, searching for something to

talk about. "Hey, I'm helping the police with a murder," she finally said.

Natasha reacted immediately. "You are? What are you doing? How did the police get to you?"

"One question at a time, please." Carlin told Natasha about her friendship with Harry Floyd and his request for her help on the Franklin murder. "I ended up finding not one but three ADAs who'd heard a Maserati mentioned in the course of a drug investigation."

"What's an ADA?" Natasha asked.

"Assistant district attorney. Those are the guys who actually try most of the criminal cases. The only time I even saw the actual district attorney was my first day on the job."

"It sounds like the DA's office is chopped liver compared to your friend *Harry*." Natasha emphasized his name flirtatiously.

Carlin laughed in response. "It's not exactly what you're thinking. Harry Floyd is in no way a romantic possibility. He's married. Besides, this is a guy who would eat his own mother if he thought it would advance his career."

"Well," Natasha insisted, "he certainly seems to have a soft spot for you."

"Yeah," Carlin admitted, "he's been great to me. But trust me, if I ever got in his way, he'd mow me down so fast, I wouldn't even see it coming."

Carlin had never said this before, even to herself. But as she thought about it, she realized it was true. Harry Floyd was a great friend. But, boy oh boy, would she hate to have him as an enemy. On the other hand, the days she'd been spending with him were proving to be the most exciting of her summer. In fact, the most exciting hours of her life.

"So what did your friend Harry find out from the three names you gave him?" Natasha demanded eagerly.

"Actually, I'm supposed to call him tonight. Do you mind if I use your phone?"

"It's in the bedroom. Can I listen in?" Natasha led the way to a small room in back, handing her a white princess phone.

"Harry? Carlin. What did you find out?"

Natasha watched a triumphant smile emerge as her friend

held the receiver to her ear. Moments later, the smile faded. As Carlin hung up the phone, her eyes were ablaze.

"What's the matter? Didn't your information help?"

Carlin sank back onto the bed, obviously frustrated.

"Actually, it helped a lot. In fact, one of my three guys turned out to be the driver of the car that killed Jackie Franklin."

"So why do you look so unhappy?"

"Harry says that Marshall Pittard, the driver of the Maserati, has major dirt on a drug czar in Washington Heights. According to the district attorney's office of the borough of Manhattan, this information entitles Marshall Pittard to a jail sentence of exactly zero years." Carlin didn't even try to keep the disgust out of her voice.

Natasha tried to find words that would make her friend feel better. "If his information leads to someone who's doing even more harm . . . "

Carlin barely even heard her. She thought back to the night they'd found the body, how the girl had looked sprawled out on the ground. According to Harry, Jackie Franklin had been only nineteen when she was killed. And from all her bruises, it was clear that she'd suffered horribly even before she was dead.

"Natasha." Carlin's voice was stricken. "You had to see that girl. She was like us, she was a kid. The fact that someone could run her over like a, like an empty soda can and get away with it . . . I don't know, it's horrible."

"Well, maybe when you get your law degree and you work in the district attorney's office, you'll make things better." Natasha knew she wasn't really comforting Carlin, but she couldn't think of anything smarter to say.

"The DA's office doesn't seem to make anything better," Carlin found herself responding. Jesus, was that how she really felt? she wondered, suddenly hearing herself. She began to think about all her plans. Law school. The bar exam. Maybe even becoming an ADA herself. What a waste, she thought, making an effort only *after* someone's been hurt.

Carlin leapt up, her eyes suddenly focused on something Natasha couldn't see. "You know what? I *am* going to make things better, but it's not going to be in some female version of a gray flannel suit." She reached out and grabbed Natasha's hand. "Are you still gonna make me dinner when I'm Police Officer Carlin Squire?"

1983

15

The small figure lay on its side, at first neither decidedly male nor female, just smooth, milky white skin shimmering under the studio lights, from the tiny narrow neck to the softly rounded bottom. The knees were hidden from view until slowly and expertly the figure rolled over toward the camera, first the lower body, revealing the vulnerable penis of a young boy. Then his chest and shoulders came into view. Finally the face was revealed with its large brown eyes and a tiny upturned nose.

Why, he couldn't be more than five or six years old, Carlin thought, horrified, as the tape continued to roll on her VCR. She could barely stand to think about what whoever was operating the camera must have done to entice a small child to feign adult sexuality this way, nor could she imagine what kind of future this child could possibly have. Obviously he had been carefully trained for this performance.

Repulsed, Carlin shut off the VCR. One thing she knew for sure, this cameraman was not going to be allowed to continue his "art," not if she had anything to do with it. At least there was some satisfaction in that. She picked up the telephone.

"Harry Floyd, please," she said as the telephone at Midtown North Precinct was picked up on the first ring.

"Sergeant Floyd." His voice was crisp.

"It's Carlin. Guess what? We've got Quantrell."

"What do you mean?"

She could hear the suppressed excitement in his voice. For months, the superintendent of the building on West Fifty-third Street had been suspected of child pornography, but no one had been able to prove anything. Up to now, there'd been rumors and gossip, plus the disappearance of a seven-year-old boy from Ninth Avenue, but no child had been willing to testify against the man, no adults had come forward to say outright that their son or daughter had been approached or molested by the fifty-year-old Quantrell. Everyone in the neighborhood seemed to know enough to urge their young children away from the yellow brownstone with the green shutters, but no one knew enough to convict him of a crime.

Until now, Carlin thought with satisfaction. Maybe she'd thought of Quantrell's hiding place because the case wasn't hers. Sometimes distance made it easier to put the pieces together. She felt proud as she looked down at the cassette tape in her hand. What would you think of my choice now? she wondered as Harvey Armistead, her senior advisor at Harvard, came into her mind. "If I believed you'd stick to it for more than a month or so, I'd advise you against it, Miss Squire," he'd said contemptuously when she'd informed him of her decision to join the police force. "If I know my girls, you'll probably be married in a year and the mother of two within five years."

She'd felt like strangling him. Not that her parents had been much nicer about it. "Four years down the damn drain," her father had said, an odd satisfaction in his voice. Even her mother had sounded uncertain. "If that's what you want, dear ... ," Lillian Squire had said tenuously. Only Nancy Erickson had been honestly enthusiastic, hosting an impromptu dormitory party the night after Carlin had told her about her plans, at which all the guests were presented with water guns. Thoroughly wet and completely exhausted, the two had sat up until four in the morning trading fantasies of how exciting life for both of them would turn out to be.

It had been three years since Carlin had graduated from Harvard and come through the six months of Police Academy training, two and a half since she'd been assigned to a precinct in Brooklyn. Nothing at the academy had prepared her for street patrol in the wilds of Bedford-Stuyvesant, with Hasidic Jews and blacks vying for territory, while the crime rate soared.

She had been there for only a few weeks when she got a bird's-eye view of the worst New York City had to offer. A special narcotics unit had zeroed in on a heroin dealer on

Pitkin Avenue. Carlin had been one of a dozen backup cops surrounding the small brownstone building as the detectives in charge banged on the front door.

But this dealer had no intention of giving himself up. Instead he barreled through the entrance shooting wildly at the men in front of him, killing two and leaving the third critically injured as he attempted to run down the steps. Every member of the backup team began to shoot, including Carlin. In fact, when he fell, facedown, in a heap at the bottom of the stairs, no one was quite certain who had fired the bullets that actually killed him.

Carlin had been sent home after filing her report, advised to seek counseling within the department to deal with the psychological after-effects of what she had witnessed. And she'd felt okay after a couple of days, although the sight of someone getting shot would never grow routine. What had begun to wear her down was the constant stream of drug trade, users and dealers, bringing the neighborhood to its knees. It was a simple drill, really. Street crime up, look for the users. Young men and women overdosing from a bad shipment of dope, go after the dealers. The work was unremittingly grim.

Meanwhile, just as he'd predicted, Harry Floyd had gone on to become a detective and passed the sergeant's exam. As an extra bonus, he'd been transferred to Midtown North, one of the most interesting precincts in Manhattan. She and Harry had stayed friends, meeting every few weeks for dinner or a drink. Harry had been obsessed with the Quantrell case since October, when the little boy disappeared. Harry talked and conjectured, while Carlin listened. No proof had been found in Quantrell's apartment, even after they'd obtained a search warrant in January.

"We tore that place up," he'd said as he described the six-hour examination of Quantrell's one-bedroom apartment. "This guy has five sets of dishes and fifteen pairs of designer blue jeans. And sure, he's got photo equipment. A video cam, a Polaroid, two Nikons, even a kid's Brownie camera from the early nineteen fifties." Harry'd shaken his head disgustedly. "But the only tapes we found were a complete selection of Hollywood musicals and the only still shots were family vacations in Yosemite when Quantrell was growing up in California."

Carlin shared Harry's frustration. His instincts were great. If he thought Quantrell was sour, it was very likely true. Suddenly she'd had a hunch.

"Harry," she'd said after a few moments' thought, "how about I borrow some of those movies? Just for the weekend," she'd wheedled as she'd watched him start to say no.

She now twirled the phone cord around her fingers in satisfaction as she prepared to share her discovery with Harry. Her hunch had panned out. "You know those tapes of movie musicals you took, the ones with *South Pacific* and *Oklahoma* marked on the boxes?" Carlin asked, the satisfaction evident in her tone.

"Sure," Harry replied.

The edge of hope in his voice had been joined by something else, a note of apprehension almost, but Carlin felt too excited to notice. "Well, somewhere between 'Bali Hai' and 'Many a New Day' the scene changes radically."

"What do you mean?"

"I mean that on every tape, beginning somewhere about an hour and a half in, some poor kid gets to be naked. On each six-hour videotape, the middle three hours or so is Quantrell's dirty work."

"Jesus." Harry was silent for a minute or so. "Listen, that's dynamite," he finally said, his tone slightly withdrawn.

"And one more thing," Carlin added, too excited to notice, "there's got to be a way to find where this stuff is done. A loft space from the building next door shows through on some of the film, and there's a huge mural on one wall. Some kind of surrealistic stuff, cartoonish almost. Bright colors, oversized figures. Very distinctive. Somebody's gotta recognize it and ID the studio space."

"Terrific, just terrific," Harry murmured. "How about I reward you with dinner tonight and you can give back the tapes?"

"No way tonight. My friend Natasha is fixing me up with some artsy downtown type. But I can drop the tapes off. We're meeting at Fiorello's at seven-thirty. I'll swing by the station afterward. Okay?"

"Great." Harry lowered his voice. "Listen, I'm not gonna be able to give you credit on this. You know, it's not exactly kosher for a Brooklyn officer to be viewing Manhattan evidence."

Carlin couldn't have cared less. The dual pleasures of working with Harry and getting a pervert off the street would keep her going for weeks.

"I may have some good news for you, though," Harry continued. "In fact, I may have good news for both of us."

"Good news like what?"

"Good news like I'll tell you when you get here. There, I've given you incentive to skip dessert or avoid a sexually transmitted disease."

"God Almighty," Carlin said, hanging the phone up.

Very funny, she thought, walking over to the small closet in her bedroom. Well, at least that was one benefit of having no sex life: sexually transmitted disease was one problem she didn't have to think about. On the other hand, what to *wear* for a date was a big problem, she thought critically as she appraised her meager civilian wardrobe. What will contestant number one have on, she wondered, conjuring up an image of Natasha's friend. All she'd told Carlin was that he was a fashion photographer originally from England. Carlin imagined a diminutive man with a nasal voice wearing a striped Savile Row suit. Perhaps he'll call me a "bobby," she mused as she selected a short pleated skirt and a baggy turquoise sweater. "Stop it," she said out loud, realizing she was already beginning to hate this man she'd never even met.

She held the garments in front of her and peered at herself in the mirror. Not only aren't you giving this guy even a hint of a chance, but you've made sure to look as boring as possible, she admitted. Vowing not to defeat herself quite so easily, she put the skirt and sweater back, and took out a dark red sweater dress, one she knew hugged her curves and lit her pale winter skin.

Arriving at the Italian restaurant just across the street from Lincoln Center, she was pleased to have made the switch. The man leaning against the wall in front of the maître d's station was attractive in a striking way, at least for the Upper West Side. His thick, prematurely gray hair stood straight up in a brush cut, and a diamond stud graced his left ear. Dressed in nubby tweed woolen pants and a short leather jacket, Derek Kingsley was an unusually good-looking man.

He raised his arm in the direction of the maître d'. "Perhaps you can arrest him for rudeness," he said, assuming Carlin to be his date without a moment's hesitation.

"What exactly has he done?" she asked.

Before he had a chance to respond, the maître d' walked the few steps to where they stood. "If you had waited until eight, when everyone leaves for a concert," he whined, "you wouldn't have forced me to make you stand here like this." He nodded toward Carlin, as if those words had constituted an appropriate greeting, and walked huffily toward the back of the restaurant.

"Voilà," Derek said, smiling.

Carlin laughed along with him. Many of the tables were being emptied as concertgoers seemed to leave en masse for Lincoln Center, so the maître d' returned almost immediately to seat them in a booth.

"You *are* Derek?" Carlin asked, smiling, as she removed her coat and laid it on the seat beside her.

"Indeed." Derek smiled back, seeming to enjoy what he saw. "Natasha described you perfectly. In fact, she told me exactly what dress you'd probably be wearing."

"Oh, God, what do you think that says about my wardrobe?" Carlin replied with dismay.

"I think it says something about your priorities versus your friend's," he answered, making it sound like a great compliment. His slight British accent made everything he said sound both cultured and slightly ironic, yet there was genuine warmth in his eyes as he spoke.

"Perhaps it's time to let Natasha dress me in addition to orchestrating my social life. That could be the answer to everything." Carlin noticed she was acting like herself this evening, something that didn't always happen on first dates. In fact, she thought, that was something that probably hadn't happened since . . .

Willfully, she made herself concentrate on Derek. "So what exactly is it you photograph?" she asked, realizing suddenly how little Natasha had told her about him.

"It's quite boring, I assure you. Beautiful women wearing beautiful clothes. That's all of it."

Carlin looked dubious. "Most men wouldn't find that boring at all."

"Pardon me for being disingenuous. Actually I like what I do a great deal. But it's not as fascinating as what you do, not by a long shot. How did you decide to become a cop?"

As wine and a vegetable antipasto were placed in front of them, Carlin spoke about her three years on the police force. Derek asked question after question. She entertained him with descriptions of her months in the Police Academy, studying all the minority cultures that made up New York City under her social science teacher, the myriad laws and procedures that went into even the smallest infraction, not to mention the hours of calisthenics and physical conditioning that every future police officer had to perform in order to graduate.

"Do you actually practice putting handcuffs on people and such?" Derek asked, sounding astonished.

"Would you want to try it on some 250-pound drug dealer without any rehearsal?"

Derek raised an eyebrow in response. "Very little seems to faze you. Surely there must be aspects of police work that are forbidding."

Carlin had no intention of confiding her occasional fears to a near stranger. Purposely misunderstanding him, she decided to stick with things the police force didn't allow her to do. "Well, I can't own a liquor store and I can't live in the district I work in."

She watched him see her evasion for exactly what it was. But he let it pass.

"I'll tell you what. Let's go downtown after dinner and try out some spots that might surprise even you. How about it?"

"Sure, but I have to stop on Fifty-fourth Street for a couple of minutes. I have some stuff to return to a friend."

"Dare I hope this is police business?" Derek leaned forward as he asked.

Carlin thought for a moment. Derek Kingsley was a photographer, just the kind of person who might be able to figure out where the Quantrell films had been made from a description of the mural she'd seen. That's not all, she realized. He might even be able to draw up a list of duplicating houses willing to process this kind of slime.

Would it be right to tell him about the Quantrell case? She ran through the material in her mind. Finally she decided to go ahead. Sparing the names and exact addresses, she told him about the child porn king of the West Fifties. She was pleased when Derek came up with the name of an artist whose work matched the description of the mural she'd seen. It would be a cinch to talk to him and zero in on where his stuff was hanging. And Derek also knew of a place in the West Thirties where pornographic films were duped.

"A friend of mine, Max Zipkin, worked there early in his New York career. He lasted three weeks, but it was enough for him."

"How can you be certain it would be the exact same place?" Carlin asked.

Derek shook his head. "Oh, I doubt it's that studio. But it's a small filthy world. Guys in this line of work are busy protecting their own skins. They'll probably lead you in the right direction with even the most minimal pressure just to get you off their own tails. If the players are the same as they were a couple of years ago, you should be able to zero in on them in no time."

He smiled. "It sounds like your work is going to turn this whole case around," he said, taking her hand in congratulation, holding on to it several moments longer than was actually called for.

Uncomfortable and pleased at the same time, she extricated her hand as she answered. "Actually, no one is to know I had anything to do with this. I'm not with Midtown North. I'm not even in a precinct in Manhattan. Harry could get into trouble for giving me those tapes."

"In that case, I'm honored that you chose to share the information with me." Derek's British accent made the phrase seem intimate and significant, causing Carlin to feel terribly vulnerable somehow.

"Let's go and do my errand, then all the rest of tonight's decisions will be up to you." Carlin kept her voice brisk. "May I share the cost of dinner?"

Derek smiled as he called the waiter over. "No, Officer

Squire. I'm pleased to say that photographing beautiful women allows me the luxury of generosity." He handed his credit card over to the waiter without even glancing at the bill. "Feel free to cook for me next time. That is, if I'm not being presumptuous in suggesting that there'll be a next time."

Carlin felt unexpectedly attracted to this man. Still, she had no intention of sewing her heart to her sleeve, at least not in one date.

"Perhaps you could draw up a list of your food allergies and I'll take it under consideration," she replied with a caustic smile.

"Go easy on the organ meats," he answered back as he signed the bill and stood up. "Ready?" Not waiting for a response, he lifted her coat and held it up for her.

Derek was clearly interested when ten minutes later their destination turned out to be the Midtown North precinct on West Fifty-fourth Street. She took in his fascination as he scanned the array of police vehicles parked on both the sidewalk and the street. It was nice to be with a man who found her world interesting. In fact, she was enjoying this evening more than any she'd had in years.

"I'll only be a minute," she said, laying her hand lightly on his sleeve. "I just have to return the tapes to Harry."

"Can I stick with you?" he asked.

She wondered what Harry Floyd and Derek Kingsley would make of each other. It would have been fun to find out, but bringing Derek into the station with her might not be such a good idea.

"Would you mind terribly waiting out here?"

He looked disappointed.

"Well, come on inside, but I think you'd better hang out in the lobby."

Derek opened the doors for her, then peered around at the empty beige walls and ordinary terrazzo floor, the large rectangular counter walling in numerous police officers busily at work. Carlin went off in search of Harry Floyd.

When she and Harry emerged from the elevator together a few minutes later, they found Derek in friendly conversation with the desk officer.

"So Thursday afternoon's good for you," Derek was saying as they approached.

"Are you moving in?" Harry's voice was friendly, but his policeman's eye was carefully evaluating Derek Kingsley.

"Harry Floyd, Derek Kingsley," Carlin said quickly.

Derek extended his hand, then answered Harry's question. "Actually, Officer Graham has offered to allow me to do a photo shoot here next week. I've a job to do for *Vogue* that would be sensational in these surroundings."

"Perhaps Detective Graham would like to run that past his sergeant before making any promises." Harry's rebuke found its target as the desk officer reddened in embarrassment.

"Sorry, sir."

Harry's tone lightened. "I guess the idea of some beautiful models draped over our green plastic chairs isn't such a bad one. Let me check it out with the chief, and maybe we can get it done."

Detective Graham gave him an appreciative nod.

"But I have better news than that." Harry wrapped his arm around Carlin as he continued to address the desk officer. "There's one beautiful woman who's gonna be here with the detectives permanently. Detective Third Grade Bert Graham, I'd like you to meet your new colleague, Police Officer Carlin Squire. As of Monday, she's being reassigned to Midtown North as my sergeant-operator."

Carlin could barely contain herself as the men in the room turned toward her curiously. The transfer to Midtown North was a dream come true. This was the essence of New York City, from the Broadway theater district through Hell's Kitchen. And being Harry's sergeant-operator meant driving him every day, taking part in every move he made.

Derek turned to Carlin, interested to see the excitement in her face. "What does that mean?" he asked her.

But Harry answered instead, including the whole room in his response. "It means the team of Brooklyn College and Harvard University is about to revolutionize the study of crime from Forty-fourth Street to Central Park South."

A slew of derisive comments met his exclamation.

"Wait and see, my cynical friends. This little lady and I are about to be the Batman and Robin of West Fifty-fourth."

His enthusiasm embarrassed Carlin, but she was too excited at the prospect of working with Harry to put up a fuss.

"Speaking of Batman"—the voice came from a well-dressed middle-aged man stepping off the elevator—"that was great work on Quantrell, Harry. You nailed that bastard, and I'm damned proud of you."

Harry beamed with pleasure. "Chief of Detectives Hal Farris, I'd like you to meet my old friend, Carlin Squire."

"So you're the Harvard girl. A pleasure to meet you."

Being described as "the Harvard girl" wasn't exactly music to Carlin's ears, but confronting one's future captain the minute you were introduced didn't seem wise. She kept her response at "Happy to meet you too."

"Harry, thank you for everything. Derek and I have to go, but I'll talk to you tomorrow, okay?"

"Baby, you'll talk to me tomorrow and the day after that and the day after that. From now on, it's Floyd and Squire." He raised an imaginary glass in a toast and gestured grandly to the entire room.

"I don't know how to thank you," Carlin said to Harry as he put his arm around her and began walking her toward the exit.

Harry's voice became a whisper. "Tonight, the *thank-yous* are on me. That was great work you did." Not even Derek, walking only a step behind, could hear what he was saying.

"He's not shy, your friend Harry," Derek observed as they headed up the street.

"No," Carlin smiled, "*shy* is not a description anyone would use for Harry Floyd. But he's the smartest cop I've ever seen. You don't know what a big deal this is for me."

Derek was quiet for a minute or so. "I'd say taking credit for your work on that case must have been a big break for him. Not to mention gaining points with the brass for your gender and your education."

"Derek, you really don't understand. Harry Floyd just gave me the biggest opportunity of my career. I'm about to learn everything there is to know about this whole city. Harry's handing it to me on a plate."

Derek nodded in apparent agreement. "You're absolutely right. Now let's go celebrate."

The rest of the evening seemed to fly. First, Derek led Carlin to Visiones, a jazz club on MacDougal Street, where a quartet led by an alto sax player performed its own magic on the music of Duke Ellington. As they entered the small room, several of the patrons waved to Derek. Even the bass player winked at them as they took their seats. After the set was finished, they went on to a couple of other dimly lit clubs farther downtown, Derek finding a host of familiar faces at each one.

"Is there anyone in New York you don't know?" she asked breathlessly as they left a table of magazine editors and went off to dance to a band from Chicago at CBGB.

"I don't know *you* anywhere as well as I'd like."

"And how many women have heard that sentiment?" Carlin said more testily than she intended.

Derek looked at her quizzically, but said nothing. For several minutes, they moved around the floor, Carlin enjoying the sensation of being in his arms. Derek was sure of himself on the dance floor, shifting easily when the band switched into a salsa rhythm. What a pleasure, she thought, leaving all the decision-making to someone who was so good at it.

For years now, she'd been on her own in every way. At Harvard, at the Police Academy, even at the precinct in Bed-Stuy, every move she'd made, she'd made by herself. She had become so used to being solitary that she'd forgotten how sweet it could be to have someone else take charge. Closing her eyes, she didn't resist as Derek pulled her closer, kissing her lightly on the lips, then more deeply. I don't know this man at all, she thought for a second, then gave herself up to the luxurious sensations she was feeling.

"Carlin." The sound of his voice was a surprise, as if she'd been wakened out of a dream. "I want you to come home with me tonight. I want to make love to you."

"Gosh, how adult!" She was nonplussed by his directness, wishing to hide behind jokes.

Derek refused to smile. "I am an adult, as are you. I won't insist if you don't want to come with me." He stopped moving to the music, just stood there, his arms around her, looking directly into her eyes. "You're the most unusual woman

I've met in a long time and I have no intention of playing childish games."

Leaning down to kiss her again, he placed his arms around her waist, slowly raising them up her back, swaying now to the Latin rhythm.

Carlin responded to his kiss, bathed in a trail of heat.

Suddenly he pulled back. "If you want to come, say so. I won't force you."

"Of course I will." The words came by themselves. Carlin felt she was hearing them for the first time as she spoke, as if they had a mind of their own. It was so easy to give in to Derek, to be led.

And an hour later, as they lay across the king-sized brass bed in his Spring Street loft, it was so easy to give in to his caresses, to get lost in his accomplished hands, his long sinewy body.

He made love to her with his mouth, opening her private places with his tongue, reminding her of what she'd been missing for so long. When finally he entered her, his hardness felt familiar, as if she'd known him before, loved him before. As he thrust deeply, surely inside her, Carlin felt tears coming to her eyes.

"Why are you crying?" Derek held himself back as he noticed the wetness on her lashes.

"It's been so long . . . ," she stammered. She'd been so alone, she'd forgotten how wonderful it could be to connect with someone, to allow herself to *feel*.

Derek said nothing. He simply eased back into his rhythm, held her fast as he felt her body clenching in pleasure. When his own pleasure came several moments later, she held him tightly, feeling his rush of satisfaction.

"You're so beautiful," he said moments later, running his hands over her breasts and the flatness of her stomach.

"I am probably the least beautiful woman you've seen in fifteen years," Carlin responded, looking up at the magazine covers that graced one wall of the bedroom.

"Carlin, I'm not talking about the poreless perfection of a fourteen-year-old professional model. You're an original, a real person, for God's sake."

Carlin flushed with pleasure.

"Listen, didn't you tell me a police officer isn't allowed to live in the district that the precinct is in?" Derek was leaning on one elbow, peering down at her as he continued to explore her body with one hand.

"Yes." Carlin felt entirely relaxed. Even the one-word response was hard to get out of her mouth.

"That means you're going to have to leave your apartment." He paused. "Move in here with me."

Suddenly Carlin came startlingly alert. She could hardly believe what she was hearing. "Have you lost your mind?" she exclaimed. "We met six, seven hours ago."

"Take a chance. I know it's right. Trust me." Derek licked each breast slowly, teasing her nipples hard with pleasure.

Carlin longed to give in to him again. The whole evening was like a magic ride in a fantasy playland. How easy it would be to just say yes.

"I'd have to be crazy," she murmured as her hands explored his powerful shoulders, the downward tapering of his well-muscled back.

He grinned as he began caressing her in earnest once again. "Be crazy, Carlin. You *need* to be crazy, I can tell."

"You're the embodiment of evil, aren't you?" Even as she said it, she knew she was going to agree.

1984

16

Carlin lowered the window of the rental car she and Derek had picked up early Friday evening, squinting into the bright sunlight as she let the warmth bathe her face.

"You shouldn't do that, you know. You'll look a hundred when you're forty. Besides, it causes skin cancer." Marissa Foreham's over-educated tone cut through Carlin's moment of pleasure as effectively as a carving knife.

Grinning in the driver's seat, Derek spared Carlin from having to answer. "Skin cancer generally occurs when a person spends more than two hours per decade in the sun," he said, catching Marissa's eye in the rearview mirror.

"Pardon me for living," Marissa answered petulantly. "I was only trying to be helpful." She twisted in her seat, grabbing the attention of her husband, Spencer, who'd been staring out the window, carefully ignoring the conversation. "You know, people are so allergic to learning anything. Even here on the island. All the way out on the jitney, this lady in front of me kept looking around to give me a dirty look just because I mentioned how many fat grams there were in the granola bar she was eating."

Unable to hold her husband's attention, she leaned forward, once again directing her remarks to Carlin and Derek. "You know, people think they're being healthy eating that stuff, but granola has enough sugar and starch to take you down in your prime."

Derek pulled the car into the parking lot of the Tuck Shop, peering at Marissa as he let himself out. "Exactly how many early granola deaths have you actually witnessed, Mar?" he asked laughingly.

"Have all the fun you want at my expense," she answered,

joining him in the parking lot. "I, for one, see no reason to throw my life away."

Carlin got out of the car and walked into the ice-cream parlor. "Hot fudge sundae, please. Two scoops of vanilla, and lots of whipped cream and nuts."

She knew without looking that Marissa would be open-mouthed at her choice. In fact, she didn't even like ice cream particularly, but she couldn't help herself. Derek was the one who was good at dealing with annoying people. His great gift was staying completely honest without ever losing the ability to be kind. Carlin, however, couldn't help causing a little trouble when she was around people she didn't care for.

This is a new low, she thought to herself, as a young waitress handed her the enormous pile of goo loaded into a large paper cup. She began eating, her appetite disappearing completely with the first sickeningly sweet bite. I'm not punishing Marissa; I'm punishing myself. Suddenly Derek was at her side. Grabbing a plastic spoon, he dipped it into the sundae and raised it to his mouth.

"Shall I help you with that?" he asked, before popping it into his mouth.

"Yes, please," Carlin said gratefully. "In fact, would you take the whole thing?"

"We can share it," he said cheerfully. Looking up to see Marissa and Spencer ordering their frozen yogurt, he lowered his voice. "Although as I remember, you don't much like vanilla, and positively loathe whipped cream."

"Guilty, guilty, guilty." Carlin smiled and handed the sundae to Derek. "The devil made me do it, I swear."

"No, darling," Derek answered, kissing her lightly on her nose, "the devil's the one who's going to accompany you to hell when you're struck dead by the sun when we go back outside."

Carlin laughed. It was easy to laugh here, easy to forget the rest of the world even existed. Shelter Island was such a beautiful place. Hidden between Sag Harbor to the south and Greenport to the north, they'd had to take a ferry to get there. With mile after mile of woodland disguised within a perimeter of white beaches, this felt more like Cape Cod than New York. The only drawback was that a visit to Shelter Island meant staying with Marissa and Spencer, whose massive white dream house on exclusive Dering Harbor unfortunately had the two of them in it.

Spencer had been mentioning the possibility of a weekend visit since Derek had started doing some spreads for *The Good Life,* the magazine Spencer had founded a few years before. Once Carlin had entered Derek's life, the invitation had naturally been extended to include her as well. But it was hard for Carlin to warm up to people who made almost no attempt to hide their disdain for her job. They were clearly uncomfortable at having a police officer in their social circle, someone they considered ignorant, not worth wasting time on. Derek didn't care much for the Forehams either, but as usual he simply overlooked their foibles and made the best of the situation. Carlin realized it was important for Derek professionally that he stay friendly, so she continued trying to be a good sport about their get-togethers, resolutely attempting to ignore both Marissa's grating personality and her superior attitude.

"It's just a cottage on the water," Spencer had said each time he urged them to visit the island, his tone clearly conveying how grand the "cottage" must be. And grand it was, with huge white pillars hugging a massive stone terrace, six bedrooms, five bathrooms, and a screened-in porch large enough to hold a convention. Spencer had taken the previous week as vacation, while Marissa, who had stayed in the city to rework one of the two or three articles she wrote a year, had joined him late Friday afternoon. Derek had offered her a lift, but she'd preferred the Sunrise jitney. "I *live* for those hours of freedom," she'd said to Carlin over the phone Thursday night. Irritably, Carlin wondered just how many hours Marissa had that weren't free.

"Why do they call it a jitney, anyway?" Carlin muttered, low enough so her host and hostess wouldn't hear. "It's a bus, just like what I used to take from Westerfield to Coleville. A big, crowded bus."

"It's a bus for rich people," Derek answered in a voice equally soft.

"You know, Carlin," Marissa called out from across the

room, "you might spend some time studying up on nutrition, although I guess *your* crowd prefers donuts."

Carlin looked at her evenly. "They do say one a day keeps the doctor away."

Derek took a last swipe at his sundae and threw the cup into a large wastebasket. Throwing one arm around Carlin's shoulder, he walked over to Marissa and threw his other around hers. "Time to get back to the water, isn't it, ladies?"

Climbing back into the car, all four were quiet for a few minutes, but Marissa couldn't bear the stillness.

"What is it you do when you're on patrol?" she asked, sounding bored despite the face that it was *her* question.

"I don't really go out on patrol," Carlin answered. "For a while now, I've been a sergeant-operator. That means I work with the sergeant, and go everywhere he goes."

Derek cut in proudly. "In fact, Carlin herself just passed the sergeant's exam. Came in number one."

There was a red car with an M.D. license plate in the Forehams' driveway as Derek turned in and parked behind it. Marissa waited until he'd shut off the motor before answering. "I'm sure the competition must have been very stiff," she said with a smile as she made her way out of the car.

Carlin stayed seated as Derek answered for her. "Not quite as stiff as it used to be at Harvard, I would guess," he said softly, rubbing the back of her neck before opening his door.

Marissa looked back in surprise. "Carlin went to Harvard?" she asked, looking none too pleased to hear it.

"Graduated with a three-seven, didn't you, honey?" he asked innocently, as Spencer joined his wife on the driveway and they walked through the side door that led to the kitchen.

Carlin got out of the car and walked around to Derek. "Thanks, but it's not necessary. They don't have to love me." She looked up and smiled. "That is, assuming I don't have to love them."

Derek stroked her cheek lightly. "You just have to love me."

"Ben, you made it!" Marissa's shriek of pleasure rang out from inside the house. "Did you bring that beautiful nurse with you, the one from the emergency room you were talking about last week?"

Carlin froze. It couldn't be, it just couldn't be. But the M.D. plates, the mention of an emergency room. Ben Dameroff might well know the Forehams; Tash could have introduced him. After all, she'd been on the cover of Spencer's magazine several times.

Derek looked at her. "Is something the matter?" he asked, his arm coming protectively around her waist.

"No, of course not." She forced herself to calm down. "It must have been a ministroke caused by the hot fudge." She caressed his hand gratefully. "I'm fine."

Inside her head, she felt as if she were screaming, *Please don't be Ben Dameroff, be some other doctor from some other emergency room.* She looked at Derek as they walked toward the house, so handsome in his tan shorts and navy Izod shirt. She had come to count on him for his humor and his affection. He was so different from anyone she'd ever known. So even, so damn nice. Her life had finally become content. Okay, so contentment wasn't ecstasy. But it was a great deal better than the loneliness that had preceded it. Or, she admitted to herself, than the turbulence that had come before that.

Please, she begged silently. Don't be here. Don't trample on the peace I've finally found.

"Ben Ginsburg, this is my very best photographer, Derek Kingsley, and his lovely girlfriend, Carlin."

Carlin didn't even notice how patronizing Spencer sounded as she watched a fiftyish, gray-haired man turn to smile at her and extend his hand. Thank you, she was saying silently as she put out her hand in return.

"Are you sure I couldn't pass for a hooker if I wore my old dress blues?" Carlin's voice was shaking from the cold as she whispered into the microphone hidden in her bra. Clothed in a skimpy orange skirt with a tiny black leather jacket that didn't quite cover her midriff, even the over-the-knee white boots couldn't help keep her warm as the subzero February wind blew over the Hudson River.

"Yeah, Cambridge."

She heard Harry Floyd answering her through the tiny receiver hidden in her ear.

"Very few things turn a fella on faster than a nightstick, a set of cuffs, a can of Mace, and a gun."

The voice changed to the higher pitch of Officer Richard Overton. "Nah, Harry. The real turn-on is the ten-pound shoes."

The sounds of raucous laughter and static flooded her ears. There was no question that Harry and Richard, warm and cozy in their car, were getting a big kick out of watching her shiver.

When Carlin had first become a police officer, she quickly discovered one of the traits universal among cops: the immediate testing of their fellow officers, followed by an instant judgment that would stick for the rest of their official lives. Cops were not known for giving second chances. She'd dealt with all that when she joined the force.

How clearly she remembered her first week in Bedford-Stuyvesant, sent out on foot patrol to a neighborhood known to have the highest murder rate in all of Brooklyn. There she was, all alone, her partner having dispatched himself to some phantom task she was sure didn't exist. She made it her business to walk tall that day, maintaining a visible presence on the street. When her partner returned late that afternoon, an approving smile on his face, she was sure he'd been observing her, and knew he'd share his opinion with the rest of the precinct.

That had been a test she *had* to pass. But it came as a surprise to her that making number one on the sergeant's exam, then gaining her detective shield two months later, seemed to set her up for another round of testing.

Not that she had any right to complain. Without Harry, there was little chance she'd have been selected as a detective. Every rank from sergeant through captain was based on a civil service exam, and if you ranked high on the list and a job opened up, you could pave your own way. But making detective was completely different. Supposedly based on some kind of merit, it had everything to do with having a friend in the right place, and Carlin had been lucky enough to have Harry. When fellow officers suggested she go to her rabbi, she knew just who they meant.

But mentor or no mentor, Harry enjoyed watching her pay

her way. "You figure this one out, Cambridge," he would say, his tone proud as if claiming her as his discovery, yet half-taunting her with the possibility of failure. Tonight's hooker patrol was a perfect example. Not that Carlin hadn't been undercover as a prostitute dozens of times before, but choosing the coldest day New York had seen since 1952 to stake out a guy who had robbed and beaten nine different ladies of the night was Harry's idea of a great assignment for Carlin. Besides, he almost never took street assignments anymore. Sergeants generally stuck to overseeing events, not taking an active part in an operation like this one.

All the way over to Twelfth Avenue, he had teased her about how long she might have to walk around before seeing any action, how toasty the car would be as he and Richard sat watching her from across the street. Noting the huge grin on his face when she got out of the car, she wasn't about to give him the satisfaction of seeing her hesitate. She only smiled when she heard him talking loudly to Richard about whether "windchill" was a meaningful concept, making sure he could see she wasn't slowing down. Marching boldly to the dark empty stretch across the street, she walked back and forth, from Fifty-second Street to Fifty-third, with a wiggle in her hips and a cigarette hanging from her mouth. Despite their teasing, she knew that having Harry and Richard as backup was enough to ensure her life. They might relish watching her tough it out in the frigid air, but they would never let anything happen to her.

She'd already been approached by several men, most of them pulling up in cars with New Jersey license plates to proposition her. In the past, she might have taken them in as johns, arrested them for solicitation. But tonight she wanted one special guy. It was close to one in the morning, two hours after she'd first started walking the avenue, when a tall heavy man in a blue ski parka, a woolen hat covering most of his face, came up to her and used the phrase that three of the injured prostitutes had mentioned after their attack.

"Whores don't deserve to live."

As the man spat the words out, he stood directly in front of her, putting his arms around her like an embrace. His hold was anything but affectionate. One hand circled her neck, choking her for a moment, as he yanked her handbag off her shoulder. Sticking the small purse in his pocket, he grabbed her by her hair and pulled his other arm back, about to slam his elbow into the side of her head. Suddenly Carlin drooped, seeming to faint, but when he reached down to get a grip on her lowering body, she jabbed the pointed toe of her boot into the front of his ankle as hard as she could.

The man dropped to his knees in pain, clutching his ankle, shrieking curses at her in some indecipherable language.

Without a second's delay, Carlin whipped her gun out of her shoulder holster. "Hold it right there. You're under arrest."

Harry and Richard were right behind the man as he turned, obviously intending to make a run for it. Both officers grinned when Carlin pulled the man's arms behind his back. She quoted his Miranda rights while she attached handcuffs to his wrists.

"You sit in the front seat, Cambridge," Harry said, a twinkle in his voice as the quartet moved toward the car. "It'll be warmer."

"How about next time you play the hooker?" Carlin tossed back at Harry, causing Richard to laugh out loud.

"That was nice work, Carlin," her squad commander said two hours later as she waited for Harry on the first floor of the precinct. "I'm seein' more promotions in the offing." He gave her a friendly pat on the back before walking out the door.

Carlin shrugged off the compliment. She didn't see Harry coming up behind her, looking anything but amused.

"Let's go, President Squire," he mimicked, as he tapped her smartly on the shoulder. "I'll drive you home now."

They went outside and got into Harry's car.

"Do you have a favorite route to Soho, Your Highness?" he continued as he turned on the ignition.

"Ease up, Harry." Carlin refused to take his teasing seriously and was too tired to notice the tightness around his mouth. The only thing she felt capable of thinking about was crawling into her bed. Although her regular hours as a detective were two day tours, followed by two night tours, then two days off, she'd been working both shifts for almost two weeks in order to catch this guy.

Harry looked over as he drove. "You should take a couple of days to yourself."

"Derek would certainly appreciate it. How does your wife feel about getting a regular weekend with you once every six weeks?"

"Marilyn probably likes it. I'm not exactly a dream to live with."

Despite her closeness to Harry, Carlin had met his wife only a few times. He liked keeping his family separate from his work, and no matter how many hours they spent together outside of the precinct, how many dinners they shared, Carlin still seemed to constitute "work."

"It must be hard on the kids."

Harry's two sons were seven and eight now.

"Ah, Harry Junior and Georgie couldn't care less if I'm home or not. Just so long as they've got their TV." Harry didn't seem fazed by their lack of appreciation. "How about your boyfriend? How does he cope without you?"

Carlin laughed. "You know, I'd love to believe he couldn't live without me, and God knows with these hours I'm practically never there, but Derek knows every single person in New York City. You walk into a restaurant, into a party, into a museum, and Derek greets everybody by name. He's the most gregarious person I've ever seen. He just doesn't have the tortured psyche every other New Yorker seems to take for granted." She smiled as she thought about him. "There's a lot to be said for a wealthy, happy childhood," she added, laughing.

"He was a rich kid?" Harry's tone was half-interested, half-resentful.

"His family lived in a huge flat in London, plus a manor in the Cotswolds. His mother and father doted on him, and after Oxford he experienced immediate success in the career he loved." She paused and looked over at Harry. "What would Derek possibly have to be tortured about?"

They both laughed, but Carlin felt slightly uncomfortable. After all, Derek's happy life hardly let her off the hook. She really should try and make more time for the two of them.

She so rarely got to go to the parties he had to attend to cultivate new clients. He'd even gone to the Caribbean alone, spending two days on a photo shoot, then adding another ten days as vacation; he'd asked her repeatedly to join him, but she just couldn't get away then. It's not fair to him, she admitted to herself.

"Marilyn used to complain about the long hours all the time," Harry said. "Now she has her own friends. I think when I retire she's gonna make me leave the house every morning and not let me come home until late at night."

Carlin thought for a minute. "Actually, Derek never complains. In fact, he's completely self-reliant." She smiled as she turned toward Harry. "Does that mean I can stop feeling guilty?"

They both chuckled as he pulled the car in front of the eight-story building Derek's loft was in.

"Get some rest, Cambridge," Harry said as Carlin pushed the car door open. "You need it."

"All I need is two hours' sleep, three at the most," she assured him, stifling a yawn as she swung her legs out.

"Right. Listen, I don't want to see you until late tomorrow morning. In fact, make it afternoon." He squeezed her hand good-naturedly. "The dead are pretty certain to stay that way for the next twelve hours or so, you know."

Carlin grimaced and waved good-bye. Leaning against the padded wall inside the industrial elevator, she was so exhausted, she almost fell asleep before she arrived at the top floor. But, as she let herself into the huge, dark loft space, her senses instantly came awake. It was after three in the morning and Derek would be asleep. But she heard a noise coming from the area he used as his studio. Quietly she eased the door shut and pulled her gun from its holster. She tiptoed silently across the highly polished wooden floor, holding her breath to listen. As she entered Derek's office, her hand inadvertently brushed an envelope that stuck out from between some file folders on the desk. The papers clattered to the floor. Instantly, the lights from the rear of the studio flashed on and Derek's voice rang out.

"Carlin, is that you?" he cried out urgently.

Her gun was firmly in her hand as she walked past the wall

separating his work space from their living area to see a naked Veronica Slater, one of Derek's photo assistants, hurriedly pulling on a shirt.

Carlin stood where she was, too shocked to speak, while Veronica threw on the rest of her clothes quickly and ran out of the apartment. Derek, naked as well, was sitting on the edge of the bed.

"I had no idea you'd be home this early," he said, surprisingly matter-of-fact when they heard the door close.

To Carlin, he suddenly looked like a stranger. "That's all you have to say—you didn't think I'd be home so early? Not something better, like 'I was drunk,' or 'I was drugged by terrorists,' or 'This isn't really me, it's my twin brother just come back from the great war,' or something!"

Derek looked at her, incomprehension all over his face. "Darling, I've never lied to you. Nor have I ever monitored your activities. It never occurred to me that this would upset you so."

"What planet are you from?" Her sharp sarcasm couldn't keep tears from welling up in her eyes.

"Darling, I'm so sorry." He came to her side, putting his arms around her.

She pulled back immediately, holding still for a few seconds, blinking back the tears.

Finally she felt her voice would come out steady. "Exactly what kind of relationship did you think we had?"

Derek's utter sincerity was as shocking as his words. "We are two people who love each other and live together."

"And sleeping around is part of loving each other and living together?" she asked agitatedly.

"Honestly, darling, I never would have done it if I'd known how much it would hurt you." Even now, his tone was more confused than guilty.

Carlin was disheartened and exhausted. She forced herself to calm down. Arguing with him was stupid. "It seems we were handed two different rule books at the door." Her voice was bitter. "God, I knew you were charming, but I hardly thought that charm extended to sleeping with your friends."

She hated the way she sounded, especially with Derek looking more like a baby lamb suddenly hit over the head by a completely new concept than like a man who'd just broken a sacred trust.

She frowned, disgusted with herself as much as with him. "Derek, this isn't working. I won't be turned into a shrew. A relationship should consist of loyalty and fidelity. Not just . . . well, good fellowship." Wiping the remaining tears from her cheek, she walked away. "I'll pack up my stuff in the morning. Right now I'm just too tired."

Derek looked stricken. "Darling, you can't leave. Listen, I'll never sleep with another woman." His voice became placating. "Now that I know how much it bothers you, I promise it will never happen again."

Carlin stared at him. It's astounding, she thought, noting the honest bewilderment in his eyes.

"I fail to believe that English people, or photographers, or those who live south of Houston Street, or any other piece of the population to which you belong have a separate charter. People who choose to live together do so because they want to be faithful to each other. That's what commitment means."

He looked at her with the expression of an assiduous pupil studying the times table.

"You never heard of this before?" she asked in astonishment.

"I've never lived with anyone before."

She would have thought his response glib if it weren't for the simple way he'd said it.

Derek came up beside her, rubbing her arm slowly with his hand. "There's a lot I don't know about all this, but you have to believe I love you. Please, please don't walk out of here."

She felt overwhelmed with disappointment. Yet she could see that he meant it when he said he loved her. His beautiful artist's face held nothing but heartbreaking sincerity. There was one further question she had to ask.

"Exactly how many times have you done this?"

His voice shook with emotion as he responded. "Oh, Carlin, how can I answer that? I won't lie to you; I never have and I won't start now. It seems that even one time would have been too many."

It was clear to Carlin that his pain was genuine. Whatever their differences, this was no stranger. This was the man she had fallen so happily in love with. But it wasn't at all clear whether she could ever trust him again.

When Derek spoke, his head was bent, as if in prayer. "I will swear to one thing. This was the very last time."

Carlin studied him for a long moment, thinking of everything they'd shared. Could she throw it all away?

"Next time," she said gravely, "it's over for good."

1991

17

"Mr. Isaacs is cleared for his cardiac bypass on Tuesday. He's the first case, seven A.M. Mrs. Herbert's lung biopsy will be at one." Helen Afton hurriedly flipped through the papers on her crowded desk as she spoke, wanting to be sure she told Dr. Dameroff everything in this quiet moment with him. It was rare that he stopped by her desk for messages; she usually had to catch him on the run. "I'm sorry the surgery's broken up like that, but the OR couldn't manage a block of time. There's a pediatric case in between your two."

"That's fine. Thanks, Helen."

"Dr. Ladd called. You can reach him after five. Oh, and don't forget grand rounds after the department of surgery meeting tomorrow."

Ben nodded. "Do you know what the talk's on?"

Helen consulted her pad of notes. "It's 'Acute Aortic Dissection.' Dr. Everts is lecturing."

"Okay, but—"

He paused, hearing the private line ringing in his office. "Excuse me, I'd better grab that."

Ben turned and headed toward the door. He didn't see Helen staring at his retreating back or realize that as usual she was thinking he was far and away the best-looking doctor in all of Mercy Hospital. Just because she was fifty-two and married for a thousand years, she thought, didn't mean she couldn't still get a little flutter in her stomach when he fixed those big brown eyes on her. And he was a damn sight nicer than a lot of the other surgeons, too. He had the decisiveness and self-confidence a surgeon needed, but he was blessedly free of the arrogance that often went with a job involving split-second life-or-death decisions.

Shutting the door behind him, Ben crossed over to his desk. He'd had the private line installed when he first moved into this office because he liked dealing with his personal calls himself. Once Sara came along, it had turned out to be a necessity. Right now, though, he hoped it wasn't Sara who was calling; he had a lot of paperwork to finish up and didn't really have time to talk. The thought made him feel slightly ashamed of himself.

As he reached for the phone, he rubbed his eyes, fatigue suddenly settling in on him. Not surprising, he supposed, considering he'd operated on a car-accident victim at midnight, then went straight on to perform abdominal surgery until 4 A.M. on a seventy-year-old man who'd been stabbed leaving an all-night deli. At eight, he'd been back in the OR for a previously scheduled pacemaker insertion.

Usually, his arrangement with the hospital seemed ideal. He maintained a private practice at Mercy while acting as a trauma surgeon for the emergency room. Using the hospital's facilities, he was spared managing and paying for an office, staff, supplies, and everything else that went along with running a private practice. The hospital supplied all that. In exchange, he and another caradiothoracic surgeon, Morton Ladd, split duty as trauma surgeons, operating on the emergencies that came in, and teaching their skills to the residents who were part of the training program. Ben got a salary from the hospital and Mercy split the fees from his private patients. Overall, it seemed like the best of both worlds, enabling him to take care of his private patients and still experience the exciting pace of a busy emergency room. But when his emergency-room duties collided with his private-practice responsibilities—as they had today—the demands on him were all-consuming.

Days like this one always brought back memories of internship, the indoctrination process into medicine he'd gone through the year after graduating from medical school. He recalled the grueling schedule, being on call and working thirty-six hours straight, then having one night off to catch up on sleep before going back for another thirty-six hours. There must have been some nights when he actually got some rest while on call, but those weren't the ones he remembered.

What stuck in his mind were all those other times, he and his team having just dozed off on the narrow cots in the on-call room, when—invariably, it seemed—a patient would go into cardiac arrest. Every one of their beepers would go off at the same time, sending them racing down the hall to the appropriate room, pushing aside their overwhelming exhaustion, summoning up the adrenaline from out of nowhere to save a life.

It had been harrowing and exhilarating, and he had thrived on it. That was why he had chosen this specialty, where emergencies and long hours were the price of staying a part of that excitement, the thrill of those life-or-death victories. But, hey, he thought wryly, I was twenty-six then and now I'm an ancient thirty-three. He knew all too well how high the burnout rate was for doctors who did emergency-room work.

He spoke into the receiver. "Hello."

"Ben, honey, it's me." Sara Falklyn was soft-spoken and Ben usually found her voice soothing. At the moment, though, he wasn't eager to talk to her.

"Hi, darling," he said, wanting to give her the enthusiasm she deserved. "How are you?"

"I'm great. But we haven't spoken in the past couple of days, and I hope you're going to be able to steal away for just a little bit tonight."

"Tonight?" Ben frowned, glancing down at his schedule. Damn. He hadn't noticed it, but in fact he'd circled today's date and made a notation of *anniv* next to it. It had been a year since they'd begun their affair, and he knew from a few things she'd let slip that she was planning to make a big deal of it. Even worse, he saw that he'd inadvertently also made a dinner date with Natasha and her boyfriend Ethan for nine o'clock. As much as he loved his sister, at this point he was so tired, he frankly didn't much feel like keeping that date either. The situation wasn't helped by his suddenly spotting a stack of pink telephone messages waiting to be returned.

"Sara," he said gently, "I hate like hell to do this, but could we celebrate another time?"

"Ben, you can't mean that," she replied, disappointment making her voice break a little.

He sighed. "I'm sorry, I really am. I promise to make it up to you."

"But it's been almost three weeks." Her voice was tinged with anger now. Ben found it ironic that she was pressing him this way. After all, she was the one who was married, the one who was usually unavailable.

Her voice softened. "Please, Ben, I really miss you. Besides, this is a special day and I want to share it with you now, not some other time. It turns out I can't spend the evening, but I was counting on a few hours with you."

He glanced at his watch. A quarter to five. It was wrong of him to forget. And it *would* be nice to see Sara.

"Why don't we meet at my place at six-thirty? We can have some champagne together."

"Great. See you then." She hung up.

Ben sat down and reached for the pile of phone messages, plowing through as many of the calls as he could in the next half hour. Then he took off his white lab coat and exchanged it for the navy overcoat hanging on a hook behind the door. If he hurried, he could make it to the jewelry store on Madison Avenue that Sara loved so much. He said good-bye to Helen, who was gathering up her things to leave, and raced out of the hospital.

It was unlikely he would find a taxi in the middle of rush hour, but keeping an eye out for one, he walked briskly across Seventy-ninth Street toward Madison Avenue and then headed downtown. If he recalled correctly, the store was in the low sixties. The November night air was brisk and refreshing, making him feel he was giving his mind a much-needed airing-out as he strode along. He spent way too much time cooped up in his windowless office and the examination rooms, not to mention the OR. But he wouldn't change it for the world. The hope of attaining his dream was what had kept him going after his mother's death, what had driven him when he was working his way through SUNY Binghamton, three jobs at a time.

He'd worked so hard to raise the money for college, winning every scholarship he could compete for along with his jobs, but even that hadn't been enough. The truth was, it had been poker that had gotten him through. After he joined a local high-stakes game as a freshman, poker had paid for nearly a third of his expenses. He'd continued playing poker throughout medical school at Columbia, though even his winnings weren't enough to keep him from having to take out sizable loans to pay for those long years of training. Still, he certainly felt the pressure of the stakes, and it robbed him of any enjoyment in playing. The better he got at it, the higher he raised the stakes, and the more he grew to hate the game. Even now, nothing in the world could induce him to sit down to a card game.

Adelman Jewelers was open until six, so he had twenty minutes left to pick out a gift for Sarah. As he entered the small shop, tiny bells on the door jingled faintly. An overly made-up woman behind the counter smiled at him.

"Good evening. May I help you, sir?" she inquired politely.

"Yes, thank you." Ben immediately began to look down at the gleaming display cases, wondering on earth he could pick on such short notice. "I need a gift for a woman, an anniversary sort of gift."

"Ah, yes. A wedding anniversary." The woman nodded. "Maybe something associated with the number of years you're married. Unfortunately for the lady, I see you are far too young for the diamonds of a sixtieth." She laughed at her little joke.

Ben looked up sharply, oddly jarred at the thought of being married to Sara. But when he spoke, his tone was mild. "No, not a wedding anniversary actually. Just a regular gift. A pair of earrings, I suppose."

He sighed. This was so unoriginal. Besides, he didn't have to be told he was going to buy something ridiculously overpriced to assuage his guilt at forgetting their anniversary. It suddenly came to him that he was trying to throw money at the fact that he didn't really care about forgetting. *That* was what he was feeling guilty about.

Leaning down, he inspected a selection of bracelets and earrings with intricately carved heavy gold charms. Although he wasn't especially interested in them, Ben knew from Sara that these pieces were what the shop was known for, and she had a bracelet from here that she adored. She'd mentioned several times that she would love to have a pair of earrings to go with it. What was carved on the pieces hanging from that bracelet? He cast around helplessly in his memory. Coins? Horses, maybe.

Ten minutes later, he was on his way home, a five-hundred-dollar pair of earrings with dangling cupids in a small velvet box in his pocket. Five hundred dollars for earrings, he thought grimly. There was a time ... Well, there's no point harping on that, he told himself. Sara deserved something nice. At least it was taken care of and he could get home in time to meet her.

Sprinting the last two blocks to his apartment on Sixty-ninth Street, Ben waved hello to the doorman who let him into the building and made it up to the fourteenth floor just before six-thirty. Yanking off his coat, he opened the refrigerator door to make sure he had a cold bottle of champagne, then grabbed two stem glasses from a wooden rack on the far wall. There was nothing around to serve with the champagne. Quite the celebration, he chided himself.

He had just loosened his tie and began washing his face when the doorbell rang. Towel still in hand, he went to let Sara in. She stood in the doorway holding a large shopping bag, her blond shoulder-length hair perfectly in place as always, her makeup minimal but expertly applied, her clothes expensive and tasteful. She smiled at the sight of him, and he smiled back. No question about it, he was very fond of her.

"Hello, sweetheart," she said, coming inside to kiss him softly on the lips. "I'm so glad you could get away."

"And you? No trouble getting out?" Ben asked, taking her coat.

"He's not due home until midnight. I don't know—meeting, surgery ... Frankly, I've lost track. One excuse is as good as another."

Ben nodded. Sarah's husband, Dean, was an orthopedist at Mercy, which was how she and Ben had come to meet in the first place. It had been at a hospital fund-raiser, a big black-tie dinner. Dean Falklyn had accidentally slammed into Ben as he turned away from a group of people, spilling his drink on Ben's jacket and stepping hard on his foot. Far from apologizing, Dean had walked off in annoyance, as if *he* had been put out. Ben had promptly forgotten the whole thing, but later that evening, while his date was fixing her hair in the ladies' room, Sara Falklyn had come over to say she was sorry for her husband's rudeness. She'd insisted on taking Ben out to lunch the next week to make up for it. Ben saw no need for such a magnanimous gesture, but he hadn't wanted to embarrass her by refusing.

Of course, as she admitted later, the lunch was about seduction, not apology. She knew Dean had been cheating on her for years, but she had always remained faithful to him. Until Ben. Much later, she confessed that one look at him that night at the Mercy dinner and she'd known she was going to pursue him. It was utterly out of character, she'd laughed, but for once she'd made a quick decision and stuck with it. She had taken matters into her hands then, and she continued to manage their affair now, always keeping things running as smoothly as possible. As she often told Ben, she was satisfied with what they had. As far as she was concerned, they could go on forever this way. But she was always careful to keep their liaison a secret; she knew Dean would go wild if he ever thought she'd dared to cheat on him, despite his own ill-concealed flings. Besides, she had her ten-year-old son to think about.

She went into the kitchen with Ben and started taking things out of the shopping bag. Cheese and crackers, strawberries, a bottle of chilled Dom Pérignon, and a small white box tied with red ribbon from one of the most expensive bakeries on the Upper East Side.

"It's just a small chocolate cake," she said, as she placed the box carefully on the counter. "But every party needs a cake."

Ben smiled as he watched her move easily about the kitchen, setting the food out on plates, totally at ease in the familiar surroundings.

"How come you were so certain I'd be totally unprepared?" he asked in amusement.

She laughed. "I didn't see any point in taking a chance. No reason we can't have a special celebration, even if it's just a couple of hours."

"I do have some champagne, I'll have you know," he said teasingly.

She carried a tray with the hors d'oeuvres out into the living room. "You've got enough on your mind, Ben."

Ben retrieved the jewelry box from his coat pocket and set it down next to the couch. He glanced at his watch surreptitiously. Ten to seven. He was meeting Natasha and Ethan at a restaurant down on West Twelfth Street—some impossible hot new spot, the kind of place Natasha loved—which meant he had to allow time to get there. Christ, he should be paying attention to Sara instead of planning his itinerary. No question about it, he'd been shortchanging her for a while now, distracted when they were together, his attention elsewhere.

He kissed her as she handed him a glass of champagne. Of course, theirs had never been a passionate affair. Somehow, he had just slipped into it. The last thing he would have envisioned for himself was a long-term affair with a married woman, especially one who was the wife of a physician at Mercy—albeit an especially obnoxious one whom he didn't know and almost never had occasion to see—but he soon understood that the marriage meant nothing to Dean Falklyn.

Ben and Sara were comfortable with one another. He was able to relax with her. That meant a lot, considering how difficult he found it to trust people. Few were permitted to penetrate the wall around him, the wall built so long ago upon the lessons taught him by Margaret Wahl and J. T. Squire. He had worked hard to keep himself from becoming bitter about the betrayals of his youth, but he couldn't change the fact that there was a darkness inside him, a cold place of loss. The emptiness would hit him suddenly, making him wonder what could ever fill it. Usually, he was able to push the feeling aside, and he was satisfied with that, choosing to look into it no further.

"To us," Sara said, leaning over to give Ben another kiss as she raised her glass.

He put his arm around her and brought his mouth to hers. She was warm and soft, so comforting at the end of a long day. And there were so many long days, so many solitary nights too. Solitary years was more what it felt like to him, although that wasn't actually the case. Before he'd met Sara, there had always been women in his life once the demands of his medical training had let up enough for him to have time for them. But no one important, no one he really wanted to hold on to.

He stroked her hair, then took her champagne glass from her and set it down on the coffee table. She put her arms around him as he continued to stroke her back, her shoulders, pulling her close and fitting her against him. Sara broke away and stood up, holding out her hand. Taking it, he stood up and they went into the bedroom, quickly shedding their clothes as they walked. They lay across the bed, their kisses growing more heated as Ben caressed her breasts, her buttocks, moving his hand between her legs, gently stroking her as she became wet. He probed with his fingers until, with a moan, Sara reached down to guide him inside her. He thrust deeply, over and over, her hips rising up to meet his. At last, she pulled him to her, burying her face in his shoulder, tensing, then shuddering. Ben permitted himself to let go, the feeling a welcome release from all the tension of the day. The two of them lay together quietly for a few minutes, Ben feeling completely relaxed for the first time in weeks.

Later, they moved back into the living room, Ben in a white terrycloth bathrobe, Sara in the pink silk robe she kept at his apartment. She served Ben a large slice of chocolate cake, then cut herself a sliver. As she settled back on the couch, Ben handed her the velvet jewelry box. Her eyes lit up with surprise and pleasure when she opened it.

"Oh, sweetheart, these are so beautiful. I can't believe you remembered." She leaned over to kiss him. "You're wonderful. Beyond wonderful."

She hastened back into the kitchen to retrieve another box from the shopping bag she'd brought, a present wrapped in silver paper with an enormous red bow. "Now you," she said.

Ben pulled off the bow. They'd made love, celebrated with champagne and delicious cake, were exchanging gifts. So why did he suddenly feel the emptiness again, the old feeling he'd grown so used to over the years, the sense that something was missing? He shook his head to rid himself of it, opening the box to lift a black cashmere sweater out of the tissue paper. Would it be better if Sara lived with him, if she left her husband for good and moved in? No, even if she decided she was willing to, he knew it was better the way it was. They would just go on this way, being comfortable. But wouldn't it be nice to feel passion again? The thought came out of nowhere, startling him. He remembered all too well how long ago it was that he had felt genuine passion. It wasn't a place in his memories he wanted to go back to.

"Is it the right size?" she asked anxiously.

"Exactly what I needed," Ben said, holding the soft sweater up against his chest so she could see that it would fit, hoping he sounded sincere.

From her seat at the bar, Natasha kept an eye on the door for Ben while she continued her conversation with Ethan.

"Saint Bart's? What do you think of that?" she asked, furrowing her brow as she considered her own suggestion. She took another sip of her sparkling water, musing aloud. "Maybe too popular already. We need an island nobody's ever heard of."

Ethan Jacobs laughed. "Natasha, let's just pick a place that we think will be pleasant."

Natasha immediately caught herself. God, was she crazy, slipping up like that. She always made certain that her actions seemed spontaneous, as if she never planned anything or cared what anyone ever thought about her. That was part of what Ethan liked, she was certain. He had no idea how hard she worked at it.

He, of course, always seemed to know what was right. It drove her nuts, because he didn't *care* at all; he just did what he felt like doing and somehow it turned out to be the right thing, even the *hip* thing. Appearances didn't concern him, and the idea of doing anything because it was trendy or hip was completely unappealing to him. He had loftier goals, she knew. Ethan was so committed, so *good*. It was there in everything he did, in the causes he supported, the things he believed in, and, most importantly, his work. As a director he'd been compared to everyone from Bergman to Costa-Gavras. His early films were considered works of lyrical beauty; the more recent ones had been a radical departure, described in the press as masterfully executed, gripping, and suspenseful.

The other models at her agency had almost died of envy when she'd begun dating him. Ethan Jacobs was probably the most eligible bachelor in all of New York. And *she* had won him. With each step along the way, she'd been sick with fright that he would dump her. She'd lain awake countless nights planning her moves, calculating what would please him. She'd waged successful campaigns for many other men, always willing to reinvent herself for them. But none of them had been as important to her as this one. And somehow, miraculously, the relationship kept getting better. When she realized that she actually had a chance with him, she'd begun to put more energy into Ethan than into modeling, canceling assignments so she could go on location with him, making sure she was always available. The modeling didn't matter. Winning Ethan was far more important.

Modeling had been a triumph, too, of course, and she never stopped marveling at how she had fulfilled her childhood dream. Although her success had come quickly, the whole business had started out tough and had only gotten tougher over the years. The constant rejection in the beginning, the obsession with her weight, the fear of losing her looks. Even when she was in her early twenties, she'd dreaded getting up every morning because she never knew what that first glance in the mirror might bring. Between her constant starving to keep her weight down and the energy she'd put into staying popular with the photographers, bookers, and other models, she'd worn herself down over the years.

Becoming a big name didn't bring the satisfaction she'd expected, either. It still seemed that no matter how much money she made it would never be enough; she hoarded every dime, certain she'd lose it all somehow and be left alone in the world with nothing. Even worse, she'd been in constant fear of sliding from her perch near the top, always wondering if today was the day the bookings would stop coming, if she'd suddenly be yesterday's news. Once she had turned twenty-seven, she'd officially stayed that way for about four years. She didn't know how much longer she could hide the fact that she was actually thirty-two; she suspected plenty of people knew the truth anyway and gossiped about it behind her back.

Thank God that was nearly all over now and she wouldn't have to worry about it anymore. Ethan was the best thing she had ever done. Desirable, rich, and so handsome with that jet black hair and those huge hazel eyes. Most incredible of all, he actually seemed to love her. *He* would be her life's work from now on.

"Hey, there." Ben was suddenly beside them, planting a kiss on Natasha's cheek. "Sorry I'm a little late."

Natasha threw her arms around him. "Ben, it feels like I haven't seen you in a year."

He laughed. "That's probably true, but it's *your* schedule that's the busy one." He turned to Ethan and they shook hands. "How're you?"

Ethan smiled. "Good to see you again."

"I caught *Finelli's Angel* a couple of weeks ago and I really enjoyed it," Ben said. "How did you ever get Peterson Stoddard to play the guy who loses the girl?"

Ethan shrugged. "It was a good part and Stoddard saw that." He grinned. "Besides, it looks like he'll be nominated for an Oscar, so I guess being second banana has its rewards."

"Ethan," Natasha urged, "tell Ben about the award *you're* getting from the film critics for directing it."

"Okay, Natasha"—he laughed—"now Ben knows." He signaled to the maître d'. They were led to a table off to one side, but still near the entrance.

"Is there anything a little quieter?" Ethan asked politely. "It's kind of a family dinner. Maybe a table in the back?"

The maître d' frowned. He wanted to please the famous model and movie director so they would return, but he had no intention of permitting them to go unseen in the back. What good was attracting celebrities and then letting them hide so the restaurant couldn't get any mileage from their presence? He weighed his decision.

"I'm so sorry, Mr. Jacobs. If something opens up, we'll be happy to move you."

Nodding amiably, Ethan held Natasha's chair for her. When the three of them were settled, Ethan turned to Ben.

"We'll order some champagne, Ben, if that's all right with you. We've got something here to celebrate."

Ben smiled. "It seems to be a celebrating kind of night. What's the occasion?"

A broad smile lighting up her face, Natasha extended her left hand to display a ring with a large diamond.

"Here's our big news, Ben. Isn't it incredible?"

Ben gazed at his sister's shining eyes. Other people perceived her as supremely confident, but he knew better. He'd assumed her self-doubts would pass as she got older, but if anything, they'd gotten worse.

Yet tonight she seemed different. My God, he thought, she actually looks *content*. It was a word he would never have thought he could have used to describe his sister. Maybe she had finally found something in Ethan to bring her the kind of peace Ben wouldn't have believed was possible.

He took her hand. "Tash, that's fantastic."

He leaped up to hug her and plant a big, loud smooch on her cheek, causing her to laugh and smack his arm in reproach. He and Ethan exchanged a quick hug as well.

"Congratulations, you two. You're really made for each other."

Natasha laughed lightly as she reached up to smooth her hair.

18

As the violinist played softly in the background, Ben took Leslie Jacobs's arm and escorted her the short distance to the front of the room. The two of them then separated to stand at opposite corners of the *chuppah,* turning to watch Ethan approach. He took his place between them, fidgeting uncharacteristically and clearly uncomfortable in his tuxedo.

Finally it was Natasha's turn. She looked so extraordinarily beautiful that her arrival was greeted with an audible intake of breath from many of the people in attendance. Her long, ivory matte jersey dress had been created especially for her by Alain Gerard, one of New York's foremost designers. Ben wasn't surprised that Natasha had forgone a traditional wedding gown and veil for this somewhat slinky and highly sophisticated dress; it was totally in keeping with the image she'd carved out for herself. And she did look magnificent, no question about it. The simple design of the dress served to underscore her figure, while the pale color was exactly right to set off her creamy complexion.

The finishing touch was Natasha's flowing red hair, its cut and color fussed over by so many experts in the course of her career that neither the style nor shade could be improved upon. She appeared to be wearing virtually no makeup, although Ben knew from Natasha that the natural look she sported required hours to achieve. Her only jewelry was a pair of emerald earrings, a birthday present from Ethan. She held a small bouquet of pale pink tea roses with both hands, but while her expression was serene, Ben noted that her knuckles were white as she grasped the delicate flowers.

Ethan held out his hand, and she turned to him with the same brilliant smile that had earned her so many magazine covers. As the rabbi began the ceremony, Ben reflected again on what a good marriage this was. Ethan was a solid guy who would take good care of Natasha. Ben chided himself for thinking of her as a child who needed someone to look out for her. But hell, he was her big brother, and she would always be his baby sister.

Contentedly, he listened to the words of the wedding service. His attention drifted slightly, and he looked out into the audience. This small library in the Tribune Club was just right for accommodating the thirty people here. Afterward, another hundred people would be coming for the reception. Ben smiled, remembering Natasha's histrionics over Ethan's request that they restrict the number of invitations to the reception, and his further insistence that he wanted even fewer people at the ceremony itself. She never complained to Ethan, but Ben sat through half a dozen phone calls in which his sister agonized over how she could exclude so many of the people in her industry. Ben was sorry she hadn't gotten what she wanted, but he had to admit he thought this was a good decision on Ethan's part. In fact, having gotten to know him better over the months since Natasha and he had gotten engaged, Ben found he liked Ethan more and more. He was genuinely flattered when Ethan asked him to be his best man. It was a nice touch, he thought, having Ethan's sister Leslie as Natasha's maid of honor, while he stood up for Ethan.

What a shame their father couldn't be there to see Tash get married, Ben reflected. But the passing of years hadn't been easy for Leonard Dameroff. He had aged poorly, suffering from a host of maladies. At the moment, he was having difficulty with his circulation, and he'd told Ben that traveling so far was just too much for him. Of course, Ben was well aware that Leonard's usual depression wasn't helping. Damn, if only I could get him on some medication, Ben thought. He was both saddened and annoyed by his father's resistance to taking anything. But no one had ever diagnosed Leonard's clinical depression in the earlier years, and the kind of drugs that were around now to treat depression hadn't even been available back then. The problem was that Leonard was completely unwilling to try anything at this stage in his life. He wasn't going to change.

Ben had been disappointed by Tash's indifference to their father's absence today, but he felt it wasn't his place to comment on it. Natasha hadn't made much effort—none, if he were going to be honest—to stay close to Leonard once she'd left Westerfield, so her reaction didn't surprise him. Still, it bothered Ben. He had always tried to compensate for Tash's coldness by calling his father frequently, conferring with the doctors who treated his various ailments, making sure Leonard's life was as comfortable as possible. Visiting was another story, however. Ben was no better than Tash in that respect; he could never seem to find the right time for a trip upstate. On Monday, he resolved, he would plan a visit to Westerfield, force himself to take a few days off, come hell or high water.

Feeling better, he took a closer look around him, scanning the well-appointed room with its book-lined walls and dark oak paneling. The Tribune Club was about as exclusive as these places got. How like Tash, he thought in amusement; she won't wear a wedding dress, but she chooses the most traditional place in the world for the wedding itself.

Suddenly he froze. Of course, it wasn't as if he hadn't expected to see her. But somehow he just wasn't prepared. He took a deep breath, steeling himself, and observed her watching the bride and groom.

She was different, strange to him, yet so familiar at the same time. Carlin was far more beautiful than before, he realized, her face reflecting a self-assurance he'd never seen there when they were younger. Seated quietly next to a tall gray-haired man who held her hand in his lap, she seemed completely at ease with herself.

The flood of memories that overtook him was almost too much to bear. He saw his mother, and all the events surrounding her violent death. God, how he hated those memories, so unspeakably painful even now. He'd become adept at running from them, but here was Carlin dredging it all up again.

Yet at the same moment, he was bombarded with images of the two of them as teenagers. He remembered their fever for each other the night they tried to crash some ridiculous dance, so young and naive but so sure of what they wanted. He could smell the perfumed air of the lakeside that night, the taste of her pink lipstick, the soapy clean scent of her neck. And the night they'd made love for the first time, all cramped up in his car outside the diner on the way back from Natasha's first fashion show. Jumbled pictures were coming back in a sweet rush. He could feel Carlin's skin as he caressed her, the two of them lying naked together in those magic hours they stole here and there. Or walking home from school, his arm around her, her hand stuck in his back pocket, oblivious to anyone but each other. And ringing the bell to her parents' tiny apartment on a Saturday night, barely able to wait until she appeared at the door after they'd been apart during the day.

Just then, Carlin's gaze shifted and she caught his eye. They stared at one another for a moment. What the hell had been wrong with him all those years ago, holding Carlin responsible for what happened to his mother? After the horror and suffering he'd seen as a doctor, the scandal of their parents' affair seemed awfully insignificant now. Blaming Carlin for that was unimaginably crazy and childish. Looking at her now, all he felt was an overpowering desire to go to her, put his arms around her, to do . . . he didn't know what. But he didn't want to be angry at her. With a shock, he realized he didn't even want to be apart from her. Slowly, he started to smile.

The man sitting beside Carlin leaned over to whisper something in her ear, breaking the spell. Humiliated, Ben looked away. He'd made an idiot of himself, that was for damned sure. What the hell was he thinking of, gawking at her like a lovesick kid? She wasn't giving him a thought, probably hadn't for years. In all this time, despite being Natasha's closest friend, she'd never once made an appearance anytime he was with his sister. Of course, he'd always made sure to stay away when he knew Natasha and Carlin were getting together, but that wasn't the point. Here he'd made a friendly overture to her, and look at what happened.

It had always annoyed him that Natasha continually insisted on filling him in on Carlin's accomplishments. He knew all about her Harvard education and how well she was doing in the police department. But he was willing to bet Carlin had never expressed the slightest interest in *his* career, or given two seconds' thought to the fact that he'd lived up to his vow of becoming a doctor.

The muffled sound of breaking glass caused Ben to look back at Ethan, who had just brought his foot down hard on the white cloth wrapped around a wineglass. As Ethan and Natasha kissed, Ben smiled at the expression of genuine happiness lighting up his sister's face. If only this would bring her some real peace of mind. Maybe, he hoped, Ethan could finally make her feel good about herself.

Ben and Leslie followed the couple out of the room.

"Tash, you know what I wish for you, don't you?" Ben kissed his sister and put his arms around her.

She smiled up at him and wrapped her arms around him in return. "I know, Ben."

"You deserve all the happiness in the world. I love you." Giving her a long hug, he then relinquished her to the other guests who had begun emerging to offer their kisses and congratulations.

He escaped to the bar, knowing he could avoid Carlin there in the crush of other guests arriving for the reception. It wasn't until he went into the dining area for dinner that he finally saw her again. He watched as she and her date located their place cards. How could Tash have been so stupid, he wondered irritably, as the man held Carlin's chair for her; although Tash had had the decency to place them at separate tables, their seats faced one another directly. Every time he looked up, he would glimpse her just one table away. He quickly moved over two seats, unobtrusively switching the place cards. At least that was a little better. When one of Natasha's model friends sat down next to him, he immediately asked her to dance, pleased to leave the table altogether.

It turned out that quite a few of Natasha's female friends wanted to dance with him, so Ben found himself occupied throughout most of the meal. Yet, when he finally sat down to grab a bite, he couldn't help staring at Carlin and her date, laughing together, looking every bit the ideal couple. Ben didn't have to be told that the anger he felt toward Carlin's boyfriend was irrational. *Damn it.* Of course, he could go on over and be friendly, but why should *he* be the one to make the overture? If she'd wanted to talk to me, he thought in annoyance, she'd have done it before this.

"Why don't you ask her to dance?"

Startled, Ben looked up. Natasha was standing there, clearly having caught him staring at Carlin.

"Go on, Ben," his sister urged him. "For old times' sake, if nothing else."

"You've never struck me as someone interested in reliving old times," Ben snapped at her. "Why should I?"

Natasha shook her head, too happy to be hurt. "Haven't you two punished each other enough?"

When Ben didn't reply, she leaned down and kissed his cheek. "I adore you anyway, but I *wish* the two of you would make up. I've been caught in the middle of this cold war forever. Besides, you two *have* to be together. I'm never going to stop believing that."

Across the room, a woman in a broad-brimmed black hat waved to Natasha and she headed off, smiling and saying quick hellos to guests on the way. Watching her retreating back, Ben was ashamed of himself. Of course he was behaving like a lunatic. For God's sake, he was a grown man. There was no reason he should be thrown by seeing a girl he used to date as a teenager.

He turned back to look at Carlin. Her date's chair was empty and she was talking to the man on her left as she sipped her coffee. Ben got up and, quickly buttoning his jacket, strode over to her table, smiling at her as she caught sight of him approaching. This time, she returned the smile.

He was unprepared for how happy it made him feel to be standing so close to her.

"Hello, Carlin," he said softly.

"Hi, Ben." Her eyes seemed luminous to him. She spoke teasingly, but in a careful tone. "Are we actually talking to each other?"

He laughed. "Maybe not talking, but how about dancing? That seems pretty neutral."

She nodded and stood to take his hand. "I'll even let you lead," she said with a grin.

They made their way to the dance floor and turned to face one another. Ben felt as awkward as a boy as he slid an arm around her waist. Carlin took a step forward to move closer. In that instant, everything changed. No longer unsure of himself, Ben pulled her to him, his arm encircling her more tightly as they began to dance. He couldn't believe the sensations taking hold of him. Being with her was so absolutely right, having her close to him again—this was the only place he wanted to be on earth, the only place worth being. He inhaled the delicious scent of her hair, felt the softness of her cheek coming to rest against his.

Trying to regain his bearings, he pulled back. Christ, get a grip, he ordered himself. She turned her face up to his, and he was stunned to read in her eyes that she was feeling the same thing.

"I remember another time we danced together," she said softly. "After Tash's first modeling job ... when we drove home together ..."

The first time they had made love. So she was thinking about it, too.

Before he could speak, her date appeared next to them, a look of displeasure on his face.

"Darling, could I borrow you for a moment?"

Carlin turned to him.

"Derek Kingsley, this is Ben Dameroff, Tash's brother."

Derek extended his hand, speaking rapidly. "Your sister's a sensational girl. Carlin and I love her to pieces."

Carlin and I love her to pieces. Obnoxious jerk. Ben had an impulse to punch this man right in the face. But who was the obnoxious jerk now, he thought; Derek was Carlin's lover, while Ben was nothing to her anymore. Carlin's lover. With a supreme effort, he put his hand out in return.

"Forgive my rudeness, but Carlin and I have to run," Derek said, attempting to steer her away.

"Derek, please," Carlin said, unsuccessfully attempting to keep the annoyance out of her voice. "There's no reason for you to yank me off the dance floor. We can wait another few minutes."

"I'm so sorry, darling, but there's been rather an emergency," he said.

"What's happened?" Carlin asked in alarm.

"It's all right, but please, let's go." He paused for emphasis. "It's important."

Carlin turned back to Ben. "Forgive me. I don't know what's going on, but . . ."

"I understand." Ben had no wish to be the fifth wheel here. Besides, whatever had transpired between them on the dance floor was over, as if it had never happened. "Nice to see you again."

There was sadness on Carlin's face as she nodded, then walked off, Derek putting a proprietary arm around her.

Ben went to the bar over in a corner of the room and ordered a Scotch. He downed it quickly, unwilling to accept how rattled he was. A second drink in his hand, he left the room, searching for someplace, anyplace he could be by himself for a few minutes.

He entered another of the seemingly endless number of small libraries. Ben sat down heavily in a leather armchair, sipping at his drink and wondering what the hell had come over him. *This* was why he worked so hard to stay in command of his life, why he preferred to get his excitement from his work rather than his love life. It was far too painful any other way. Perhaps Carlin had returned his feelings for the moment, but that was just a fleeting throwback to old times, a momentary nostalgia. She had a longtime lover, and she was doubtless very happy with him.

He got up and went to the door. It wasn't fair to Natasha for him to disappear from her wedding. Stepping out into the hall, he glanced down the long passageway to his left. There was Carlin, emerging from the ladies' room all the way at the end of the hall, her head bowed as she searched for something in her purse. When she looked up and saw him, she froze where she was. Slowly at first, he began walking in her direction. She stood completely still, her eyes locked on his. He moved faster and faster until he was there, gathering her in his arms as he brought his mouth to meet hers, her purse falling to the floor as she reached up to put her arms around him. Their kiss was one of exquisite hunger, driving out everything else around them. He was stunned by the power of his need for her, rising in him with such ferocity he could barely breathe. He couldn't remember the last time he'd experienced a wave of such intense desire. He moved his mouth along her face, her eyes, her neck, tasting every inch of her.

"Ben," he heard her whisper. "Oh, sweet Ben."

He wanted to tear off her clothes, to sink down to the floor with her right here, right now.

Then she wrenched herself away from him, her breath coming in gasps as she backed up, out of his reach.

"Ben, I—"

He never heard what she was going to say, because Derek's voice rang out in annoyance from down the hall.

"Carlin, are you coming or not?"

Carlin practically jumped, guilt and fear on her face. Ben could almost hear her thoughts, wondering if Derek had seen them kissing. She bent down, hastily retrieving her purse, then hurried down the hall without looking back.

Ben leaned against the wall, fury and shame competing inside him. She'd wanted him to kiss her. Hell, she wanted him to make love to her. So what was she doing, what game was she playing? She'd brought up all the demons of the past for him, encouraging him to follow the desire she'd stoked, then jerked him around like some dog on a leash. He knew he was being irrational, but his anger made it impossible for him to think clearly. Christ, he had made it so easy for her. He'd been pathetic, practically begging.

In one swift turn, she'd demolished his entire sense of self-control. That might not have been the worst thing in the world to someone else, he knew, but it felt that way to him. As long as he was in control of his emotions, he believed he could handle whatever came. And he *was* in control, he'd proved it to himself time and time again. Why had she kissed him? So she could go off with her boyfriend, fuck him silly while she laughed at the thought of her old flame Ben Dameroff still lusting after her? She had brought him pain in the past; it seemed that she always would. When would he ever learn?

Carlin followed Derek out of the Tribune Club, but waited under the building's vast awning while he went into the street to hail a taxi. She kept her eyes down, desperately trying to compose herself. She'd lost her mind in there. Not that it surprised her. From the second she'd seen Ben walking to the front of that room during the wedding, she'd known he had only to touch her and she would go to pieces. It had shocked her at first to see him transformed from the lanky teenager she remembered to the mature man he was now, the firm jaw filled out, the dark hair with a touch of gray here and there. He looked older, but so handsome she'd felt her stomach practically drop to her knees when he passed her row, his strong profile fixed straight ahead.

For God's sake, she was nothing to Ben Dameroff anymore, that was obvious. He'd never made any effort to see her. She doubted he'd deigned to ask Natasha anything about her in all this time. He was a successful surgeon after all, just as he'd vowed he would be, and from what Tash had told her, his life was filled to the brim with his work. She imagined there was plenty more going on besides his work, but she'd never chosen to speculate about his love life.

But, oh God, when he'd looked at her during the ceremony, she'd been caught up in a flood of feeling that caught her completely by surprise. She'd been unable to move or react. It was as if Derek had radar, leaning over at that moment to distract her, breaking the connection between her and Ben. All during the reception she kept telling herself to go over and talk to him; there was really no reason not to. But somehow she couldn't make herself do it. And there were so many women flocking to his side, obviously trying to make an impression on him. Then, when he'd asked her to dance, catching her up in his arms that way . . .

"Hop in."

Carlin's head jerked up as she heard Derek's voice. He stood at the curb, pulling open a cab door.

"Coming."

She tried to keep her voice even as she walked past him and got into the car. How long was it since she'd professed such shock at finding Derek in the arms of another woman, since they had agreed to start over and do it right? Of course, she had assumed it would always be Derek who would be the problem when it came to this sort of thing. Yet she had thrown herself at Ben in the hallway just now without a thought of Derek. All she'd cared about at that moment was

Ben. Kissing him, touching him. The depth of her need for him was so great, she'd had to pull away, afraid that she might do God-knows-what right in the hall there.

As the cab moved away from the curb, she looked out the window. She wondered how much Derek had seen. Her heart was still thumping wildly from a mixture of desire and fear. I can't believe what I just did, she thought. I must be the biggest hypocrite who ever walked the earth.

Ben Dameroff was a ghost from the past, but one instant of contact and she was thrown back to a place she'd never dreamed of going again. The awful part was how furious he must be with her right now. She'd flirted with him, held on to him for dear life on the dance floor, practically begged him to make love to her with a hundred people around, and then run off with her boyfriend like a little tease at the high school prom. Carlin shut her eyes, wishing she could blot it all out. She'd behaved abominably.

What she had to keep sight of was that she had committed herself to Derek Kingsley. He was the man she lived with, the man she had chosen. That was what she had to remember.

19

"Cambridge, you give education a good name." Police Commissioner Rodriguez was practically beaming as he watched Carlin write the name "Amos Richards" on the perp column of the Midtown North homicide board.

"I should say so," Lieutenant Ernie Fallon, squad commander of the precinct, joined in. "Last month she came in first on the lieutenant's exam, you know." He chuckled appreciatively. "A few years ago, it was first on the sergeant's exam. Now first on the lieutenant's."

"Enough, guys." It wasn't modesty that stopped Carlin from wanting any further praise, but the probability that Harry would walk in any minute.

Ernie saw her glancing at the door to his office and guessed who it was she was looking for. Fallon lowered his voice as he continued.

"Poor bastard," he said, shaking his head.

Commissioner Rodriguez looked confused.

"Harry Floyd," Fallon explained. "Carlin's busy protecting her pal. The guy waited eleven years for a lieutenant's exam to be offered. *Eleven years.* Then Cambridge goes and scores number one, Floyd was number two, can you beat it? She aced him right out of the top spot."

Fallon chortled, and the commissioner began laughing as well. Carlin was horrified. This should have been a moment of glory for both herself and Harry. They had just succeeded in finding the man who had robbed and murdered three different jewelers on West Forty-seventh Street during the previous six months. They had spent long days and nights questioning every store owner, customer, and bystander, following up every lead they could find. Then they'd conducted a computer search of the entire Northeast corridor, uncovering a trail of major theft that went all the way from Richmond, Virginia, to Boston. Finally amid the mountains of data, they'd come up with Amos Richards, who was virtually certain to be found guilty based on solid detective work. To Harry, that's what being a detective meant, but to those around them it seemed pretty much of a coup. Even so, she knew he was desperate for the recognition he expected from the lieutenant's exam. But it was Carlin, not Harry, who had triumphed.

She glanced again at the door. If Harry came in and heard Fallon telling the story one more time of how Carlin beat him, it wouldn't be their mutual success he'd be left thinking about. She was constantly surprised at how insensitive most of their colleagues were. Civil service exams were given when they were given, no rhyme, no reason. So Harry, who qualified as a sergeant years before she did, had been forced to wait over a decade before taking the lieutenant's test. Carlin had had to wait a much shorter time. And, yes, she had been lucky enough to score number one, but she wished everyone would stop making such a fuss about it. She and Harry had made a great team from the moment he'd first brought her onto the detective squad. Even when she'd matched him in the rank of sergeant under Squad Commander Fallon, and taken charge of a separate unit, they benefited from working together unofficially on case after case. To Carlin, it was their joint efforts that really mattered, not her supposed victory over him on one stupid exam.

And Carlin wasn't a fool. She loved Harry, owed him her detective shield plus much of the credit on the bulk of her biggest cases, but he was not a man to take being bested easily. His ambition was a standing joke around the precinct. Even *he* could be amusing on the subject. When her promotion to lieutenant was promulgated before his, as it was sure to be, given her ranking, he wasn't going to like it one little bit.

"Isn't some bigwig buying us lunch?"

Carlin almost jumped when she heard Harry's voice. How could she be thinking this way, she mused, as she took in the real Harry Floyd. This was her friend. Not some ambitious bastard who was about to punish her for succeeding.

"Yeah, Manuel, how about some gastronomic praise?" Harry said expansively. "I'd say Amos Richards is worth about three vodka martinis at Gallagher's. Right, Cambridge?" Harry put a friendly arm around her as he addressed himself to the commissioner.

Rodriguez was happy to agree. "How about you, Carlin? Vodka martinis or maybe a great bottle of wine?"

"Actually I was thinking more of a huge sirloin."

"As long as it's on the commissioner, I'm right behind you." Squad Commander Fallon pulled his overcoat off a chair.

As hour later, two rounds of drinks had heightened the color on everyone's cheeks when the commissioner proposed a toast to Carlin and Harry. "To the best two detectives in New York City."

Carlin raised her wineglass with pleasure, but as she turned toward the commissioner, she saw something that stopped her. Across the restaurant she had caught the sparkle of a diamond stud and a head of gray hair. Even as she was registering the fact that Derek was there, she couldn't help but see him run his hand over the arm of the woman seated alongside him. She recognized the woman, a stylist who often worked for a bunch of the Hearst magazines. That's what would have brought him to the West Side, she thought, a shoot for Hearst. Derek and the woman had been friends even before Carlin had moved in with him, that much she knew. But he's too damned tactile, she said to herself, slightly annoyed for a moment.

When the woman raised her other arm and passed her fingers slowly over Derek's lips, it became obvious that his touch had not been just a friendly gesture. Carlin worked hard to keep her face impassive as she watched the two of them lean in for a long kiss.

Sickened, she turned her back on them, praying none of the men at the table had noticed her distress.

"Harry, I've got to get home," she said abruptly.

"Sure, kid, I'll run you right downtown."

Carlin found his voice suspiciously sympathetic, so it

didn't surprise her when he started talking about it once they were in the car.

"Some men, they just can't help themselves." Harry patted her arm sympathetically as he drove down Broadway. "I mean he loves you and all. Anyone can see that. But a guy like Derek . . . to him it's like spreading the wealth."

"You're telling me he couldn't *not* cheat on me if he tried," Carlin said caustically.

"Cambridge, if I hung out with the babes Derek sees every day, I'd probably have left Marilyn and the boys in a ditch along the turnpike fifteen years ago."

Carlin felt outraged, although deep inside she knew Harry was trying to be funny. "What is it with you? Are all men so selfish and vain that you have absolutely no conscience?" Unbidden, the image of her father came into her mind.

Harry realized how he'd sounded. "Hey, listen, as far as I can tell, Derek really loves you. This extracurricular stuff probably means next to nothin'."

"Well, it happens to mean a great deal to me," she replied, perilously close to tears.

She sat in silence as Harry drove past Fourteenth Street. Was it as insignificant to Derek as Harry suggested? she wondered. She thought about their years together, his tenderness when they would make love, the occasional weekends when all-day movie or gallery marathons would be followed by elegant dinners or long massages in the privacy of the loft. Whatever his flaws, his generosity and kindness were real.

Which should leave only one possibility, she thought. Namely, that he couldn't possibly love me. Yet, deep inside, she knew that wasn't true. Slowly she accepted the truth. Harry was absolutely right. Derek *did* love her. That much hadn't been faked. But, apparently, he couldn't help himself when it came to other women, even if it meant he risked losing her.

Harry pulled the car up in front of her building. Thanking him for the lift, she waved and went inside. Harry sat in the car for a few seconds, putting off the trip home to Staten Island. Finally pulling out into traffic, he caught a glimpse of himself in the rearview mirror. Now what are you smiling about? he asked himself, noting the slight tilt of his mouth.

Could he be *enjoying* the notion that Carlin, too, had her ups and downs?

It made him feel bad to realize that he could take any pleasure at all in a friend's distress, but, damn, it was just the least bit satisfying that Carlin Squire's life was less than perfect. Certainly her career wasn't suffering. He thought about the conversation he'd had with his wife the night he told her about the results of the lieutenant's exam. *I told you she'd be sitting on top of your head,* Marilyn had whined when he quoted the rankings.

She had never trusted Carlin, sure the younger woman was using him, sucking up all his expertise and advice, certain to leave him in the dust when she'd gotten everything she wanted. At least Marilyn had gotten past the first few months of his friendship with Carlin, when she thought the two were sleeping together.

His wife was dead wrong about Carlin, Harry was sure of that. He knew that she would do anything for him, was his fiercest ally, in fact. But that didn't stop him from feeling her breath on his neck every once in a while.

I wouldn't wish Carlin any real harm, he said to himself as he drove south, but a little boyfriend trouble shouldn't kill her.

As Carlin entered the loft, she couldn't stop herself from thinking about how upset Derek was going to be when he found out what she had witnessed, how unprepared he would be for her anger.

The image of her mother flashed into her mind. She pictured the years of Lillian sitting patiently in the living room, knitting, waiting. It shocked her to realize that she held her mother almost as responsible for her father's ongoing cheating as she did J.T. himself. Lillian's total lack of courage, her passive silence on the subject gave him virtual permission.

Suddenly she felt furious with herself. What the hell am I worrying about Derek for? I've always been more concerned with protecting his feelings than my own. There was no excuse for what he'd done, what he continued to do despite his promises to her. And what did she do? Sit around worrying that *he* might be upset. I must be crazy, she thought.

With renewed energy, she marched over to their living area

and stopped in front of his closet. Opening the massive oak doors, she began pulling his suits off their hangers, paying little attention as they fell in a heap on the floor. Brooks Brothers, Paul Stuart, Barney's—the labels flew through her hands. By the time she'd cleared the racks, the floor resembled an expensive bazaar.

Not satisfied with just the contents of his closet, she walked out to his work area and collected several cameras plus an enlarger and dozens of boxes of film. With grim satisfaction, she walked them back to the bedroom and spread them on top of the pile of clothing. Then she walked over to the side of the bed, reached down under the end table, and lifted the New York telephone book. She thumbed through until she came to the listing she wanted.

It was only an hour later when the truck marked SALESIAN MOVING AND STORAGE pulled up to the front of the building. It took her less than fifteen minutes to heave the clothing and camera equipment into the huge empty boxes provided by the movers.

Carlin smiled as she filled out the packing labels also provided by Salesian. TO DEREK KINGSLEY, they read. CARE OF THE AMERICAN EMBASSY, TOKYO, JAPAN.

Let's see how long it takes you to track everything down, she thought to herself as she turned to pack up her own things and tried to decide where she would go.

1994

20

Carlin waited patiently in front of the coat check in the first-floor entryway of the Four Seasons as the young woman behind the counter rummaged through masses of fur coats. She could feel the stares of one of the men in a large group behind her before she felt his light touch on her shoulder.

"Carlin? Carlin Squire?"

She turned around to face his frank evaluating gaze, no glint of recognition in her eyes.

"It's Tony Kellner. You know, from Westerfield."

Carlin gave him a long look and finally smiled back. "Tony Kellner! Is that really you?" She couldn't have sounded more surprised. Natasha's old high school boyfriend looked like a better-fed version of his teenage self, his dark gray Armani suit and confident smile all attesting to a successful adulthood. She noted his eyes doing a similar appraisal of her as his face broke into a friendly smile.

"So how's your friend Natasha?"

Carlin couldn't help laughing. "It certainly didn't take you too much time to get to that question. She's fine."

"I've seen some pictures of her." Tony sounded curious.

"Her career's been pretty spectacular," Carlin began, "and, of course, she's been married for about three years to Ethan Jacobs. You know, he directed *Harbors of Granite*."

Tony shrugged. "Yeah. I guess I'd heard she'd gotten married."

The coat-check attendant was holding Carlin's short leather jacket for her. Carlin placed her arms through it, gathered up her purse and a leather carryall, and moved back to allow room for the people behind her. Tony followed as they stood at the foot of the stairs leading up to the Grill Room.

"And what are you doing with yourself these days?" he asked politely.

"Actually, I'm a freelance writer. Corporate brochures, that kind of thing. This fancy lunch was courtesy of an old friend from college." She and Harry had discussed telling him the truth about her profession. After all, there was no reason an old acquaintance couldn't be a police officer. But they had quickly agreed it wasn't worth the risk. She looked at her watch and shook her head. "I'd better be getting back to the office I'm working in this week." She pulled on her gloves, then looked at him fondly. "I'm sorry we don't have more time. I'd love to know what you're up to."

"Why don't we get together for lunch? It's been years since I've spoken to anyone from Westerfield." Tony couldn't have sounded more eager.

"Well, sure. I'd love to." Carlin held out her hand as if to say good-bye.

"How about next Thursday? We could make it right here if that's all right." He took her hand and gave it an affectionate squeeze, waiting for her response before he let it go.

"Okay," she answered after a second or two. "Next Thursday then. Is one o'clock okay?"

"One o'clock it is. And if Natasha's around, why don't you bring her along?"

"I'll be glad to." Carlin smiled at Tony for the last time and walked out onto Fifty-second Street. The words *When hell freezes over* were audible only to herself as she made her way toward Park Avenue.

"You're sure he didn't suspect anything?" Harry drummed his fingers on Carlin's desk as they went over what happened.

"Swear to God." Carlin held her hand up as if she were a Girl Scout taking an oath. "As far as he knew I had just finished lunch." She laughed a little. "It's lucky he didn't take any longer or my feet would have given out."

It had been just one year since Harry's promotion, and he'd become a lieutenant with the Twentieth Precinct on West Eighty-second Street. Carlin's promotion had come through two years earlier and the plum position of squad commander opened up right there in Midtown North. Now she was in

charge of the entire Midtown North detective division. Before
Harry's move to the Twentieth, their friendship had cooled a
bit, but now that each of them was in charge in different precincts, they once again found themselves discussing cases
over lunch or dinner a couple of times a month. When Harry
had mentioned the name Tony Kellner over pizza one night,
Carlin recognized it immediately and insisted on helping.

"You're absolutely certain he didn't notice you looking for
him before he came up to you?" Harry's fingers continued
their nervous dance.

Carlin reached out and took his cheeks in her hands, her
eyes boring into his as she answered slowly. "Harry, I was
posted near the ladies' room on the first floor. The minute I
saw him coming downstairs, I walked over to the coat check.
He didn't see me watching for him. No one else knew I was
watching for him. *He* asked *me* to lunch. It all went exactly
according to plan. The bait has been placed on the hook, the
butter knife has plunged into the jar of Skippy, the key is now
in the lock, the thread is in the needle, the cheese is resting
on top of the mousetrap . . ."

"Enough! I surrender!" Harry's explosion of laughter made
several of the detectives outside Carlin's door look up curiously, gazing through the glass wall separating her office
from their long row of desks. Harry's return visit to Midtown
North had caused quite a stir.

Carlin ignored her staff and kept talking. "I never made a
big enough dent in Tony Kellner's life for him to suspect
anything. In fact," she said, obviously disturbed by the notion, "the only thing he was really interested in talking about
was Natasha Dameroff. She's the reason he was so eager to
plan a lunch date within twenty seconds of seeing me there.
As if I'd ever let her get within a hundred feet of him."

"Ah, Natasha the dish," Harry said, raising his eyebrows
lasciviously.

"Enough," Carlin said grimly.

Harry was happy to return to the subject of Tony Kellner,
who had been a thorn in his side for months. "Well, if your
pal Natasha likes all the cash and all the jewelry and furniture
that it can buy, she'll do well to keep away from Mr.
Kellner."

* * *

As Harry told it, Tony had made it big in New York. Well dressed, seemingly polished, he was known in certain circles for his elegant dating service. Rich women all over the tristate area were happy to pay thousands of dollars and engage in long, private interviews in his Central Park West apartment.

I have two men in mind for you, he would say to almost every one of them, his eyes intent, his voice thoughtful. *One of them is absolutely perfect, I just know it.* And within a week or two, a man would call. Someone charming, apparently well heeled. The only problem was that while the women were out on their arranged dates, their apartments or houses would be stripped clean.

When Harry started running his investigation, his sole complainant was a rich widow who lived in a triplex in the El Dorado, a famous cooperative on Central Park West at Ninetieth Street. But within months, when two more single women living in lavish apartments also found themselves robbed while out on a date, he made the link to Tony Kellner's dating service. Twice he'd tried setting up police-women as decoys, but so far it hadn't worked. In both cases, the women went out on a couple of dates, but their apartments remained untouched.

Still, Harry was dead certain Kellner was his man. So when Carlin heard about the investigation and realized she'd gone to high school with the guy, Harry was happy to let her in. Maybe, with her old connection, she'd be able to come up with something.

"Just remember, Cambridge"—Harry's eyes twinkled as if he were about to make a joke they were both in on—"when we stick it to this character, the pleasure is all mine."

Carlin knew just what he meant. For Harry, this wasn't just about cooperation. It was *his* bust, *his* collar. She shook her head in undisguised contempt. "Now, now, Harry. Far be it from me to interfere with your pleasure."

After leaving Carlin in front of the restaurant, Tony Kellner had gone straight home. There were half a dozen phone calls he wanted to make, not the least of which was to check out a potential new fence for artwork. Valuable paintings were a bitch to dispose of. The conversation would be brief, mostly to arrange an initial meeting; he would never discuss the sensitive matters of his business over the telephone. Then he needed to place a call to Bob Ames, a minor partner in the dating service. Annoying as he was, Bob was useful.

As he sat down at the long, black desk in his study, he smiled and paused for a minute, reflecting on his meeting with Carlin Squire. Boy, that was a name he hadn't thought of in years. Natasha's little pal, the one whose father was in that sleazy motel with Natasha's whore mother. There she was, right in front of him at the Four Seasons.

The reason was so obvious: she was meant to bring Natasha to him.

Just thinking of her began stirring up the old feelings of black rage. At least he had the satisfaction of knowing that no woman had ever been able to do to him again what Natasha Dameroff had done. He'd made goddamn sure of that. She'd sucked him in, gutted his heart, and stolen the best he had to give. When he had *proven* he would do anything for her. But, hell, given half a chance, any woman would probably do pretty much the same thing to a man. He'd wised up after the lesson taught him by Miss Dameroff. No, he thought, a smile on his face, this was one guy who no longer took any shit from women. No, indeed.

He swiveled his chair around to look out at Central Park. Usually, the incredible view calmed him down, but for some reason today, he only felt his agitation growing. The memories were coming back, that day Natasha had dumped him—right at her own mother's funeral, for Christ's sake, the bloodless bitch. He couldn't believe it, couldn't fathom how, after he'd made that phone call just like she'd asked, she kicked him out on his ass. As if *he* were responsible for the fact that her lowlife mother got herself killed. What was she doing in that dump with another woman's husband anyway? Getting smashed by a truck only served the bitch right.

But it was amazing how his parents' religious crap had addled his brain. He'd wake up with the sweats every night for weeks after it happened, one nightmare after another about that damned phone call, hearing the fear in Kit Dameroff's voice when he told her about the phony car accident, reliving the sick feeling when he put the phone down, knowing the two people in that motel room were half out of their heads because of what he'd told them. He knew he was going to burn in hell for eternity.

It would have been an entirely different matter if Natasha had been by his side. That was the way it should have been, the two of them bound together by their secret, their love cemented by what they had shared. They had been destined to be one of the greatest couples of all time, anyone could have seen that. But she abandoned him. He didn't know what the hell to do, and of course, he'd done the stupidest thing of all by running off and joining the navy.

Tony stood up. He didn't like the way he was feeling. He crossed over to stare at the sculpture on the bookcase, a Degas figurine worth a small fortune. He'd fenced paintings and sculptures equally valuable, but he wasn't stupid enough to keep any of them around his own apartment. This one he'd bought legitimately, and it was his personal favorite. He stared at the girl's impassive face.

He'd gotten over Natasha Dameroff and moved on. Of course, he knew she'd become a big-deal model; any fool recognized her face nowadays. So he could have reached her easily if he'd wanted to. But he'd never tried to exact any revenge for what she'd done to him, even though God knows he was entitled to. But, hell, he had a great life—she may even have helped him get to this point. He chuckled. Perhaps he actually owed her a thank-you.

Returning to his desk, he opened up the small memo book where he jotted down notes in a code that was indecipherable to anyone but himself. He flipped through the pages, rapidly taking in the names and descriptions of various women who had been interviewed in the past month for his dating service. It was time to select that next lucky gal to go out on one of his fabulous arranged blind dates, when she could be conveniently relieved of all her worldly belongings while she dined on escargots and some fancy-ass veal dish at an expensive French restaurant.

Tony relaxed a bit. He *loved* his dating service. It was such a perfect cover; he got such pleasure getting rich women to virtually beg him to rob them. The process never failed to amuse him, having those pathetic creatures sitting in his living room as they sipped wine and told him their most personal fears and secrets. There were so many of them, too. They just kept coming, with their fake blond hair, their designer clothes, the rail-thin bodies they struggled so desperately to hang on to at the gym seven days a week. If they only knew how much he detested them, how he could hardly wait for those nights when he sat at home at one in the morning with a snifter of good brandy, envisioning them arriving home from their dream dates to find that the loot they didn't deserve in the first place had vanished into thin air.

Naturally, the crucial selection had to be made with infinite care. Once he'd picked a candidate, he still had her checked out thoroughly. There was no such thing as being too careful in his business. Although he couldn't be certain, he was convinced that the cops had tried to sniff him out at least once with a decoy, that babe in her forties a few months back. She *seemed* to check out, but his instincts had told him to steer clear, and his instincts were rarely wrong. He hoped that was the first and only time; if not, he'd escaped by sheer good luck. After that, he'd tightened his security checks. Still, he was keeping his eyes open.

He continued perusing his notes, but something was wrong. With annoyance he realized it was the image of Natasha Dameroff, her face long ago branded into his brain, hovering at the corner of his mind, ruining his concentration. No point wasting time now, he told himself, trying to regain his focus. She would get hers eventually. He smiled grimly at the thought of just how soon "eventually" was going to be.

21

The bloodied body of the twenty-seven-year-old woman looked broken, like a doll thrown across a room by an angry child. Carlin found herself shivering, despite the early summer temperature. Terri Madison's remains had been located in an alley behind a Cuban-Chinese restaurant on West Forty-seventh Street by one of Midtown North's patrol officers at five o'clock that afternoon, two bullets in her head, a New York City telephone book placed carefully just beneath her feet.

"Hideous."

Carlin looked over to see Harry Floyd standing beside her, sympathetically eyeing what had been a slender, beautiful young woman.

"Was the name circled?" Harry asked, knowing he couldn't touch the phone book until forensics had finished their work.

Carlin nodded yes. "Same red pen, same stupid stars around it."

"We're gonna get this guy, make no mistake about it." Harry's voice was taut.

"You certainly are," the voice of Deputy Inspector Reed Malone boomed in behind them, "that is, if you two wish to continue receiving paychecks from the City of New York."

Carlin turned around to see Malone bearing down on them, the mayor and the police commissioner right behind him.

"Their keen interest should really help." Carlin kept her sarcasm to a whisper as she and Harry greeted the newest arrivals.

She wasn't surprised at the unusual level of interest in a street crime. After all, this week alone, Terri Madison was the third victim whose name had been circled in red pen, garishly surrounded by red asterisks, in a telephone book left near the body. Undoubtedly the police lab would find that the two bullets used to kill her came from the same gun as those found in the first two bodies. But that would not be the most striking similarity between crimes one and two, and today's crime number three.

"We've gotten confirmation on the address," Carlin said to the mayor and the commissioner.

The first two victims were Mary Abbott, a sometime sculptress recently separated from her banker husband, and John Robles, owner of a small printing and copying service in the West Village. Mary Abbot was found at ten at night on the steps of a small building on West Fifty-fifth Street, her body shielded by the low concrete wall behind which the brownstone's dwellers housed their garbage cans. Robles had been located in an alleyway on West Seventy-third Street. Both bodies were accompanied by the phone books, their names set off by the red pen markings. But even more important, at least to the squad commanders of the Twentieth and Midtown North precincts, was the fact that both Mary Abbott and John Robles lived at 400 West End Avenue. According to the yellowed phone book placed at the latest victim's feet, so did Terri Madison.

"We're pretty sure we're going to find the killer among the other tenants," Harry said confidently.

Malone's voice chimed in. "Make sure you scour every foot of the Upper West Side. There's no guarantee the perp lives in that building. No guarantee at all."

"And do it in our lifetime." The mayor's smooth baritone did not disguise the threat in his voice.

With bodies found in both their precincts, Carlin and Harry found themselves officially assigned to the same case. It was clear to them that their careers would suffer a little more each day until the Phonestalker, as the city's best-selling tabloid had dubbed him, had been put behind bars.

Two days later, in the darkened back room of Tom's Pizzeria, it was hard to believe that summer had even started. In just forty-eight hours, the thermometer had fallen over twenty-five degrees, making late June feel like mid-April. Carlin held her slice of whole wheat with tomatoes and cheese at an angle, letting the overflow of oil roll off in large dollops onto the paper plate.

"Cambridge, that's disgusting," Harry Floyd said as he took an enormous bite of a pepperoni, mushroom, meatball, and pepper combination.

"Not as disgusting as the fat factory you just shoved into your mouth." Carlin took a careful bite of her slice and chewed thoughtfully. "So what's going on with you? The kids, the wife? Any progress on Tony Kellner? Got any theories on the Phonestalker?"

Harry laughed. "Like you care about my pukey little life or what's happening with your old pal Kellner, which as you well know is at this very moment a big fat nothing."

"Okay, so let's hear what your people have dug up," Carlin went on brightly.

"I think the butler did it."

"Harry, you are screamingly funny." Carlin took another bite of her pizza and returned to the crimes that had become an obsession for both of them.

Harry took a swallow of Coke. "We're pretty sure the doer's gonna be a former tenant. Seventeen people have moved from that building in the past two years, some of them kicking and screaming at maintenance increases and building noise and so on. One of those guys has gone psycho."

"Maybe." Carlin didn't look convinced.

"Who do you think did it," Harry asked, noting her expression, "a disgruntled long-distance operator?"

"I don't know . . . It all feels, well, too pat." She took another small bite of pizza and chewed thoughtfully. "Like this crime is somehow, well, designed."

"Designed?" Harry looked dubious.

"It's too perfectly put together—the phone books, the same address—all such a neat package." Carlin knew she sounded ridiculous, yet her instincts were running on overtime. She tried to explain the feelings she'd had since the second victim had been found. "Abbott and Robles, now Madison. All three are quiet, pay their rent on time, go to work, live their lives. None of them has wild parties, they don't really even know each other, according to the superintendent. It just doesn't feel as if they're really as connected as they seem."

Harry didn't bother to hide the scorn on his face. "They lived in the same goddamn building. You don't call that a connection?"

"I don't know," she replied, at a loss to explain what was pure gut feeling. "Maybe I'm just nuts."

Harry laughed as he agreed with her. "Now you're talking."

"I thought Dustin Hoffman's Willy Loman had real subtext. George C. Scott was all surface." Elliott Shillansky's fork was poised in midair as he held forth.

Carlin looked over to Natasha and Ethan across the table, bored despite the liveliness of the conversation. What's the matter with me? she thought, irritated with herself. Here she was, seated beside New York's most eminent theater critic, *straight, single* theater critic, as Tash had said only ten or twelve times before introducing them, and all she wanted to do was go home and look over the Phonestalker file one more time. She forced herself to listen as Elliott continued his lecture.

"Elliott," Ethan interrupted him, "we've been hogging the conversation all night." He ran his hand down Natasha's cheek. "I haven't even seen you all day. How was the shoot?"

Natasha nestled against him. "It was great. The newest commercial has me walking in the park with these two huge mastiffs." She smiled at Carlin and Elliott. "Evidently they think women pick their perfume to please their dogs."

"Is this the latest in the Forager line?" Carlin asked politely.

Natasha nodded yes.

Ethan smiled at his wife. "Over a million dollars a year to walk in the park for a day!"

Elliott looked shocked. "Is that true?" he asked, an expression of horror on his face.

"Sort of," Natasha replied as modestly as she could. "Now, just as I'm practically over the hill, Forager has made me their spokesperson." She laughed lightly. "All those years I was in my twenties, I was dying for this kind of contract. Suddenly, at thirty-five, the sweet life gets hand-delivered to me." She sounded almost apologetic as she addressed herself to Elliott. "Not so bad for a high school graduate, I guess."

Carlin could see how uncomfortable this conversation made Elliott Shillansky. Whether he couldn't bear modeling talk, or he simply couldn't keep the focus of conversation off himself, he quickly got back to the discussion he'd started earlier.

"It's like what Woody Allen did in *Hannah*," Elliott continued, not bothering to complete the title of a movie Carlin had never gotten to see. "Everyone thought the attention was on Farrow and Hershey, but it's really Wiest who holds the piece together."

"That's so much horseshit." Ethan laughed good-naturedly and winked at Carlin. "You're just trying to impress your date," he said.

Shillansky smiled benignly at Carlin. "I certainly wouldn't mind impressing such a beautiful woman," he said, but he quickly turned his attention back to Ethan. "You couldn't be more wrong about Woody, however."

Carlin did her best to concentrate, but it was impossible. Elliott Shillansky's world was a mystery to her, and not one she particularly cared to solve. The conversation washed over her as she found herself tuning out once again. Only when Elliott began a diatribe about a Shaw play he'd seen performed in London a few months earlier did one of his phrases stick in her mind.

"It's just a red herring, Ethan. You didn't understand it at all. It had nothing to do with what was really going on."

Elliott's face was growing flushed as he rode this subject for several minutes. Finally Ethan cut him short with a question about the British cast.

But the phrase lingered in Carlin's mind. *Red herring.* Why was she so obsessed with those words? Suddenly she knew.

"Carlin, you're a million miles away." Natasha's voice nudged her gently.

"Listen, I'm terribly sorry, but my head is throbbing." Carlin turned to Elliott. "Would you forgive me if I saw myself home?"

Elliott looked more confused than concerned. "Not at all, but let me take you."

"Please, don't bother." Carlin nodded apologetically toward Natasha's obvious disappointment. "There are a hundred cabs right out front." She held her hand out to her date. "Thank you for dinner. It was a wonderful evening"—she looked over at Natasha and Ethan—"and I wouldn't want to spoil it for everyone."

"Are you sure you're all right?" Natasha asked.

"I'll be fine, I promise." Carlin kissed her friend on the cheek and made her way to the door. More than fine, she thought to herself as she settled into a yellow cab.

Back home in her apartment, Carlin sat on the floor of her living room, looking out over the Hudson River. She knew she'd lucked out three years before when she'd broken up with Derek and found the small, relatively inexpensive two-bedroom apartment on Riverside Drive and Eighty-third Street, but on a night like this when she needed to think, she thanked her lucky stars all over again. Watching the boats make their way down the Hudson, even getting a glimmer of green from Riverside Park right outside her door plus the view across the river, all of it helped to soothe her. Stacked around her were files from the Phonestalker case, including copies of every interview her detectives had held with people who lived in and around 400 West End Avenue.

The stately co-op was just a few blocks from her own building, and several times she had walked West End from Seventy-ninth Street to Eightieth, hoping for some kind of inspiration. But it wasn't inspiration that had given her the clue. It wasn't even the days and weeks of collecting bits and pieces, then putting them together with care. It was that casual mention of a red herring.

She studied the profiles of the three victims. Mary Abbott had lived in the building for fifteen years. Her two children, Joan and Elaine, were away at college. Abbott had no enemies. Even her estranged husband spoke well of her. It seemed that after twenty years of marriage, he had suddenly announced a new sexual preference, and moved in with a man he'd met two years before. Not only didn't there seem to be hard feelings, but Mary and her husband and his lover celebrated every Christmas together, and all three of them plus the two daughters had shared a house in Quogue over the Memorial Day weekend a few weeks before the murder.

John Robles, who lived three floors above Mary Abbott, had two small children—a daughter, three, and a son, five and a half. According to his wife, Sylvia, he was a dedicated husband and father who spent every moment out of his print shop playing with his kids. The business made a fair, not fabulous amount of money. He owed no one and hated no one, she'd said. Carlin had pored over every line of every interview with his two employees and numerous aunts, uncles, and cousins. They all seemed to agree with Mrs. Robles. John Robles had lived the kind of life that was extraordinary only in its simplicity. Nothing about him seemed to single him out as a potential murder victim.

Terri Madison was a different story. Now this was a woman who could inspire feelings other than respect and love. She had been returning from a Sunday afternoon performance of a new musical at the Manhattan Theater Club when the killer had stopped her. As in the other crime scenes, a copy of the New York City telephone directory had been placed at her feet. What set this crime apart from the other two was the personality of the victim. Virtually everyone interviewed from the theatrical community referred to Madison's ambition and her uncanny talent for taking center stage at every opportunity.

In fact, *Terrible Twos,* the show she'd been about to open in at the Manhattan Theater Club ten days after the murder, had been developed by another cast at a regional theater out in San Francisco. It seemed the original star, Ellen Moscow, had worked with the piece for two years, performing almost gratis as the writer and director polished it over time. It had been only a short while after rehearsals in New York started that Terri Madison had introduced herself to the show's director. Then, just a few weeks later, Ellen Moscow was notified that she was now understudying Terri Madison. When Carlin's people had interviewed the cast, no one bothered to be nice.

While Ellen Moscow didn't gloat outright, she didn't pretend to be unhappy that her competition had been eliminated. "Do you know how many Manhattan Theater Club productions have gone to Broadway?" she'd demanded of the detective who'd questioned her. "It's a dream career break for an actress." Beginning with *Ain't Misbehavin'*, she went on to list almost a dozen shows that had made their leading ladies household names.

Brian Midland, the play's author, was also outspoken. Recasting the lead had been done without his okay, and he, too, seemed glad that Madison was out of the picture. "Not that I wished her dead," he'd insisted to the detectives.

Madison also wasn't much of a relative. Her grandmother, who lived in Brewster, just about an hour from the city, hadn't seen her granddaughter in over a year. One sister, living in Albuquerque, talked to her only every couple of months or so, and a brother working at a service station in Montclair, New Jersey, had stopped speaking to her completely several years before. She had no boyfriend. It seemed that Madison was too busy with voice lessons and dance classes and auditions on both coasts to bother with the opposite sex. And while there were two roommates, one a secretary, the other a flight attendant, neither of them had had much to do with Madison outside of sharing the Con Edison bill every month.

So presumably, Carlin thought, leaning back against the sofa and shutting her eyes for a few minutes, there have been three victims, each picked for some unknown reason. The perp could be a complete psycho who knew none of them, or someone who hated all three.

It just didn't feel right. It was as if the killer were trying to prove how crazy he was. No, there was a motive, a specific point to all of it. If only she could see what that point was.

She got up and paced. Yes, the victims all lived in the same building, but there was no real connection. Maybe the killer wanted it to *appear* that they were connected. *Red herring.* The words echoed in her mind.

So who was the real target? Suddenly it seemed clear. One of the three victims was universally despised. Carlin could think of half a dozen people with a motive to kill Terri Madison. She replayed their faces in her mind. She knew which one it was.

Going over to her desk, she scanned a couple of the interviews Ellen Moscow had undergone. Damn, she thought. Moscow had already seen every youngish female detective at Midtown North within the past couple of days and would recognize their faces. If somebody were going to go undercover as an actress, it would have to be Carlin herself. Okay, she thought, grinning. I guess it's time to repeat your high school triumph in *West Side Story*.

"I hope I don't actually have to sing," she said out loud.

Carlin stood in the center of a large circle of people at the Manhattan Theater Club as the false bio developed by the detective squad of Midtown North was recited by Doug Towne, the director of *Terrible Twos*.

"So please say hello to our new star, Caroline Sessions."

Carlin felt the name change was necessary, although all these people were strangers to her; her part in the investigation, at least up to now, had never included direct contact with acquaintances of the victims. She looked closely at Ellen Moscow as the announcement went on. Moscow's face revealed obvious disappointment. Nonetheless, within moments after Towne finished talking, Moscow had come up to her and congratulated her, even asked if she wanted some help learning the choreography.

"I won't be starting to rehearse until the day after tomorrow," Carlin explained. "There's some stuff I have to finish up for the company I'm leaving in Boston."

The bio of "Caroline Sessions" had her starring at Boston's Charles Theater in a Tennessee Williams revival due to close the next evening. Carlin dearly hoped that if something were going to happen, it would happen before she actually had to show up in rehearsal. This was a wild card, and if it didn't work out, she'd look more than foolish. *Idiotic* would be the least of the adjectives hurled at her by her peers. As for her superiors, it would be a miracle if she weren't demoted to cleaning up Midtown North rather than heading it up.

Moscow continued talking as Carlin put on her coat and picked up her bag. As the two walked together toward the exit doors, Carlin noted that Moscow had asked her home address and travel plans, all as casually as could be. Suddenly,

Carlin felt especially pleased at the thought of the three detectives who would be protecting her for the next few days.

There was no way to return to the precinct that afternoon without blowing her cover if someone were following her. So it was only four o'clock when Carlin got home to Riverside Drive. She found three messages on her phone machine, one from Harry Floyd, telling her she was crazy, another from the deputy inspector, filled with dire warnings in case she was wrong. The third made her smile. It was from Derek Kingsley, asking her to dinner. She returned the call, promising to meet him the following night at Ernie's, a noisy Italian restaurant just a few blocks from her apartment.

Hanging up, she felt unexpectedly happy. She had twenty-four hours with absolutely nothing to do, and she decided to make the most of it. Cut off from her usual demands, she picked up a novel she'd been longing to read and savored every page. When she finished, she sank into bed and watched David Letterman interview Demi Moore. So this is how normal people spend their time, she thought as she closed her eyes and sank into sleep.

A little before eight the next evening, she left the apartment to meet Derek. She smiled as she walked down Broadway. Derek might have been a ridiculous choice as a steady boyfriend, but he had proved himself over and over as a valuable friend. He still couldn't quite understand why she refused a romantic involvement with him, and he never would get the concept of fidelity. But he was always there when she needed him. He had claimed to find the two months it took to retrieve his wardrobe and his photography equipment from the Tokyo embassy quite funny, and had immediately insisted on staying in Carlin's life. And soon enough, Carlin had realized that was fine with her. It didn't come near solving the loneliness that crept into her soul every now and then when she allowed herself to slow down long enough to feel anything, but seeing Derek every month or so inevitably cheered her up.

Natasha often warned her that her friendship with Derek was keeping her from moving forward with her life. Sometimes, she got even more pointed. "The one man for you is right across Central Park, and you know it," Tash would de-

clare when Carlin refused invitations to dinner parties where
Ben Dameroff was sure to be a guest. Carlin still couldn't
bear to think about him. Maybe Natasha was right, maybe
Derek had protected her from thoughts of Ben. But there was
no way she was going to struggle with that one again. And
from her memories of their last encounter at Natasha's wedding, there was no way Ben was about to get involved with
her again either. Should she and Ben ever run into each other,
Carlin would be surprised if he even spoke to her.

The sharp honk of a bus horn nearby startled her. Realizing
she hadn't been paying attention to her surroundings, she
glanced around nervously. No one would do anything right
here, she thought, taking in all the people on Broadway, not
to mention the plainclothes cops walking behind her. On a
June night like this, there must be at least twenty-five people
within fifty feet of me, she thought, attempting to quiet the
small voice of fear inside her chest.

Still, her instincts warned her to be on guard. She continued walking, but one minute later, as if from out of nowhere,
Ellen Moscow stood next to her, a gun deftly digging into
Carlin's ribs from under the actress's voluminous silk pleated
top.

"Turn left on Seventy-seventh," Moscow whispered force-
fully.

Slowing down almost to a stop, Carlin answered back in a
conversational tone. "Ellen, put the gun down. I am not an
actress. I'm Lieutenant Carlin Squire from Midtown North.
Three guys have you covered and you're under arrest for the
murders of Mary Abbott, John Robles, and Terri Madison."

"I said, turn left." The girl didn't seem to have been listening to Carlin. Holding the gun steady against Carlin's side,
she put her arm around Carlin's shoulders and forced her to
move forward.

Carlin was a little surprised by the girl's strength. I hope
those guys can see what's going on, she thought, as she felt
herself moved by the relentless force of Ellen Moscow. The
actress had a viselike grip on her shoulder, yet her mouth
smiled gaily, so anyone passing them on the busy sidewalk
would think they were two friends out for a particularly
chummy walk.

Carlin tried again. "Ellen, I'm not who you think I am. I'm squad commander of the Midtown North Precinct, and the two men behind us are about to arrest you for murder. Please don't make it any harder for yourself than it already is."

This time the woman stopped, still holding her gun to Carlin's waist. Looking behind her for the first time, the actress saw the two plainclothesmen approaching, and for a second it seemed she was loosening her grip on Carlin's shoulder.

Suddenly Derek's voice rang out from down the street.

"Carlin, the restaurant's this way."

The two officers looked up at the unexpected interruption, and Ellen Moscow's face took on a confused expression. Carlin watched what followed as if it were happening in slow motion. As Derek approached from Seventy-sixth Street, the two detectives following her came up behind them, their guns out of their shoulder holsters, aimed straight at Ellen Moscow. Other passersby stopped and stared when the girl pulled her gun from Carlin's side and began walking away. Carlin's voice followed her.

"Stop, damn it," she cried out. "Don't make things even worse."

Ellen whirled around. Carlin could see the agony in her eyes as she raised the gun and fired off two shots with deadly accuracy.

There was a burning sensation in Carlin's stomach, and she felt a hot stickiness spreading across her shirt. My blood, she thought calmly, almost as if none of this had anything to do with her. I'm hit. Trying to take a step forward, she stumbled and dropped to her knees. Everything seemed to be slipping away from her. Struggling to remain conscious, she felt herself being eased to the ground.

"Carlin. Oh, Jesus . . ."

Derek's voice was frantic, and for the life of her she couldn't figure out why. Then there was the screaming of a siren, but it seemed miles away.

"Officer down," she heard someone yelling as she felt the excruciating pain of being lifted.

Suddenly she was in a hospital, with more people yelling at one another across her. She closed her eyes against it all, feeling as though she herself were fading away, leaving the chaos and noise behind. When she opened her eyes again, she was staring into the face of a doctor in a green cap and mask, his dark eyes holding hers. Those eyes.

"*Oh, God,*" she whispered, "*it's you.*"

22

Carlin felt as if she were floating through space, only now and then picking up a thread of conversation, a few bars of music, anxious whisperings of strange voices. When she finally woke up, her eyes squinting in the bright sunshine coming through the picture window, she found herself alone in a large white room. She looked around, taking in the bare walls, the antiseptic odor in the air, finally the many tubes threading mysteriously under the clean white sheets that covered her.

Only after she was awake for a moment or two did she begin to feel the searing pain in her lower body, the throbbing a few inches beneath her waist that was unfamiliar yet seemed to have been going on forever. Then she became aware of the stiffness in her neck and upper back. Moving seemed impossible. Slowly she raised her right arm, surprised to see the IV tube taped to her hand. She didn't even attempt to turn her head and see where the plastic tubing came from.

"Don't try to move, honey." A crisp-looking young nurse came through the door, her voice authoritative. She approached the side of the bed, lowering the metal railing and easing her hands under Carlin's body, moving her into a different position.

"Is that better, dear?" The nurse peered at her, then cushioned Carlin's head with her hand, raising it gently as she rearranged the pillows underneath.

Carlin felt the muscles of her shoulder ease, although the searing pain in her abdomen continued unabated. "Is there anything you can do about the rest of me?" she asked, trying, not very successfully, to smile.

"Got you covered," the nurse answered, holding up a hypodermic needle filled with a whitish liquid. "That should do it," she said as she injected it into Carlin's thigh.

Carlin felt the relief almost immediately. She was practically asleep as she heard the nurse pad softly out of the room.

When she opened her eyes, she would have sworn it was a couple of hours later, but when the same nurse drew back the curtains covering the window to reveal bright sunshine once more, she discovered she had been asleep for almost twenty-four hours.

"That's right, you missed a whole day. But you need the rest," the woman said, returning to the side of the bed and smiling down at her. "How's the pain today?"

Carlin smiled back. "Better," she answered, as she mentally catalogued her body to see if that were indeed true. She found she could stretch her legs a bit, the throbbing in her abdomen having calmed to a dullish ache.

Suddenly she remembered the face behind the mask. The memory of that brief moment in the operating room filled her with an odd mix of dread and anticipation. "Has Dr. Dameroff been in to see me?" she asked tentatively.

"Oh, he's been in a lot since the surgery, but you were sleeping every time," the nurse answered brightly. "Of course, now that you're on your way, he won't need to come by so often."

Carlin was embarrassed to feel her eyes tearing up in disappointment.

"Are you in pain? Do you need this?" the nurse asked, holding up a hypodermic.

"I don't think so," Carlin answered.

Harry's booming voice came from the doorway. "Take it while you can get it."

Carlin looked over, smiling as the big red-haired man seemed to fill the whole room. "Is that your official opinion or a boyhood remnant from the late nineteen sixties, Lieutenant Floyd?" Carlin asked, grinning at him affectionately.

"Wouldn't Dr. Dameroff like to be listenin' to the two of you!" The efficient young nurse wagged a finger at them as she walked out of the room.

Carlin's smile crumpled at the mention of Ben's name, leaving her eyes suspiciously bright, tears threatening. Harry walked over to the side of the bed, picking up a box of tissues from a small table and offering them to her.

"You in that much pain, Cambridge?" he asked nervously.

Carlin shook her head. "I don't know what's the matter with me." She reached for one of the tissues, holding it tightly in her hand, trying to hold the tears back.

"You know, sugar, you've still got a hell of a lot of anesthesia running through you. It's kind of a truth serum, they say." Harry sat down in a brown leather chair right next to the bed and grabbed one of her hands. "So exactly what truth are you trying to cover up here?"

Despite her best efforts, Carlin felt the tears begin to course down her cheeks. "You know who my surgeon was, don't you?"

Harry shook his head. "Nope."

"Ben Dameroff. Brother of Natasha Dameroff, who is the ex-girlfriend of Tony Kellner."

"Aha," Harry said, releasing her hand. "So what does Ben Dameroff have to do with the waterworks you're so eager for me not to see?"

"I can't really blame him," she said sadly. "Frankly, I'm surprised he didn't kill me while he had me on the table."

"Excuse me?" Harry moved his chair so he could watch her face as she talked. "Well, this is much more interesting than the average hospital visit to a downed colleague."

"I wish I found it so amusing," Carlin answered glumly.

Harry took her hand one more time. "What exactly happened between you and this Dameroff guy to make him want to murder you?"

Carlin felt torn. The last thing she wanted to share with Harry was the lurid scenes of her childhood, but whether it was the anesthesia or not, something made her long to unburden herself. "You're sure you're up for this?"

"Beats working."

Carlin began to talk about the past. Harry smiled benignly at the story of their high school romance, but when she got to the events at the Starlight Motel, he looked more serious.

"That's a lot for a couple of kids to carry around with them," he said as she finished. "You're still in love with this guy, aren't you?"

Oh God, she thought, wishing he hadn't asked. After all these years, could it still be true?

Carlin was spared having to answer by the entrance of Deputy Inspector Reed Malone. "It's good to see you here, Floyd. Maybe Squire can solve a few of the other crimes in your precinct while she's sitting on her duff."

Harry dropped Carlin's hand and stood to face Malone, his cheeks reddening. Malone went right on, throwing a comradely arm around Harry's shoulder, as if the two of them were in on a big joke. Whatever Harry was thinking stayed buried beneath the artificial bonhomie.

Carlin felt sick to her stomach. From the vantage point of this hospital bed, guessing right on the identity of the Phonestalker didn't seem like such a big deal, especially since she'd almost gotten herself killed in the process. But watching Harry try to control himself was torture, like monitoring a time bomb to see if it was going to blow. What's the matter with him? she thought. Harry knew damned well he was one of the best cops in the city of New York, why did he have to go from Jekyll to Hyde every time he sensed competition? She just didn't have the energy for this. Her head began to throb.

"Listen, guys," she said weakly, "I'm really exhausted." She closed her eyes.

"Sorry for staying so long, slugger," Harry said, his voice tight.

"It was great work, Squire," Malone said, squeezing her hand softly.

Carlin kept her eyes shut when the men had gone. That's all I need, she thought miserably, having my friend Harry needled into becoming an enemy. It was bad enough having one antagonist operate on me . . . At the thought of Ben, she shifted on the bed. I wonder what else can possibly go wrong, she thought as she tried to find a comfortable position.

"Well, well, well."

Carlin's eyes flew open. There was Tony Kellner standing right over her bed.

"If it isn't Lieutenant Carlin Squire."

So there *is* one more thing that can go wrong, she thought. Keeping her face expressionless, she looked up at him. Tony was dressed in a blue blazer and a pair of expensive-looking tan slacks, his elegant appearance out of place in the stark hospital room. In his hand were a bunch of newspaper clippings. Knowing procedure, she expected that a patrolman was posted at her door, but, of course, she realized, there would have been no obvious reason to stop Tony. Ellen Moscow was in custody. Why should there be danger from this obviously well-heeled citizen?

Tony held up the clippings so she could see the headlines. COP GIRL GETS PHONESTALKER! TOP FEM COP SOLVES SERIAL MUR DER! Carlin had had no idea that the New York papers had made her into such a hero.

"So why didn't you mention you were a police lieutenant?" Tony's voice was smooth, but she couldn't miss the anger flashing in his eyes.

Carlin stalled for time as she tried to make her brain work. "You must have been surprised," she said as calmly as she could.

"You could say that," Tony said, sarcastically.

"You know, the day I ran into you at the Four Seasons, I was actually on duty." Carlin held his gaze squarely.

"What kind of case were you on?" The question sounded merely polite.

"I can't tell trade secrets to a friend." Carlin forced a smug twist to her mouth. Anything even bordering on the apologetic would just make him more suspicious. "Suffice it to say, I done good."

Tony was taken aback. Clearly he had expected a more thorough cover-up. Carlin was amused to realize that her answer had unsettled him.

"So does my being a cop mean I don't get flowers or candy?" She was almost purring.

Tony said nothing, considering her. She could practically see the wheels spinning. He'd come here certain she'd been setting him up. But she was making him reconsider, maybe even making his social-climbing ass uncomfortable for forgetting the niceties. Suddenly she felt too tired to go on with this particular charade. "Tony, maybe you could come back in a few days when . . ." Carlin stopped in mid-sentence as Ben Dameroff entered the room.

"Sorry to interrupt."

In his white coat, stethoscope strung around his neck, Ben looked crisply handsome. Carlin felt her heart constrict, her former nervousness with Tony Kellner not nearly comparable to the fear now silencing her.

"Why, you're Ben Dameroff." Tony Kellner put out his hand.

"How do you do." Ben offered his hand but it was clear he had no idea who Tony was.

"Westerfield High School. Tony Kellner." He grinned broadly. "Natasha's old boyfriend."

"I guess we've all grown up, haven't we." Ben sounded pleasant enough, though he didn't appear especially pleased to see Tony.

"Are you two still an item?" Tony looked from Ben to Carlin.

Ben answered for both of them. "I operated on Carlin a few days ago."

"How cozy," Tony said.

"Would you mind leaving us alone for a few minutes?" Ben asked him, any trace of warmth gone from his voice.

"Not at all." Tony smiled at Carlin a little too carefully. "I'll try to stop back and see you again while you're here." Obviously he was still having trouble deciding whether Carlin was on the level.

She returned his smile, managing to look sincere. "That would be nice."

As Tony walked out of the room, Ben approached the bed. "I'm going to check the dressing." His tone couldn't have been more professional as he reached under the white sheet and drew up her hospital gown. "Is Tony Kellner a good friend of yours?" he asked as he gently explored the bandaged area.

"Not particularly," Carlin just managed to get out.

"Am I hurting you?" Ben withdrew his hand quickly, searching her face for pain.

Carlin felt as if she had stopped breathing. Having Ben Dameroff so near, feeling his cool touch was enough to paralyze her like a teenager with a crush. She forced herself to speak evenly, to meet his eyes. "I'm fine. Do whatever you have to."

Ben continued to examine her, his smooth fingers every now and then coming in contact with the skin surrounding the bandage. It was fascinating for Carlin to watch him work. Not surprisingly he seemed utterly at ease. Carlin even felt herself relaxing under his expert touch. But his next words caught her up short.

"So the Harvard graduate decided to become a cop."

She couldn't believe her ears. Had he really made such an obnoxious crack? Her voice suddenly came back in full, along with the capacity for instantaneous rage that Ben Dameroff had been inspiring since they were toddlers. "Somehow exhibiting my superiority to sick people didn't sound as appealing to me as it did to you."

Ben's retort came so quickly, it might as well have been twenty minutes since their last fight instead of nearly twenty years. "I bet ordering around a whole department filled with men really does it for you." He glared at her, aiming his next words like bullets. "I certainly hope your performance at my sister's wedding helped you develop your skills."

Ben pulled the cover up around Carlin's waist and crossed to the doorway. "The stitches look fine. Dr. Aranow will attend to you until you go home." Without waiting for a response he strode out, slamming the door behind him.

Carlin couldn't even try to control the tears. She lay in bed weeping until she was too exhausted to continue. She longed for Ben to return, even as furious as he was, just for a few minutes, just long enough for her to explain, to apologize, to beg his forgiveness. She lay there, spent and miserable, looking out the window at what had become a bleak twilight. It was no good wishing. She knew he would never come back.

23

Carlin felt dizzy as she sat on the pure white sofa watching Ethan Jacobs's friends circulate. It had been such a short time since Natasha had whisked her out of the hospital, from her bed to a cocktail party within the space of an hour or so. Tash had seemed almost feverish as she'd put Carlin's few things into a small bag and wheeled her out to a waiting car. She'd explained that her husband's cronies from last year's Cannes Film Festival were in town and asked would Carlin mind stopping by for just a few minutes. But it made little sense to Carlin, who longed to go right home. She'd tried to talk Natasha into driving her straight home, but Tash had insisted. Carlin knew something was going on. Tash seemed almost too bright, as if she were engaged in some frantic dance of deception. Carlin had asked what was wrong, but Tash dismissed her question with a wave. It was terribly confusing.

Tash had to be aware that Carlin shouldn't be at a cocktail party under the circumstances. After two weeks in the hospital, she wasn't in much pain, but she had little stamina. Sitting in the plush richness of Tash's living room, Ethan's cultivated friends speaking in what must have been at least four different languages, wasn't enough to distract Carlin from her discomfort. She knew she belonged at home, but she couldn't even slow Natasha down long enough to ask that she take her to her apartment. Tash was everywhere, distributing drinks, emptying ashtrays, acting as if she were a fabulously entertaining maid instead of a hostess surrounded by an army of helpers.

Carlin could deal with the bizarre juxtaposition of this party and her clinical surroundings for the past two weeks; what she was having a problem with was seeing Ben's picture on the mantelpiece. For two weeks, she'd prayed that he would return to see her. She'd rehearsed an apologetic speech six different ways, hoping he'd come back. But he'd stayed away, just as he'd said he would. Damn you, Ben, she thought, her eyes tearing, as she looked at his picture one more time.

Ben got off the elevator, but he stopped outside his sister's door. What am I doing here? he asked himself, dreading the cocktail party. He had nothing in common with a bunch of European actors and directors, as little interest in foreign movie people as they would have in an American surgeon. But Natasha had insisted he show up. He'd begged off with every excuse he could muster, but she refused to let him off the hook. Finally, he'd given in.

It hardly mattered, he thought, pressing the doorbell. The last couple of weeks avoiding Carlin had been pure hell—how could this be any worse? A maid let him in, ushering him toward the living room. Ben stood in the archway leading to the noisy crowd. He looked around the room, hoping to see even one vaguely familiar face. Suddenly he spied Carlin, pale in a black pants suit that seemed to be swimming on her. She was seated on the couch, obviously exhausted. Natasha appeared at his elbow, quickly kissing his cheek and urging him into the room.

"What's Carlin doing here?" he demanded.

Natasha felt as if she were caught in a trap. What was I thinking when I invited Ben? she wondered frantically. "I'm in the middle of taking her home from the hospital. I thought she might enjoy spending some time with people after two weeks of IV's and bandages." She heard the frenzy in her voice, but she couldn't imagine how to make Carlin's being there sound any less crazy than it so obviously was. She couldn't let Ben even suspect the real reason she'd needed Carlin there.

He wheeled around to face her, noting her high color. Either she knew enough to be embarrassed or something else was going on, but he was too furious to figure out which it might be.

"Carlin has no business being at a party. She was just discharged. What the hell were you thinking about, bringing her here?"

"I thought she'd have a good time. After all, for the next few weeks, she's going to be recuperating at home. What's wrong with a few minutes of socializing?" Natasha felt stung. Ben was so rarely angry with her.

Ben wasn't about to argue any further. He started toward the sofa, knowing what he had to do. Whatever else lay between them, he was Carlin's doctor. She certainly shouldn't be at a party on the day she was released from the hospital. Looking at her sitting there, pale and listless as the talk flowed around her, Ben stopped for a moment. How could this woman make him so furious and weak all at the same time? Seeing her surrounded by people eating canapés and carrying drinks reminded him all too strongly of the day she'd walked out on him at Natasha's wedding without even a backward glance.

But as he watched her, a large man carrying a plate filled with sandwiches and appetizers plunked down beside her. Ben saw Carlin go white, her hand moving to the site of the surgery, as if the jostling had upset her wound. Without waiting another second, he strode over to the couch. Carlin looked up, shocked to see him, as he put his arm under her elbow and forced her to stand.

"Come on, I'm taking you home," he said firmly.

Carlin allowed him to take her hand, following wordlessly as he led her to the door. Only when he had eased her into his car, parked right out front, did she speak.

"Thank you for getting me out of there." She hardly looked at Ben as she curled into the seat. "I had no idea how exhausted I was."

"You had major abdominal surgery, you idiot. How could you let yourself be dragged to a party?" Ben's worry made him sound furious.

Carlin was too fatigued to allow herself to be drawn into a fight. Having given him her address, she sat quietly, looking out. As he drove across town, she tried to remember all the apologies she had composed, but none of them would come to mind. All she could think about was how it felt to be seated next to him. If he weren't so angry, if she weren't so exhausted, she could just reach across and touch him, take his hand. But she stayed where she was, just gathering her strength as he pulled up in front of her building.

He said nothing as he got out of the car and came around to her side, opening the door. She felt dizzy as she stepped out, stumbling slightly on the sidewalk. He reacted immediately, picking her up and carrying her into the lobby.

Winding her arms around his neck, she breathed him in, the clean scent that hadn't changed since he was a boy. I won't mess it up this time, she vowed to herself, the familiar strength of his body cushioning her as he walked.

"Try and put me down," she whispered, holding on to him for dear life. "Come on, I dare you."

Ben stopped and smiled down at her, the words obviously touching something inside him. He suddenly looked younger somehow as he carried her into the elevator. Only after he'd taken her into her bedroom and placed her on the bed, pulling the covers up around her and easing a pillow under her head, did he answer her.

"So I've put you down. Now what?"

Carlin pushed herself up on her elbows. This was the moment she'd been dreaming of. Please, she begged herself, don't mess this up again. "Ben, at the hospital. I was stupid. I know you didn't mean to be insulting. And that scene at Natasha's wedding. I never meant to tease you, I wouldn't hurt you on purpose for anything, I swear it."

To her surprise, Ben began to laugh. "We're some pair, aren't we?"

He eased her head back down on the bed once again, but this time he eased himself alongside her. Ever so gently, he pulled her into his arms, kissing her softly on the mouth as he held her tightly.

"How about instead of insulting each other," he said, "we admit that we love each other, that we belong together for the rest of our lives."

Carlin felt the warmth begin to flow through her. Once again he kissed her, but this time she returned his kiss, urging him closer. For the first time in years, she felt completely safe. "I love you, Ben. I always have, I always will. Please promise never to leave me for a single second."

Ben couldn't help but smile. "How about this . . . I promise not to leave you until one of us gets thirsty or we have our next big fight, whichever comes first."

They both grinned as he leaned down to kiss her one more time. Eagerly they tasted each other, their tongues exploring familiar territory, their shared longing building as it always had. Ben forced himself to pull away from her. "I'd better start to remember that I'm your doctor," he said as he eased her back to a comfortable position. "We don't have to rush," he whispered, kissing her lightly on the neck, "we have the rest of our lives."

"I'm sure Carlin is fine, Tash. After all, Ben is her doctor and he's the one she left with." Ethan Jacobs had to raise his voice to be heard over the din of the party. "It just seems such a shame for you to leave with all our friends here."

Natasha bit her lip. She hated disappointing her husband, but this was one night she simply had to. "Really, Ethan, I'm sorry, but you don't know what it's like when Ben and Carlin get together. Honestly, two weeks of hospitalization could be thrown right out the window."

"They aren't teenagers, honey, they're grown-ups. If anyone knows how to behave, it's Dr. Benjamin Dameroff."

"Ethan, I'll be back in no time at all. Please stop nagging at me." Natasha knew she sounded ridiculous, but the clock was ticking. Already she was an hour late for the most frightening appointment of her life. If she wasted any more time, she might have to pay an enormous price.

Without allowing her husband to say another word, she slipped out of the room, grabbed her bag, and ran out to the elevator. As she waited for it to arrive, she fumbled through her wallet, looking for the white piece of paper that held her instructions. There it was, finally, folded any number of times, hidden behind her driver's license and some old photographs of herself and Ethan.

"Central Park West and Sixty-second Street, please," she said breathlessly, smoothing the piece of paper out as she entered a yellow cab. Leaning against the back door of the taxi as it sped uptown, she reread the words above the address: *Tony Kellner, seven o'clock, Friday night.* A burning sensation spread through her stomach, the familiar pain she'd lived with for so many years.

It was a warm night, but Natasha found herself shivering. Her pink linen suit, with its long sleeves and silk blouse underneath, didn't keep her from feeling chilled to the bone. It was the way she'd felt since noon the day before, when she'd first received Tony's phone call. Long time no see, he'd whispered when she got on the line, like an old friend on Christmas Eve. But this wasn't Christmas and he wasn't just an old friend. He was the one person who could tear apart everything she cared about, everything she'd worked so hard for. His voice had become smoother over the years, his manner polished and sophisticated. But his demand to see her tonight hadn't been a request; it had been a summons.

She pursed her lips as she thought about Ben upsetting her plans. Saying she had to take Carlin home and stay a while to take care of her would have been a perfect excuse for leaving Ethan's party. Here she'd been praying for Ben and Carlin to get together again. But why in heaven's name did they have to pick tonight to do it?

More importantly, why had Tony Kellner called her after all these years? Could it be just to say hello? She doubted it. Did he want to rekindle their romance? That just didn't seem possible. He had to know about her marriage to Ethan. They were in and out of the New York papers every few weeks, and Tony said he'd been in New York for years. Besides, as slick as he sounded on the phone, he might still be angry with her. After all, the last time she'd talked to him had been at her mother's funeral, the day she broke up with him. Tony had been miserable. Miserable and furious. Well, she thought, he certainly has gotten over his misery. But what if he's still furious—furious enough to rake up the past? Natasha was seized with a bout of trembling so acute, she noticed the taxi driver looking at her through the rearview mirror. I've got to get hold of myself, she murmured under her breath.

The sense of dread that started with Tony's phone call began to harden into pure terror. What if Tony still blamed her for that phone call, so many years ago? What if he threatened to tell Ethan? Or worse yet, her brother and Carlin? My God, she thought, if they even had a hint of what she'd urged Tony to do, she'd be dead to them. As dead as Kit Dameroff, she thought, as the picture of her vibrant, beautiful mother came to her.

It doesn't matter how frightened I feel, she realized, watching her hands shake as she held them in her lap. Whatever Tony Kellner wants from me, I'm going to give him. No matter how much money he asks for, I'll find some way to get it. Money was what she had plenty of. For the first time she felt grateful at the knowledge of how little money meant to her husband. The truth was she could take almost any amount from their account and he wouldn't even think to ask about it. Suddenly she felt better. That's right, she thought. I'll walk in, hear him out, and give him whatever he asks for. She took a deep breath and tried to compose herself. By the time the cab slowed down in front of the enormous block-long building, she managed to ask the doorman for Tony Kellner without betraying any nervousness at all.

"Well, don't you look lovely for our first date." Tony was leaning in the doorway, staring at her, as she got off the elevator on the twentieth floor.

Natasha felt a stab of fear. The words "first date" terrified her. She thought of responding angrily, but decided that politeness would be more effective. "Hello, Tony. You certainly look all grown-up."

Tony smirked at her. "I'm glad you approve; it should make things much pleasanter for you." He disentangled his long body from the door frame and held out his hand. "After you."

"You have a beautiful apartment," she said too brightly.

"How handy that you like it. You're going to be seeing a lot of it."

Natasha walked toward the large window at the end of the long living room. He's scaring me on purpose, she said to herself. "Your view of the park is terrific. In the winter you must be able to watch the iceskating at Wollman Rink."

Tony came up behind her, standing so close she could feel his breath on the back of her neck. "Why don't you take off your jacket, Tash? You'll be more comfortable."

"Tony, I'm fine. I'm just fine." Natasha heard the hysteria beginning in her voice. I'm going to stay calm, she vowed to herself as she backed away from the window and walked toward a curved white sofa positioned against a wall. "Why is it you've asked me here?"

"We're in no rush, sweetheart. We've got lots of time to catch up." Tony's pleasure was obvious.

Natasha began to walk toward the front door. "My husband is waiting for me. I promised him I'd be home by nine."

"You're not going to be home by nine. Perhaps you'll want to call him." Tony walked over to a white phone on a granite-topped mahogany end table, picking up the receiver and holding it out toward her. "What's the number again?"

"Tony, put the damn phone down. I'm not calling my husband and I'm not staying another minute." She reached a hand toward the doorknob, but he was across the room instantly, blocking her exit.

The smug smile was gone from his face. Now his real feelings were all too evident. Frightened, she backed away from him.

Tony followed her with his eyes, but he didn't move. At first, he didn't even speak. Natasha thought she was as petrified as she could possibly be, but a few minutes later, when he finally began talking, she realized her fears were just beginning.

"Natasha, you owe me," he said, his voice husky with rage. "You've owed me for years, and now you're going to start to pay."

Natasha turned her back to him, slowly reentering the living room, trying to figure out what to say. "Listen, Tony, everything that happened back then, it's all in the past." She pointed to the plush furnishings and lavish oil paintings gracing the walls. "We're both adults now, both successful. We did a terrible thing when we were kids, and now we're both sorry."

"Stop babbling." Tony stood straight in front of her, eyeing her with distaste. "*We* didn't do anything all that time ago. *You* did. You made an idiot of me, and"—he smiled— "incidentally, you killed your mother."

Natasha put her hands over her ears. It was all she could do to keep from screaming.

"Tony," she said, "we were kids. Kids do stupid things. *I* did a terrible thing. You're absolutely right."

"Yes you did." His voice was disturbingly calm. "And now you have to pay."

"Anything. You can have whatever you want. I have money, lots of money." She was begging.

He looked at her disdainfully. "In case you haven't noticed, I already have plenty of money."

"Tony, I know every famous model. I can introduce you to them, fix you up." Natasha couldn't believe herself. How low have I sunk, she thought. Yet she wouldn't take the words back.

"Now, Tash, why would I want another woman with you right here?" His eyes hardened as he approached her. "Let's get a little more comfortable."

Imperiously he walked behind her and lifted the linen jacket from her shoulders, tossing it back onto the couch.

"You're cold," he observed as she began to tremble uncontrollably. "Don't worry, you won't be cold long."

Without another word, he leaned down, kissing her softly on the back of her neck as he passed his arms over her shoulders, sliding his hands down the front of her blouse. "They've held up very nicely," he said, as he unbuttoned the top of her blouse and grabbed under her bra for her breasts.

Natasha was pinned against him from behind, already feeling his arousal as he pasted his body against hers. "Tony, please stop this. I'm not going to sleep with you, if that's what you're thinking. You can just forget it."

Tony continued stroking her breasts as he answered her. "Natasha, not only is it going to happen, but it's going to happen many times. Or would you prefer reading about our childish prank in the tabloids? Your husband should get a real kick out of that." His hands trailed down to the waistband of her skirt, digging underneath to the softness of her belly before snaking around to the back where the skirt fastened.

This can't be real, Natasha told herself as he unzipped her skirt. She was desperate to run out of the apartment, away from his clammy hands, his disgusting demands. But if I do, I'll lose everything, she thought, the reality of that sinking in. She felt his hands ease beneath her skirt one more time. My husband, my brother, my best friend. They'll hate me for the rest of my life. Now his fingers were inside her underpants.

I'll have nothing. No career, no life. Tears began to slide down her cheeks. Since she was a little girl disaster had felt only inches away. She had planned so carefully, prepared so diligently so that every pitfall could be avoided. But now disaster was here. And there was absolutely nothing she could do about it.

Tony's fingers began to probe her vagina. With one arm around her breasts, he locked her close, while with the other, he became more insistent, jabbing into her, practically lifting her body off the floor. Suddenly he stopped, wheeling her around so she had to look right at him. When she lowered her chin, he raised it roughly, locking her eyes with his own.

"Why should I do this for you?" he asked. "After all, I could have the pleasure of watching you do it for yourself." Roughly he pulled her skirt to the floor, then tugged at her underpants. "Come on, Tash, let me see what you can do for yourself."

Natasha couldn't move. She stood in the puddle of her discarded skirt and panties, staring at him with wounded eyes. Tony stared back.

"I guess we'll have to save that for another day." He lifted her off her feet, carrying her to the sofa and laying her down on her back. Quickly, he tugged at his pants with one hand while his other arm kept her pinned down. Within a few seconds he was on top of her, peering at her body under the open blouse, the sheer white bra he hadn't bothered to unclasp. "Now, Tash. Let's see how much you've learned."

Natasha began to scream as he rammed himself into her, but he quickly covered her mouth with his hand. She was trapped beneath him, unable to move as he drove into her over and over. Finally he was finished. When he kissed her tenderly, running his tongue around her mouth as if he were tasting a lollipop, she thought she would die.

"Was that as nice for you as it was for me?" Tony might have been talking to a friend, concerned, loving. But his garish smile revealed just how fully he appreciated her pain. "I have a surprise for you, sweetheart."

Oh God, she thought. What else could he possibly be planning?

"Bob." Tony's voice rang out as he raised his head toward a darkened alcove. "It's your turn."

Natasha gasped as a short man with tortoiseshell glasses walked toward the sofa. He was shirtless, clad only in chinos and a pair of brown tasseled loafers, an excess of dark curly hair covering his body.

"How can you make me do this?" Natasha begged Tony.

Silently, Tony withdrew from her and rose up to a standing position. Within seconds, the man had taken Tony's place, his hands eagerly searching her breasts, his tongue engorged in her mouth. Pulling away from her for a moment as he lowered his hands to the zipper of his pants, it was he who finally answered her. "Baby, you're gonna love it."

24

Ben shifted restlessly in the airplane seat, his long legs cramped in the row's narrow confines. He leaned back against the headrest and gazed at the night's blackness outside the plane's small window. The medical journal he'd intended to read on the flight remained unopened in his lap.

The elderly woman sitting beside him had said little so far, but now she looked up from her book and gave him a smile.

"Tight quarters for you, I guess," she offered sympathetically.

Ben turned to her. With a tremendous effort, he summoned up the hint of a smile. "It's all right, really."

"Would it be safe to guess you're a doctor?" she went on, gesturing toward the journal. "Going to Albany on medical business?"

The last thing Ben felt like doing was getting into a conversation. Not today, for God's sake, not while he was on his way to his father's funeral. But he didn't have the heart to be rude.

"No, just family business," he replied, hoping it would end there.

"Oh, are you from Albany?" The woman twisted in her seat to get a better look at him. "My people have been there for over seventy years. What's your name? I'll bet I know your parents."

"Actually, I'm from Westerfield," Ben said. The flight seemed interminable. Would they never get there?

"My sister lives in Westerfield." The woman grew more animated. "Has a blue house on Lookout Lane. You've probably seen it, they always have an American flag out front."

Without meaning to, Ben tuned out her voice as she went on.

He sighed, wondering if it had been better this way, Leonard's dying suddenly of a heart attack. Would it have been easier to deal with if Leonard had been sick for a while, when it would have been obvious that the end was coming? Ben could have prepared himself psychologically. Easier for whom? he admonished himself. This way was quick and relatively painless for his father. It was odd, because there were so many things wrong with Leonard, yet there had never been any sign of heart trouble. That was the last thing Ben would have guessed would kill him. But he'd had a massive coronary as he was walking home from the grocery store, and it had all been over in a matter of minutes. Well, Ben thought unhappily, I'm finally making that trip home to see Dad.

Natasha didn't even know. She and Ethan were off vacationing, traveling around Morocco with no set itinerary and no way for Ben to reach her. Ben frowned. Why am I pretending she'll be grief-stricken? he asked himself. She didn't hate Leonard, of course. She simply didn't care much about him. There was no doubt that of the two of them, Ben was far more upset about losing his father than his sister would be. But she would never have skipped the funeral. She would have been right here beside him on the flight. At the moment, he would have given a great deal for the comfort of her presence.

The woman sitting next to him finally noticed his preoccupied air and abruptly broke off her monologue, returning to her book with a displeased expression. Sorry, Ben thought, suddenly feeling so weary, he barely had the energy to rub his tired eyes.

The funeral was tomorrow at ten. He considered who might be there, old names and faces flashing through his mind in a parade of ghosts from the past. Oh, Dad, you poor bastard, he thought sorrowfully. Here was a guy who never meant anyone any harm, yet his life was full of rotten luck. First, there was old Grandpa Dameroff, that son of a bitch with the two wives. Jesus. Ben shook his head, still marveling after so long at the sheer outrageousness of his betrayal. Then, Dad losing his money and his big house, and having to move to their sad little apartment in Westerfield, the crummy store where he toiled like some kind of invisible clerk, his savings disappearing with Margaret Wahl. Kit's death was the final blow. After that, it was as if Leonard had simply been marking time. Just getting frail, the aches and pains coming one after another; above all, he was alone.

Christ, thought Ben, without Carlin, that's where I was probably headed. Letting the years slide by, pretending it was all right because I had my work, but always by myself when it came down to it.

After the night of Natasha's wedding, he had been forced to face the truth of it. Carlin had infuriated him, but she'd also made him feel the passion he didn't know he was still capable of. He couldn't go on pretending that what he had with Sara Falklyn was anything more than a pleasant convenience. It wasn't fair to either Sara or him, and he'd ended it.

Carlin was the only woman he loved, it was as simple as that. Suddenly, he felt a frantic need to be with her. But, of course, it was too soon after the shooting for her to travel.

"We're beginning our descent now." Blessedly, the pilot's voice interrupted his thoughts. "We should be on the ground in just a few minutes."

Ben took a deep breath. This was a time to be thinking about his father, not himself.

The plane finally came to a stop. The woman next to him gathered up her purse and coat. Ben gave her a smile, which was met with a stony look as she turned and left. He retrieved his bag from the overhead compartment, then made his way off the plane. Outside the terminal, he headed to the taxi stand and got into the first cab in line.

"Well, I'll be damned. Ben Dameroff."

Startled, Ben looked at the taxi driver who had just spoken. He was in his mid-thirties, with a long thin face and brown hair.

"Don't recognize me, huh?" The man twisted around in his seat and extended his hand. "Joe Lenstaller. You know, from high school."

Ben took a closer look, now able to envision the boy this man once had been. He'd barely known Joe back in high school—Joe must have been a year or two behind him—but he recalled seeing him around.

"How are you?" Ben shook his hand.

"I'm okay, thanks." Joe nodded. "Driving a cab, making a living. Never left the old place. Not like you." He took in Ben's suit. "Heard you became a doctor. Good for you, buddy. You made something of yourself."

Embarrassed, Ben wasn't quite sure how to respond. "Thanks."

Joe's face grew somber. "But you're here for your dad's funeral. I'm real sorry about his passing."

Seeing Ben's expression of surprise, Joe hastened to explain.

"Our dads played pinochle together, that's how I know. They were in a game with two other guys every Thursday night. They must have had that game going ten years at least."

"Really?" Ben had no idea his father played pinochle at all, much less was part of a standing game. Good for you, Dad, he thought.

"Nice guy, your father. In fact, I was planning on taking *my* dad to the service tomorrow." Joe paused for a moment respectfully, then spoke again. "I guess you want a lift back to Westerfield, huh?" He faced front again and looked thoughtfully at Ben in the rearview mirror for what seemed like a long time. "Ben Dameroff," he finally murmured. "Oh, God, Jeez."

Ben looked at Joe questioningly. But Joe turned the key in the ignition without saying anything else. It was a full ten minutes before he spoke again. Then, as if nothing had happened, he resumed his small talk, catching Ben up on the whereabouts of their former classmates.

They pulled in front of the apartment complex. The meter read sixteen dollars. Ben reached for his wallet.

"Hey, forget it," Joe protested.

"Come on, now." Ben sat forward, attempting to hand a twenty-dollar bill to Joe. "Please."

"No way."

Ben smiled and dropped the money on the front seat next

to Joe. "Thanks, but I can't let you do that. . . . See you to-morrow morning?"

Left standing on the sidewalk once Joe had pulled away, Ben stopped to look at the run-down, dirty building. This was the moment he had been dreading. Slowly, he entered and rode the elevator upstairs.

He supposed he should have expected it, but he was still sadly surprised by how dilapidated and depressing the apartment was. Clearly, Leonard had never thrown anything out or bought anything new, and the furnishings were old and shabby. Ben wandered around the clutter aimlessly, throwing out old newspapers and junk mail here and there, but mostly picking things up and putting them down again, not yet ready to start packing it all away. This was the sum of both his parents' lives, all they'd left in the world. Threadbare chairs and old dishes, not a lot more. A bunch of useless stuff that could be gotten rid of in an afternoon.

In his parents' room, he opened the closet door, flipping through Leonard's few suits and shirts, everything worn to the point of shapelessness. Off to the side, he spotted something he'd never noticed when he'd still lived here. Leonard had kept a few of Kit's dresses. Ben took them out of the closet with a sad smile. Untended for so many years, they hung limply on the hangers, the colors washed out. They gave off a musty scent. He remembered all three of them: the pale blue one she'd worn so often, the one with the red and yellow flowers she put on when she was going someplace a little bit special, and the black one with sequins for important occasions. The sight and feel of the dresses in his hands instantly brought her back to him. Hanging them up again, he was overcome with sorrow—for himself, for both his parents.

He spent a sleepless night in his old room, uncomfortable in the hard, narrow bed that was too short for him now, painfully aware of the thin, worn sheets and blankets, the discolored curtains and wallpaper. By the moon's light, he stared at the pennants on the wall and his old desk, his old schoolbooks messily shoved into the bookcase nearby. Everything was faded, as if it were slowly disappearing. It was a relief when the dawn came and he could get dressed and go out to a nearby coffee shop for breakfast.

* * *

"I love you, too. See you in a couple of days."

Ben hung up the phone, glad he'd been able to catch Carlin. Their conversation was brief, but it made him feel better just to hear her voice. Then, steeling himself, he went into the room where people were beginning to gather. His eyes immediately went to the plain brown casket at the front. He'd been in earlier that morning to see it and to sign the necessary papers for the burial. They had opened the coffin, giving him one last chance to say good-bye to his father. Ben had stared quietly at Leonard, lying peacefully, his arms at his sides, dressed in his best suit.

"Such a lovely man." A gray-haired woman he didn't recognize came up to him. "I'll dearly miss him."

Ben racked his brain, but he didn't have a clue who she might be. Maybe an old customer from the store. He thanked her and she moved away, leaving him on his own. He glanced around the room. Nearly twenty people had come to the service but he knew only a few of them. There was Lillian Squire talking to a couple across the room. He started to walk over to her when he was caught up short by the sight of J. T. Squire coming toward him in his wheelchair, a warm smile on his face.

Ben clenched his fists even as he told himself to relax. J.T. was the last person in the world he expected to see at his father's funeral. Had he gotten over the insane notion that the Dameroffs were to blame for his being crippled? Ben knew that he blamed Kit, Leonard, and, somehow, even him for what happened. J.T. hated them all. But maybe he'd come to understand how wrong that was. Maybe he'd even grasped that he held some responsibility himself by being in that motel room with Kit. No, Ben decided bitterly, that was probably too much to expect from old J.T.

"A terrible day, Ben, a terrible, terrible day." J.T. looked up at him from the wheelchair, shaking his head forlornly.

Ben took a closer look at him. J.T.'s complexion was gray, the skin slack around the jaws, with bags under his eyes. The black hair J.T. had always been so proud of was still thick and as dark as ever, obviously dyed. It was clear he had once been handsome, but the deep frown lines around his mouth etched in over the years gave him a nasty expression that took away from what attractiveness might otherwise have remained. As far as Ben was concerned, the face now reflected the man. He was reed-thin, dressed in a navy blazer and neatly pressed gray slacks, but the collar of his shirt hung loosely around his neck. His bony knees jutted out from under his pants as his useless legs lay pressed together, tilted over to one side of the chair.

Ben was torn between pity and the desire to choke him. But if the man had the decency to pay his respects, Ben could be decent back.

"Yes, J.T., it is terrible" was the best he could manage.

"Where's your sister?" J.T. asked, making no effort to hide his curiosity. "Why isn't she at her own father's send-off?"

Ben flinched. "She's traveling. Unfortunately, she can't be reached."

J.T. nodded. "Such a shame. She should be here, of course." He gave Ben a wily smile. "I myself wouldn't have missed this for the world."

You son of a bitch. Ben took a step back, trying to contain his anger. The bastard had come to gloat.

Ben kept his voice low. "Maybe you can learn something from my father today, J.T. Because you know so little about what it is to be a real husband and a real father. In fact, you know pretty much nothing about what it is to be any kind of a real man."

He walked away, although not before he saw the fury flash in J.T.'s eyes. Ben was somewhat startled; he had never quite realized the depth of J.T.'s hatred for him.

He spotted Joe Lenstaller in the doorway, escorting a frail older man who was clearly his father. That must be Leonard's pinochle partner, Ben thought, although he seemed much older than Leonard had been, probably in his eighties. Glad for the distraction, he moved toward them. As he approached, the older man was pulling his arm away from Joe and lost his balance. He fell, hard, onto the marble floor just beyond the carpet, and let out a cry of pain.

Ben hurried over and knelt beside him as Joe started to lift his father up.

"Wait a second, Joe," Ben said, gently but expertly feeling

along the man's arms, legs, and hips. A man this elderly and fragile could easily break a bone in a fall. As he checked, Ben spoke soothingly to the frightened man. "It's okay, Mr. Lenstaller, you're fine. Nothing to worry about."

He and Joe helped him to his feet. "Ben, I'm sorry," Joe said. "You've got enough to deal with today. Thank you, but please don't worry about us anymore."

"Don't be ridiculous, Joe," Ben responded. "If there's anything I can do . . ." He looked at the elder Lenstaller, who was still shaken. "Are you feeling all right? Why don't we get you some water?"

"I'm okay," the older man managed.

As he was leading them inside, a man stepped out to announce that the service was about to begin.

"Go on," Joe urged. "Thanks."

Nodding, Ben went to sit down in the first row. He gazed at the casket as he heard the sounds of everyone else settling into their seats. Then the rabbi approached the podium and began to speak.

Joe Lenstaller pulled his cab up in front of the red brick apartment building. He hadn't called ahead, but he was pretty sure he would find Ben inside; he'd still have plenty of things to take care of after the funeral yesterday. Joe remembered the unpleasant process of packing up after his mother's death. But he hoped he could persuade Ben to take a break. The time to tell him was now or never.

Ben appeared surprised to see him, but Joe was relieved to note he didn't look annoyed at the intrusion. Dressed in jeans and a white shirt with the sleeves rolled back, he was, just as Joe had guessed, in the middle of filling up cartons and huge black trash bags.

"Hey, Ben," Joe said as he entered, "I know you're busy, but I wanted to get you out for a break. Buy you a beer, or at least a cup of coffee."

"Thanks, Joe." Ben smiled. "That's nice of you."

Joe shrugged. "Hell, it's the least I can do after what you did for my dad and all."

Ben waved it off. "Come on, I didn't do anything."

"Okay, okay, whatever you say. But let's get out for a few minutes."

"Sounds good to me." Ben grabbed his jacket, rolling down his shirtsleeves. "I have to admit I'm getting punch-drunk by now from packing."

They headed toward the coffee shop a few blocks away, the same one Ben had eaten breakfast at the day before. As they walked, Joe pointed out changes in the neighborhood, telling Ben how many shops had closed or changed hands, and how the few jobs available in Westerfield had dwindled with every year.

Sliding into a booth at the restaurant, Joe called out to the waitress to bring them some coffee and two pieces of cherry pie.

"The pie is exactly what you need," he told Ben. "Trust me."

Ben laughed. "I think you're right."

Settling in, Joe gave him an admiring look. "So you really left this hole and became a doctor. Even after your dad lost all that money with the Wahl dame."

Ben was taken aback. "Is there anything about me you don't know?"

"Come on, Ben," Joe said offhandedly, "everybody knew about Margaret Wahl running off with those families' savings. It was no secret."

"I guess not," Ben reflected.

"But it didn't stop you. You went on to college and med school, the whole bit."

The waitress set down two steaming cups of coffee. Joe put four cubes of sugar in his and reached for the metal pitcher of milk. "Still, I suppose you were mighty happy when she was arrested."

Ben stopped stirring his coffee. "Are you serious? I haven't heard anything about her since it happened."

"You're kidding." Joe raised his eyebrows in disbelief. "Yeah, she was arrested in Pennsylvania a few years back. Pulling the same kind of scam, but this time they got her. She went to jail."

Ben shook his head, taking it in. "That's good, Joe. It's so long ago, it's like a bad dream now. But back then it seemed like that woman had wrecked my life forever." He went on, almost as if he were thinking out loud. "I was never quite the happy-go-lucky kid, but she sure—"

He caught himself up short. "Sorry. Those days are long gone." Raising his spoon, he gave a flourish. "And justice has been served. Let's celebrate." He turned to the waitress who was passing by their table. "Miss? Could you make those pies à la mode?"

Joe grinned. "So, tell me, where do you live now? In New York, I suppose."

"Manhattan," Ben said with a nod. "The East Side."

Joe hesitated. The perfect opening. He took a deep breath. "I know another kid from around here who's living there now. Tony Kellner. Remember him?"

"Sure," Ben replied. "My sister's old beau. In fact, I've seen him. Carlin is sort of friendly with him, although I'm at a loss to know what she likes about the guy. He doesn't seem like much to me. Never did."

"Carlin Squire?" Joe's eyes opened wide. "Are you two still together?"

Ben smiled. "With about a hundred-year break, yes, we're back together. This time for good, I hope."

Joe looked down at his coffee unhappily. "Holy Jeez," he muttered.

The waitress brought their plates of pie. Ben watched Joe, waiting for him to speak again. But he said nothing.

"Joe, that's the second time you've gone all quiet on me like that," Ben finally said. "There's something going on here, but I can't figure what."

Joe looked up at him and took a bite of pie, chewing slowly. "Good pie, isn't it?" he asked, as though he hadn't heard Ben. He paused. "You know, back in high school, I was just about the biggest jerk around."

If Ben were unprepared for this abrupt change in subject, he didn't show it. "We were all jerks, I would say," he replied with a smile.

"Nah, not like me," Joe went on. "I was always goofing off in school, spending my money on fancy clothes I didn't need, drooling over girls I couldn't have. And I was lazy, too, I really was."

"Hey, those aren't exactly crimes," Ben said. "You're being hard on yourself."

"No, really, I was kind of a creep." Joe hesitated. "Like, I had this motel job, working the front desk. And I used to"—he faltered, then forced himself to go on—"listen in on the switchboard, stuff like that."

"Yes?" Ben's tone grew quieter as he realized that this was leading somewhere.

"I worked two nights a week plus Saturdays at the Starlight Motel. To get money for clothes, mostly." Joe stopped.

"The Starlight Motel," Ben repeated. He nodded. Then he put down his fork and waited, not moving a muscle.

Joe continued, the words coming more painfully now. "So this one night I'm at the front desk and a call comes in, asking to be connected to one of the rooms. I put the call through. But I listen in. And suddenly, the guy's voice changes, he makes it sound like he's older. He's telling the lady on the phone that there's been a car accident."

"The lady," Ben echoed. "My mother."

Joe took a deep breath. "Yes. I mean, I knew your mother and Mr. Squire were coming there. I'd seen them for a few weeks. But I never told anybody, not anybody at all."

Taking a sip of coffee, Joe pieced together his next words. "I mean, I considered telling them it was all a joke, ringing the room myself after they hung up. But then they came tearing out of the place and took off in his car." He hesitated, uncertain if he should go on. "Where I sat, I couldn't see the exit from the parking lot to the road. But I heard the crash, and I knew right away what happened."

Ben only looked down into his coffee.

"I know I should have told somebody, Ben, I know I should have," Joe said agitatedly. "But I was a kid, and I was embarrassed 'cause I'd been listening in, doing something wrong. Do you understand? I was ashamed and afraid I'd lose my job."

Ben spoke slowly, without emotion. "It doesn't matter much, Joe. It's not like you knew who it was."

"But I *did* know who it was," Joe said emphatically. "I knew right away."

Ben stared at him.

"It was Tony Kellner."

All the color drained from Ben's face. "Tony Kellner? You're talking about Natasha's boyfriend?"

"He had that stupid southern accent for so long after he moved here. As soon as I answered the call, I recognized his voice. But when he was talking to your mom, he changed his voice completely. You wouldn't have known it was him in a million years."

"*He* made that call?" As the idea sunk in, Ben's words were loud and angry. "*Are you sure?*"

Joe nodded miserably "When I saw you in my cab yesterday, I realized you had a right to know. I mean, I always told myself it didn't make any difference. Nothing was going to bring back your mother or make that J. T. Squire walk again. But you're a nice guy and . . ."

Ben's face seemed to have turned to stone. When he spoke this time, his tone was icy. "There's no mistake? Tony Kellner?"

"There's no mistake," Joe said sadly. "All I can do is say I'm sorry I never told you before."

"I understand."

Without another word, Ben slid out of the booth and walked toward the door. Joe watched him leave. He felt the guilt all over again, feelings he had forgotten about. But he was glad he'd gotten it off his chest. Maybe it's years too late, he thought, but at least I did the right thing. He swallowed hard. I hope.

25

Grinning broadly, Ben practically bounded across the threshold as Carlin opened her door to let him in.

"Hello, sweetheart girl," he said tenderly, coming forward to take her in his arms. "I can't tell you how good it feels to see you."

Her arms went around his neck. "Feels like years instead of days since you left. I'm so sorry I couldn't be at the funeral with you."

They exchanged a long kiss, momentarily lost in each other, until Ben finally pulled away.

"How do you feel?" he asked, his hands on her shoulders as he searched her eyes.

"I'm fine, really and truly." She grinned. "Don't look at me as if I'm going to break."

"Yes? Not too much pain?"

"My biggest problem is being cooped up in this apartment for so long. I'm going stir-crazy."

Ben encircled her waist with his arms. "So," he said seriously, "if you're feeling fine, exactly how fine would you say fine is?" He kissed her lingeringly on the mouth. "Fine enough for that?"

"Yes, definitely," she answered, smiling. "More, please."

His lips went to her throat, then slid lower as he opened the top button of her blouse and his tongue delicately traced the rise of her breasts.

"Fine enough for this?" he asked.

"Ummm. Absolutely," she murmured.

His mouth never leaving her, he ran his hands over her breasts and down her waist, reaching around to unzip her skirt. They both heard the skirt fall to the floor. "What about this?"

He unbuttoned her blouse and slipped it off her shoulders. "More than fine enough," she whispered.

Their mouths met again as she helped him take off his jacket and tie. She untucked his shirt from his pants and opened it, running her hands along his chest. "And you?" she said. "How do you feel about this?"

"I feel pretty good about it." Ben reached around and picked her up in his arms like a baby. He carried her toward the bed. "Do you think we can—"

"We have to," she interrupted softly. "I couldn't stand it if we didn't."

Ben gently deposited her on the bed, then hurriedly removed the rest of his clothes.

"I could look at you, hold you, forever," he said, lying down alongside her, helping her slip off her bra and underpants. "All I wanted while I was away was to be with you. I love you so much."

She ran her hands along his chest and shoulders, swept up by the sensation of touching him again. How was it possible that every time was as thrilling as the first? Softly, she kissed his face, his neck, sliding down the length of his body, her lips roaming along his chest to the hard flatness of his stomach. She slid her hands around to his buttocks. Her breasts brushed against the velvet hardness of his penis and she heard him groan. He reached down, pulling her up so he could kiss her mouth hungrily.

Their kisses grew more intense. He cupped her breasts, gently stroking and teasing the erect nipples, then brought his mouth to them, leisurely sucking first on one, then the other. The sensation of his warm tongue was unbearably exciting.

"Ben . . . ," she whispered.

"God, I love you." His voice was a husky whisper in reply as his hands trailed down her stomach to stroke the soft insides of her thighs. As he kissed her breasts, her belly, her thighs, his fingers explored her welcoming wetness, sliding in and out so slowly she could only moan with the pleasure of him.

She gasped as his tongue found her center, caressing her

with long, slow licking. Then, suddenly, he gripped her buttocks, burying his face in her as if he couldn't get enough. His tongue moved faster and faster, and she writhed beneath him, her hands in his hair, holding him to her, the pressure inside her mounting. She wrapped her legs around his back, her breath coming in short gasps. Not moving his mouth away, he slipped two fingers inside her. She felt herself explode, crying out as the waves of her passion rocked her. Ben slowed down, holding her around the waist until her savage shuddering subsided.

He moved up beside her and they lay quietly, arms and legs intertwined, Carlin's breathing returning to its normal rate. She gave a deep sigh of satisfaction, turning to look into his eyes as her finger traced the outline of his jaw.

"God, Ben, that was . . ."

"Just the beginning, I hope." He brought his mouth close to hers, savoring her. Then he lightly brushed his lips against hers. "There's no way to get enough of you."

In response, she put her hand behind his head and brought his mouth to hers again, this time kissing him deeply. She wrapped one leg around his, and gently pressed against him, rolling over with him so that he was on his back and she was above him. Then she sat up, her hands stroking his chest.

His eyes locked with hers as his hands ran along her narrow waist and up to her breasts. "So beautiful . . ."

Reaching down between them, she stroked him gently, seeing how much he wanted her, feeling her own desire growing again. She guided his penis to her, touching him with more urgency. With delicious slowness, she lowered herself onto him. For a moment she sat perfectly still. Then, she began to move above him, almost imperceptibly at first, then faster and faster, harder, her hands on his shoulders, her body controlling his.

"*Jesus.*" Crying out with the exquisite torture of it, he suddenly reached to grab her at the waist, taking control. He held her tightly against him, preventing her from moving at all as he thrust deeply. Moaning, she dug her nails into his shoulders.

Suddenly, he stopped once more and, still inside her, sat up, hugging her to him. Her legs went around his waist and they rocked together. Frantically, their mouths met, their kisses ravenous as they drove themselves on and on.

Carlin's body trembled with the force of spasms overtaking her. *"Ben ..."*

He held her against him and together they let their release come, lost to everything but each other. When it was finally over they stayed locked in their embrace for a long while, her face buried in his neck, neither of them wanting it to end.

Their breathing still ragged, they lay down together again. Carlin snuggled into the crook of his arm.

Tenderly, he reached over to wipe her hair, damp with perspiration, away from her eyes. "Are you all right?"

She smiled up at him, running her hand along his arm. "All right doesn't even come close."

He grinned. "Well, actually, I meant your stomach. That kind of activity wasn't exactly what I would have prescribed for a postop patient."

She laughed. "Hey, I've got my doctor here with me if there's a problem, right?"

"Absolutely."

She raised herself up on one elbow. "It just dawned on me that you must be starving. If your plane got in at five and you came straight here, you haven't had anything since lunch." She glanced at the clock by the bed. "It's after eight."

"A little hunger was a small price to pay to see you," he said. "But I wouldn't argue with the idea of getting something to eat."

"Should we order in Chinese food? The place down the block is like lightning."

"Perfect." Ben hopped up. "Direct me toward the menu. I'll call while you rest. The truth is that was a bit of overexertion for a woman in your condition, you know."

"In my condition?" Carlin echoed with a laugh. "You make it sound like I'm pregnant."

For a brief moment, the two of them looked at one another as the significance behind Carlin's words sunk in, each one envisioning the situation in which those words would be true. They both smiled.

A half hour later, they were happily ensconced under the covers, manipulating chopsticks and balancing plates heaped high with steaming food on their laps, an array of white take-out containers on a bed tray.

Carlin reached for her glass of soda next to the bed and looked over at Ben. "I'm so happy you're home."

"Not as happy as I am." He picked up the container of sesame noodles for a second helping.

"Was it awful?" Her expression turned somber. "I still wish you'd let me come with you. I was well enough to travel up there."

He shook his head. "Thank you for wanting to go, but you just didn't need to make a long trip like that."

Carlin was quiet for a moment. "I feel so sad about your father. It's been so long since I last saw him, but I always liked him, you know that."

She sighed. "God, Ben, everything from Westerfield is slipping away, as if our past never even happened. Every time I talk to my mother, something else from the old neighborhood has closed, burned down, just disappeared. Having your father go . . ."

Ben nodded. "I know. It's as if the past is just disintegrating into dust."

Carlin took another bite of food. "Maybe it's that way for everyone who leaves a small town. Maybe it always seems as if the world you grew up with has been stamped out of existence once you walk away from it."

They were quiet for a minute.

"You know, honey," Ben said carefully, "I want to talk to you about something out of the past. It's important."

"Something good or bad?" she asked lightly.

Ben spoke unhappily. "Not something good."

Carlin tilted her head. "Are you up to telling me? Would you rather wait?"

"It's about Tony Kellner.'"

Carlin was instantly on guard, although she kept her expression neutral. "Um-hmm," she said noncommittally.

"You're still seeing him now and then?" Ben asked.

"Now and then," she repeated carefully. It was important to maintain the secrecy of any undercover operation, but the fact that Ben knew Kellner meant she'd had to be especially careful not to let anything slip. "We're having lunch tomorrow as a matter of fact."

"Carlin." Ben looked pained. "Tony Kellner made the phone call. *He* made the phone call."

She looked puzzled. "What phone call?"

"To the Starlight Motel."

Carlin put her chopsticks down and stared at her plate for a moment, then repeated his words as if unable to comprehend them. "Tony Kellner made the call to our parents?" She shook her head. "No, no. It's not possible."

Ben turned slightly to lean closer to her. "Yes, it *is* possible. It's true. I saw Joe Lenstaller in Westerfield. You probably don't remember him from high school, but he was there. He worked at that motel back then, and he *listened in* on the phone. He knows it was Kellner. He told me himself."

Carlin stared at him. "Back when Tony was Natasha's boyfriend?"

Ben nodded.

Her voice was practically a whisper. "But why?"

"I don't know. A prank?"

Carlin looked away. Suddenly, she set her plate on the night table and got out of bed.

"It's pretty hard to believe, Ben, I have to tell you," she said coolly as she got her robe from the closet and slipped it on. "Excuse me for a minute. I'm going to the bathroom. I'll be right back."

Without waiting for a reply, she walked across the room as slowly as she could manage. It was difficult to resist the urge to run. She'd barely opened the bathroom door and gotten inside when she started gasping for breath, her composure deserting her altogether. Without warning, the wound in her stomach began to ache. She sank down onto the edge of the bathtub, feeling the hot wetness of tears on her cheeks.

Tony Kellner wasn't just the head of a burglary operation. He was the one who had destroyed their childhoods, blown their families to bits. And she was in the midst of befriending him as part of an undercover operation, having to make nice to him and win his trust and affection. It was one thing to buddy up to him when it was just a job. But it was another thing to go on doing it now that Ben had told her this.

She tried to clear her head and think, but it was impossible to focus. She was getting so close to making the case, she could feel it in her bones. This was exactly when her intimacy with Kellner counted most. But had he put her father in a wheelchair and killed Ben's mother? If it were true, she couldn't imagine how she could continue. She pictured her father and Kit Dameroff in that room, answering the telephone and running in fear out the door, replaying it in her mind's eye just as she had a thousand times since it happened. But this time, she envisioned Ben's mother talking to Tony Kellner, imagined him on the other end of the phone pretending to be a cop, then hanging up and laughing gleefully as her father and Kit raced out to the car. She heard the crash in her mind, could almost taste the blood that she'd later learned had been splattered everywhere. Bile rose in her throat. I could kill him with my own two hands, she thought.

Carlin stood up and went over to the sink to splash some cold water on her face. She opened the medicine cabinet to find the jar of aspirin and quickly took two.

Of course she knew what she would do. She would go right on with her undercover work. She was a cop and she would never go outside the law for revenge, even if it was for her own family. That could never happen; she could never permit it to happen. Nor would she back out in the middle of a job.

Her mind clicking, she was already assessing the situation. There was no way to prove he made the call, no way to make him pay through the system for what had happened so long ago. All she had was the chance to catch him at what he was up to now and make him pay dearly for that. It would tear her apart, but when she got back to work, she would face him just as she'd been facing him up until now. She'd be the best friend this bastard ever had, and sooner or later she'd crucify him.

She glanced in the mirror to be sure she appeared composed before leaving. She didn't want to hide out in here too long; Ben would wonder what had happened to her. Her hand on the doorknob, she paused. What the hell would she tell him? Maybe she *could* confide in him about the investigation. But even as the thought crossed her mind, she dismissed it.

Given how angry Ben was about Kellner now, it was too risky. Unhappily, she opened the door.

Ben was relieved to see Carlin come back to the bed. He had put his plate aside and was just sitting there quietly, waiting for her. He'd assumed she would be shaken by the news, and she had seemed to be at first. But he was confused by her sudden coolness and the way she'd just gotten up and left.

"Are you okay?"

"Of course, darling." Carlin gave him a slight smile as she slipped off her robe and climbed back in bed beside him.

"So now you know about him." Ben's voice grew tight. "What I can't understand is how this guy has the nerve to want to get friendly with you."

Keeping her voice casual required every ounce of willpower she had. "It's strange, it really is. Interesting."

It was Ben's turn to stare at her. "Are you out of your mind?" he asked in disbelief. _"Interesting?"_

She went on, her stomach churning. "Well, yes. It's an interesting theory."

He threw back the covers angrily and got up, pulling on his pants without a word. Buckling his belt, he looked hard at her. "Perhaps you didn't follow," he said in a clipped tone. "We're talking about the man responsible for my mother's death, the reason your father is a bitter cripple." He saw the pain flash in Carlin's eyes. "But this was just a sweet young boy playing a little joke, right? No reason for you two not to pal around."

The bed suddenly felt cold. Carlin pulled the covers up. She had to force herself to speak, struggling to keep her words measured. "You haven't proved he was the one. All you've got is some kid who says he was eavesdropping. That's no case."

Ben clenched his jaw in anger. "Stop it, Carlin. Whatever you're doing, stop it right now. I'm not buying this."

She looked away. She should certainly have known better than to treat Ben like a gullible child. Desperately, she cast around in her mind for some other way to justify the unthinkable. But she needed time to figure out how to deal with this.

"You could be right, and I'm being irrational," she said to him gently. "Listen, maybe I can't take it all in so suddenly.

Or maybe I can't face my real feelings about it." She hoped he couldn't see what agony these lies were for her. "I don't know . . . ," she trailed off.

"Well, *I* sure as hell don't know." Ben's mouth was set in a tight line. "It's not that I want you to be miserable and suffer, but Carlin"—he searched for the right words—"all this time, we've waited to know who was responsible. I'd pretty much given up on ever finding out. Now we know. You can say there's no proof, but I believe Joe Lenstaller. The way I felt when he told me—you don't seem to feel anything at all. No anger, no grief, no desire to strike back. What's going on with you?"

She looked at him helplessly, not trusting herself to say a word.

He looked back at her, as if he were seeing her for the first time. "I guess I assumed we shared the same feelings about what happened. But obviously I don't know what you feel about it. Somehow, we look at this very differently."

"Ben, please, let's not allow this to ruin our evening. Come back to bed." She gestured toward the food. "Let's finish our dinner."

Ben studied her for another moment, then nodded resolutely. He sat down on one side of the bed and picked up his plate from the night table.

"Fine." He resumed eating his dinner, which was now completely cold. Her appetite gone, Carlin nonetheless retrieved her plate as well and forced herself to take a bite of moo shu chicken, trying to hide her misery. She wondered how she would get through the rest of the evening. Ben thought she had no feelings, no reaction to his terrible news. She pictured her father, so thin and pale, bitterly wasting his life in a wheelchair, all because of an idiotic prank. The truth was she wanted to shriek in fury. Most of all, she wanted to see Tony Kellner burn in hell. But all she did was sit there, watching Ben pretend to be absorbed in his food. He was right there beside her, but it felt as if he'd gone a million miles away.

"Harry, did I call too early for a little chat?"

"Come on, Cambridge, in this house there's no such thing

as too early. The kids like to greet the dawn every day. They think they're damned roosters or something."

Carlin laughed. It was the last thing she'd expected to do, given how grim the night before had been. She and Ben had made it through dinner, but he had left shortly afterward, claiming surgery early the next morning. Ordinarily that wouldn't have stopped him from spending the night with her. But after their conversation about Kellner, there was a wall between them that was a mile high.

She had been up most of the night, debating whether she could tell Ben the truth about why she had to go on being friendly with Kellner. It was nearly 4 A.M. when she'd convinced herself that it was well worth it to violate the secrecy of the operation. Still, a voice inside her insisted that she run it by Harry first.

She'd waited as long as she could before calling, but she knew he must be wondering what she could want at this hour. Pulling her bathrobe around herself more tightly, she sat down on the edge of her bed, wincing at a slight pain in her abdomen as she shifted position.

"I'm sorry to bother you." She hesitated, hearing Harry waiting patiently on the other end of the line. His kids came into earshot, yelling at one another in the background. "It's about Tony Kellner. And Ben."

Harry knew about Carlin's relationship with Ben, although the two had never met. "I'm listening" was all he said.

"Ben went home for his dad's funeral and found out that Kellner was responsible for his mother's death. The same accident that crippled my father."

There was no response on the other end of the phone, but Carlin could almost hear Harry's mind working. She'd told him her father had been injured in a crash, but she'd never explained the exact circumstances. It wouldn't take Harry long to figure out what was going unsaid, but she pressed on.

"Kellner made a phony phone call, pretended to be a cop. He's the one who sent them rushing out into that car crash."

Harry exhaled slowly. "Jesus, you're sure it's the same guy? That's small-world stuff in a mighty ugly way."

"Harry, the question is, can I tell Ben why I have to be buddies with Kellner?" Carlin talked more quickly, wanting to convince him. "He can be trusted with it, I know it. And if I don't tell him, I can't imagine what the hell he's going to think is wrong with me. From his perspective, it's insane for me to be friends with this guy, given what I know about him."

Harry's response was immediate. "No way."

"But Harry, come on, this is my—"

"You make up some excuse, Cambridge, but you don't blow this case by worrying that your boyfriend is going to be teed off at you." Harry's tone made it clear he had no sympathy for her situation. "Too much time and money has gone into this guy. Don't even consider screwing around with it. And let me tell you, I don't like this sudden involvement with your sweetie and Kellner. I better not hear that your guy interacts with Kellner in any way. Keep him far away from this."

"Won't you at least think about it?"

"Here's what I'm thinking about," he said in annoyance. "I'm thinking about the good doctor doing something stupid. He could cause Kellner to leave town, or change his activities somehow. Besides, I don't care how good his intentions are, you can't guarantee me that he won't accidentally leak that there's an investigation. His old grudge could wind up blowing us out of the water."

Carlin had half-expected Harry to react this way, but she was taken aback by his vehemence, his coldness. "Harry, Kellner put my father in a wheelchair."

"So what are you saying?" Harry snapped. "You want off the case? I don't like the conflict-of-interest possibilities brewing here, but you're the best contact I've got with our boy, so I'm overlooking them. But you don't even think about talking on this one. Do we understand one another?"

Carlin bit her lip. Of course. Kellner was Harry's case and he was expecting a big payoff in the department from it. Naturally he'd be furious that she would even consider talking about it.

"You're right, Harry," she finally said, knowing better than to waste time arguing with him. "I won't say anything."

His tone instantly became more jovial. "Attaway. Listen,

I'll see you when I see you, but now I've gotta try and force my kids to eat something before they run out of here today."

"See you, Harry."

Carlin sighed heavily as she hung up. She couldn't go behind Harry's back and tell Ben, not after the years she'd spent with Harry and the trust she'd worked so hard to earn. Ben would just have to trust *her* and realize she knew what she was doing.

She stood up and headed for the shower. Sure, she thought sarcastically, Ben won't have any problem accepting this. After all, what's a little senseless death among friends?

Marilyn Floyd walked into the kitchen just as Harry was hanging up the phone.

"Who was that?" she asked.

"Just Carlin," he answered.

Reaching for the carton of orange juice in the refrigerator, Marilyn paused and looked over at her husband.

"Isn't it a little early in the morning for Wonder Woman to be walking all over you?"

"Knock it off, Marilyn," Harry snapped. He turned away, but his wife's barb stung.

What would the big boys think if they knew their superstar girl had just made a request no amateur would even consider? With her luck, he thought bitterly, they'd probably award her the Nobel prize.

Ben had gotten home just a few minutes before. He was changing out of his suit into jeans and a faded sweatshirt when he heard his doorbell ring. Christ, he was exhausted and didn't feel like seeing anyone. A long day of emergencies hadn't helped any after his dinner with Carlin the previous night. He hadn't slept well when he got home, lying in bed unable to stop thinking about their conversation. It wasn't just that he was puzzled by her reaction to learning about Tony Kellner. He was also shocked at how quickly and sharply it had separated them. Christ, he hadn't even spent the night. Being with Carlin again had been the one thing he'd been longing for the entire time he was in Westerfield. Yet he was so thrown by her reaction to his news, he'd just wanted to be alone.

He recalled their lovemaking earlier in the evening, and the way she felt nestled in his arms. It was a mistake to leave her. Being together was what mattered. He wouldn't let anything separate him from Carlin again; it was a vow he'd made, and he intended to keep it.

Still, it didn't mean *he* was going to let Kellner off scot-free.

The doorbell rang again, more insistently this time.

"Okay, okay, coming," he yelled out as he hurried to pull the door open.

"Hey, big brother."

Ben was happily startled to see Natasha standing in the doorway. Tan and glowing, her long hair cascading around her shoulders, she wore an open trench coat, beneath which she paired a severely starched white blouse buttoned all the way up with the briefest black leather miniskirt. He gave her a hug.

"When did you get back? You were so vague about your plans, I didn't have a clue when you'd turn up."

"We got in last night." Natasha threw her coat down on the couch and sat down. "The trip was incredible. We had such a fantastic time."

Ben sat down in a chair facing her. "Well, you look wonderful. But then again you always do, no matter what."

"The divine thing that is me," Natasha said sweetly.

He laughed.

"Now tell me everything I've missed," she said to him.

The happy expression faded instantly from his face. "Oh, Tash, I'm making idiotic small talk and you don't know."

"Know what?" She looked alarmed.

He spoke gently. "Dad died while you were away. The funeral was on Tuesday. I had no way to get in touch with you. Otherwise I would have told you right away, of course."

Natasha looked somber for a moment, but if she felt any pain at the news, it wasn't evident. "You went to the funeral in Westerfield?"

Ben nodded.

She looked contrite. "I'm sorry I wasn't here for you, Ben. That makes me feel bad, you going there and doing all that by yourself. You dealt with the apartment and everything?"

"It's all taken care of."

She took this in. "That was a lot to get stuck with. I'm really sorry."

When she didn't say anything else, he finally spoke again. "Do you want to know what he died of?"

Momentarily startled, she quickly recovered. "Well, naturally I do. But I assumed it was old age. Natural causes sort of thing."

"He wasn't that old, Tash." Ben tried to keep himself from sounding reproachful. This was the reaction he'd feared from his sister. But there was certainly no point trying to make her grief-stricken if she wasn't. "It was a heart attack. He had it on the street walking home. It was over right away."

"Oh, no, he died right on the street?" she groaned. "What a lousy way to go. Dad's rotten luck holding up as always."

She got up and went to the window to look out, her back to Ben. "He had a sad life and a sad death," she said softly.

Ben waited, but she continued to look out at the view below, keeping her thoughts to herself.

"Tash, there's something else." He leaned forward on the couch. "You remember your old boyfriend, Tony Kellner?"

He thought he saw her back stiffen slightly at the name.

"I remember him," she said without turning around.

"When I was in Westerfield I found out something about him." Ben paused, uncertain how to say it. "He was the one who made the call to the Starlight Motel. He pretended to be a cop and told Mom and J.T. about the fake car accident."

Natasha didn't move, didn't say anything.

"Are you okay?" Ben asked. "I know it's a big shock. But I met a guy back home who actually heard the phone conversation. He knew it was Tony."

Natasha turned to gaze impassively at her brother.

"Ben, does that make any sense to you? He was my boyfriend. Why would he do that to my mother?"

"I don't know," he replied, shaking his head. "I've racked my brain trying to figure that out. All I've got are guesses."

She waved a hand dismissively at him. "Maybe your friend heard something, but I'm sorry, it just couldn't have been Tony. That's impossible."

"No, no, it was," Ben insisted.

She shook her head and spoke slowly, as if she were clarifying a point to a two-year-old. "No, Ben, the guy was mistaken. That just didn't happen." She made a face to indicate how foolish the idea was. "Tony loved me back then. He would never have done anything to hurt me. I guess you were happy to think you found the person responsible, but it's just not true."

Ben ran his hand through his hair. First Carlin, now Natasha. Both of them were acting as if he were off his rocker.

Natasha crossed over to grab her coat.

"I'm sorry, but I've got to run. I just popped in to say hi and invite you and Carlin for dinner tomorrow night. Not at the house, at a new restaurant I found on Twenty-third Street. Will you come? Around nine-thirty?"

Ben was taken aback at the abruptness with which she changed gears, but he tried not to let it show. "I'll have to check with Carlin, but if it's okay with her, we'll be there." He would call her as soon as his sister left.

"Great. I'll call your office with the address." Natasha leaned over to kiss his cheek. "Good-bye, gorgeous doctor brother." She laughed playfully. "How *do* those nurses resist you? Or do they?"

Natasha heard Ben laugh in spite of himself as he closed the door after her. She walked down the carpeted hallway and turned the corner. Leaning back against the wall, she waited for her heart to stop pounding.

As she stepped inside the elevator, she tried to calm herself. Ethan was meeting her at a bar down the block for a quick drink before he went into an all-night editing session. She couldn't let him see her looking shaken like this.

She smoothed her hair and set her face in a pleasant expression. It seemed like the past was determined to catch up with her one way or another. But she was going to do everything in her power to outrun it.

26

Ben ran to beat the changing traffic light at Columbus Circle and turned onto Central Park West. Walking briskly, he spotted the building ahead, the address spelled out in white letters on a dark green canopy. Intent on his destination, he didn't notice Carlin's car parked nearly ten yards beyond the building's entrance.

In the process of eating a bagel, Carlin stopped in mid-bite as she caught sight of Ben approaching. She hadn't told him she was spending the last of her sick leave staking out Tony Kellner's apartment. She slid down in her seat so her face was hidden, letting out a small cry at the stabbing pain the sudden motion caused in her stomach.

His face set with grim determination, Ben yanked open one of the heavy glass entrance doors.

Oh no, she said to him silently, *what are you doing? Please stay away.*

Ben had started across the lobby when the doorman stepped in front of him.

"I'm sorry, sir," he said, the apologetic tone in his voice muted by annoyance at the way this man expected to breeze into his building. "How can I help you?"

Ben stopped. "Please ring Anthony Kellner. Tell him Benjamin Dameroff is here to see him."

He waited as the doorman picked up the house phone and spoke into it. There was a long pause. Finally, the doorman said, "Yes, sir, very good," and hung up. He looked at Ben. "The far elevator at the end of the hall. Twenty D."

"Thank you."

Tony Kellner opened his door with a wide smile. In a quick glance, Ben took in the custom-made shirt, silk tie, and charcoal gray pleated pants that belonged to an obviously expensive suit.

"Well, well, Ben Dameroff," Tony proclaimed, ushering him in. "What a surprise. It's always so nice to get together with old friends. To what do I owe the honor of this unexpected pleasure?"

Ben stepped inside the apartment. The living room was furnished with exquisite antiques, and carefully designed lighting set off the magnificent paintings lining the fabric-covered beige walls. For a moment, Ben was taken aback. He hadn't realized Kellner was quite so well off. It occurred to him that he half-expected the guy would somehow have been punished for his past deed. But in fact, it would appear that, so far in life, he'd been rewarded.

Turning to face Tony directly, Ben spoke sharply. "I'm not here to resume old friendships. You may have been Natasha's boyfriend, but you were nothing to me."

Tony frowned. "You're the one who came to see *me*, Ben," he said with mild reproach in his voice. "I don't know why such harsh words are called for."

Ben recoiled at the phony politeness. "Why don't we just get to the point." He fixed his gaze on the other man. "I know what you did."

"What I did." Tony echoed his words with an amused expression. "Well, that hardly narrows it down for me, old buddy. I've done a lot of things in my life."

The anger rose in Ben. "Cut the crap right here, Kellner. I'm talking about the call to the Starlight Motel. I'm talking about the death of my mother. And about Carlin's father."

Tony nodded, as if a distant memory were slowly returning to him. "Yes, I remember that. Your mother and her father were having a little get-together in that motel. A small party for two, shall we say?"

Ben's eyes flashed. "Whatever *we say*, you scared the wits out of them—"

"Or—you could put it—the pants off them," Tony interrupted in an amused tone. "But, no, I guess the pants were already off them by the time all of this happened."

Ben stared at Tony. "Your little joke drove them straight

into that truck. But now I know." His voice dropped down to a cold whisper.

Tony's expression turned to one of confusion. "What are you going on about, Dameroff? What joke?"

"Cut it out," Ben snapped. "What the hell reason did you have to tell them their children were in a car accident? What kind of son of a bitch are you?"

Tony took a step back as if shocked by the accusation. "Now, listen, I found out about their seamy affair like everybody else did—afterward. But I didn't make any such call, and that's the truth."

"You lying bastard," Ben spat out. "You don't even have the guts to admit you did it. You always were a slimy little loser."

Tony's friendly demeanor vanished. His tone was icy. "What makes you think you can come into my house and start calling me names? Or that I care about you and your petty problems from that crappy little town? Hell, some people might even say the two of them deserved it."

Ben stared at him. If there had been an inkling of doubt in his mind before, it was gone now. "I want an explanation. My sister and I are entitled to one. And so is Carlin."

"Oh, now you speak for Carlin as well," Tony said sarcastically.

"Where do you get off even talking to her?" Ben yelled. "You destroyed all of us. How do you have the goddamned gall? You're keeping far away from her from now on, you understand me?"

Tony seemed to be mulling something over. Then he gave a short laugh. "What makes you think she wants that? Too precious to consort with the likes of me, eh?"

"Stay away," Ben warned, his fury mounting further.

"Now *you* listen to *me*," Tony snapped, his eyes threatening as he moved closer to Ben. "Your adorable Carlin doesn't need any protecting by you. Before you go telling me what a lowlife I am, you look a little closer to home. Carlin's done a few things you might not find perfectly to your liking."

"You've got nothing to say about Carlin that I want to hear," Ben yelled.

"No, I don't guess you want to hear how much I give her

each year, how long she's been on my payroll and on the take from how many others."

Ben felt his fury explode inside him. *"You filthy son of a bitch."*

Tony wagged a finger at Ben, his voice singsong but his eyes menacing. "There you go calling those names again." He folded his arms across his chest. "Not so pleasant to hear, is it, that your beloved Carlin is just a corrupt cop, salting it away for a rainy day. At the rate she's going, she'll be able to retire well before she's sixty-five."

Without thinking, Ben swung with all his might. The impact was so powerful it sent Tony crashing down. He reached out to the couch to pull himself up onto his knees, holding his jaw with his other hand as blood dripped from his split lip onto the white silk sofa.

Ben took a few steps back, his anger unabated, as disgusted with himself now as he was with Tony.

Tony turned his head to look up at Ben. "Get out," he managed to say.

In a few quick strides, Ben was out the door, slamming it behind him. His mind was reeling. The guy had killed his mother and now had the nerve to say ... He couldn't even think about it, it was insane. Seeing Ben approach, the doorman quickly pulled open the door for him. He raced out without a word, not thinking about where he was headed. Carlin taking payoffs. Jesus, what a way for this bastard to deflect the spotlight from himself.

His head down, Ben kept walking, entering Central Park just across the street from the building. He was trying to ignore it, but something in the back of his mind kept pushing forward, demanding to be heard. If Carlin really was on the take from Tony or for whatever reason, wouldn't it explain why she acted so strangely? It would be the best reason in the world to look the other way when she found out what Tony had done in the past, to act as if it simply weren't worth pursuing. If she had a vested interest in keeping Tony happy, she would want no part of Ben's stirring up trouble.

Of course, the whole idea was impossible. Still, Carlin was only an underpaid detective. They'd never discussed exactly how much she made, but like everyone else, he knew cops weren't the highest-paid people in the world. She was single, and had had to take care of herself all these years. For all he knew, she'd also had to take care of her mother and that good-for-nothing father of hers as well; he must have had some pretty steep medical bills.

She'd grown up with very little and she'd given up the opportunity to have something more when she chose to join the police force. Maybe she'd come to regret that decision. Or maybe she'd seen a way to do what she liked and still have a little financial compensation. A long time had passed since their childhood together; was it possible she had changed more than he knew?

He sat down on a park bench. It was ridiculous.

It would explain a lot.

No. This wasn't just anybody, this was Carlin. No.

He leaned forward, burying his face in his hands. He hadn't called Carlin since their dinner two nights ago, despite his promises to himself to make up with her right away. The hospital had paged him just after Natasha left his apartment the day before, and he'd had to go back for an emergency. All this morning he'd been in surgery. As soon as he'd finished operating, he'd headed straight to Kellner's apartment. Now, suddenly, he was wondering if he should call her just yet. Maybe he needed to wait, sort things out in his mind. He couldn't harbor these kinds of suspicions about her, but how could he come right out and ask her?

Let's say I do ask her, he reflected. If she's not taking bribes, she'll deny it. But if she is, she'll deny it just the same. He felt a sickening stab of fear at the possibility that he might not know for sure if he could believe her.

27

Holding the telephone slightly away from her ear, Carlin tried to decipher the message being delivered through Port Authority's public address system at the same time as she registered Ben's unanswered phone, now on its seventh or eighth ring. Her mother's bus would arrive any minute, which would make a real conversation with him impossible for the next couple of days. Damn him, she thought, knowing how unreasonable she was being, how dare he *not* have an answering machine in this day and age.

That's not what's really bothering me, she acknowledged, as she walked away from the phone booth toward the platform where the bus from Westerfield was due to pull in. After all, he might not have an answering machine at home, but that didn't begin to explain why he hadn't returned her calls to his office earlier this morning and twice yesterday. He carried a beeper day and night, and his office staff *never* neglected to give him his messages.

How many days had it been since their unpleasant dinner? Two, three maybe. And not one word from him. So he was angry at her. Well, damn it, she wasn't too pleased either. What the hell was he doing marching into Tony Kellner's apartment yesterday morning? And what the hell was he doing not calling her back?

Carlin looked at her watch and realized her mother's bus was just about due. Better put a happier face on, she thought, although she felt mildly resentful in that quarter as well. It had been weeks since the shooting, yet only now was Lillian coming to see her. Sure, her parents had called every Sunday, although each time Carlin had heard her father's voice in the background five or ten minutes into the call: *It's long dis-*

tance, Lillian. Time is money. Yeah, Dad, she'd felt like saying last time her mother had put J.T. on the line, too bad I
didn't die in the shooting. You could've used all that telephone money on a new tie or something. And Lillian of
course had said nothing back to him, simply hurrying her
conversation along with her daughter, trying to be as nice as
she could without rocking the damn boat.

God, what kind of baby am I turning into? Carlin repri-
manded herself. I'm thirty-six years old and I'm still mad at
my mommy and my daddy. Grow up. Shaking her head as if
she could shake her thoughts away, Carlin walked up to the
gate and stepped outside onto the platform. There it was, the
red bus from upstate New York, rounding the turn. Be nice,
she instructed herself as it came to a stop right in front of her.
Your mother is a wonderful woman, and your father's idiosyncrasies, however unpleasant they may be, aren't her fault.

Lillian was the first passenger to disembark. "Oh, darling!"
Her arms flew around Carlin's neck. "I was so worried about
you." She stepped back to take a better look. "Are you really
all right, dear?"

Carlin hugged her mother in return. How could she have
thought to be angry? "Oh, Mom, I'm fine. In fact, if it
doesn't get too hot in the next day or so, I'll be able to show
you all of New York, walking, running, roller-skating, whatever proof of full health you require."

Suddenly, it felt terrific having her mother right here with
her. Whatever hoops J.T. put her through, Lillian was always
in Carlin's corner. Happily taking her mother's arm, Carlin
walked to the side of the bus and took Lillian's small cloth
suitcase from the bus driver's hands. "So, Mom, what do you
want to see in the Big Apple?"

Lillian smiled conspiratorially. "You know something, I
feel as if I've been living in New York vicariously for the last
fifteen years. I've always loved this city, in movies and
books, that is. I know we have only forty-eight hours, but if
you promise you're really well enough, I'd like to see every
inch from the Bowery to Harlem."

Carlin looked at her with surprise. "How do you know
about either one of those places?"

"Oh, honey, I've been coveting a trip to New York since I

was a teenager. Your father never wanted to come here, even before the accident. I think he likes a smaller arena."

An hour later, Lillian's bag had been deposited in Carlin's apartment and the two women were walking around the boat pond in Central Park. Gleefully, Carlin watched her mother's fascination at the mechanized boats being raced across the placid water. When a little girl tripped and fell right in front of them, she watched in amazement while Lillian lifted the child up, comforting her as she transferred her into her father's arms, falling into immediate and exuberant conversation with the well-dressed man and his highly manicured wife. Within minutes they were deep in the competing philosophies of small-town versus large-city living.

"Now, my daughter and I are off to Zabar's," Liilian exclaimed to the couple, as she took Carlin's arm and led her toward the west side of the park.

"How in the world did you come to hear about Zabar's?" Carlin asked, as they emerged from the park right across the street from the Museum of Natural History.

Instead of answering, Lillian turned and pointed downtown. "The Dakota's just down that way a few blocks, right?"

"Yes, Mom," Carlin answered, smiling now at her mother's unexpected expertise. "You knew that from the murder of John Lennon, right?"

"Well, yes, that too, I suppose. But actually, it was mentioned in *Time and Again*. I read it a few years ago. You know, the Dakota was one of the first buildings built in this neighborhood."

Carlin found herself laughing out loud. As they toured the Upper West Side, going from the food bazaars of Zabar's and Fairway over to Riverside Park, where Lillian requested a viewing of the houseboats at Seventy-ninth Street, then all the way up to Grant's Tomb, Carlin was nearly exhausted while Lillian was still bursting with energy. Even after they walked back down West End Avenue and turned into Carlin's building, Lillian was the one who busied herself making tea and preparing tiny sandwiches of smoked salmon they'd brought from Zabar's.

Carlin relaxed on her sofa, enjoying the sight of her mother eating a sesame bagel for the first time in her life. Lillian's cheeks were still reddened from the long walk; her gray hair, ordinarily so neat and plain, was full and damply curled from the summer humidity. For the first time, Carlin could appreciate how attractive Lillian must have been as a young woman. In Westerfield, none of it seemed to show through. In fact, Carlin could suddenly remember her mother when she herself was only five or six years old—her mother had to have been a few years younger than Carlin was now. But even then her mother had seemed much older. In early photos, J.T. was the one people noticed; Lillian always seemed pallid and worn. Yet look at her today! Where had all that vibrance, all that energy come from?

The phone rang, interrupting Carlin's thoughts.

"Why don't I get it, dear," her mother said, signaling for her daughter to stay put on the sofa. "You've done quite enough for today."

Carlin leaned back, luxuriating in her mother's care.

"Hello." Lillian's voice was sprightly. Yet when she next spoke, her tone had altered, now an apologetic murmur that was all too familiar to Carlin.

"The aspirin's right in the bathroom, in the right-hand drawer, next to the toothpaste. I'm sorry you had so much trouble finding it." Her mother slid down onto a straight-backed chair, her posture suddenly revealing deep fatigue. "No—" She was speaking so quietly now, Carlin could barely hear her. "I'm not due home until the day after tomorrow. . . . Well, perhaps I could, but Carlin has so much planned for me here."

It's unbelievable, Carlin thought, knowing full well who was on the other end of the phone and just what he must have been saying. One day away, no, eight or ten hours away, and her father was already asking his wife to come home. She watched Lillian struggle with herself. Obviously her mother didn't want to leave, but already an expression of resignation was sneaking across her face.

"Let me get back to you later, dear. . . . Yes, I'll call before nine-thirty, I promise. Let me see how much I can accomplish for Carlin before I make any final decisions."

Thoroughly dejected, Lillian hung up the phone. "I'm

sorry, darling, I didn't even put you on the phone with your father."

"Please." Carlin held out her hand, as if warding off a blow. "It's hard enough watching you contend with him. I consider your omission a favor." She saw her mother frown in obvious disapproval. "Sorry, Mom. I shouldn't have said that. I just lack your saintliness when it comes to my father."

"My saintliness?" Lillian was confused. "What on earth do you mean?"

Carlin hesitated. The last thing she wanted to do was offend her mother. "Oh, I guess I mean your ability to put up with Dad. I mean, his selfishness never really bothers you."

Lillian looked at her daughter in amazement. "Is that what you really think? My Lord, I get so angry at your father, well, I don't know what I feel like doing." She gave Carlin a long searching glance. "You're a woman now. I don't have to hide behind platitudes. The truth is I've almost left him any number of times. In fact, before the accident with Kit Dameroff, I got as far as looking for a furnished room a few miles out of town. I was waiting for you to graduate so I could go out on my own."

Carlin was openmouthed. "You mean you knew about the affair?"

"I'd known about your father's behavior for years. But while you were little, there didn't seem to be much I could do about it. Then, when you were a senior in high school, just when I was nearly ready, your father was crippled in the accident. I couldn't leave him then. You never would have forgiven me."

"Never would have forgiven you!" Carlin sat up straighter. For a moment she debated saying the things that were rushing into her head, but she decided to go ahead. "Do you remember Derek Kingsley?"

"Of course I do. In fact, I always wondered what broke the two of you up. He sounded like such an interesting man."

"Mom, it was you who gave me the strength to break up with him. Derek *was* a nice man. In fact, we're still friends. But when we lived together he made a habit of cheating on me. More than once I found him with another woman. And I almost let him get away with it." Carlin chose her words carefully, trying to find a way to say this nicely. "I always saw you as forgiving and understanding. And for a while I had the urge to be the same way, to take what he had to give without expecting the loyalty he obviously couldn't deliver, no matter how much he might have wanted to. But then I pictured you, knitting or cooking or just sitting around looking depressed and sad while daddy went out at night. I couldn't bear to live my life that way. I forced myself to break it off even though part of me wanted to stay in that cocoon forever."

Lillian didn't seem upset at all. In fact, she smiled as her daughter spoke. "I'm very proud of you, Carlin. Amazed, in fact, by your resilience."

Carlin was relieved by her mother's response, glad to see that Lillian looked anything but humiliated. In fact, she was glowing, either from pride in her daughter or from the intimacy of such an unusual conversation. Carlin decided to tell her mother the whole story.

"Would you like to know what I did to break up with Derek?" she asked, a grin on her face.

"What was that, dear?"

Her mother's expectant look turned to an explosion of laughter as Carlin answered. "I mailed all his belongings to the American embassy in Tokyo."

Still laughing, Lillian reached for a tissue to wipe at her eyes, which were tearing in merriment. "I wish I'd had the courage. Actually, I'd give anything to have my own life."

Carlin looked puzzled. "So, why don't you?"

"Oh, everyone in Westerfield would think I was a witch for even contemplating such a thing."

"I, for one, would admire you." Carlin leaned forward and took her mother's hands. "And everyone who knows you in Westerfield would stand up and cheer."

Lillian looked doubtful.

"Who would take care of him, the way he is? I mean, selfish or not, he really can't do much for himself stuck in a wheelchair."

Carlin thought of two patrolmen who'd been injured when she'd been at the precinct in Bedford-Stuyvesant. One had been a widower without any children, the other a confirmed bachelor. She remembered the many discussions surrounding their care when they realized their injuries were permanent. "The Visiting Nurse Service, Mom," Carlin answered gently. "That's what they're for."

She could see that her mother was actually considering her suggestion. Lillian still seemed uncertain, although a hopeful flush had begun to rise on her cheeks.

Carlin pictured her father as he'd been the last time she'd visited Westerfield the year before. Even in his wheelchair, he took the trouble to be perfectly dressed and smoothly combed as Lillian had taken him outside for his daily walk. Knowing she was speaking the truth, she half-whispered her next words, cold as they sounded.

"I bet he gets someone else to fetch and carry before the smell of your perfume fades."

28

"Don't be surprised to hear the words 'Captain Carlin Squire' one day soon," Captain Fallon said, smiling at Carlin, then twinkling at the mayor, seated just to the right of the podium.

Gracie Mansion was filled with officials from both city government and the police department, on hand to congratulate Carlin as she received a special commendation for her work on the Phonestalker case. Standing next to Captain Fallon, Carlin blushed with both pleasure and embarrassment. She tried to catch Harry Floyd's eye as she saw him scowling from the center of the second row of seats, but he was looking past her, seemingly fascinated by the newspaper blowups the mayor's staff had posted on the walls behind the speaker's platform. She couldn't bear to imagine what he must be making of all this praise heaped on the head of his closest colleague.

LONE WOMAN OFFICER THWARTS SERIAL KILLER screamed the headline from *Newsday*, GIRL COP GETS HER WOMAN was the even less dignified banner in the *Post*. Carlin couldn't bring herself to look at those accounts. As far as she was concerned, her hunch on the Phonestalker could have cost innocent bystanders their lives, given what had actually happened on Broadway that terrible night. Even now, more than six weeks after the event, she was still trying to figure out how she could have played it so no one else was endangered by her trap.

But, deserving or not, it was still fun to be the center of attention. Today's ceremony at Gracie Mansion was being covered not just by all the city papers, but by a number of upstate newspapers as well. She knew her mother would get a kick out of reading about her daughter in the *Westerfield*

Herald, which had actually sent a reporter all the way down to Manhattan to cover the proceedings. Carlin smiled as Captain Fallon finished his talk and an array of flashbulbs went off, all directed straight at her.

If only the rest of my life was filled with excitement, she thought ruefully, forcing herself to hold a smile for the mass of cameras. Ben hadn't called once. When today's furor was over, she knew she would go back to feeling the pervasive sadness that had followed her around since that horrible night when Ben had told her about Tony Kellner. If only she'd been free to tell Ben the truth, she thought for the thousandth time. Harry Floyd seemed to have read her mind. Coming up to give her a hug as the ceremony ended, he whispered into her ear.

"Come on, Cambridge. Let's go have ourselves a drunken blowout dinner and make believe life is just dandy."

"So your smile is just as real as mine, huh, Harry?" Carlin whispered back, taking his arm and following him out the door.

"Now let's do some real celebrating," Harry said twenty minutes later as they sat in a darkened corner booth at Bill's, one of the few restaurants on Columbus Avenue to remain exactly as it was pregentrification, forty or fifty years before.

"Here's to you, Carlin. You were right, I was wrong about that Moscow babe."

"Now that's what I call gracious," Carlin replied, laughing. "Listen, if you hadn't trained me right, I never would have been able to get to the bottom of my grocery bill, let alone a murder. Here's to you."

Harry took a long time before answering. "I happen to agree with that," he said finally, taking a swallow from the shot glass in front of him and polishing it all off. "Here's to me," he said in a somber tone, as he lifted the empty glass and waved to the waiter standing against a pillar a few feet away.

"Maybe we should order some food," Carlin suggested. "It wouldn't be all that nice to wind up a celebration by getting sick."

"Sure," Harry answered, turning his attention to the waiter, who was placing a new shot glass of Scotch in front of him.

"Two cheeseburgers, make them deluxe. After all"—he raised the glass and pointed it toward Carlin—"this lady is a bona fide New York City heroine."

"I believe," Carlin replied, taking the glass out of Harry's hand and sipping from it before replacing it near his table setting, "when a cop mentions the words 'heroine' and 'New York City' in the same sentence, he isn't usually talking about a human being."

Harry cringed at the terrible joke, but Carlin felt it succeed in breaking the slight tension that had seemed to linger since the ceremony at Gracie Mansion. During dinner, they retold every police joke either one had ever heard, ending with a series of bad puns.

It was over two hours later that Harry signaled for the check.

"Forget it, Harry," Carlin said, swiping it out of the waiter's hand before Harry had a chance to take it. "This one's on me."

Harry reached out. "Come on, Carlin. This is *your* celebration."

"Forget it," she answered. "I owe you this and just about everything else."

Harry raised his hands in acceptance and sat back in his chair as Carlin placed her American Express card on top of the check.

"This poor guy deserves a fortune for putting up with the two of us today," she added, as the waiter placed the credit card form and a ballpoint pen in front of her and walked back to the bar.

"And they say women are bad tippers," Harry replied, laughing.

Carlin held up the form and squinted at it. "The only problem with atmosphere and authenticity is the ancient lighting. Here," she said, handing the form to Harry, "you do the paperwork. I've always wondered if they really check the signature. Now I'll know."

"So the young Harvard graduate's senses are failing her! Age is finally catching up to you," he said with satisfaction. "It's about time."

"Oh, please," she said defensively. "My eyesight's perfect. There's no light in here."

Harry looked at her with exaggerated doubt, although she was absolutely right. Carlin was in near darkness, while one small yellow bulb was lit over his right shoulder. He read the numbers—barely—and placed the form back down on the table. "Since this one's on you, I'll leave a hundred percent tip. Okay?"

"Whatever makes you happy, Lieutenant Floyd," Carlin answered with mock sincerity.

"No, I guess I'll take it down to about twenty. After all," he said, "now that you're in your failing years, you'll need every penny you can save."

Carlin took up the challenge in his voice. "I can out-see you any day of the week."

"Not a prayer," Harry sneered back as he squinted down at the form and signed "Carlin Squire" with a flourish.

Carlin continued her challenge. "Highways in darkness, the bottom line of directions on the back of a bottle of dishwasher detergent, *The New York Times* stock exchange page at dusk."

"Will there be anything else?"

Carlin and Harry both jumped at the waiter's voice, both starting to laugh as they realized that neither one had seen him approach.

29

Still catching her breath from the spasms that had shaken her as she vomited, Natasha stood at the sink putting toothpaste on her toothbrush. Her stomach was aching, even after just having thrown up everything in it. Hurriedly, she brushed her teeth, then went into the bedroom and opened her top dresser drawer. She uncapped the small brown vial of Valium. *Shit.* She was almost out. But she certainly wasn't about to forgo taking some now. Besides, she needed something to calm her down from the pills she'd taken this morning. She swallowed one, then hesitated, and quickly downed another. Wiping a light film of perspiration from her forehead, she hoped she would get some relief from them. Lately it seemed like the more pills she took, the less they did for her.

There was no putting it off any longer, she had to get dressed and go. She was in the process of buttoning her blouse when she heard the door downstairs slam. She froze. *Damn.* She hadn't expected Ethan to be home for lunch today. She had to be out of here in forty-five minutes.

"Tash?" Her husband called up to her from the bottom of the stairs. "You home, honey?"

"Up here, sweetheart." She forced her voice higher to make it sound more cheerful.

"My meeting was put off an hour, so I came back for a quick bite."

Natasha ran a brush through her hair and hurriedly applied some flesh-toned concealer beneath her eyes, though she suspected it would do little to hide the dark circles. She attempted a composed expression as she padded down to the first floor of their duplex to greet Ethan, who was standing in the foyer, caught up in a magazine article.

"Hi." She came forward to kiss him on the cheek.

"Hiya." He looked up, dropping the magazine on a table. "It says here that Walter May is twenty million over budget on *Fiasco* and everybody's furious about it. Not that you can believe these stories, but I wonder. You know, I said it would take more money to do it right."

"It's not your headache," Natasha replied with a smile. Ethan had turned down the job of directing *Fiasco* because he'd finally been given the go-ahead on his latest project, a script titled *Waterfall* that he'd been trying to get made for over five years. "You having second thoughts about not taking that job?"

He shook his head. "No, of course not."

Natasha put both arms around him. "You and I both know that *Waterfall* will be your best yet."

"Thanks," he said with a smile, leaning forward to kiss her.

They stood there for a moment. Then, slowly, his smile faded and was replaced by a look of concern.

"Tash," he said haltingly, "I try never to tell you what to do, you know that. But I can't help wondering if you're not getting a little bit too thin. You look pale, honey. Are you eating enough?"

Natasha turned her face away and broke free. She tried to keep her tone easy as she took a few steps back. "You can never be too rich or too thin."

Ethan frowned. "Come on, Natasha, you know how much I hate that expression. Seriously, you don't seem like yourself. You're almost—gaunt. You sure you're okay?"

She turned and headed toward the kitchen. "Ethan, you're being ridiculous," she said annoyedly. "I'm the same as always. Now come with me and we'll get you some lunch."

Her heart was beating frantically as she walked away, hoping he wouldn't answer. She made it all the way to the kitchen without his saying anything, and with relief she escaped into the other room.

She'd wondered how long it would take him to notice. Despite her best efforts, she couldn't erase the signs of her nights spent tossing and turning in fear, getting barely two or three hours of sleep and then only with the help of tranquilizers, needing yet different pills to get going in the morning.

And she certainly had no interest whatever in food. She thought of all the years she'd struggled to keep her weight down. A few visits with Tony Kellner is all anyone needs, she thought bitterly. Since he'd reappeared, not only couldn't she bear the sight of food, but she'd thrown up every single time she prepared for a trip to his apartment and then again as soon as she got back home. Today would make the fifth time she was going—or rather, that she had been *summoned*—to see him.

Frantically, she slapped together a roast beef sandwich for Ethan, setting a place for him at the large wooden table in their eat-in kitchen, and putting out precut crudités and his favorite sweet pickles. She glanced at her watch. Half an hour before she had to go.

"Ethan, come and eat," she called out as she poured him a tall glass of mineral water and squeezed a piece of lemon into it.

He entered the room, looking surprised. "Wow, what fast service. I didn't expect you to fix me lunch, Tash. I would have done it."

She smiled sweetly. "My pleasure. I ate already, but I'll sit with you."

Taking a seat, she gestured across the table, willing him to hurry.

He sat down gratefully and picked up the sandwich. "Ummm, roast beef. I shouldn't be eating red meat, but I thank you from the bottom of my heart."

Just eat it and leave. Please, she begged him silently. Under any other circumstances, she would have been delighted to have a few extra minutes alone with her busy husband. She watched him, hoping he couldn't tell how miserable she felt.

"I put the editing facility on notice that we might run a few weeks over," he said, taking a bite of his lunch.

Do it like you mean it, bitch. Natasha started in her chair as Tony's voice echoed in her head. Oh, God. Smiling and nodding at her husband, she prayed her face wasn't giving her away. Her heart was pounding, and she rubbed her perspiring palms together.

She'd been lucky up until now, managing to get out to

Tony's without much difficulty. But one of these days Ethan was going to question her more closely when she dashed out of the house, or worse, catch her in one of the lies she'd been telling to explain her absence when she'd had to leave in the evening. She never knew when Tony would decide he wanted her; once, she'd had to appear two afternoons in a row, then not again until ten at night a week later. The tension was unbearable.

Ethan went on. "This could be a late night. I'm sorry, but I'll get home as soon as I can."

Bend over for papa. Natasha squeezed her eyes shut, trying to drive away the memories, the image of Tony's leering face. *You love it, baby, don't you? Tell me how much.*

With a little cry, she sprang to her feet, trying to cover her agitation by quickly busying herself at the sink. Ethan, finishing his sandwich, looked up.

"You okay?"

"Of course." She thought her chest would explode from the pounding of her heart. "I just remembered . . . it's Lainie's birthday tomorrow and I meant to get a gift."

"Oh, that reminds me. Phil Whitby's wife is throwing him a birthday party. You know, the writer from . . ."

Natasha stood at the sink, her back to her husband, nervously biting on a cuticle, making it bleed. Finally, *finally,* she had something worth holding on to. She loved Ethan more than she had believed she could ever love any man. And she had even begun to believe he genuinely loved her back, that their marriage might last. But if Ethan found out what kind of a person she really was, that she had caused her own mother's death and kept that terrible fact a secret, there was no question what would happen.

And when Ben and Carlin learned the truth—she couldn't even stand to imagine what their reactions would be. They would despise her, and rightfully so. Two-faced liar that she was, the person who'd ruined their lives and then played the loving sister and friend right to their faces. They'd never speak to her again as long as she lived. Oh, God, she was going to lose them all. The teetering house of cards that was her life would be struck by a tornado. And no matter how hard she'd tried, she couldn't find a way out.

Tony was waiting.

"Coffee, Ethan?" she asked sweetly, praying he would refuse.

He glanced at his watch and started to rise. "I'd better run. Thanks for lunch. See you later, sweetheart."

With a quick kiss, he was gone. Natasha folded her arms on the table and put her head down on them gratefully. Thank God. Heavily, she got herself up and into the bedroom to finish getting dressed. She began to shiver with fear, and grabbed a sweater from her closet. Ten minutes later, she was in a taxi heading across town.

By the time the cab pulled up in front of Tony's building, Natasha's stomach was in agonizing knots. She handed the driver a five and two singles.

"Keep the change," she said absently, stepping out of the cab onto Central Park West. It wasn't cold, but she pulled her sweater more tightly around her.

Usually the doorman was around to announce her, but he didn't seem to be anywhere in evidence at the moment. I wonder what he thinks of these little visits of mine, she thought cynically, a married woman appearing in the middle of the afternoon. He probably knows exactly what I'm doing upstairs. No, she amended, not exactly. He would assume I'm having a happy little affair with one of his tenants. He might not figure on Tony's pal Bob, or the side attractions like the handcuffs and burning cigarette last week.

Her stomach knotted up again as she recalled her terror at being cuffed to the bed for one of Tony's leisurely sex sessions. Still in the restraints, she had lain there sobbing afterward, which only served to annoy Tony. As punishment, he had lit a cigarette, and for what seemed like an eternity, threatened to burn her, bringing the cigarette so close to her skin, she could feel its heat. Several times, he had convinced her he was really going to do it, and finally she had wet the bed in fear. Disgusted, he let her go.

She closed her eyes against the memory as she stepped into the elevator. For a moment, rage welled up in her with such force, she couldn't breathe. Why doesn't he just kill me and get it over with? But, of course, he was enjoying this. He had no interest in seeing it come to an end.

Who knows what he had planned for her today? She reached into her purse, grabbing another Valium and gulping it down as the elevator door opened. It doesn't matter what he's got in mind, does it? she asked herself in despair. He can do whatever he wants. If I want him to keep quiet, I don't have any choice but to go through with it. She started shivering violently.

Tony let her in wearing only a towel wrapped around his waist. His hair was till wet from the shower.

"Hey, baby," he cried exuberantly when he saw her, "it's great that you could make it. I had an incredible game of tennis this morning, and I'm feeling absolutely fantastic."

Natasha stared at him. His mood was different every time she showed up. Last time he had been cold and aloof, as if her presence were an irritation to him. Here he was acting as if she'd come for a date. Without realizing it, she clenched her hand into a fist and rubbed it against her stomach, trying to massage away some of the pain there.

"You look delicious." Tony stepped closer and nuzzled her neck. "Ummm . . ."

She shut her eyes tight. *God, why are you doing this?* she asked silently. *Are you going to make me pay forever?* Maybe Ethan would understand, maybe Ben and Carlin could learn to forgive her. She almost laughed aloud at how ludicrous the thought was. Ethan wouldn't even find her worth spitting on. She envisioned the icy hatred in her brother's eyes and Carlin's blazing fury. Tony had her. Completely.

Tony's voice dropped to a seductive whisper. "I thought maybe we'd bring it on into the bedroom."

He took her arm, his fingers holding her so tightly that she winced as she walked. When they got to the bed, he sat her down.

"You know," he said pleasantly, "that tennis game pretty much wore me out. This seems like the perfect time for you to fly solo, Natasha. Give me a little show, if you get my drift."

He went to his dresser and picked up something there. When he turned back to her, she saw what it was: a bottle of Discovery, one of the perfumes she'd been promoting as part of her modeling contract with Forager. The campaign they'd done with her had turned it into one of the leading perfumes in the country. To the public, her face was inextricably linked with that bottle. Tony held it out to her. Jesus, what now?

"You're going to do yourself today, honey," he said, obviously enjoying himself. "But I don't expect you to get hot the way I know you can without a little help. I figured this bottle made you a bundle, and, hell, I know that would be a real turn-on for *me*." He ran his hand up and down the tall cylinder of glass and stroked its rounded top. "Why do you suppose they made it this shape? It's almost like it was meant for this."

Natasha was too horrified to move or say a word. She thought she might vomit again right there all over herself.

"I got you the big size. So come on, now, baby, use it. Pretend it's me inside you, making you beg for more. I'm just gonna sit here and watch the show."

Her voice came out in a strangled rasp. "No."

His eyebrows shot up. *"No?"*

"No. I won't."

Shaking his head with disbelief, he set the bottle back down on the dresser, then reached across her to pick up a fresh pack of cigarettes from the night table. "You surprise me, sugar."

She sat perfectly still, mesmerized by the sight of his hands as they tore the cellophane off the cigarette pack and crumpled it. There was no way in the world she could do what he was telling her to do. But how could she not?

Natasha became aware that the top drawer of the night table was slightly ajar. Something black and shiny inside it caught her eye. A gun.

I could grab it and blow my brains out all over his bedroom, she told herself. *At least this would finally be done with.*

Tony opened the pack slowly and tapped it against the side of his hand just enough to nudge the first few cigarettes partway out. He put one in his mouth. His tone suddenly became serious. "Before we get started, I think you should know that your brother was by to see me about that special little phone call."

Natasha's head jerked up, fear in her eyes. "Ben was here?"

"The son of a bitch had the nerve to accuse me of making the call, demanding explanations, carrying on like a horse's ass. The bastard actually swung at me, if you can believe it." He smiled. "But I kept your little secret. I protected you, baby, like I always do. Right?"

Tony paused as if waiting for her to agree. Then he picked up a piece of white paper that was resting next to the perfume bottle and waved it at her. "I took the liberty of writing a little letter, setting down what happened back in Westerfield. I've also gone into the details of our affair now. You know, how you seduced me, how you've kept coming here despite my protests that you're married and it isn't right. I've made it clear that my conscience is forcing me to speak." He nodded thoughtfully, putting the letter down. "What we have between us is pretty terrific, but there's something to be said for turning the letter over to the right people and seeing what happens. It's a temptation."

He gazed at her impassively for a moment, fingering the unlit cigarette in his hand. Then he turned away again toward the dresser. "Where's my damn lighter?"

Panic was coursing through Natasha with such force, she was afraid she would black out. Even with what she'd gone through, there was still no way to be sure he would keep quiet. She imagined Ethan reading that letter. The vomit rose in her throat. *And there was no way out.* No matter what she did, she could never be sure of Tony's next move. She could feel the perspiration on her upper lip. Her head began to pound.

"Six hundred dollars I paid for that lighter," Tony was muttering.

She was trapped. Helplessly, endlessly, waiting for him to destroy her one way or another. She trembled with rage and desperation. It couldn't go on. It couldn't.

It didn't have to. She sat, frozen with the realization of what she was about to do.

No longer thinking about anything at all, she swiftly reached out and opened the night-table drawer just enough to pull out the gun. Leaping up, she gripped it with both hands and aimed at Tony's broad back, instinctively spreading her legs apart to brace herself and locking her arms straight ahead of her.

"No, you bastard," she whispered fiercely. "I won't let you!"

She shot, her hands rock-steady. Once, twice, three times.

The noise exploded into the room. Tony's flesh was ripped apart by the bullets, his blood spurting out in every direction. He half-spun around, but slipped to the ground before he could face her. Blood began seeping out around him in a dark pool.

Immobilized, Natasha stood there. After the noise of the shots, the sudden silence was eerie. She was surprised at how completely still Tony was, his eyes staring up at the ceiling. His hand still clutched the cigarette. That was it, as simple as that. It had happened so quickly.

She went around him to the dresser. As she reached out to take the letter, she paused. The stationery had a letterhead imprinted on it, but it wasn't Tony's. It was from Hearn Management Services, and the message was a short typed one.

Dear Tenant:
  Due to repair work being done on the boiler Tuesday morning, there will be no hot water in the building between 10 A.M. and 2 P.M. that day. We regret any inconvenience this may cause you.

Natasha stared at the piece of paper, clenching her fists. Tony had just been playing another of his games with her. Looking back down at his body, her eyes narrowed with hate. She had to resist the urge to kick him.

She took several deep breaths, waiting until she was calm again. Then, gathering up some of her skirt in the front, she wiped off the gun and, still holding it through the fabric, replaced it inside the drawer. She quickly walked to the door and left, pausing to wipe off both sides of the doorknob and the doorbell with her skirt as she exited. Taking the service elevator downstairs, she left through the building's side entrance, emerging unnoticed onto Sixty-second Street.

30

Carlin looked with dismay at the enormous stack of folders crowding her desk. One day off being feted at Gracie Mansion, and the paperwork became a mountain. She took a quick glance at her watch. Two-eighteen. Could she get through this ton of paper before her monthly four o'clock meeting with Captain Fallon? Fatigued by the very thought of it, she rubbed her eyes. As always, she wished someone would interrupt her with something pressing, something *interesting*.

Police lieutenants shouldn't go around wishing for action, she chided herself. In her line of work, something interesting would probably translate into something horrible having been done to some innocent citizen. But an afternoon of quiet desk work wasn't enough to keep her from thinking about why her home telephone refused to ring, why Ben Dameroff had gone from being the center of her life to an emptiness that seemed to grow deeper and more painful every minute the phone stayed silent.

She looked up with surprise as the phone suddenly trilled.

"Squire," she answered breathlessly, hoping against hope that Ben would be the voice on the other end.

"From the sound of your voice, I gotta believe you were dying to hear from me, Cambridge." Harry Floyd's unmistakable baritone echoed through the receiver.

"Man of my dreams," Carlin replied, aching with disappointment.

Harry chuckled. "Well, I'm glad you feel that way 'cause your other boyfriend's not gonna be calling anymore."

"What?" Carlin was frozen with fear. Whatever did Harry mean? What did he know about Ben?

"Nosiree, you're not gonna have Mr. Anthony Kellner of Central Park West to kick around anymore." Harry's tone carried more satisfaction than sadness.

Carlin tried to clear her head before asking any more questions. Harry wasn't talking about Ben; he was talking about Tony. "Please spit it out. What happened to Tony Kellner?"

"He was discovered in his apartment this morning, dead as a doornail. Probably happened yesterday sometime."

Carlin was silent. Good God, she thought, Kellner was dead. "Any idea who did it?" she asked finally.

"Person or persons unknown. You got anything you wanna share with me?" Harry inquired. "After all, you knew this guy."

"Not off the top of my head," Carlin answered, keeping her voice light. "Listen, though, how about faxing me whatever paperwork you have on it? Who knows, maybe I'll be able to catch something."

Harry hesitated. "Sure, sugar, I'll send you whatever we have. The medical examiner won't be finished until later on today, but you're welcome to the rest of it. But don't forget, this one's mine."

"I'm not looking for a collar, Harry, just a little background to satisfy my curiosity."

"You got it, babe," Harry said, hanging up the phone.

Within minutes, Sergeant Conklin was delivering a file of fax papers to her. Carlin picked up the file and turned her chair around. This was one time she didn't wish to be seen by the detectives seated on the other side of the glass window fronting her office. Fear was coursing through her like electricity. She tried to concentrate on the details of the crime report, but all she could take in was the fact of it: Tony Kellner had been murdered by person or persons unknown. It terrified her to imagine even for a second that the person might very well be known. At least to her.

If I ever find out who made that call, I'll kill him. Ben Dameroff had made that threat almost twenty years before. Could he have carried through on his promise?

Oh, that's impossible, she thought, forcing herself to breathe deeply, to slow the panic that had her in its grip. A thought flashed across her mind. Ben wasn't even supposed to be in town yesterday or today, she realized. He'd been due at a medical conference in Chicago the night before last, wasn't supposed to get back until tomorrow. She could swear she remembered him telling her that, that is before he stopped communicating with her entirely. Swiveling back around in her chair, she reached across the desk and grabbed at her calendar. Swiftly she turned the pages. There it was, marked by a red line across three dates. *Ben in Chicago.*

A flood of relief almost made her lay her head on her desk, but a quick look through the glass demonstrated how many witnesses she would have to that act. This case would be handled exactly as every other murder was handled. In fact, she realized, not at all proud of her thoughts, if ever someone deserved to die it was Tony Kellner. It was all she could do not to feel thankful to whoever the person had been who had taken the initiative of killing him.

At least it hadn't been Ben. Then, unbidden, a small doubt crept into her mind. What if he hadn't gone to Chicago as planned? Well, of course he did, she thought. It was a conference, not some dinner date or even surgery, she reassured herself. But the worry lingered. Carlin found it difficult to concentrate.

Finally, she reached out for the phone. Please, God, don't let me be right, she thought as she dialed the familiar number.

"Helen," she said as Ben's secretary answered on the second ring. "Hi, this is Carlin Squire. I know Ben is out of town, but there's a message I wanted to leave."

"Hello," the woman replied cheerfully. "That's fine, but you don't have to bother with a message. You can talk to him yourself as soon as he gets out of surgery. It should be only an hour or so from now."

Carlin couldn't keep her voice from shaking. "I thought he'd gone off to Chicago."

"No, actually that meeting was postponed. Shall I tell him to call you at any particular time?"

Carlin could barely respond. "Anytime," she answered finally, knowing full well he wasn't likely to return her call whatever time she might suggest. Especially if he had stayed in New York to commit a murder.

She felt as if she were going crazy. I can't just sit here, she decided. She looked at her calendar for the next day. Nothing that wouldn't wait. Grimly, she went back to the file on Tony Kellner and began writing names and numbers furiously on her desk pad. There was no way Ben Dameroff could murder anyone. She'd never believe it, not in a million years. But, whatever the truth was, she was going to get to it.

It was all she could do to get through the three-hour session with Ernie Fallon. As her captain droned on about shift changes and survivor-benefit alterations sought by the Patrolmen's Benevolent Association, Carlin couldn't stop glancing at her watch. Usually these monthly meetings were of great interest to her, but tonight the concerns of the precinct took a distinct backseat. Finally, at seven-thirty, the meeting over, Carlin taxied over to the East Side. She'd debated using one of the squad cars, but this was personal. At her direction, the driver stopped in front of a large white building on York Avenue in the high Eighties. She asked the doorman to ring Michelle Miller, and took the house phone in her hand when the buzzer was answered.

"Ms. Miller, this is Lieutenant Squire from Midtown North. I wonder if I might have a few minutes of your time."

The voice answered yes and buzzed back.

"Fourteen B," the doorman said, as he pointed her toward an elevator to the left. Michele Miller lived in a spacious two-bedroom apartment, whose large windows featured perfect views of the East River.

As she was led inside by a tall, slender woman in her middle thirties, Carlin apologized for appearing unannounced.

"It's all right." Michele Miller's response was muffled as she raised a handkerchief up to her face.

"I'll try to be brief, but I understand you were the person called to identify Mr. Kellner's body. You must have been a good friend of his."

The woman lifted her red-rimmed eyes to Carlin. "Tony Kellner was my fiancé, Lieutenant. Today has been the worst day of my life."

"I didn't realize you two were so serious. When was the wedding going to be?" Carlin asked matter-of-factly, hiding her surprise. Tony had never mentioned a girlfriend, let alone a fiancée.

"Actually, we were just about to set a date."

Carlin sneaked a glance at the woman's left hand. There was no ring on her fourth finger.

"This is a beautiful apartment," Carlin observed, walking over to gaze through a window. "Is that the tower at La Guardia?" Carlin pointed to a spot in Queens, the borough visible across the expanse of water.

"Yes, it is," the young woman answered. "In fact, Tony always said it was the spectacular view that sold him on this apartment."

Carlin looked at her quizzically. "I thought Tony lived on Central Park West."

"Well, yes, of course." Miller's response came quickly.

Almost too quickly, Carlin thought.

"Actually that was as much a business space for him as a living space. As soon as we were married, he was planning to move in here with me."

"And what is it you do?" Carlin asked.

"Well, I used to model. Now I'm thinking about going into real estate. I've been taking classes Wednesday afternoons all summer."

Carlin turned to look back at the view. In other words, she thought, putting the woman's answers into her own words, Tony owns this place lock, stock, and barrel, and you have no visible means of support. There's no ring, and I'm betting there was never going to be a wedding. He might even have been about to dump you. That gives you a motive for murder, which you don't want me to know about.

"What kind of man was he?" Carlin asked disarmingly, making her way back toward the couch. "May I?" she asked before taking a seat.

"Please," Miller replied, sitting on a white brocade chair across from her. "Tony Kellner was, well, he was the most creative man I ever knew. You must know about his dating service. I think he must have had the top ten percent of this city as clients, I swear it." Michele Miller's eyes almost fluttered as she enthused. "He was creativity itself. And kindness. He would talk about those women as if they were his children."

Miller muttered on, sniffling occasionally, until Carlin rose to leave. Amazing, she thought, as she walked to the front door. The man Michele Miller described had about as much in common with the Tony Kellner she knew as Billy the Kid did with the pope. "Thank you, Ms. Miller. Let me leave you my card in case you think of anything else you wish to tell me."

Miller put her hand out to take the card and held Carlin's for a few seconds before drawing back.

"There's someone else I trust you're talking to. Robert Ames, Tony's business partner. I'm sure he'd have a lot to tell you."

Miller's eyes gleamed with something indefinable. Okay, Carlin thought, I'll bite.

"They were good friends?"

"Well, let's say that Tony was a good friend to Bobby, a very good friend." Miller opened the door and held it for Carlin.

"You have me curious," Carlin said, leaning against the open door rather than walking through it.

"I can't say much more than that, Lieutenant. I just think you'll want to talk to him. Bobby owed Tony everything, as far as I could tell. In the last few months Bobby seemed to have kind of an *attitude.* Tony mentioned it a few times."

"Okay," Carlin said, walking out to the long, carpeted hallway. "You have my number if you want to get in touch."

With that, she walked toward the elevator. As Miller's door closed behind her, Carlin pulled her notebook out of her purse. Robert Ames. The address was on Third Avenue, probably somewhere in the Thirties. Okay, Michele. Mr. Ames will be my first stop tomorrow morning.

Robert Ames greeted Carlin at his apartment promptly at eight-thirty the next morning. With his eyes covered by tortoiseshell narrow-rimmed glasses and his blue pin-striped suit fitted perfectly to his short, compact body, Ames looked like every second or third man on the streets of his neighborhood. Third Avenue in the lower Thirties had become a haven for young professionals who were single, well-off, and eager to meet each other.

"Our service caters to women of a certain social standing;

therefore, the men we have them meet are signed on only after an exhaustive researching process," Ames said almost pro-
fessorially in response to Carlin's first question.

"Does that research center on their habits and personalities,
or does it focus on their financial position?" Carlin kept her
tone businesslike.

"Actually," Ames replied with a salesman's smoothness,
"both matter greatly to clients such as ours."

Carlin listened closely. She could easily imagine this man
and the Tony Kellner she knew so well oiling lonely women
with hope as they took them for all they could.

As Carlin pressed him on his feelings toward Tony Kellner,
Ames became almost elegiac.

"He was the best business partner any man ever had,"
Ames was saying over and over again, "the most loyal friend
in the world. Generous to a fault."

"And exactly what fault would that be?" Carlin asked, deliberately misunderstanding him.

Ames looked at her critically. "I meant to say he was generous, not that he was flawed."

Carlin went right on. "Mr. Ames, we can use all the help
we can get. Can you think of anyone who might have wished
him harm? Perhaps even a customer who was left displeased?"

Ames raised his hands in mock helplessness. Oh, if I only
could be of service, they seemed to say as his face registered
the utmost sympathy.

Carlin doubted he had any particular interest in helping the
police at all. Robert Ames seemed altogether intent on pre-
senting a tidy picture, one that might well be smudged by uncovering a murderer. Nonetheless she pressed him again.

"Is there anything you can think of to tell me, anything at
all?"

Ames lifted a hand to wipe some invisible perspiration
from his face, with drew Carlin's attention to the thick, dark
hairs covering his wrists and knuckles. Suddenly he seemed
more like an animal just waiting to spring than the attentive
young businessman whose profile he'd seemed to fit so perfectly.

"There is one person you might want to talk to," he said,

choosing his words carefully. "Tony had a girlfriend, a woman named Michele Miller. He'd broken up with her a couple of months ago, but she was still living in an apartment he owned uptown. You might want to—"

The ringing of the telephone interrupted his train of thought.

"Hey, Bro." He spoke enthusiastically as he heard his caller's voice. "I've got someone here, the police actually, looking into Tony's murder."

Carlin watched him listen intently to the person on the other end.

"No, not this afternoon. Too much to clean up. I'll try to get up there on Sunday. We'll kill them, you know we will." He laughed as he spoke. "Catch you later. Bye now."

"Sorry," he said to Carlin, hanging up the phone. "My brother's a tennis pro at a club up in New Rochelle. We were supposed to be in a pairs tournament this weekend, but with Tony's death and all . . ." Suddenly, he seemed to remember he was talking to a police lieutenant. "Sorry. You don't care about that. Anyway, aside from Michele, I don't know anyone you should talk to. Tony was my best friend. I hope you find the guy who did this and stick him in the electric chair."

"New York is not a capital-punishment state, Mr. Ames," Carlin answered without irony. "Thanks for your help."

Leaving him her card, Carlin left his apartment and began walking slowly up Third Avenue. So, according to Ames, Tony Kellner was a saint and Michele Miller was about to get the shaft. Carlin considered both of these hypotheses. The second part was exactly what she herself had suspected. Was Tony about to put Michele Miller out on the street, as Robert Ames had suggested? Would she have been angry enough to shoot him?

Carlin pondered Robert Ames's other contention, the one that had Tony Kellner cast as an angel. She found it hard to believe that Tony would have been anything but slimy as a partner. By the time she reached Grand Central, she'd figured out a way to get at the truth.

At three-fifteen, Carlin was taking a tennis lesson from Stuart Ames at the Beach and Tennis Club, overlooking the Long Island Sound in lower Westchester. *I have to get good by next Saturday,* she'd stressed over the phone, identifying herself but not bothering to mention her profession. Stuart was taller and more solidly built than his brother, the same vast store of body hair thickly covering his arms and legs. After twenty-five minutes of volleying—"Turn to the side and bring your racquet back!"—Carlin didn't have to feign fatigue as she begged him to let her rest for a few minutes.

The last time—for that matter, the first time—she'd picked up a racquet had been one weekend at Nancy Erickson's parents' country house during sophomore year. She was grateful now to be sitting over an iced tea, chatting with Stuart Ames for the rest of her assigned hour. Casually, she mentioned having met a Robert Ames who resembled him.

"That's my big brother," Stuart said enthusiastically. "How do you know him?"

"Actually, I thought of using his dating service, although eventually I chickened out." Carlin affected the coy glance of a woman with one foot in the dating waters. "I met your brother a couple of times, but mostly I dealt with a man named Anthony Kellner."

Stuart looked at her and grimaced. "Funny you should say that. Tony Kellner was just killed."

"Killed!" Carlin was all dismay. "How awful for your brother. They must have been such close friends."

"They were close enough," Stuart answered, his tone guarded.

"Well, I thought Anthony Kellner was one of the sweetest men I'd ever met." Carlin leaned toward him intimately. "In fact," she almost purred, "I hoped he would ask me out himself. He was such an intelligent man, so hardworking and sincere."

"Yup." Stuart Ames continued to keep his thoughts to himself.

"In fact, it's interesting that your brother was on staff," Carlin said, a shrewish edge creeping into her voice. "He must have gotten there after I met Mr. Kellner, because he didn't seem to think much of his staff. It seemed as if he had to do just about everything by himself."

"You know something," Stuart answered, obviously annoyed, "Tony Kellner was a son of a bitch. As far as I was concerned, he was cheating my brother blind. I'm telling you, he lived like a king, while Bobby was doing most of the work. No man deserves to be killed, but, honestly, I'm not going to weep any tears over Tony Kellner and neither is my brother."

Carlin replayed the conversation in her mind as she traveled back to Manhattan. So Robert Ames wasn't going to cry over the death of his beloved business partner. And Michele Miller was about to be forced out of her palatial apartment by America's sweetheart. Might either of these people have wished the man dead? Sure. Carlin tried to reassure herself with the two new suspects she had managed to unearth.

Yet, somehow, she kept hearing Ben's voice, over and over again.

If I ever find out who made that call, I'll kill him.

31

J. T. Squire swiped drunkenly at the bourbon bottle, grabbing it by the neck and pouring himself another drink. The amber liquid splashed over the sides of the glass onto the table. He cursed at the waste. Setting the bottle back down, he noticed it was nearly empty. What the hell was he going to do about getting some more today?

"You rot in hell, Lillian," he yelled to the empty room. *"You stupid, ugly bitch. You go right to hell and rot there."*

He used both hands to bring the glass to his mouth, careful not to spill any more. That idiotic woman. She was nothing, a boring, fat old lady. He'd done everything for her. Provided her with a good home, a kid, and a husband who stayed with her through thick and thin. She'd gotten lucky when she'd landed him all those years before; he should have married a classier babe, and definitely more of a looker. God knows, he'd had opportunities to leave her along the way, plenty of them. But he'd stuck it out, returning to this dump day in and day out, putting up with her incessant chattering.

"And what does she do?" he demanded in an angry shout. When he's crippled, confined to a goddamned wheelchair. *She leaves him.* Runs off for an entire weekend—two nights, no less—to visit that harebrained friend of hers over three hours away. Right on the tail of going to New York to visit Carlin, she takes off on yet another merry little jaunt. What would happen now? Who would take care of him, wash up and cook his meals, help him when he had to take a leak, for Christ's sake? Apparently she didn't give a good goddamn. She tells him she's left a meat loaf in the refrigerator for his dinner and waltzes out the door, as calm as you please.

Don't worry, J.T., she'd said as she packed her suitcase not

even two hours before, I've made arrangements for you with
the Visiting Nurse Service. Someone will stop by tonight. Besides, it's not as if you're completely paralyzed. It's only your
legs. Plenty of people with worse problems than yours take
care of themselves just fine.

"Give me a frigging break," he muttered. Swallowing the
last drops in the glass, he freshened his drink once again.
Could he call the liquor store to deliver more bourbon? Was
there any cash in the house to pay for it? He had no idea how
Lillian managed these stupid things. But the idea that he
could sit here and starve to death didn't concern her.

Strangers should take care of him, that was fine by her.
She gets it into her head that she wants to take off and, boom,
she's gone. It was bad enough when she'd gone to New York
City; he'd had to put up with neighbors helping him out. But
he knew she wouldn't impose on their neighbors more than
once. This new arrangement meant she would be free to leave
him any time she wanted. He shook his head. Just like that,
she abandons her husband.

"In sickness and in health, you bitch," he yelled. "You took
a vow. You *swore*. Remember that?"

He slammed the glass down on the table. Lillian had been
acting up like this ever since she'd gotten back from New
York. She'd started talking back to him, telling him she didn't
like the way he spoke to her, that he took her for granted. A
couple of times when he'd asked her for something, she actually refused, claiming it would be good for him to do it
himself. Yesterday she'd even told him there was no reason
he couldn't help out around the house more, maybe make the
bed or do the dishes once in a while. He'd really lost his temper at that one, but when he finally smashed an ashtray
against the wall, she'd come to her senses and backed off
with an apology.

Then, on top of it all, just this morning she'd told him she
was joining a beginners' bridge club that met every Tuesday
and Thursday night. What the hell was going on here? Now
this, a weekend spree. Never asked for permission, nothing.
Just goddamned *informed* him that she was going.

Of course, he knew who was really to blame. It was all
Carlin's fault. He'd let his wife go for one crummy visit to

New York and this was the result. Carlin must have told Lillian to do all this stuff, and brainwashed her until she agreed. He could just envision the two of them huddled together, plotting it out.

His eyes narrowed. Hell, it was because of Carlin he was in this damn chair to begin with. She and that Ben Dameroff had brought the whole thing on. If Carlin and Ben hadn't always been off together—no doubt screwing their brains out—whoever made that call couldn't have convinced him and Kit so easily that both their kids were in an accident. If it had just been Ben, or even Carlin, he would have been a lot more levelheaded, not gone tearing off like a lunatic that way. But the way the news came in, *both* kids hurt, Kit's wild panic . . . It threw him off completely.

And now look at him. In disgust, he punched his unfeeling legs, so scrawny and useless. Someone had wanted to play a joke on his daughter and Ben, but *he* had paid the price. Of course, no one ever acknowledged it. God knows, his daughter had never even apologized. And Ben Dameroff—well, he'd grown up to be the most arrogant one of them all. The big *doctor.* It made J.T. sick.

Those Dameroffs were nothing but trouble and always had been. If Leonard had been able to satisfy his wife, Kit wouldn't have seduced him that night in the store and dragged him into the affair. That Kit was just another stupid bitch, full of herself and what she wanted. But nothing ever happened to that family. Of course, J.T. had had the satisfaction of seeing Leonard Dameroff buried before him, but so what? The girl in that family, that Natasha, had gone on to be a rich model; Lillian had bored him silly for years with stories about her from Carlin. Ben, of course, had it easy, now that he was a doctor. Worst of all, Carlin had gotten back together with that bastard. Hell, it was probably Ben who told Carlin that Lillian should stop taking care of her husband.

It wasn't right. J.T. rubbed his bloodshot eyes. He was sick of those Dameroffs, sick of them getting what they wanted. Including his own daughter.

He leaned his head back and shut his eyes, worn out by it all. It was quiet in the room except for the occasional noise of a car passing outside. He sat like that for a long while, wondering when the right people would pay for what had been done to him.

Slowly, an idea started to form in his mind. He lifted his head up again and opened his eyes, his mind suddenly clear and sharp. Sure, it would probably come out sooner or later that he was lying, but in the meantime, he could certainly give Dr. Dameroff a run for his money. He smiled.

Wheeling himself into the bedroom, he stopped before the small desk in the corner where Lillian always sat to pay the household bills. He yanked open several drawers before locating some stationery and a pen.

For a few moments more, he reviewed in his mind just what to say. Then, with a broad grin, he started to write.

Slamming the door behind him, Ben raced inside his apartment. He tossed his jacket over one of the chairs at the dining room table and dropped his briefcase nearby. Hastily, he grabbed the newspaper, left on the table along with his mail by the cleaning lady. He tore through the second section, running his eyes across the columns, searching.

Just a few minutes earlier, he had been coming uptown on the subway after attending a charity function for the hospital, a boring evening of bad food and long speeches. He was anxious to get home and try to reach Carlin again. He knew she'd been calling his office, and she had to be wondering why she hadn't heard back from him. But at first, he'd been so thrown by her attitude about Tony. And then, after he'd confronted Kellner only to hear Carlin was taking money from him, he'd hesitated again. But he couldn't keep running away from whatever he might find out. He loved her, and needed to be with her.

He had tried to reach her earlier at the station, but she was out and he hadn't left a message; he didn't want her to call back and get him when he was rushed with patients or distracted. The call was too important. When he got back to his apartment, he would keep trying until he got her at home tonight.

The woman sitting next to him on the subway was reading the newspaper, and he casually glanced down it, noticing a small headline stating that a man had been shot in his Central

Park West apartment. As he idly read the first paragraph over the woman's shoulder, the name *Anthony Kellner* jumped out at him. But just then, the newspaper's owner had abruptly turned to the next page. Fortunately, Ben's stop was next. He had run all the way from the station to check out the story in his own copy of the *Times*.

Finally, on page nine, he found it. He dropped down into one of the chairs to read. So it was true: Tony Kellner had been murdered.

Ben sat there motionless for a few minutes. Then he got up and went into his bedroom, slowly loosening his tie as he walked. Changing from his suit into a pair of jeans and a T-shirt, he reflected that it was entirely possible that Tony Kellner had other enemies, and maybe quite a few of them. But there was no question about it: Carlin had the motive to kill him. If what Tony had said was true, and Carlin was on the take from him, he had a lot of power over her.

He pondered it some more. Perhaps something in their arrangement had gone terribly wrong, and Carlin had gotten violently angry, angry enough to kill him over it. Or perhaps Tony was about to expose her to the police department, just as cavalierly as he did to Ben. Knowing what her career meant to her, Ben could imagine she would go to just about any lengths to stop him. She might have resorted to murder to keep Tony quiet.

Ben went back out to the dining room, shaking his head. He just couldn't make these scenarios jibe with the Carlin he knew. *The Carlin I think I know,* he reflected uneasily.

There was another possibility that was just as terrible, but that undeniably rang truer. Perhaps Carlin hadn't been so forgiving after all when she'd found out about Tony making that phone call. Maybe her apparent indifference—the attitude that had frustrated Ben so much—had merely been a way to conceal her real fury.

He thought back on her relationship with her father, back to the dapper, handsome guy J.T. had been before Tony performed his dirty work. Carlin had worshipped him, always turning the other cheek, refusing to see what a pathetic excuse he was for a father. No, there's no way in hell she could really be that forgiving, Ben decided. I didn't think it made sense when I first saw how calm she was about it—and I was right.

He stopped where he was as another thought occurred to him. Maybe Carlin had already known it was Tony who had made the call, even before Ben told her. Maybe she planned the whole friendship with Tony to hide her real intent of getting revenge. She might even have known for years, been biding her time until the moment to take action was just right. Carlin was a police officer. She would know just how, when, and where to do it. He imagined her face, her expression of determination when she made up her mind to do something. But this time he was imagining her with a gun in her hand.

Ben stood there, knowing he should get moving, but somehow unable to. He had resolved to talk to Carlin tonight, to patch things up and get back together. But that was before—before he'd found out about Tony Kellner's murder.

What would he say to her now?

32

"You see, Carlin. I told you a run would make you feel better."

Natasha pulled slightly ahead, as if to quicken their already brisk pace. She squinted at the sunlight reflected off the calm water of Central Park's reservoir.

"Is this the most beautiful day you've ever seen?" Natasha grinned at Carlin and began to run even faster.

"Hey, Tash, slow down. I played tennis yesterday for the first time in about ten years, and my legs could come to a complete stop at any moment."

Natasha slowed slightly. "I thought policewomen were supposed to be prime physical specimens."

Carlin laughed. "I feel like a specimen, all right. The kind you slather on a piece of glass and put under a microscope." She looked over to Natasha, beautifully turned out in perfectly fitting shorts and a T-shirt so white they looked new. Somehow she seemed different today, much more relaxed than she'd been in months.

"What are you so happy about?" Carlin asked finally. "Or does spending about a thousand dollars on a running outfit just brighten your day?"

"Why shouldn't I be happy?" Natasha tossed the question back at her. "I've got a husband, a brother, and a best friend I love, the career I've wished for all my life . . . What would I have to complain about, for God's sake!"

Carlin nodded. "I guess that's true. Although I must say, all of that has been true for years, yet somehow you seem to be blooming." A thought entered her mind. "You're not pregnant, are you?"

"Jeez, no." Natasha seemed alarmed at the question. "Now there's a career breaker for you."

"Not necessarily," Carlin responded. "I mean getting shot in your apartment, now that's a career breaker." Suddenly she caught herself. "Sorry, Tash. You and Tony Kellner went way back. I don't mean to be sarcastic about the love of your high school life."

"I don't think of Tony Kellner and the word 'love' in the same sentence," Natasha said. "He was awful in high school and got worse after that."

Carlin nodded in agreement. "Actually, you're more right than you know. Tony Kellner was under investigation when he died. I couldn't tell you about it before, but now it's pretty much an open secret."

Natasha smiled grimly. "In New York, it seems like you hear about some kid getting killed for his running shoes every couple of weeks. I wouldn't be surprised if someone bumped Tony off just for his Armani suits."

Carlin regarded Natasha with surprise. Implications about the dating service and the criminal acts behind it had appeared in one of the papers the day his murder was reported, but no one had said anything about the way he dressed.

"Gee, Tash, how do you know about Tony's fabulous wardrobe? He certainly didn't dress that way at Westerfield High."

"Oh, Tony called me," Natasha answered evenly. "It was right after you ran into him. He asked me to meet him for a drink at the Carlyle. I was curious, so I went." She shook her head in a display of disgust. "Before he finished his glass of white wine, he invited me back the next day for a nooner. Can you imagine!" Natasha laughed as if it were the silliest thought in the world.

Carlin frowned. "You should have mentioned it to me. I'd have found some way to make him leave you alone."

"Don't give it another thought," Natasha replied. "Somebody else seems to have taken care of it. Tony Kellner is never going to bother another human being ever again."

"You preparing for the exam already?"

Marty Browne's Philadelphia accent, with its high-pitched

whine, identified him before Harry even turned around in his seat.

"Can't a man have even one slice of pizza without being hounded?" Harry sounded as if he were teasing a friend, but in fact the sight of big, blond Sergeant Martin Browne was enough to spoil his lunch. He quickly closed the book that was in his lap.

"Come on, Floyd," Browne said nasally, pulling up a chair and placing a tray with three slices of pepperoni pizza down on the plastic tabletop, "you need me to keep you sharp."

Harry emitted a long sigh. "I'm as sharp as I'm gonna be, and that's sharper than you'll ever be."

Browne laughed as if Harry's comments didn't hurt a bit, but Harry knew that couldn't be true. Martin Browne had trailed Harry Floyd on every civil service exam, every police appointment, over a twenty-year period. If Harry came in third on the sergeant's exam, Marty came in fourth; Floyd number two for lieutenant, Browne number three. Every promotion Martin Browne received came six months or a year after Harry Floyd's.

But not when it came to making lieutenant. Since Harry had nabbed the lieutenant's job in the Twentieth Precinct, no other squad commanders had left and Browne hadn't been able to move up. Browne's number three might not qualify him for a lieutenancy for years. If ever. And Harry knew that Martin still smarted from being bested every single time. Not so different from the way he himself felt about Carlin.

Martin Browne was more than aware of Harry's resentment every time Carlin moved ahead, and he never waited long to take advantage of Harry's Achilles' heel.

"The captain's exam is coming up in three months. You getting ready to be beat out by the Harvard brain trust one more time?"

"Too bad nothing's opened up for you, Marty, or else you could be competing right along with us." Harry peered at Marty's sergeant's stripes with a derisive grin.

Martin regarded him cynically. "Like you're really sorry."

Harry clapped him on the back. "It would give me something to look for below my own name when the captain's results are posted."

Browne wasn't about to give Harry the satisfaction of a frown. Instead he doubled his attack. "I hear your old friend Squire's on the rise."

"She's a smart girl," Harry acknowledged dismissively.

"More than a smart girl," Browne protested. "I hear you and she are the only contenders for the President's Task Force on Crime. And you know they're going to pick Squire."

Harry felt as if he were being punched in the stomach. "You don't know what you're talking about," he protested, trying to keep his face a mask. He was shocked. Being on the task force was the opportunity of a lifetime, a solid year of high-profile research into national criminal activity that would culminate in reporting to Congress. He didn't even know he was under consideration, much less that it had come down to just him and Carlin.

"Hey, I'm just telling you what I heard." Marty took a large bite of pizza, chewing carefully. "You know, Harry, with her work on that Phonestalker thing . . . Well, face it, she's everybody's favorite girl."

He watched with satisfaction as Harry's face revealed some of the anger he'd been struggling to contain, then continued his needling. "And, after all, she is a *girl*. Imagine, a woman in that position. It would protect the mayor's political ass for years to come."

Marty smiled at Harry with amusement. "I'm telling you, Harry, before your kid graduates from high school, you're going to be seeing Carlin Squire at the head of every Saint Patrick's Day Parade." With that, he swallowed the last bite of pizza and crumpled up his emptied paper plate. Standing, he aimed it straight into a large wire trash basket a few feet away. "Well, that's it for me, Harry. Thanks for sharing the table."

Harry watched Marty amble toward the exit. He had a feeling that a smile of triumph would be creeping across his face just about now. God, what a loathsome creep Browne was. No wonder Harry always beat him, the guy was a fool.

But however stupid Martin Browne might be, this time he'd probably turn out to be absolutely right. Carlin would undoubtedly get that appointment. She'd be the one who rocketed to national prominence, and he'd be left in the dust.

Yeah, the big boys just loved Carlin Squire. He'd heard Fallon on the subject of her greatness too many times already.

It seemed so damned unfair. Here he'd put in years more than she had, worked a damned sight harder to get where he was. For Christ's sake, he had a wife and two kids to support while she had her rich doctor boyfriend to pick up every stinking check. Harry Junior was applying to colleges now, with the little one close behind. How much was four years of college nowadays? A hundred thou? More than that? So my kids go to a cheaper school, so what? he thought to himself. Brooklyn College was good enough for me, it'll be just fine for them.

Not that Carlin had had to make do with a local school. No, Harvard was what had been waiting for her. Sure, she claimed she was poor when she was a kid, but her kind of poor ended up in the Ivy League, not on the Seventh Avenue subway. What was her childhood really like? he wondered. Her parents must have had plenty stashed away to set her up like that.

He frowned in displeasure. What if she had stretched the truth about some other things? he thought uncomfortably. What if Marilyn had had her number on day one, and it had taken him this long to catch up? He thought about what his wife's reaction would be when he told her about the task force, which would be Carlin's next triumph. You taught her everything she knows, Marilyn would say, and now she gets to laugh at you all the way to the Oval Office.

Carlin Squire had been the one person right in front of him for too many years, and if he didn't do something about it, it would be her ass he'd be expected to kiss for the rest of his life. Oh, God, he thought miserably, how long had Marilyn been predicting something like this? Suddenly, in his gut, he understood how right she'd turned out to be. I've been like an idiot two-year-old, he thought, his face reddening in humiliation. Marilyn was the smart one all along. Carlin's been playing a shell game with me for years. Oh Harry, my good friend, my rabbi. Bullshit. She's been out to beat me on every field in every event.

Well, for once Martin Browne had been helpful. The memory of his smug little face rejoicing in Harry's future misery was just enough to move him to action—action he should have taken years before. Harry's eyes narrowed. It was perfect timing. Years ago, he wouldn't have had such a good opening. But here it was, right in front of him. An opportunity just waiting to be seized.

Harry leaned against the wall of Captain Fallon's office. "I don't quite know how to say this." He bowed his head as if weighing the consequences of his words. "I guess there's no other way but to spit it out."

Fallon looked at him curiously.

"I think Carlin Squire might have had a motive in the murder of Tony Kellner." Harry sounded almost contrite as he said the words.

Fallon raised his head questioningly. "Kellner was the dating service guy, the one you were working on, right?"

Harry nodded yes. "There are some things about that investigation you probably don't know." He paused, as if reluctant to go on. "For instance, Carlin knew every detail of the operation." Harry waited a beat, enjoying Fallon's full attention. "But here's something you don't know. I found it out myself just a couple of days ago. Tony Kellner was the guy responsible for making Carlin's father a permanent cripple."

"He what!" Fallon's face held shocked disbelief.

Slowly, Harry revealed the facts Carlin had told him about the accident in Westerfield years before.

"I'm sorry about this, Captain." Harry sounded desperately sincere. "I've been Carlin's friend for fifteen years. But even your best friend can't protect you in a situation like this one."

Fallon thought for a moment before he reacted. "Wouldn't Carlin have been on duty the day Kellner was killed? I'm sure she can account for her time."

"Actually," Harry replied smoothly, "I'm not so sure she can. The day Kellner was killed was the day of the celebration at Gracie Mansion. Carlin left after the ceremony and took the rest of the day off." Harry shook his head sadly.

Fallon stared at Harry for a long time. All he could see was the sadness of one old friend facing the worst kind of truth about another. Finally he cleared his throat and put out his hand. "This can't have been easy for you, Harry. Thanks."

Harry walked out of the office and quickly made his way out. He thought about the day Tony Kellner was killed. He'd spent every minute of that day with Carlin. If he let himself, he knew he could even summon up what a good time they'd had, laughing over a few beers and a burger in that bar.

Forget it, Floyd, he said to himself as he walked toward his car. You did it and it's over. For a moment he felt sick with shame as he unlocked the Chevrolet's front door. Quickly he countered it with fifteen years of stored-up bitterness.

"Let's see what that Harvard education can do for you now," he said out loud in the privacy of his car.

Walking into the kitchen to pick up the phone, Carlin was surprised to hear Ernie Fallon's voice on the other end. It was eight o'clock at night, long past the time he might normally call. In fact, she thought to herself, he almost never called her at home.

"What's going on, Captain? Something wrong?"

Fallon's voice exploded. "Goddamnit, Squire, you've been holding out on me. Withholding information from the police is unfit behavior for a civilian. For a cop, it's unforgivable."

Carlin was taken aback. "What are you talking about, Captain?"

"I'm talking about the murder of Anthony Kellner." Fallon's voice had become coldly official.

Carlin held her breath.

"Exactly when were you planning to tell me about your relationship with Mr. Kellner? I'd vaguely heard that you'd known him years ago, but you never bothered to mention just how deep your real relationship went, or that you had an excellent motive to murder this guy."

Carlin was startled into silence. Almost nobody knew about Tony Kellner's role in Kit and J.T.'s accident all those years ago, but that was obviously what Fallon was referring to.

"I'm not exactly sure what you mean, Captain." She stalled for time as she tried to decide how much she had to tell him.

Of course she should have informed the department about Tony Kellner's role in her life the moment he turned up dead. But that would have meant throwing Ben to the wolves. Even *she* was afraid he had murdered Tony. But maybe she was mistaken, and that wasn't what Fallon was referring to. There was no way he could have found out what had happened in Westerfield all those years ago. No way at all. She'd told no one.

No one except Harry Floyd, she suddenly realized as the captain began to speak once again.

"What I mean"—the captain picked his words carefully—"is that unless you can account for the hours from noon to six on the day you collected your award from the mayor, you are officially on notice as a suspect in the murder of Anthony Kellner."

"But, Captain"—her anger exploded over the telephone line—"I couldn't have killed Tony Kellner. Haven't you checked where I was? Didn't you ask Harry Floyd? Didn't he tell you I was with him?"

"Harry Floyd watched you leave Gracie Mansion alone." Fallon's voice dripped with disapproval. "Don't try and hide behind your friends, Squire. It's not just unprofessional, but cowardly. Consider yourself on suspension as of right now. Tomorrow you can go down to the station and turn in your gun and your badge."

The phone went dead in her hands. Carlin put the receiver down slowly, then dropped into a kitchen chair. How could he? she thought, Harry's face flashing into her mind. The man who'd always been there for her, who'd brought her along on the force, who'd enabled her to achieve so much!

That was it, she suddenly realized. She knew how hard it was for him to watch someone else succeed. She remembered wondering, all those years ago when they worked on case after case as colleagues, what would happen if her success ever interfered with his.

Well, now she knew. The question was What the hell was she going to do about it?

33

Ben emerged from one of the examining rooms, holding a manila folder containing the medical records of the patient he had just finished with.

"Helen," he said, pausing at the secretary's desk and laying down the chart, "I want to see Mr. Ballantine again in two weeks. He says he feels great, and he doesn't see any reason to come back for his final postop visit, but I need to check his wound one more time."

"Is he getting dressed now?" Helen asked.

Ben nodded. "I've explained to him that it's the final part of his surgical care. But he's waving me away."

Helen smiled. "I guess you should take it as a compliment if he thinks he doesn't need any more looking-after."

"It's—"

Ben was interrupted by the appearance of two men. Massively built, they both wore white shirts and dark slacks, and one sported a loudly striped tie. There was something about their dour expressions that made it clear they weren't seeking Ben's medical advice.

"May I help you?" Helen asked.

"You Dr. Benjamin Dameroff?" the one with the tie asked brusquely, looking past her at Ben.

"Yes, I am. What can I do for you?"

"I'm Detective William Hurley. This is Detective Dan Mannis." Detective Hurley produced a badge and flashed it at them as he spoke. "We're going to need you to come with us for a little while, Doc. It's in regard to a Mr. Anthony Kellner."

Ben nodded. "What's this all about?"

Detective Mannis took over. "We'd like you to come to the station with us to answer a few questions."

Ben gestured to the people in the waiting room. "Look, I can't just walk out now. I have patients here."

"We appreciate that," Mannis replied flatly. "Nonetheless, we're still going to have to ask you to come with us."

There was a momentary silence. Helen looked worriedly from the two men to the doctor beside her.

"Isn't there something else that can be worked out?" Ben asked in annoyance. "I'll answer questions, but not this way. What are my patients supposed to do?"

"*Now,* Dr. Dameroff." Hurley wasn't interested in negotiating.

"I'm just supposed to drop everything and walk out of here with you two?"

Mannis nodded. "That's about it."

Ben looked from the men to Helen and back again, his lips an angry line. "How long will this take?" He slipped off his lab coat as he finished asking the question.

"I can't say, Doc."

"Helen, you'd better reschedule everybody." Frowning, he walked over to his private office and tossed his white coat over a chair, then reached around to retrieve his suit jacket from a hook behind the door. He took his beeper out of one of the jacket pockets and secured it to his belt. "This is really something."

"Don't worry," Helen said reassuringly, "I'll take care of things."

"I'll check in by phone if they let me," Ben told her as he walked around to join the men in the hallway. "Page me if there's any kind of emergency. If you really can't get hold of me, you can ask Dr. Shapiro to help out."

One detective held the door open for Ben and the three of them stepped out into the waiting room. The patients already seated there looked up in surprise at the sight of their doctor, dressed in a suit and tie instead of the white coat they were used to seeing, obviously on his way out.

"Mrs. Simon, Mr. Van Hull, I'm sorry, but we'll have to reschedule for tomorrow," Ben said apologetically. The detectives moved impatiently to the door, indicating they didn't want to stand around while he made speeches. "Something's come up and I have to leave now."

"Are you all right, Dr. Dameroff?" Mrs. Simon rose in concern as her eyes took in the two men with him.

"Perfectly fine," Ben said in a reassuring tone. "I just have to take care of something."

Hurley touched Ben's elbow as if to guide him out, but Ben yanked his arm away. When they had stepped out into the bustling action of the hallway, he turned to the man.

"It's not bad enough you embarrass me and frighten my patients, is it?" he said quietly, controlling his anger so no one else could hear. "Keep your damned hands off me."

An internist Ben knew came around the corner and took in the scene of Ben glowering as he strode down the hall toward the elevator, one man on either side of him.

"Hi, Ben," he said amiably as he passed.

Ben forced his features to relax into a smile. "Hi, Mark."

He continued smiling and greeting the other hospital personnel who walked by. But his smile disappeared as they finally stood waiting in front of the elevator.

Jesus, he thought, I suppose I should be thankful they're not putting handcuffs on me. Maybe he was just being paranoid, imagining that everyone could tell he was being led away by the police. But the whole business was so humiliating.

What were they going to ask him when they got to the police station? Fearfully, he thought of Carlin and of the questions they might ask about her. He was willing to tell them the truth about his own relationship to Kellner. But, hell, he wasn't going to talk about her, there was no way. He was unsure what his rights were here and if he could refuse to answer questions. The only thing he was certain about was that he had to get a lawyer, and fast.

At the sight of her boss entering the office, Helen jumped to her feet behind the desk.

"Dr. Dameroff, are you okay?" she asked anxiously.

Ben nodded. He'd been feeling as if he were in a state of shock ever since he'd left the police station late the day before. But there was no point in alarming his secretary any further.

"Good morning, Helen. I'm fine," he said easily. "It turned out to be nothing, really. Just a big waste of time. Let's forget it ever happened."

She picked up a pile of telephone messages. "Here are your calls. The one I think you'll want to know about first is Dr. Rawlings. He wants to see you in his office right away."

Cyrus Rawlings was the chairman of his department. Ben took the messages. "He didn't say what it was about?"

"No."

"Thanks, Helen." Ben went into his office and shut the door.

Had Rawlings gotten wind of what happened yesterday? Ben wondered wearily. That's what it had to be: he'd heard that the police were questioning him about a murder. Most meetings were arranged via memos and phone calls between their secretaries. There was no reason to be summoned to the department head's office out of the blue other than to discuss the—what the genteel, Yale-educated Rawlings would undoubtedly call—*situation*.

God, it had been so much worse at the police station than he'd anticipated. Ben would have laughed if he weren't so bitter. Here he'd been worried about Carlin's getting nailed for Kellner's murder. But they'd soon made it clear that they suspected *him* of killing Kellner, for Christ's sake. At first, Ben had answered freely when they'd begun posing simple questions about how he knew Kellner and so on. But when it became evident what direction the questions were taking, he'd clammed up, saying he wanted a lawyer present. The police hadn't liked that; he wasn't being accused of anything, they'd insisted, and they expected him to provide the information they needed.

Then, walking home from the station, he'd had the shock of seeing Carlin's name in the newspaper headlines. Apparently, he was wasting his time trying to protect her; he wasn't the only one who suspected that she might have murdered Kellner.

Still, it was all speculation. His own dealings with the police were far from over, that much was for sure. But right this minute, there were two immediate questions to be resolved: what had Rawlings heard and what was he going to do about it?

His private line rang. Glad at the distraction, he answered it.

"Ben, dear, hello."

"Sara?" Ben spoke with surprise. He and Sara Falklyn hadn't talked since he'd broken off their affair. "How nice to hear your voice," he said, genuinely meaning it.

"Ben, Dean told me the police came to see you yesterday about that murder case. Are you all right?"

So the damage was worse than he feared. Even someone as removed from him as Dean Falklyn had gotten word through the grapevine about Ben's command performance yesterday. Every person who worked in Mercy must have been filled in by now; it was probably the morning's conversation over coffee and Danish up and down the hospital's halls.

"Thank you, Sara. It wasn't the way I might have chosen to spend my afternoon, but I emerged intact."

"Ben," she said reprovingly, "tell me the truth. Are you in trouble?"

"Honestly, I don't know yet." That *was* the truth, but he was beginning to wonder how long it would remain that way.

"Nobody's actually suggesting you had anything to do with it, are they?"

He didn't respond.

"Oh, my God," she said, shocked by the implication of his silence. "Please, if you think of the slightest thing I can do to help . . ."

Ben was touched that she had gone out of her way to give him this show of support, a man who had called it quits on her. Of course she had handled the end of their affair with the same elegance with which she handled everything else, but that didn't mean she'd been pleased about it. He spoke admiringly. "Thank you, Sara. You're quite a lady."

"We're still friends, or at least I'd like to think so. I'll always be there if you need me."

"You're a wonderful woman," he said sincerely. "Now, please, tell me how you've been doing. Dean's not giving you a hard time, I hope."

"I can't believe you want to talk about my marriage at a moment like this."

"I want to hear how you are."

"Well, okay. You won't believe this, but about a month ago, I finally got fed up, once and for all, and I told him I was leaving him. I meant it, too."

"You were ready to do it?"

"I was. And he knew it. Well, he was so stunned that I would actually have the nerve to do such a thing—Ben, it was as if he became a different person. He begged me not to go and swore he'd turn over a new leaf."

Ben hid his skepticism. "What did you do?"

"At first, I didn't believe him. But he really seemed to be trying, and I agreed to give him another chance. We're trying to start over again." Her voice was enlivened at the prospect of a happy ending.

"I hope it works out for you, you know that," Ben said warmly.

"Thank you."

"And whatever I can do for *you,* just name it . . ."

Her tone grew serious again. "My life is simple. But yours is getting a lot more complicated. I'm worried about you. Promise you'll call if I can help."

He hesitated. "There is one thing . . . I guess I'd better face up to it, and sooner would be better than later."

She responded immediately. "Tell me."

"It looks like I'm going to be needing a good criminal lawyer. I have a lawyer, but we're talking about someone who knows how to handle a murder trial. My guy isn't the right one for that. Would you know any names?"

"Is it really going to get that far?" she asked, horrified.

"I don't know. But I'd better be prepared."

"Oh, God." Her tone told him how upset she was. "I'll start working on it right away."

"I appreciate it," Ben said gratefully.

"And, Ben"—her voice was soft—"this will go no further. I may be back with Dean, but he doesn't have to know your business, right?"

"Thanks."

"I'll get back to you by this afternoon, tomorrow morning at the latest. Will that be soon enough?"

He smiled into the telephone. "Thank you, Sara."

They said their good-byes. As soon as he'd hung up, Ben asked Helen to dial Cyrus Rawlings's secretary to say he was on his way over if Dr. Rawlings was free now.

He removed his suit jacket and reached for a freshly laundered white lab coat. *Too bad I don't have a suit of armor,* he thought as he hurriedly buttoned it. *It looks as if I'm going to need one.*

Carlin stood beside her answering machine, letting it screen the telephone call. When she heard Sergeant Conklin's voice leaving her a message, she grabbed the receiver.

"Hello, it's me, Conklin. I'm here."

"Lieutenant?"

"I assume you've been told," she said without preamble.

"It's ridiculous, totally ridiculous, the idea of you killing that guy," he answered.

Carlin felt heartened by his fury. It was good to know someone was on her side.

"Listen, Lieutenant," he continued before she could say anything else, "I don't know if I'm supposed to be telling you this, but there's some news from Billy Williams, the detective from the Twentieth who was sent up to your hometown."

Carlin stiffened, afraid of what was coming. "Yes?"

"I guess you know this doctor who lives on the East Side, Benjamin Dameroff." Conklin's voice was apologetic. Obviously someone had told him about Carlin's relationship with Ben. "Well, Williams dug up a guy named Lenstaller, someone who it seems went to high school with both of you. He had information that must go back almost twenty years."

"Oh." Carlin felt sick. She knew exactly what information Joe Lenstaller had.

"It came out that Dameroff's mother was killed in an accident that happened because of a phone call made by Kellner." Conklin hesitated, then went on, picking his words carefully. "I guess your father was in that accident as well. Anyway, these idiots in the department now have you and Dameroff as their favorite suspects." He waited a few seconds, hoping she would say something. "They brought him in yesterday for questioning."

Oh, Jesus, Carlin thought. "I appreciate your telling me."

"Ahh, I'm sure you'll be cleared in no time. They're a bunch of stupid bastards, every single one of them."

Conklin's outrage warmed her as she hung up the phone. So they'd found out about Ben's connection to Kellner. She'd figured it was coming, but hearing about it was still something of a shock.

The phone rang again. She ignored it, letting the answering machine pick up. This one was from *Time* magazine. Grimly, she listened as the reporter left his name and number, urging her to return his call before he had to go to press without a comment from her. *Time.* Well, we've really hit the big leagues now, she thought wryly.

Too restless to sit still, she went into the living room. The damned phone hadn't stopped all day, reporters from the newspapers, producers from talk shows, everyone wanting a comment or an appearance from the fallen angel. It was the New York newspapers that had broken the news, but the media from all over had jumped on it, obviously knowing a hot story when they saw one. IS HERO COP REALLY KILLER COP? Carlin had thought her heart would stop when she saw that headline. The paper had run a picture of her accepting the award from the mayor after the Phonestalker case, then had gone to town with the story about the hero who'd caught a serial killer and was now under suspicion herself for murder.

Internal affairs had questioned her twice, and it was crystal clear now that Harry had deliberately lied about being with her on the day Kellner was killed. She could still hear the questions coming rapid-fire at her, the way they exchanged glances of disbelief with one another at her protests.

Where were you that day?

I was with Harry Floyd.

Sorry, but he's not covering for you, so give it up. You got an alibi or not?

What are you talking about? Harry's my alibi. Not that I should need one, for Christ's sake.

Floyd's told us where he was, and it wasn't with you.

The pain of Harry's betrayal was too much to handle.

She'd have to face that later. At the moment, though, she needed to find out who the hell the murderer was.

The problem, of course, was that every road still led to Ben. Other people connected with Kellner had some kind of motive, but his was the most compelling. Everything else aside, he looked even more guilty avoiding her this way. If he wanted to clear himself, he should be working with her to do so. By staying away . . .

This was ridiculous. Carlin glanced at her watch. Five-thirty. She should be able to catch him in his office. Grabbing her purse, she hurried from the apartment. She wasn't going to sit around speculating. She *had* to find out whatever she could.

Taking a deep breath, Carlin knocked on Ben's office door. She'd waited nearly an hour for him to finish seeing patients, and had pleaded with Helen not to tell him she was here. Her heart was in her throat as she waited for a reply to her knock.

"Come in."

With a supreme effort, she controlled her growing nervousness and entered the room.

His eyes opened wide with surprise. He stood up to greet her, but there was a guardedness about him, and she tried not to let him see how hurt she was by it. She didn't know if she wanted to cry or lash out in anger.

"I wasn't expecting you," he said neutrally as he gestured to a chair. "Please come on in and sit down."

"I don't think we have to be quite so formal, do we?" she asked. He seemed so completely removed from her. Come on, she reminded herself, remember what you're about to do here.

"I saw the newspaper headlines," he went on, more hesitantly now. "I'm sorry about the publicity. That can't be easy on you."

She weighed her words. "I understand you're getting some unwanted attention yourself. They took you in yesterday?"

He smiled wryly. "You're on top of things as usual. Yes."

"Anything result from that?"

"The police let it slide for the moment, but I suppose I'll be hearing from them again." He shook his head. "The fallout came when I got back here. Seems the powers that be at the hospital aren't too keen on having a suspected killer in their midst. They didn't exactly throw me out, but I have a lot of vacation time accumulated, and they *suggested* that this would be the perfect time to take it. Today's my last day, until further notice."

"Really?" Carlin said sympathetically.

He sounded weary. "The news is traveling at the speed of light. Patients are calling to ask questions, and those who've heard are canceling right and left. Before this is over, it will probably succeed in destroying my practice altogether."

"I wouldn't say *my* career is going anywhere soon, either," Carlin put in. "The department, the press—they're all over me."

Ben just looked at her.

She summoned up her courage. It was time.

"Look, Ben, we have to talk about this. Whatever reasons you've had for avoiding me, let's put that aside. It's just you and me, all alone now, so please, please tell me the truth. I know how hard this is for you, and how helpless you must feel. But we're the ones who know what happened back in Westerfield, and I understand why you would have done it."

"Excuse me?" Ben raised an eyebrow.

"I need to know. Please believe that I won't abandon you. I'll try to help you in whatever way I can. But you have to tell me. Did you kill Tony Kellner?"

"What?" His rage exploded with such force that Carlin shrank back in her chair. *"Are you serious?"*

"Look at the motive you have," she said agitatedly. "You'd vowed to get whoever made the call. It's not hard to imagine that you made good on that promise. I saw how angry you were when you found out about him."

"I don't believe this," Ben yelled, smacking the desk with his palm. "Have you lost your mind? To suggest that I'd shoot a man. Is that what you think of me?"

Carlin's voice rose in response to his. "Don't scream at me. There's plenty of circumstantial evidence against you, and it's the kind of evidence that sends people to jail. I'm trying to help you."

"Help me?" He was wild-eyed with anger now. "This is

your idea of helping me, accusing me of murder?" He shook his head disgustedly. "All this time I've been worried about how to cover for *you,* and you come blowing in here suggesting I'm a cold-blooded killer. *You're* the one who needs help."

"What's that supposed to mean?" Carlin shot back. "You know perfectly well all that stuff in the papers is a bunch of crap."

"And if there's more than what's in the papers? A few things that might come out later, things you don't want to come out?"

"What the hell are you talking about?"

"Kellner told me you were taking bribes, for starters—"

"Bribes?" Carlin's eyes opened wide with outrage. "He told you that I—and you *believed* him?"

"How am I supposed to know what the hell to believe?" Ben was struggling to regain control of his temper.

Carlin was so angry, she could barely get the words out. "To think that you could have bought such a lie—"

"Hell, I punched him in the face like some stupid schoolkid," Ben shouted. "But then he was killed, and what am I supposed to think?"

She leaped to her feet. "What are you saying?"

He stood to face her across the desk. "Don't act as if it isn't possible. He told me he had you on his payroll. And *you* had the same motive I did. It occurred to me just like it's occurring to everyone else that you took justice into your own hands to make sure he paid for what he did. Maybe you weren't quite as cool as you pretended to be when I told you Kellner made the call. You're a cop, so you certainly know how to use a gun."

"How could you dare say that!" she yelled furiously. "Is that how you think we settle our scores?" She spat out the words sarcastically. "Sure, cops carry guns, so why not use them to blow away anyone who annoys them?"

His eyes blazed. "Oh, but it's fine for you to accuse *me* of killing someone? I'm a damned doctor. We *heal* people, for Christ's sake. We don't cut them down in cold blood because we're pissed off."

Carlin stared at him for a moment. "You go to hell," she said coldly.

In a few quick steps, Ben came around from behind his desk and yanked open the door to his office. "I didn't ask you to come here," he snapped. "You can leave right now."

She stormed past him. "Coming here was a big mistake. But don't worry, I won't be back. Ever."

He slammed the door shut behind her so hard, the pictures on his wall jumped.

"Good."

34

Ben poured himself a cup of coffee. Absently, he stared out the window at the rising sun. For the first time in years, he didn't have anyplace he had to be first thing in the morning, and he hadn't bothered to set his alarm clock. But his habit of waking up early was too ingrained to allow him to sleep later. He sipped his coffee, wondering how long this enforced vacation from Mercy would last.

The separation from his work might not be permanent, but the one from Carlin undoubtedly would be. He thought back to yesterday's confrontation in his office, to the ugly words they'd exchanged, the look of hatred on her face when she'd left. He didn't know how to sort out the mixture of anger, hurt, and sorrow that had been consuming him ever since.

He took his coffee into the dining room. At least he had someplace to go later on, a way to escape it all even if it was just for a little while. The postponed conference with Borden and Sprague in Chicago had been rescheduled for the next day, and he had to catch a plane to O'Hare at three. Can I fill the next six hours packing one suitcase? he wondered wryly.

His eyes fell on the pile of mail he'd tossed on the table the night before; he hadn't had a chance to sort through it. On top of the magazines and circulars were half a dozen letters. What caught his attention was the return address on one of the envelopes protruding out slightly from the middle of the pile. It was his old address in Westerfield. He extracted the envelope and examined the unfamiliar handwriting as he used his thumb to open the flap.

As soon as he unfolded the letter inside, he dropped his eyes to the bottom of the page. Startled, he saw that it was signed "Cordially, J.T. Squire." What in hell is this? he wondered.

He sat down as he read.

Dear Ben,

You and I have never exactly been friends, but please understand that this letter is the greatest act of friendship I could ever perform. There's a secret I've got to unload before God takes me, before you and Carlin make the biggest mistake of your lives.

I'm sure I don't have to remind you of the tragedy that took place almost twenty years ago. You and Carlin found out the truth about me and your mother. Everybody in town found out. I've hardly had anyone be decent to me since then, even crippled as I am, wasting away in a pain that's worse than anybody can imagine. But there was one thing you all didn't find out. Kit and I weren't new at the game. I thought it was more respectful to make it seem that way, seeing as she was dead. But now that you and my daughter are together, I have to let out the truth. Your mother and I were together a long time before that. Before you were born, in fact. Back when your parents first moved to Westerfield.

This is rough, but you have to be told. You are my son. That's right, Ben. Mine. You'd better take that into consideration before you and Carlin go any further. She doesn't know about this, and I hope you'll leave it that way, for her own good.

I guess you understand now why I disapproved of you two when you were teenagers, why the news that you were back together hit me so hard. I'm sorry, but there it is.

Cordially,
J.T. Squire

Ben dropped the letter as if it were burning.

"It isn't possible," he whispered. "Oh, God Almighty, no."

35

Carlin moved restlessly in her sleep as she heard Harry Floyd urging her to quicken her pace. *C'mon, Cambridge, places to go, people to see.* She would have sworn the dream was real, watching herself walk toward him, smiling up at him, dressed as she used to be in her patrolman's uniform, her shoes shined to perfection, the weight of her gun and nightstick slowing her down. *Get moving, honey.* Suddenly his voice sounded harsher. *For a smart girl, you're awfully slow. Come on, damn it. Wake up and smell the coffee.*

It was the cooing of a pigeon perched outside her window that finally woke her. She lay still, thinking about the dream. Not that she'd ever been much for dream interpretation, but this one wasn't all that hard to figure out. Harry Floyd, turning on her after so many years. All that trust. All that love, damn it. Wake up and smell the coffee indeed, she thought, swinging her legs off the bed and sitting up straight. Here's how much he loves me, she thought. I'm on suspension from the police department, prime suspect in a murder case.

For a smart girl, I certainly was slow, she acknowledged sadly as she walked into the bathroom and turned the shower on full blast. Five minutes later, refreshed by the hot water and fully awake, she looked at her reflection in the mirror above the sink. Okay, Harry, she thought. You've had your turn. Let's see what today holds for me.

An hour later, she was on her way out of her building, midmorning sunlight blazing into her eyes. She walked down Broadway, stopping into H & H to buy a bagel. Taking her place on the long but fast-moving line of customers, she planned her day in her head. She would go back to the place she'd been to with Harry right after the ceremony at Gracie

Mansion. Harry might deny that they were there together, but *someone* had to remember the two of them. God knows they'd sat there long enough.

"One poppy seed, please," she said to the man behind the counter as she came to the front of the line. The bagel was warm in her hands as she gave the man a dollar and collected her change. She walked outside. Would the bar even be open at this hour? she wondered. Worth a try, she decided, realizing she had nothing else to do with her time.

The walk to Bill's took only ten minutes, but Carlin was relieved to find the door unlocked. It took a few seconds for her eyes to adjust to the dimness of the bar's interior, but she finally spied the bartender, busily wiping out beer mugs with a large white dish towel.

"Hi," she called out as she walked over.

"Hi, yourself." He lifted an eyebrow in apparent surprise as he saw her approach.

She could see him take a quick look at his watch. Obviously most customers didn't begin to arrive until later in the morning. Was it the same man who'd been behind the bar the day she and Harry had been there? She was almost sure it was.

She forced herself to smile at him, hoping an air of friendliness would make it easier for him to remember her, as she so desperately needed him to.

"I have a little problem, and I wondered if you could help me with it," she offered, as she relaxed onto a bar stool.

"Shoot," the man replied, smiling at her in return.

"I was here the other day with a friend of mine, a tall man with red hair. We were here for a few hours, eating burgers and drinking at a table in the back." She indicated the booth she and Harry had sat in.

The bartender looked at her curiously.

"I wonder if you remember me," she asked. By now she was certain she recognized him.

The man shook his head, the friendliness disappearing from his face. Carlin could imagine what he was thinking. Not only didn't it look as if he recognized her, but whatever she wanted only seemed to point to trouble.

"Sorry," he finally answered. "We serve about five hundred burgers and five thousand beers every week. My memory usually lasts from the time someone orders a bottle of Bud to the time I place it down in front of them."

Carlin couldn't afford to give up. "Is the waiter here from Monday night? He was kind of tall, with light hair, early twenties maybe."

The bartender turned his back to her, choosing to stack the glasses he'd been washing in a cabinet under the bar. "We've got one waiter and that's my son, Brad. He'll be here in about forty-five minutes or so, if you feel like sticking around."

It was obviously the last thing he intended to say.

Half an hour later, the young waiter—whose face she recognized immediately—entered the bar. But as he sauntered over to her after a whispered conversation with his father, she realized he wouldn't be any help.

"I don't know, ma'am. You might have been here. I just don't know. This place is so busy and so damned dark, I barely see people when they're straight in front of me." He shook his head as if to say, "Sorry."

Carlin walked through the length of the place when she left. She thought about what he'd said and realized he was right. This place was so dimly lit, no windows to let in any sunshine, only a few low-watt bulbs supplying any illumination at all. There was no way anyone could be expected to remember her and Harry. Disconsolate, she walked out into the glaring sunlight.

What now? she thought, looking down the length of the street. There seemed to be only one option: she would go home and unearth everything she could find on Tony Kellner, the notes from the murder plus anything she had from the undercover investigation. Something would occur to her. It damned well had to.

Six hours later, she sat at her kitchen table, every inch of which was covered by papers. In addition to the case file and the early notes from the dating service investigation, she'd filled several yellow pads with details gleaned from telephone conversations she'd had with every person linked to Tony Kellner after he'd been killed. Interview after interview with former clients and employees should have provided something more than vague suspicions as to who might have wanted him dead. But at the end of the day, all she had were the same terrible fears about Ben she hadn't been able to rid herself of since she'd heard the news of Kellner's murder.

What would I do now if I were in the office instead of home on suspension? she asked herself as she paced around the room trying to clear her head. She thought about all the stuff that would be available at Midtown North, all the reports from other investigating officers. Scrap that, she thought bitterly, sinking into a chair.

Suddenly a thought struck her. If I weren't on suspension, the first place I'd have gone would have been the police lab downtown. There's no way they'll let me in now, she acknowledged, standing up and starting to pace once again. She tried to think it through. Undoubtedly, news of her suspension would have flown through the entire department. Police gossip mills were some of the fastest in the world. But she had to get in, suspension or no suspension. Every piece of evidence from every case in the city was housed in that building. Whatever it took to get past the front desk, she had to do it.

Within ten minutes, she was speeding downtown in a cab. She glanced at her watch. Ten-fifteen, she noted with satisfaction. How many people would be around to stop her this late? But arriving at the imposing building, she had second thoughts. At least ten or twelve patrolmen were lounging outside as her cab pulled up. She realized how hasty her trip downtown had been. She needed to do something fancier than just show up.

"Sir," she addressed herself to the driver, "pull up to the next corner, please." A few minutes to think was what she needed. She walked into a near-empty coffee shop.

After a few minutes with a cup of coffee, she asked the counterman for change for a dollar, and walked to a public phone in the back. Taking out her phone book, she thumbed through it until she found the number she wanted.

"Police lab, Officer Citron," a male voice answered crisply after just one ring.

Carlin lowered her voice as she spoke. There was no way she wanted anyone else to overhear her end of this conversation. "Officer Citron, this is Sally Carruthers from Captain

Fallon's office." Carlin knew her imitation of Patrolman Sally Carruthers, who manned the desk outside Ernie Fallon's office, was nowhere near perfect, but she prayed it would do.

"Yes?" Citron sounded rushed on the other end.

"The captain is sending Squad Commander Squire down there to look at the stuff on the Kellner case. You've probably heard about all the flak up here."

"Uh huh."

Citron sounded as if he had no idea what she meant. Carlin wondered how true that would be. Probably he was just covering his own ass. Whatever, she thought. Just as long as he buys it.

"Well, she's out of things temporarily, but she's been active on this from the beginning, and Fallon wants her to have a go at it." Carlin waited for him to reply, then hurriedly hung up. No use talking this to death.

She didn't wait long to enter the building, grateful as she walked past the front desk that nobody seemed to recognize her. But when she arrived at the evidence room, it was a different story.

"So Sally Carruthers sent you." The tall black police officer whose nameplate read PETER CITRON couldn't have sounded more cynical.

"Actually, Ernie Fallon wanted me to come down here and take a look." Carlin kept her voice as cool as possible.

"I think I'll just call Captain Fallon at home and make sure that's correct, Lieutenant Squire." Citron placed his hand on the telephone in front of him, but seemed to hesitate. Finally he took his hand away, and looked her straight in the eye. "Listen, Lieutenant Squire. I gotta be straight with you. I know it was you on the phone a few minutes ago. If I call Fallon, he's gonna order me not to let you anywhere near the Kellner stuff. That's the truth, isn't it?"

Carlin didn't say a word.

"You know, Lieutenant"—Citron leaned forward, speaking quietly as if he wanted to make sure no one could overhear what he was about to say—"I've been hearing about you since the academy. You've pretty much been a legend in the NYPD. Getting you in more trouble doesn't feel very good. Please give me one reason not to call Captain Fallon."

Carlin could see he was being sincere. She decided that honesty wasn't just the best policy; it was the only one she had.

"Here's the reason. I've been framed, and not even by a master. I need to clear myself and I need to do it soon. I've done everything possible from my apartment. Getting into the evidence room is my last resort." She could hear her voice growing more agitated. "I swear to you I didn't kill Tony Kellner. I desperately need to find out who did." She tried to compose herself before meeting his eyes once again. "Please, Officer Citron, trust your excellent instincts and let me in."

Citron took a long look, then reached for the top drawer of his desk. Before pulling out a key, he smiled devilishly. "You guys at Midtown North get much more interesting cases than we do down here. You've got all those rich people and those Broadway people. I think I'd look great up there on Fifty-fourth Street."

Carlin raised an eyebrow. This guy certainly had nerve. Just how amusing would I find it if I weren't on suspension, and he was letting somebody who didn't belong there look at something in *my* precinct? Not so amusing, she acknowledged.

Yet, she liked this guy. And God knows, she needed him. "How about this, Officer Citron. You let me in for five minutes, and I guarantee you a transfer, that is, if and when I ever again have the authority to do so."

Citron smiled broadly and extracted the key.

Carlin leaned over and whispered her next words into his ear. "But I also guarantee you the hardest duty you've ever gotten in your life when you're under my command."

Citron walked over to the door behind his desk. As he opened the lock and led her into the evidence room, he chuckled as he heard her last words on the subject.

"And when you're working for me," she went on, "you ever let anybody do what I'm doing and I'll have your ass."

Three minutes later, Carlin was opening the box marked KELLNER, ANTHONY, and spreading its contents out in front of her. In addition to the revolver that was used in the shooting, there were only a few other items, most likely the contents of his pockets at the time of the murder plus several things that had been picked up at the scene, all wrapped carefully in plastic bags. As she opened the last of the bags, she almost gasped. Reaching gingerly inside, she withdrew a single button, colorfully decorated in blue and red hand-painted stripes.

Carlin looked behind her to see if Officer Citron was watching. Luckily, his attention had been diverted by the ringing of a phone outside. Quickly, she stuffed the button in her pocket and began placing all the other items back in their plastic wrappings.

"Thanks, Citron," she said, shoving the rest of the evidence back in the large box. "I'll get out of your hair now." Quickly she walked toward the door, her expression as normal as possible.

But as she walked out of the building, her face crumpled. So Ben really was a murderer, she thought, tears running down her cheeks. Up to now, she hadn't really believed it. But this button proved it. Only Ben could have left it there. He hadn't been wearing the sweater the day she'd seen him go into Tony's building. The only other time he could have lost the button would have been in the middle of the murder.

That button was as telling to her as his driver's license would have been to anyone else. She remembered every detail of it. It had been part of the sweater she'd made for him senior year of high school to commemorate their six-month anniversary. Even using those huge needles and that thick wool, it had taken forever to finish the navy blue cardigan. But the buttons had been the *piece de resistance*. For at least four nights in a row, she had decorated store-bought buttons with her own hand-painting.

Carlin walked up Third Avenue turning the button over and over in her hands. I swear I remember what I was feeling with every single brushstroke, she thought bitterly, finally closing her fist over it and burying it in her pants pocket. Who would have thought that childish gift could send Ben to jail for the rest of his life?

36

Carlin lingered at the edge of the boat pond in Central Park, recalling her mother's excitement as they stood there together so recently. Today, too, there were scores of people, as many adults as children, watching joyfully as the miniature boats powered their way across the water. She wished her mother were still here with her in New York, that she could cry on her shoulder, receive some small token of comfort. As it was she had assiduously avoided talking to her parents. Tony's murder probably would have been reported in the Westerfield paper, but what more could she say to them? Carlin could just imagine the phone call to Westerfield: *Mom, how're you? . . . I'm fine. . . . By the way, Ben Dameroff is a murderer.*

She fingered the hand-painted button, nestled in her pocket. She hadn't let it out of her sight since she'd discovered it—stolen it, really—the night before. Not that she knew what to do with it. She couldn't make up her mind what to do about any of it. There was no point in sharing her troubles with her mother. If a trained police lieutenant couldn't figure out whether or not to turn in a killer, how was Lillian Squire supposed to know?

Ben a murderer? It seemed impossible. But, of course, it was not only possible, it was true. Carlin had spent the entire day walking around the park, trying to think it through. Logically, she knew how and why he had done it, but she still had trouble visualizing the Ben she knew, the Ben she loved, actually aiming a gun and firing it.

The other picture she had trouble conjuring up was the one of her going to headquarters and turning him in. No matter how much sense it might have made, she still couldn't imagine doing it. Instead, she'd been wandering aimlessly in Central Park since early that morning. Standing by the boats, she suddenly knew what she had to do.

So, Carlin, she said to herself, if you know the answer, why don't you just go to a phone and try to arrange to see him? Because he doesn't love me, she answered herself. Because I don't want him to be a murderer, because I'm scared of what will happen to him if he confesses—because, because, because.

She forced herself to walk out of the park, and found a public phone on Seventy-fourth Street. Digging around in her pockets, she located two quarters. Seven-thirty. He was bound to be home by now.

She dialed, then waited anxiously as the phone rang seven times. Finally she gave up, getting her quarter back and dialing his office number. It wasn't Helen who answered.

"Dr. Dameroff's office."

Carlin quickly realized she had gotten the service. "This is Carlin Squire. Can you page Dr. Dameroff on his beeper and tell him I have to see him, please?" Carlin heard the rattled tone of her voice; she sounded more like a terrified patient than anything else.

The woman on the other end seemed unaffected by her panic. "If you need help immediately, Dr. Shapiro is covering for the doctor."

"Actually, this is personal. I really need to reach Dr. Dameroff right away."

"Sorry, dear, but he's out of town."

Carlin didn't know whether she was annoyed or relieved. "Can you tell me where he is?" she asked, knowing full well that her request was likely to be denied.

"We can't give out information of that kind."

Carlin hung up in frustration. She thought about walking back home across the park, but there was no way she could just go home, eat dinner, and go to bed. She would try Tash; she was bound to know where Ben had gone and when he would be back. She eased the other quarter out of her pocket and dialed Natasha's number.

"Finally!" Natasha's voice was a mix of relief and exasperation. "You were supposed to be here an hour ago."

Carlin didn't even hear her. "Do you know where Ben is?" she asked breathlessly.

"Ben is in Chicago at some conference or something. The question is, where the blazes are you?" Relief had faded from the mix. Now Natasha sounded angry.

Carlin finally realized that Tash was trying to tell her something. "Actually, I'm around the corner. Why?"

Natasha had eased into her usual affectionate tone. "Well, get over here quick, 'cause the reservation's for eight."

Carlin suddenly remembered what it was that Tash was talking about. Tonight was Ethan's birthday, and they were giving some fancy dinner that included German producer Wilhelm Heinemann, with whom Ethan was doing a film later that year. Damn, she thought, realizing how badly Natasha was going to take what she was about to say. "Tash, I just can't come, I'm sorry."

"What do you mean? You're right in this neighborhood and we don't have to leave for Lutèce for twenty minutes or so."

Natasha sounded fearful. Carlin knew how difficult it was for her friend when her finely wrought plans were suddenly changed. Tash was so methodical, everything in its place, every soldier in line. But Carlin couldn't imagine how she would get through a sociable evening of ingenious food and charming strangers.

"I just can't. Work has been a mess this week, and I'm dressed in jeans and a T-shirt." She looked down at herself and added, "Dirty jeans and a filthy T-shirt."

"Carlin, you can't do this to me, you really can't. It's bad enough Ben changed his Chicago trip so he's not around. Besides, Heinemann is looking forward to meeting the police lieutenant. It's all he talked about this afternoon. Please, Carlin." Natasha tried to cover her growing anxiety with playful begging. "Where are you, right at this very moment?"

"Seventy-fourth and Fifth." Carlin wished she hadn't mentioned how near she was earlier in the call.

"Well, in a couple of blocks, you'll have my entire wardrobe to choose from. Even a shower if you want it."

"Tash, please let me off the hook." Yet, even as she said it, Carlin felt herself giving in. Actually, the notion of a few hours of company didn't sound that much worse than facing the isolation of her own apartment.

"I'll see you in five minutes." Natasha's voice was relieved as she hung up the phone.

It was only three minutes later that Carlin was walking into Natasha's Park Avenue apartment.

"God, you look beautiful," Carlin said as she embraced her friend, who was dressed for the evening in a skin-tight black silk sheath, capped by dozens of strands of braided pearls circling round each other and hugging her slender neck.

"You'll be beautiful yourself as soon as we go upstairs and explore my closet" was Natasha's quick reply.

Carlin followed meekly as Tash led the way up the curved mahogany staircase, the feature that made the duplex co-op seem more like an elegant old house than a city apartment. Natasha led Carlin through the master bedroom into the walk-in closet that was as big as most Manhattan living rooms.

"And now, my pretty," Natasha said, rubbing her hands together like the Wicked Witch of the West, "what magical transformation shall we perform tonight?"

Carlin watched in amusement as Natasha flitted deftly over the racks, pulling out one garment only to go on to another. She settled on a white silk suit, its long, full skirt floating out from under what would undoubtedly be a tight-fitting jacket.

"I believe this one has your name on it." Natasha pulled the suit off the hanger and threw it over a large table that sat in the middle of the closet area. "But take your time. If something else catches your eye, just put it on." She walked toward the door. "By the way, Ethan's picking up Heinemann. He'll be back for us in exactly seven minutes." She winked at Carlin. "The bath towels are in there." She pointed to a large white cabinet on her left and swept out of the room.

Carlin looked at herself in one of the full-length mirrors. Her hair was a mess, but brushing it should do the trick. And no matter how sloppy her clothes looked, she was clean enough from her bath that morning. Besides, in seven minutes, no one could shower and dress and put on enough makeup to satisfy men who were used to movie stars. Carlin looked at the suit. It was beautiful, but so elegant and sleek. Much more Tash's taste than her own.

She decided to wander through the closet a bit, just to see if anything else appealed to her. She remembered a short navy blue cocktail dress threaded with silk, which Natasha had worn the month before. Now that would be a little more appropriate, she reflected, already imagining herself spilling red wine on the white silk suit as she sat at New York's most eminent restaurant.

She began to sort through the hangers. Aha, she thought, coming upon a short navy blue skirt, its silken threads woven through exactly as she'd remembered. So it was a sweater and skirt rather than a dress. Well, the sweater must be somewhere nearby, she reasoned, looking above the hangers to the wall of shelving.

Everything was packed in plastic bags, making it difficult to sift through quickly. She lifted a heavy pile and lay them on the table. Suddenly she took a step back.

There it was, third or fourth from the top. Carlin picked up the sweater she had made for Ben from the pile and hugged it to her chest. Oh God, she thought, holding it out in front of her and checking the buttons, hoping against hope that she had made a mistake. But right at the bottom, she saw a few navy blue threads where the hand-painted button should have been.

Had Ben left it in his sister's closet when he realized the button had come off? Was he that much of a coward? Carlin caught herself wondering at her own naiveté. Would a man who killed stop at covering his tracks? Of course not. Obviously, she had never known Ben Dameroff at all. Obviously, I don't know anything, she thought miserably, walking out of the closet toward the stairway.

Carlin held the sweater close as she descended, so lost in her misery that she didn't see Natasha coming up. They both stopped in the curve of the landing.

"That's not exactly appropriate attire for Lutèce." Natasha reached out and patted the sweater fondly. "Do you remember what you went through, trying to connect the shoulders to the sleeves?" She laughed out loud as she took a seat on the landing's top step.

Carlin sat down beside her. "My God," she said almost to herself. "If only I'd never come across Tony Kellner again." She lay the sweater out on top of her knees, fingering the place where the button should have been.

"Carlin, what are you talking about?" Natasha asked uneasily.

"Oh, Tash." Carlin touched her friend's cheek lightly before she lowered her hand to her pocket, removing the button and placing it on top of the sweater spread out in front of her, almost as if she were about to thread a needle and sew it back on.

"Carlin, what's going on?" Natasha eyed the sweater warily. Although she didn't immediately grasp the significance of what was happening, something inside her knew enough to be frightened.

Carlin sat lifelessly, the sweater grasped in her hands. She tried to form the words, but they couldn't seem to spill out in the correct order. "Ben and Tony. He hated Tony. You know . . . the phone call to the motel." Her hands began to shake as she attempted to clear her mind. She willed herself to stop trembling. "Natasha, I've been scared for a long time, and now I know there's no hope that it was a mistake. I was right all along. Your brother was the person who murdered Tony Kellner." Tears began to pour down her cheeks, and her moment of control seemed to end. "It was Ben," she cried. "He went to Tony's apartment and he shot him, just the way he threatened to all those years ago."

Natasha stared at her, horrified. "Why are you saying this?" she said, her voice in a whisper.

"Here's the proof." Carlin hugged the sweater to her chest, burying her face in its bulky warmth. Finally, she collected herself and sat up straight. Her eyes were dry now, her tone professional. "Ben wore this sweater the day he killed Tony Kellner. I found the button in the evidence lab last night."

Carlin looked to Natasha, who had stood up suddenly, walking down the rest of the stairs stiffly and standing at the fireplace, her back to Carlin.

Carlin raised her voice, but remained seated on the steps. "Ben must have left it in your closet so the police wouldn't find it." Her tone took on an edge of bitterness. "He was willing to implicate *you* to protect himself."

"Oh, Carlin, if only you had any idea . . ." Her back still to Carlin, Natasha's shoulders slumped. "I don't know how I can tell you this. But I have to, don't I?" She seemed to be talking more to herself than to Carlin. "There's no place left to run anymore. It's finally going to be over now, once and for all." She paused, thinking. "It's probably for the best."

"What do you mean?" Carlin tensed, instinctively grasping that something new, something horrible was on its way.

Natasha swiveled around to face her on the stairway, her voice suddenly charged with emotion. "Ben never left that sweater here. He hasn't seen it in years. I've had it since the two of you broke up in high school." She shook her head. "Until I saw you holding it just now, I'd pretty much forgotten it was his."

"What are you saying?" Carlin eased herself to her feet and slowly descended the stairway, not wanting to hear any more but knowing she had to. Natasha blurted out the words as if that were the only way she could bring herself to say them.

"I'm saying *I* put the sweater back in the closet. I'm saying *I* killed Tony Kellner."

Carlin stared at her, shocked and silent.

"You don't know what Tony was doing to me." Natasha's voice was fierce and tearful. "When I made him make that call to the Starlight Motel . . ."

"When you what?" Carlin gaped at her.

"Oh, Carlin, how can you understand? I cut school one day to shop for some stuff, and I saw them—your father and my mother—coming out of the motel. It was so disgusting." She was pleading now. "I told my mother I knew about it, and all she did was beg me not to tell anyone. And I couldn't . . . How could I tell my father? It would have destroyed him. And you and Ben . . . How could I do that to you?" She walked away from the fireplace and slumped down onto a white silk love seat. "But I wanted to punish her, to make her feel bad. So I asked Tony to make the call."

"And then they ran into the truck."

Natasha couldn't miss the revulsion in Carlin's voice.

"I never meant it to happen." Her eyes pleaded for understanding.

"But my father was crippled and your mother was killed." Carlin pictured her father before the accident, striding across the living room. She could picture all of them, the three kids playing some silly game on the kitchen table, Kit Dameroff, beautiful and vibrant, teasing her quiet husband, joking with Lillian, challenging J.T. when he would brag about something. So much tragedy out of one childish prank.

But that's just what it was, she reminded herself. A stupid childish act, one phone call whose consequences couldn't possibly have been foreseen by a sixteen-year-old girl. Carlin was overwhelmed by sadness. "Tash, was it worth murdering for almost twenty years later?"

Natasha didn't even stop to think about it. "Tony would have made it public. You don't know the things he was making me do."

"Why didn't you just tell me the truth? That would have ended his hold on you just as well."

Natasha looked at her blankly. "Tell you the truth? So you could never speak to me again, so my brother could hate me and my husband could leave me? So everybody in the country could read about the famous cover girl who murdered her own mother? Are you crazy?"

"But, Tash, you were only a kid. How can you think everyone would be so hard on you?" But, of course, Carlin admitted to herself, taking in the woman who'd been her best friend all her life. There was no way Natasha could imagine anything else.

She walked over and sank to her knees, grasping Natasha's hands in her own. "We're going to have to go into the precinct as soon as Ethan gets here. I'm sure he'll know a good lawyer to call."

Natasha's eyes filled with alarm. "Oh, please, Carlin, I beg you. Not tonight. Not right now." Her body became rigid with tension and her hands now clasped Carlin's almost to the point of pain. "Please, give me tonight. Just one night. Just long enough to talk to Ethan, to try and explain."

Carlin pulled her hands away and stood up. How can I let her do that? she thought. She knew what she had to do, how the Miranda warning should be coming out of her mouth right now, how she should be calling the precinct and telling them what she'd found.

Natasha watched her struggling. "I swear to you, Carlin," she entreated, "I'll turn myself in tomorrow morning. Eight o'clock, I'll be there at Midtown North. But, oh God, you have to give me just a few hours. Please, Carlin, just a few hours."

I can't. It's not possible. These were the words Carlin tried to say, but couldn't. There were too many years between them, too much love. "Tomorrow morning, Tash. I'll check in around seven-thirty. We'll go over to the precinct together."

The two old friends stared at one another silently. Carlin saw the anguish in Natasha's eyes mixed with gratitude at Carlin's decision. Carlin's eyes filled with tears. Natasha would be going to prison, her beautiful, fragile friend whom she'd loved so much. Tash had lived her whole life in fear, and fear had driven her to kill a man. Such a waste, such a cruel and terrible waste. The sorrow that swept over Carlin was so intense, she wasn't sure she could bear it.

She reached out her arms and Natasha responded immediately, the two of them coming together in a tight embrace of love and sadness.

"I'm here for you, Tash," Carlin whispered to her tearfully.

"I know," Natasha whispered back. "Thank you."

She pulled away, her eyes shining with tears. "Now you go home, okay? Ethan should be back any second."

Carlin nodded. "I'll see you tomorrow. Will you be okay tonight?"

Natasha forced a smile. "Don't worry about me. I'll be fine, I promise."

Back at her apartment, Carlin realized the night would be interminable. She was frantic with worry, obsessed with thoughts of Natasha. What is she saying to Ethan? Carlin asked herself over and over. How can she explain something that she couldn't even face herself?

She tried to occupy herself by reading, straightening up the living room, taking a shower. At eleven o'clock she gave up and went to bed, but it was soon obvious she wasn't going to fall asleep. She looked over at the clock. It was only midnight. Seven more hours to get through. I need to call her, to make sure she's all right, she thought, getting out of bed and going to the phone. She lifted the receiver, but stopped herself before she began to dial. One night. I promised her she could have these pitiful few hours. I can at least give her that much.

Still, she couldn't stop her thoughts. If Natasha had been so afraid of her old secret being exposed that she would kill to protect it, how would she bear up now that it was about to become public knowledge? Maybe Ethan can help her, she thought. He might be able to give her the strength she needs to get through this. The idea made her feel more hopeful.

How to get through this terrible night? She thought of the things she usually did when she couldn't sleep. Knowing it was fruitless, she turned the television set on, clicking it off a moment later. I can't just sit here, she thought, finally deciding she had to get out of the apartment or she would go crazy. She went to her closet, reaching for her jeans. But what if Tash called? She stopped, her hand on the hanger. She couldn't possibly leave. I should have stayed there, she thought frantically. If only I knew what was going on. Please make her call me, she pleaded silently. She stared down at the phone, willing it to ring. And suddenly, as if in answer to her prayer, it did.

"Tash," she cried, springing to answer it.

"Carlin," Ethan Jacobs's voice had a hollow ring to it. "Natasha ... Tash is dead ... in the tub ... a razor ..."

Ethan's voice broke and began a harsh sobbing that he couldn't seem to control. After a few seconds, he managed to quiet himself. "Carlin, please ..." Once more, a strangulated sound came through the wire. "I can't ..." He tried to go on, then simply hung up.

"Oh God, Tash," Carlin moaned, dropping the receiver. "No, no, oh please, no." She shut her eyes against the images flashing in her mind. Tash picking up a razor, lying down in her bathtub, the life slowly draining from her. "It's my fault, all my fault." She didn't even realize she was swaying from side to side, hugging herself as if she were freezing cold.

37

Carlin turned over on her left side, shifting the pillow one more time, attempting once again to relax into sleep. Since Ethan's call the night before, she'd been doing all she could to help him deal with Tash's death. Meanwhile, she herself felt frozen in guilt and grief, complicated by almost forty-eight straight hours without sleep.

She'd tried everything soothing music on WQXR, the sounds of the ocean from the white-noise machine that Derek had given her years before, even her own brand of meditation, but nothing would work. No matter how many ways she tried to clear her mind, the only thing she could think about was Natasha.

It doesn't even matter how awful this feels right now, she realized, opening her eyes one more time and glancing at the clock. It's going to be worse at the funeral, and worse yet as the days go on knowing she's not there.

Closing her eyes and surrendering to her own world only made her feel more alone. Not to mention guiltier. She'd tried to reason with herself. After all, she rationalized, Tash's secret was bound to be uncovered. But that thought did little to comfort her. So what if someone else would have found out eventually? The fact was, Carlin had been the one, and that had inevitably led to the death of her best friend.

Carlin sat up. She couldn't bear lying there anymore. Grabbing her robe from the foot of the bed, she pulled it on and walked out to the living room. I can't do this, she thought, catching her reflection in a small mirror, observing the destruction of the past twenty-four hours. Tomorrow, she would leave for the funeral in Westerfield. And what then? she asked herself. Certainly Ben wouldn't be in the picture anymore. They'd had their chance to be together and they'd chosen to destroy it. Would she go back to Midtown North? Back to monthly meetings and sector assignments? I can't, she realized. I can't just go back as if nothing happened.

At the very least, she needed time. Well, that's one thing I've got plenty of, she said to herself, thinking of the four weeks' unused vacation that had been building since the beginning of the year. She'd use it all. Maybe I'll stay up in Westerfield for a while. After that, I can go ... She couldn't imagine anywhere she wanted to be. A week from now, two weeks, maybe then she'd be ready to make some decisions. But one thing was clear: she had to get out of New York for a while and the sooner the better.

At least that gives me something to do, she thought, relieved at the prospect of keeping busy by dealing with everything she'd have to take care of in order to stay away for a month.

She walked into her bedroom, lifting the large brown suitcase stored on the floor of the closet and throwing it on top of her bed. Quickly, she filled it up with clothing. Snapping it shut, she thought about what other things needed attending to.

In the morning, she would call the precinct and let them know her plans. What else? Paperwork, she suddenly thought to herself. Jesus, I've been so caught up with everything, I haven't even looked at the mail in weeks.

She collected a pile of unopened letters that had lain untouched on the small table near her front door. Amid the numerous circulars were several pieces of personal mail plus a stack of bills. Everyone from NYNEX to Paragon Cable was waiting for Carlin to wake up to her responsibilities. She rubbed her eyes tiredly as she walked over to where her purse lay, removed her checkbook, and set the assortment of bills in front of her on the kitchen table.

Might as well start with the little guys first and work up, she thought. Within ten minutes, she had gotten up to the envelope marked AMERICAN EXPRESS. She opened it with some trepidation, certain that she hadn't paid them in at least two months. Sure enough, the amount she owed was enough to make her grimace, and the reproving words 30 DAYS PAST DUE shone from the page.

Carlin removed the copies of individual receipts from the body of the bill. It was annoying to go through each one individually, but she heard too many stories every day at the precinct of people cheated by thieves using stolen credit-card numbers; checking every single purchase had become a necessity. She sorted through the pages quickly, recognizing her signature, remembering each purchase as she glanced at the store name. Suddenly she came upon a signature that didn't look at all like hers. The name of the vendor read WILLIAM'S PUB. It didn't ring a bell. Confused for a minute, she removed the page from the pack.

Her eyes went to the numbers on the right. There were three separate groups: a subtotal, a tip amount, then the total on the bottom—thirty seven dollars even, the seven crossed European style. Carlin never crossed her sevens. She studied the signature scrawled across the dotted line. It read *Carlin Squire* but the handwriting wasn't hers. It certainly looked familiar, though.

Glancing back at the name of the restaurant, Carlin realized she had struck pay dirt. William's Pub must be the official name of Bill's Bar. It all came back to her, the dim light, Harry's teasing about her fading eyesight, the afterglow of what had been such a celebratory event at Gracie Mansion. This was it, all the proof she needed to clear herself of murder—and all she needed to expose Harry Floyd as the lying bastard he had turned out to be.

Carlin looked up Ernie Fallon's home number, then made a note of it and put it aside, going back to her bills as the morning sunlight was flooding through the living-room windows. At six-thirty, she decided she'd waited long enough.

"Mrs. Fallon," Carlin greeted his wife politely. "This is Carlin Squire. May I please speak to Captain Fallon?"

"Fallon." The captain sounded none too pleased to hear from her.

"Sorry to call so early, but I've got something important."

"Like what, for example?" Fallon responded impatiently.

"You asked for proof of where I was when Tony Kellner was shot. Well, I found it."

"Listen, Squire, what does that matter now? We know who did it. Your ass was out of the sling as of yesterday. Why are you bothering me with this at home at the crack of dawn, for Christ's sake?"

"This isn't about clearing me of murder. It's about Harry Floyd implicating me in a crime he knew I couldn't possibly have committed." She tried to keep the fury out of her voice, but she found she couldn't. "I told you I was with Harry when Tony Kellner was killed. Well, I just found the proof in my American Express bill."

"Absolute proof?" Fallon demanded, now fully attentive.

"One hundred percent," she replied.

Fallon responded crisply. "I'll meet you at the Twentieth Precinct at eight-thirty," he insisted. "And bring the damned American Express thing with you."

"I'm leaving for a funeral upstate at eleven-thirty," she explained.

"I don't care if you've got an appointment with the president," he countered. "You'll get that thing over to me before you leave."

Carlin showered and dressed quickly, then surveyed her apartment to see if she'd forgotten anything. As she prepared to leave, she peered at herself in the hall mirror. I don't care how exhausted I look, she thought, refusing even to add blush to her cheeks. Fallon doesn't have to think I'm beautiful; he just has to know I'm honest.

Within twenty minutes, Carlin was seated across from Ernie Fallon, as he examined the American Express receipt.

"Sickening," he muttered angrily, turning the receipt over and over in his hand. "I remember the two of you when you first came to Midtown North. Like Clark Kent and Lois Lane. Floyd was so excited about your coming. Like he was your father or something."

He shook his head disgustedly. "You two shoulda stayed friends all the way to retirement. But Harry would have had to be a different guy."

"I'm not sure what you mean," Carlin said.

"Sure you are, Cambridge. You know Harry better than anybody. You who were the only ones under consideration for the President's Task Force on Crime. With you out of the picture, it would have gone to Harry."

Carlin's eyes opened wide in surprise.

He shook his head. "The way things are, it's going to get thrown back in your lap. I hope you're ready."

Carlin just stared at him. Right now that was the last thing on her mind.

Unexpectedly, Fallon left the room, returning a few minutes later, his face sober.

"Okay, Lieutenant," he said, entering the room and holding out his hand.

Carlin stood up and put her hand out to meet his. Rather than shaking it, as she expected him to do, he held her hand in his in a more personal gesture.

"That's the end of it, Cambridge. I know you've been through hell these past few days. It's over now." He squeezed her hand lightly before he let it go.

Touched, she turned away and walked out of the room. She'd gotten almost to the building's exit when she realized there was something she had to do. Turning around, she walked to the back of the precinct, stopping as she came to the door marked LIEUTENANT FLOYD.

He was standing by his desk, loading a bunch of folders into a large cardboard box. His face was grim as he noticed her in the doorway.

"Congratulations," he said ironically.

"Why? Did I win something?" she snapped.

Harry's eyes were pure spite. "The whole shooting match, the big prize. The field is all yours, honey."

Carlin stared at him, pain and disappointment all over her face. "And that's it? All these years we had, and that's all you have to say?"

His eyes gave away nothing.

But Carlin couldn't stop now that he was right there in front of her. "You were worried that someone might beat you to the finish line, and you were damned if you'd let that someone be me, the one you brought onto the force, your acolyte, your best pupil, a *girl*, for Christ's sake." Carlin shook her head in disgust. "All this over a lousy task force?"

Harry couldn't bear to keep quiet any longer. "Of course

the princess of self-righteous indignation would have done everything different from what I did." He looked at her as if she were a laboratory animal. "From day one, you followed my every move, sucked up everything I could give you, marched ahead of me, trampling me under your feet every chance you could get. Marilyn saw it clearly all along. *I* was the idiot who apologized for you every time it happened."

"Every time what happened?" Carlin asked, astounded at his outburst.

"Don't pretend to be naive, Goddamn it." An explosion of anger left a flush of red on his cheeks as his hands clenched into fists at his sides. "The tests, the investigations, the awards. You walked away with all of it, just as you intended to all along."

Carlin looked at him in bewilderment. "What are you talking about? Civil service exams are completely standardized; how could I know I would come out ahead of you? And the Phonestalker investigation . . . We disagreed from the start. You believe I was plotting against you? My God, Harry, think about it. I never lied to you, never hid anything from you."

Harry peered at her, as if searching for the truth. Suddenly none of it made any sense. This was Carlin in front of him, a woman who'd been nothing but loyal. Always. Every step of the way. What on earth had he tried to do to her?

It had all seemed so logical when he'd been turning it over in his own mind. Once he'd started down that path, everything had fallen into place so neatly. Except that he'd been turned around 180 degrees in the wrong direction. It was his own stupidity, his own greedy need to have it all and to make sure she wound up with nothing that had destroyed his career.

Telling that lie had been so simple, just a few quick words and it was done.

He felt as if he'd been temporarily insane. Turning away from Carlin, he walked uncertainly to the window.

"Jesus, I'm so sorry."

She heard his strangled apology, watched him shrink in humiliation as he continued to look out the window.

"Good luck, Harry," she said quietly, turning and walking through the door. Oddly enough she meant it.

38

Ben dropped his valise on the rickety metal suitcase rack and hung the garment bag containing his suit in the narrow closet. The hotel room was bare and impersonal, the few pieces of furniture in it shabby, but it didn't matter; he wasn't interested in his surroundings.

Aimlessly, he wandered around, drawing open the curtains to glance out at the parking lot one floor below, getting a drink of water in the bathroom, opening his suitcase and carelessly shoving the few items he'd brought into the small chest of drawers opposite the bed.

Finally, there was nothing else to do. He sat down at the small wooden table in the corner, propping his elbows up to rest his head in his hands. The last thing in the world he would have expected was that Natasha would ask to be buried in Westerfield. She'd always loathed it here; he had no trouble remembering the countless times she'd vowed to get out and never come back.

Ben had been stunned when Ethan first telephoned him about her wishes. But when he read her suicide note, the whole thing made perfect sense.

It pained him unbearably to think of his sister sitting down to compose that note, knowing she was going to end her own life. That had to be the most alone any person could ever feel. When he saw the actual note, reading her familiar delicate handwriting and holding the thick white paper in his hands, he'd felt a stabbing grief so intense, he'd had to catch his breath. The things he considered her silly affectations—the overpriced Cartier stationery, the purple ink she used on all her correspondence—now seemed so achingly vulnerable. She'd written out the entire story of what happened for Ethan, how she knew their life together would be over once he found out what she had done to her own mother, and how she'd kept it from him.

There's been a message in there for Ben also, and he'd been crushed by the weight of her secret pain.

> *... I've hurt you the most, dearest Ben, although you're the one I love above all else. I would have done anything in the world for you, but all I ever accomplished was to deceive you. I couldn't stand to look you in the eye again. I wonder if you'll be able to ever forgive me. Please try.*

Still, as the letter went on, Ben saw there was a sort of serenity to her good-byes, such loving words for Ethan and him, and for Carlin as well. The final request was oddly comforting to him.

> *... It's because of what I did that my mother is buried in the cemetery in Westerfield. All my life, I wished she'd loved me more than she did. Maybe it was more than she could. Maybe we can find in death the closeness we never seemed to have in life.*

Ben heard Ethan moving around in the next room. He had been nearly silent during their trip up here. Ben was glad his brother-in-law had accepted his offer to drive together; he doubted that Ethan would have been in any shape to drive himself. Since Natasha's death, his sister's husband had been in a state of shock, alternately angry and despairing, unable to comprehend that his wife had kept secrets of such magnitude from him, blaming himself for not seeing that something was wrong in those weeks Tony Kellner was blackmailing her.

"Did I even know her?" he'd asked Ben over and over the night before. When his secretary summoned him home from his meeting in Chicago with the terrible news, Ben had gone straight from the airport to Ethan and Natasha's apartment. Ethan had been wild with grief, unshaven and half-drunk, his eyes red-rimmed. "How could she have thought I would leave her over this? I can't believe she didn't trust me enough to know we would have worked it out. Didn't she realize how much I loved her?"

Ben had been at a loss for the right words of comfort, fighting back his own sorrow. Ethan was practically incoherent as he tried to make sense of it all. "I didn't understand her. I didn't understand a damn thing about her. Did I know her at all?"

Did any of us know her? Ben asked himself tiredly. She was always chasing something that eluded her, never happy as herself, not even when they were kids. Why, he wondered, couldn't she have found any satisfaction in who she was?

"My sweet baby sister," he whispered sadly. "Poor little Tash."

He felt hot tears on his cheeks. Tomorrow they would bury her beside Kit and Leonard. That beautiful face, closed up in the darkness of a coffin. With a start, he recalled that he'd had almost the identical thought at his mother's funeral.

There was a fourth plot at the cemetery, on the other side of Leonard. That one was for Ben. He could remember when Leonard had purchased the four graves; he and Natasha had still been in elementary school. *I know it's not for a long time, but we're all taken care of now,* Leonard had said to Kit. Back then, Ben had thought it was disgusting to make plans for when you were dead.

We used those plots a hell of a lot sooner than any of us would ever have guessed, he thought. Now there was just the one left for him. Would he wind up there, no family of his own to take care of, the way his father had taken care of them? No daughter or son to think the plans *he* made for the future were ridiculous?

He sighed heavily. Carlin. He knew that she was here in Westerfield as well, that she'd flown in this morning and was staying with her parents.

Natasha's death had pushed Carlin out of his mind, but until he'd gotten the phone call about his sister, he'd thought about little else. Now, of course, it was clear how stupidly wrong he had been to doubt her. I let my suspicions poison everything between us, he berated himself furiously. The last time he'd seen her, their words to one another had been so vicious . . . but none of that mattered now.

J.T.'s bombshell in that letter rendered everything else unimportant. The idea that J. T. Squire could actually be his father made Ben sick. Still, it didn't really matter if it was true; Leonard Dameroff had raised him, and no matter what, Leonard was the man Ben would always consider his father. But the thought that Carlin was his sister was too horrifying to take in.

Ben stood up and began pacing restlessly. Damn it, he thought, Carlin's entitled to the truth.

Resolutely, he strode to the door.

"So I have that little half-wit to thank for all this," J. T. Squire said angrily. "Of all the twisted little—".

"Dad, please . . ." Carlin leaned forward in her chair. "Natasha's dead. You and Kit Dameroff weren't the only ones who suffered. She paid a pretty high price, don't you think?"

"No, I don't," J.T. replied hotly. "She goddamned deserved to die, the little shit."

Carlin stiffened. "That really isn't called for," she said quietly.

J.T. poured himself another glass of Scotch. "Sure, I should just accept it, forgive and forget, right?" His voice grew louder. "That's easy for you to say. You haven't spent the best years of your life in this stinkin' chair."

Carlin nodded. "That's true. But nothing's going to change what happened."

Her father yelled back in response. "Don't patronize me, you little know-it-all. This is just as much your fault, you and that jerk-off Ben Dameroff."

Carlin leaned back as if she'd been slapped. At the sound of J.T.'s raised voice, Lillian emerged from the kitchen, drying her hands on a dish towel, anger on her face. She addressed her husband sharply. "Don't you dare speak that way to Carlin. She's been through more than enough on your account."

J.T. looked over with surprise. But he recovered quickly, the corners of his mouth turning down in a frown. "How fortunate that the queen of the manor is here to straighten us out. Oh, I forgot, this is the new you. New and improved."

"I'm so glad you appreciate what I have to say," Lillian replied evenly. "I suppose that means I won't have to tell you again to leave Carlin be."

"Jeez, listen to the sarcasm," J.T muttered under his breath. He turned to Carlin. "Ever since she visited you in New York City, she's been too high-and-mighty for me."

Carlin was annoyed. "What do you mean, Dad? That she's speaking up for herself once in a while?"

"You show me some respect, goddamnit," he yelled at her. "The two of you are a pair, I tell you."

Abruptly quiet after his outburst, he slumped back dejectedly in his chair.

Lillian suddenly seemed to have lost her resolve. "It's okay, J.T. Relax now, dear," she said soothingly. "We didn't mean to upset you."

Carlin looked at her mother, taken aback at the way she had shifted gears. In their phone conversations, Lillian had told Carlin proudly that she was really making the effort to change things, that she wasn't letting J.T. get away with treating her so badly. But now Carlin wanted to yell at Lillian not to back down. On the other hand, she thought with a pang, it's not for me to tell her how to handle him; I'm certainly no expert on making relationships work.

Tiredly, she got up and went into the kitchen to pour herself a glass of red wine. She sipped at it slowly. What I wouldn't give to hear Natasha knocking at the door, she reflected. A ten-year-old Natasha. Or maybe a thirteen-year-old Natasha. She smiled wistfully. They'd had so many wonderful years together as children, she wasn't sure which age she would pick if she could go back in time.

When she thought of her friend, Carlin felt as if something had been torn from inside her. We all loved you so much, Carlin told her silently. I could have accepted the truth. I'm sure Ben could have too. What we can't accept is that you're gone.

She practically jumped at the sound of a knock at the apartment door, believing for a second that it really was Natasha on the other side. Sighing, she set down her glass and went to see who it was.

"What the hell do *you* want?"

Carlin heard J.T.'s snarling question as she entered the living room. She stopped in her tracks when she saw Ben standing there.

"You'll have to excuse my husband," Lillian began. "He's been—"

"Carlin." All she heard was the relief in Ben's voice. "God, it's good to see you."

Her stomach flip-flopped at the sight of his handsome face, his dark eyes locking with hers. She felt the same liquid weakness he'd induced in her since they were teenagers. But she held her ground and said nothing.

He came closer, his voice low. "We need to talk."

She answered coolly. "Why must it be this minute?"

"I have to tell you something, please let me," he said urgently.

J.T. interjected in a sour tone, "Carlin, you can't still be mooning over this guy." He gave a disgusted snort. "These Dameroffs are like a curse on us."

"Would you like us to leave you two alone?" Lillian asked her daughter, moving to stand behind J.T.'s wheelchair in order to take him into the kitchen.

"No!" Ben turned and answered so vehemently, there was a shocked silence in the room. "We're going to have this out in the open right now. You're going to explain it to us, J.T."

A knowing look and the glimmer of a smile flashed across J.T.'s face, but it was quickly replaced by an expression of indignation. "I'm going to explain nothing," he retorted sharply.

Ben took a step closer. "Carlin and Lillian deserve to know what you told me. That you and my mother had an affair when my parents first got here. That you got her pregnant with me. Tell them you're really my father."

Carlin gasped at his last words. Ashen, she turned to her father. "That can't be true."

He looked her right in the eye. "And why not?"

"Your father wrote me a letter, Carlin," Ben went on, still staring at J.T. as he spoke, "and laid it all out. According to him, we're half-brother and -sister. He says he and my mother started up as soon as my parents got to Westerfield."

J.T. looked defiantly from Ben to Carlin, but didn't respond. Lillian came around to stand directly in front of her husband. She gazed down at him for a long time.

When she spoke, her tone was pure ice. "Since we've been married, I've known you were many things. A lazy, vain womanizer, for starters. A selfish and a dreadful father. I could go on—it's a long list." She paused and took a deep breath. "But I never imagined that you were evil. For you to say such a thing is truly evil, J.T. What were you trying to accomplish?"

Lillian turned to face Ben and Carlin. "If my husband had ever noticed anything other than his own reflection in the mirror, he might have remembered that Kit Dameroff was already six months pregnant when she moved here. I met them the day they arrived and I knew exactly how pregnant she was. Of course, I got pregnant with Carlin a month or so later, so for a bit there we were even pregnant at the same time. I remember it like it was yesterday." She gazed directly at Carlin. "I remember everything about your childhood as if it were yesterday."

Ben's mouth was set in a grim line of fury as he turned again to J.T. "So you made this story up for your own amusement. You told me to spare Carlin the truth and stay away from her because we were related by blood. That was just your idea of a little fun, I suppose."

The older man shrugged, unconcerned. "It seemed to me that's the way it happened. But my memory may not be what it used to be."

"You never had an affair with my mother before the time she died, now did you?" Ben demanded in disgust.

J.T. gave a small apologetic smile. "Like I said, my memory . . ."

Lillian spoke again, this time with a quiet finality. "I've done the best I could, J.T. Even recently, when I finally faced up to how much I've allowed you to control me, I still tried to hold things together. But you've crossed over the line."

"What's that supposed to mean?" J.T. snapped.

She was nodding, as if to herself. "I want to be at Natasha's service tomorrow. It's too important to me; God knows, I loved that girl as if she were my own. But afterward, I'll start getting my things together."

"Don't threaten me with that crap," J.T. said menacingly.

"It's not a threat, J.T.," Lillian said to him. "I've waited too long as it is. Tomorrow I'm leaving you."

Carlin was stunned by the look of hatred that came over her father's face.

"You've just been waiting to do it." His voice grew louder. "This is your big moment of triumph, isn't it, Lillian? Walk out on your husband, let him rot in his wheelchair. That's the kind of person you are."

Lillian didn't respond. Instead, she turned to address Ben. "I'm sorry you had to see this. We've caused you enough heartache to last a lifetime, and our troubles aren't your concern."

"Please, I—" Ben tried to protest.

"No, Ben. It's way too little and far too late, but I want you to know that I hold this family responsible for what happened to yours. I'm deeply sorry."

She walked to the bedroom door. "Now, if you'll all excuse me."

The door closed behind her.

"She won't do it," J.T. said defiantly. "She can't make it on her own. No way."

Carlin stared at him in disbelief. Her father had written that note to Ben to keep the two of them apart. And even confronted with his lies, he was utterly indifferent to the pain he had willfully inflicted on both Ben and his own daughter. He doesn't love me at all, she thought numbly. He deliberately tried to destroy what I care about most in the world.

She came closer to his chair. He took a long swallow of his Scotch, then set it down on the table and looked up at her impassively.

"You wanted to hurt me. To tell that lie . . ." She could barely get the words out.

"Sorry for the misunderstanding, sugar," he said easily.

She was practically whispering. "You're a bastard. And let's be sure there's no misunderstanding about this: you'll never see me again."

With a few quick strides, she was out the door. Ben followed her into the hallway. He found her leaning against the wall, taking deep breaths to calm herself.

"I feel like this is all my fault," he said.

Instinctively, he moved to put his arms around her, then stopped himself. Did he have the right?

Carlin saw him draw back. He feels so little for me, she thought, he can't even bring himself to touch me. She looked away from him in pain.

Ben couldn't stand it any longer. He moved closer and put his hand out to touch her. "Carlin . . ."

She heard the pleading in his voice and turned to face him.

"What do you want from me?" she cried. "I know you're trying to help. But there's only one thing I want from you, and you can't give it to me."

"What are you talking about?"

It was agonizing for her to get the words out. "I want you to love me. But you don't."

"Are you crazy?" Ben grabbed her by the shoulders. "I love you more than anything in the world."

"Ben, oh God."

Suddenly, they were kissing, the need in each of them crying out urgently and finding its match in the other's longing. Hungrily, they lost themselves in the delicious familiarity of one another as Ben stroked Carlin's hair. She clung to him, wanting to forget everything else in the world. Let it all go away, she thought, as long as I can be with Ben.

They finally pulled apart. "Let's get out of here," he whispered huskily.

Outside, they started up the block, walking side by side without touching, neither one of them speaking.

"How many times do you think we've walked on this street?" Ben asked as they passed the dingy apartment complex and turned the corner.

Carlin laughed. "A hundred million at least." Her expression turned serious. "This may well be the last time, though. I'll never forgive him, Ben, never."

Ben nodded and was quiet again for a few minutes as they walked:

"You know," he finally said, "it's not that I've ever been a big fan of J.T.'s. But he *is* your father." He gave a sardonic laugh. "Thankfully, he's not mine as well."

"It was a despicable lie!" Carlin jumped in vehemently. "I

thought you always hated him. Are you telling me I should honor and obey just because he's my parent?"

"No, that's not what I mean," Ben replied slowly. "I'm saying that our parents get old and they die, and the sad truth is they're the only parents we have. You may never want to see him again right now, and maybe you won't *ever* want to. But the day may come when you change your mind. And you should let yourself if that happens."

Carlin stared at him. "You always manage to surprise me."

He kicked a small stone in front of him. "I've buried both my parents, Carlin. If the day comes when you can deal with him, I'll be around to help you do it."

She stopped walking. "You'll be around? I didn't get the impression you wanted to be around me much anymore."

Ben faced her and took both her hands in his. "I committed the unforgivable sin of not trusting you."

"Oh, Ben." Carlin shook her head incredulously. "How could you have believed those things Tony said?"

"It wasn't that I believed it. But I wasn't sure if I could *not* believe it either. I mean, you could have changed over the years. Or had some terrible secrets you chose to keep from me."

"Terrible secrets," Carlin echoed. She was quiet, then spoke softly, almost as if to herself. "Like Natasha's terrible secrets."

Ben closed his eyes in pain at the mention of his sister's name. "Yes," he said quietly. "Like Natasha."

They continued walking for a few minutes. This time, Carlin broke the silence.

"I guess it's pretty hypocritical for me to be upset with you, considering that I was sure *you* killed Tony." She looked down at the ground, ashamed. "I don't know how to apologize."

Ben expelled a long breath. "We're quite a pair," he muttered. "The two avengers."

Then, slowly, a grin spread across his face.

"What's so funny?" Carlin asked.

"Well, we both wanted justice from Kellner. I'm thinking it's lucky we didn't dare each other to do something about him."

Startled at first, Carlin began to laugh. "You're absolutely terrible." Then, her expression grew somber again. "How can we laugh, Ben? Natasha was the one who did something about him. In the end, she was the one who suffered."

"I know," Ben nodded. "I don't have an answer for that."

They stood there sadly. Then Ben reached out, tenderly laying his hand against Carlin's cheek. "The only good thing I can say is that Natasha always wanted you and me to be together. In all her fairy-tale views of the world, that was one happy ending she never gave up on. And now I hope at least that one will come true."

Carlin put her arms around his neck. "I guess I never gave up on it either. It's what I've always wanted, too."

"Forever," Ben whispered, leaning down to kiss her.

Carlin melted against him, tears of both joy and sorrow in her eyes. It was, she realized, because of Natasha that she and Ben had found each other again. The circle of our lives, she thought sadly, our losses and gains, forever intertwined. *Thank you, my friend. Good-bye.*

She drew back and looked into Ben's eyes.

"I love you, Ben. Nothing on earth will ever change that."

He answered her with another kiss, this one deeper and more passionate.

We've waited so long, she thought, her heart flooding with happiness. Finally, we're home.

If you enjoyed
Only You,
you won't want to miss
Cynthia Victor's
next exciting novel,
What Matters Most

The following is a special
advance preview

"Oh, Lainey," Riley Cole cried ecstatically, "these are dynamite."

The dark-haired little girl dug the blue sheets decorated with pictures of Supergirl out of the box so quickly, both the pillow case and a small white envelope fell to the floor.

"And what do we have here?" Lainey Wolfe smiled at the girl as she bent down to retrieve the items, replacing the pillow case in the box, then handing the envelope to Riley to open.

Eagerly, she tore at it, her eyes shining as she discovered what was inside. "That's me," she shrieked, delighted at the hand-inked cartoon of a little girl dressed in Supergirl's cape and boots. "But, Lainey, the letter in front's all wrong," she added, pointing to the enormous R right in the middle of the girl's chest. "It's supposed to be an S. You know, for Supergirl."

Lainey moved forward, her arms coming around the small girl's shoulders and pulling her into a warm hug. "No, silly, it's supposed to be an R for Riley Cole, the superest child in the state of Connecticut." She turned to the girl's blond-haired older brother, who sat across from them browsing through a soccer magazine and pretending to be paying no attention. "The superest child next to Timothy Cole, that is," she added, loosening her hold on Riley and reaching over to pick up another wrapped gift box.

Tim Cole put down his magazine and took the box from her, affecting all the nonchalance a nine-year-old could muster as he slowly undid the Christmas wrapping. When he'd lifted the lid off the box, however, he couldn't hide his excitement. "Oh, how'd you get this? Oh, wow, man, you're the greatest, I swear it."

Triumphantly, he removed the contents of the box and carried them over to his mother, who was observing from behind the couch, resting on her forearms as she leaned over, enjoying the camaraderie between her friend and her children.

"Look at this, Mom, it's a basketball signed by Patrick Ewing! And two tickets to the Knicks game next Saturday!"

"Is the other ticket for me?" Riley asked. Having unfurled her new sheets on the living room carpet, she spread herself out on them and closed her eyes as if she were about to go to sleep for the night.

"No, Riley," Lainey replied, tickling the bottom of her feet until she sat up and wrapped the sheets around herself like a protective cloak. "That particular ticket has my name on it."

Riley frowned. Farrell Cole came over to her pouting daughter and scooped her up in her arms, sheets and all. "Daddy and I have other plans for you that day, buster," she said, carrying her like a bundle to the foot of the stairway in the center hall. "If you get upstairs right now and change into a decent skirt and a clean blouse, you will reap the rewards when your brother goes out on the town with Aunt Lainey."

Riley squiggled out of her arms. "Lainey's not our aunt, silly." She clambered up three steps, then sat down and made herself comfortable.

"Well, then." Farrell lifted a finger to her forehead, pretending to be thinking deeply. "When your brother goes out on the town with Uncle Lainey."

"She's not an uncle either, Mommy." Her offended tone clearly indicated that she wasn't to be made fun of again.

Tim walked over to the staircase. "How would you know, stupid?" he said airily before bouncing his new basketball off his little sister's knees.

Riley grabbed the ball and leapt down to the bottom step, hurling the object back at her brother, who easily sidestepped the assault. Abruptly, he ran back into the living room. He returned within seconds, holding up the card that had been inside his gift.

For all of the children's lives, Lainey had been enclosing a cartoon in every Christmas and birthday present she gave Tim and Riley. Tim's first one had been when he was born. It was a sketch of a stork carrying a baby over the Connecticut state line, while a crowd of people who had climbed out of their cars stood watching and applauding. He kept it in his top desk drawer, along with all the others she'd done.

He beamed with pleasure as he examined the newest contribution to his collection. Lainey had drawn a boy with straight blond hair wearing a basketball uniform, leaping ten feet up in the air and stuffing a ball through the hoop as three aged players watched from the sidelines, all seated in wheelchairs, shawls wrapped around their shoulders. GUESS WE GOT TO THE NURSING HOME RIGHT ON TIME, read the words coming out of one of their mouths in a ballooned caption.

"Who are they?" Riley asked, grabbing the card out of her brother's hands.

Tim pulled it back, giving his sister a derisive look. "Obviously, it's Larry Bird and Michael Jordan and Isaiah Thomas," he said, pointing at each character in turn.

"Obviously, it's Karry Kird and Kichael Kordan and Kisiah Khomas," the little girl mimicked, jumping up and down on the steps.

"Stop it, both of you." Laden with bags of pretzels, nuts, and potato chips, plus an assortment of soda bottles, John Cole had come through the front door without anyone hearing him. "All this noise is going to scare off our guests. Who will be here in"—he looked meaningfully at his wife—"approximately twenty-five minutes."

"You heard your father." Farrell grabbed each of the children by a hand and pulled them up the stairs behind her.

John put down the heavy bags and extracted several of the soda bottles, carrying them over to the large table in the living room that would serve as a bar. "Thank goodness one person here is ready for this shindig," he said approvingly, looking over at Lainey, who wore a snug-fitting royal blue sweater dress that came down to the mid-calf. He frowned at the clunky black boots that completed her ensemble. "Why do all you women from Manhattan dress like you're in the army?"

"It's on the instruction sheet hanging on the wall at Balducci's," she answered. "Besides, it's a whole lot more comfortable than the five-inch heels you men would have us wear."

"Yeah," he agreed, "but where's the mystery?"

"The real mystery is how we can still be standing two hours later given what we're doing to our feet." Lainey laughed. "Time to go and pretty myself up." She started up the stairs, blowing him a quick kiss. "I'll try to make my face as festive as possible even if my feet look as if they're going on maneuvers."

She didn't look back, but she knew just what expression John Cole's face would have. Some mixture of dismay and disapproval would quickly settle into fondness, just as it had been doing for the fifteen years since he'd married her best friend.

Lainey ran her hand along the smooth mahogany railing. The lustrous wood had obviously been polished that day, as had the rosewood table holding three bowls filled with fresh flowers that decorated the landing halfway up. She stopped there, hearing the sound of Tim and Riley playing in the TV room, their noises hushed by the deep-pile carpeting. The slight fragrance of Farrell's perfume mingled with the aroma of boeuf Bourguignon and pears poaching in red wine that rose from the kitchen, all of it enhanced by the smell of the fires John had lit in the living room and the dining room.

This is what life is supposed to be about, Lainey thought, overwhelmed by a sudden sense of loneliness. She had rarely been jealous of Farrell, yet tonight the richness of her friend's life seemed undeniable. Here Farrell lived, in one of the most beautiful Colonial houses in one of Connecticut's most beautiful towns, surrounded by a husband who adored her, children who lived for her, a housekeeper to do most of the boring chores, a figure to die for, and friends by the score.

Farrell's bedroom door opened, and Lainey watched her emerge into the hallway, a vision in white cashmere, her dark silky hair down around her shoulders, her face accented by freshly applied lipstick and mascara, tiny pearl earrings her only jewelry aside from the diamond wedding band she never removed. She stood there for a moment, lost in her thoughts. Lainey was startled to see her put her hand to her chest and take several deep breaths, as if she were having difficulty.

"Farrell, are you all right?" Lainey called up to her in concern.

Surprised by Lainey's presence, Farrell hastily dropped her hand.

"I'm fine," she said quickly. "What are you up to?"

"Well, I was coming up for last-minute facial repair work, but I decided to stop right here and feel sorry for myself."

Farrell looked at her in bewilderment. "You? Why would you feel sorry for yourself? You have the most exciting life in the world."

Lainey rolled her eyes. "What would be the exciting part? My tiny one-bedroom apartment, perhaps? My job as an assembly-line worker for the Carpathia Empire? My—"

"Hold on," Farrell interrupted. "You have a wonderful job. You're a full-fledged designer, for God's sake."

Lainey shrugged her shoulders. "Meaning I copy cartoon characters onto mugs and rubber stamps, and get my wrists slapped if I so much as have them facing left instead of right."

"Meaning you get to go to a fancy office every day and interact with glamorous, creative people, and get paid for doing it."

"And I get to look at the man I love as he leaves to go home to his wife every night." Lainey sighed, coming to join Farrell at the top of the steps. "Sorry. That was tasteless. But it just hurts so much, especially on a holiday like this."

Farrell took Lainey's hand, pulling her toward the master bedroom. God, life is crazy, Farrell thought as she squeezed her friend's hand warmly. Imagine Lainey holding my life up as a model when I'm about to turn my entire world upside down. Fear and exhilaration mingled in her belly, the same mixture she used to know so well, had courted through most of her life. But all that was so long ago, before her marriage to John, the birth of her children. Now those feelings were reawakened, as tempting and tantalizing as a forbidden drug.

She thought for a moment of sharing her secret with Lainey. What a relief it would be. Quickly she stopped herself. Lainey would never understand. My God, she thought, I don't understand it myself. No. No matter how dangerous this was, it was something she had to do, something she wouldn't be talked out of.

"Let's get to that facial repair stuff before all the other guests arrive," she said, forcing lightness into her voice. She led Lainey to the antique inlaid vanity table at one end of the large room, standing behind to observe as Lainey sat down and picked up a small brush, pulling it through her dark blond, wavy hair.

Farrell watched her for a few moments, then bent down and gathered Lainey's hair in her hand, lifting it up as if to evaluate how it would look in a French twist.

Lainey met Farrell's eyes in the mirror. "Who'd have thought you'd be the one with the life straight out of *Good Housekeeping*?" She shook her hair back into its wavy disarray, and her lips turned up in a smile. "I used to imagine you ending up as a belly dancer or a bush pilot. Or, if not that, possibly in Leavenworth."

"You sound like my mother." Farrell's tone clearly indicated it was no compliment.

Lainey pursed her lips and raised her naturally low voice to a high soprano. *"Farrell may not come to the phone today. She neglected to wear her bite plate in school."*

Farrell began to laugh. "God, she was on my case all the time."

"Well," Lainey said judiciously, "you can't exactly blame her. Imagine if she had known all the stuff you did."

Farrell waved a hand dismissively. "Oh, come on. I was a model child."

Lainey laughed. "Practically a saint." She thought for a moment. "Like when you climbed out of the window at three in the morning to meet Larry Johanson in eighth grade? Or how about when you drove into New York City on a junior license and picked up that doorman from the little bistro on Second Avenue?" Lainey chose a red lipstick and evaluated the color against her face before she began applying it to her mouth.

"Gee," Farrell said, nostalgia in her voice. "Kenny Purcell. I'd forgotten all about him."

Lainey looked at her disapprovingly. "Don't sound so sentimental. That shocked even me. It's a wonder you weren't raped or killed or something."

Farrell reached for the hairbrush and ran it through her long brown hair. "I loved to shock you. I loved to shock myself, I think." And I still do, she thought.

Lainey got up and walked over to the window, peering out to observe a man and a woman leaving the house whose property bordered Farrell's from the back. She recognized Sugar and Helmut Taplinger, having met Farrell's neighbors once or twice. "But that wasn't the biggest surprise you ever handed me," she went on.

"No," Farrell said, coming up behind her. "That would have been junior year of college, right?"

Lainey nodded in agreement, easily recalling the phone call that had awakened her early one Saturday morning.

"You're marrying Mussolini!" Lainey had screamed into the phone when Farrell had announced her news.

"He's sweet and I love him," Farrell had replied, "and you're the maid of honor, so stop hollering and start shopping for a long pink dress. And never use that horrible nickname again, would you please?"

"It wasn't *my* nickname," Lainey had reminded her. "As I remember, it took you all of three minutes to call him that on your very first date."

"Well, if there were trains, he'd make them run on time, trust me. But let's forget all that. As of April twelfth, I'll be Farrell

Beckley Cole, adoring wife of John Cole. And you'll be the proud godmother of our six girls and six boys, whenever they choose to arrive."

Farrell looked at her friend, her expression serious. "You thought I was nuts getting married back then, didn't you?"

"Completely," Laincy agreed, laughing. Suddenly she noticed the intent look on Farrell's face. "Well," she amended hastily, "you turned out to be the big genius ... look at all this." She glanced around at the large room, its warmth and charm maximized by the antique iron bed, the matching loveseats covered in the deepest rose-colored silk, a hand-made throw flung casually over one arm, the wealth of pictures in heavy silver frames covering fifteen years in the life of a family. To Lainey, it seemed perfect.

Farrell's eyes were unexpectedly sad. "Not such a genius, really. Maybe just in a hurry."

"What do you mean?" Lainey asked.

"Oh, nothing," Farrell replied a little too brightly. "It's just sometimes I wonder why I settled into adulthood quite so quickly. As you know, even perfect suburban moms get occasional urges for the high life."

"According to my mother, you're already living the *ideal* life. 'Why can't you settle down like your friend Farrell?' I think you're the one she wishes she'd raised."

"She pretty much did raise me as I remember it." Farrell started walking to the bedroom door.

They both heard the doorbell and the sound of John welcoming the first guests, followed by a huge belly laugh that carried loudly up to the bedroom.

Farrell tensed. "That would be the Taplingers," she said quietly. "I've gotten kind of friendly with Sugar lately."

The bell was ringing again as they started downstairs.

"Hi, beautiful," Charlie Cole called out to Farrell as he walked into the house and handed his coat to his brother.

Farrell waved to him, then exchanged knowing smiles with her husband when she saw the woman standing next to Charlie. The brunette must have been at least six feet tall, and was slender as a willow.

"John and I had a bet, and it looks like I've won," Farrell whispered to Lainey just before they reached the bottom step. "I knew Charlie's last girlfriend wouldn't be around more than three weeks. John chose to believe Charlie when he claimed he'd finally fallen in love, but here he is with someone we've never seen before."

Lainey smiled. She'd first met Charlie at Farrell and John's wedding. John's younger brother was destined to be the handsomest man in just about any room. But he'd gotten into the kind of trouble he was forever trying to live down. At twenty-five, he'd been arrested for selling marijuana to some so-called friends, who turned out to be undercover police officers; he'd spent a year in prison.

Lainey moved off to one side, unable to shake the melancholy that had been with her since the evening began. Every man in the room seemed to remind her of Julian Kroll, the man she loved, the one man she'd never get to spend any holiday with. What would he be doing right now? she wondered, taking a seat on one of the matching white silk brocade couches. She envisioned him, dressed as he undoubtedly was in perfectly clean blue jeans or well-pressed chinos, his silky dark blond hair in a ponytail, his two little girls seated on his knee, hearing tales of Santa and Rudolph as his wife opened scores of presents at his knee. Then she imagined an explosion blowing the scene away.

Generous thoughts at Christmas, she reflected, forcing her attention back to the room. Farrell suddenly reappeared before her, sinking down to the carpet in front of Lainey in one graceful move.

"I've been making nice to my husband's business associates," she said with a sigh. "Have I stopped smiling yet?" she added facetiously. She lay her head back affectionately against her friend's knee. Farrell rubbed her temples for a few seconds as if ridding herself of a headache before reaching into the pocket of her dress and removing a tiny parchment card. On it was a caricature of a woman, obviously herself, sitting on a sunlit cloud borne by a handsome blond-haired man and two children, the boy the image of the man, the girl a dark likeness of her mother.

"It's the most beautiful card you've ever made me," she said, holding it up so its creator could appreciate it one more time. "Right now you don't quite look so sentimental. Exactly what are you conjuring up as you sit here watching my life flash before your eyes? Will my friends and neighbors show up on my next Christmas card?"

Lainey grinned. "Yes, you and your friends will be the angels circling the ceilings of heaven, while I'll be the one in uniform sweeping up the grounds, waving up to you and asking if you need anything to drink."

Farrell shook her head. "I think you're just watching so you can embarrass all of us next year with devastating caricatures of our most humiliating selves." Farrell allowed herself a tiny yawn, carefully hiding it from her other guests. "And by the way, exactly which parts of my existence suggest a visit to heaven? Driving Tim to basketball practice or picking up Riley from her computer class?" She raised an eyebrow as she saw her husband walking toward them, two fresh glasses of Perrier in his hands. "Or maybe the really heady part is being chained to sobriety by my much better half."

"I don't chain you to anything, darling," John Cole said, easing himself into a chair. "I simply keep you informed of where the straight and narrow is so you can follow it if you choose to."

Farrell gave him an odd look, then pushed up off the rug and slid into his lap, her hands affectionately messing his hair. "Who could be straighter and narrower than Mrs. John Cole, mother of two, grande dame of Meadowview, Connecticut?" She pinched an invisible bulge on her upper thigh, then raised her hand as if in horror at what it had found. "Well, perhaps there are those who are narrower."

Lainey's skeptical look said it all. "Fair is Farrell, lovely as a reed. Hear my passion, and please, please heed my need."

"Jesus, Lainey," Farrell laughed loudly. "How on earth did you remember that?"

"Please say you didn't write it yourself," John said, obviously appalled.

"The poetry," Lainey explained, "is courtesy of Fred Cioffi. Written, as I remember, in study hall. It was probably the only ten-minute period in Fred's sophomore year at New Rochelle High School during which he was paying full attention to the paper in front of him."

"I believe I rewarded him amply for those ten minutes." Farrell laughed at the memory, but stopped when she noticed the expression on her husband's face.

"Much as I hate to interfere with the 'Oh, to be a teenage girl again' hour, I have guests to attend to." He stood, gently pushing Farrell off his lap and depositing her on the chair. "We're running out of ice, if you two would like a more current project to keep you busy. We're down to the last bag." They watched him walk away.

"Poor John." Farrell looked dolefully at Lainey.

"He has nothing to worry about. After all, if you'd wanted to remain the old you, you wouldn't have married him. Right?"

No, wrong, Farrell thought, her stomach clenching in fear. Abruptly, she realized that Lainey was waiting for an answer. She tried to sound as casual as possible as she responded.

"The old me wouldn't have been hostessing this party; she would've been seduced and abandoned in some hovel in a foreign country looking forward to letters from you, describing parties like this."

Lainey shook her head. "Without the new you, I wouldn't be attending parties like this. Besides, you weren't exactly a scarlet woman. You just liked to have a good time."

"What are you two whispering about?" Sugar Taplinger plunked her large body down on the couch next to Lainey.

Farrell looked away, her expression curiously guarded.

"Farrell and I are reliving her wild youth," Lainey replied.

"And what were *you* doing all that time, Lainey?" Sugar asked.

"Oh, mostly envying Farrell, if I remember correctly."

"Mostly thinking I was an idiot," Farrell interjected.

"Well, that too." She smiled briefly. "Truly, though, I was fascinated by your courage. That has never been my strong suit."

Farrell laughed. "Oh, you're courageous enough. That is, when you decide what it is you want to do. It just takes you about a hundred years to make that decision." She raised one eyebrow meaningfully.

"What decision are we talking about here?" Sugar turned her attention to Lainey.

Lainey just smiled. "Nothing that monumental, I promise. Although we'd better see about getting some more ice before John decides to fire us both."

Farrell stood up, stretching her hand to Lainey's and pulling her up as well. "Yeah, nothing monumental. Just what to do with her life, whether or not to have children, whether or not to get married."

Lainey shot her a warning look. That Julian Kroll would never leave his wife was not a subject she felt comfortable discussing in front of Sugar. "So, Farrell, will a supermarket or a liquor store be open on a Saturday night, or will we have to forage for ice someplace else?"

"I've got a ton of ice in the freezer," Sugar offered. "Let yourself in and take as much as you want. Now, if you'll excuse me, I'm going to force Charlie Cole to dance with me. Your brother-in-law is the most attractive man I've seen since the tight end I dated at Penn State."

She got to her feet and looked toward John's brother, who was lounging against a doorframe, visibly bored as his niece and nephew tried to engage him in conversation.

"Poor Riley," Farrell said as she watched Sugar extract Charlie from the children and engage him in a spirited fox trot. "She's undoubtedly trying to fill her uncle in on her adventures with the Internet. It's amazing, you know. Somewhere in Denmark a fifteen-year-old computer whiz has a profound relationship with my seven-year-old daughter. They exchange e-mail and faxes about a hundred times a day. Erik or Ulrich—I can never tell which name is coming out of Riley's mouth—evidently has no idea of Riley's age, and on the advice of her savvy older brother, Riley isn't letting that information out." They rounded the corner into the enormous kitchen. "My greatest fear is that one of these days, some Danish teenager is going to arrive for an unannounced vacation in the United States and break my little girl's heart when he finds out his best international friend has been out of diapers for only a little over four years."

"Who's in diapers?" Riley's voice surprised them.

"Riley," Farrell said, wheeling around to see her near the refrigerator, "isn't it time you were getting ready for bed?"

"We're helping Mrs. Miles with the trays."

Farrell looked over to where her older child was removing canapes from a large silver tray to his mouth almost as quickly as the white-haired maid was setting them down.

"Tim, both of you"—she included the little girl in her gaze—"let Mrs. Miles do her work, and get to sleep."

"With all these people in the house . . . come on, Mom."

Tim picked up a tiny eclair and lobbed it over to Lainey, who caught it easily in one hand. "Thanks, sport."

"Please don't encourage them, Lainey," Farrell said, walking over to Tim and wiping his hand on a paper napkin. "When you go to Lainey's for the weekend, you can have food fights all night long for all I care."

"Come on now, guys," Lainey said. "Time to get upstairs. We're out of here, anyway. We have to go over to Sugar's house to get some more ice."

"We'll go over there for you," Tim piped up, coming to stand near his mother.

Farrell leaned down and kissed him on the cheek before heading to the door.

Once back inside Farrell's house with a fresh supply of ice, Lainey wandered through to the living room. She noticed a crush of people, whispering and looking over each other's shoulders, abuzz with excitement.

"Alanna Hayden just walked in," a pleasant-looking man in his thirties whispered to Lainey.

That *had* to be Penn's date, Lainey thought derisively. How very perfect. With a theatrically late entrance, the great Pennington Beckley had finally condescended to arrive at his sister's little party. And, of course, the sophisticated, international news producer would have to have as his date the gorgeous superbrain who covered Congress on the evening news.

Well, it's nice to know some things remain the same, Lainey thought ironically, making her way to the buffet table. Penn Beckley, five years older than Farrell and Lainey, had been the apple of every eye—his parents, his schoolmates, the football and basketball coaches, his teachers, even the Yale expert on constitutional issues who'd lectured his Problems in American Democracy class when he was a senior in high school.

"Keep an eye on that one!" the visiting professor had whispered to the teacher, a remark that made its way back to the entire Beckley family by early the same afternoon.

It had always seemed so unfair to Lainey, who visited the Beckley house almost daily all through her childhood. Everything Farrell did needed "fixing," or "improving" or "toning down," one of Mrs. Beckley's favorite expressions regarding her rebellious younger child. But Penn, ah, Penn, was perfection, his life oh so charmed. As young as she'd been, Lainey could see his parents' pride every time he entered the room. Behold the future senator, president, emperor, they seemed to think as he lifted a glass of milk or tied his shoelaces.

Lainey reached for a plate and placed an assortment of vegetables on it. Her hip rested against the table as she chewed a carrot stick thoughtfully. It wasn't just the unfairness that had bothered her all those years ago; it was the fact that Farrell never seemed bothered at all. She adored her brother, didn't seem to resent one minute of the attention showered upon him. To be fair,

Lainey realized, Penn had never been anything but kind to his little sister. And the truth of it was, every now and then, Lainey would watch him from the sidelines, guiltily admiring his longish dark hair, the deeply set, almost black eyes that had girls from his classes calling him every night of the week.

But whatever schoolgirl crush she might have harbored had been more than erased by his constant sniping at her. Sure, he was kind to his sister, but he was horrible to Lainey. She could still remember her embarrassment at the scene he caused when she wore her first cashmere sweater in seventh grade. *Elvira Flatigan,* he'd yelled from the kitchen as Lainey walked upstairs toward Farrell's bedroom. She'd run into the room and slammed the door behind her, waiting to die of shame.

Sometimes he'd eavesdrop on their most intimate conversations, never hesitating to tease Lainey about her shyness.

"Why don't you just go up to that jerk and ask him to dance?" he'd once exploded as he overheard her pour out her heart to Farrell about Stevey Roth paying no attention to her at a Friday night mixer in the junior high school gym.

"What a surprise, seeing you here without a date."

The sound of Pennington Beckley's sarcastic words almost made her drop her plate. Screw you, she thought, keeping her face impassive as she turned to look at him.

"And what a surprise watching the crowds ogle the date you picked to impress the *pauvres citoyens* in their hopelessly provincial suburb." Lainey smiled sweetly as she tossed a raspberry into her mouth

He eyed her disagreeably. "Your French is magnificent, I'm sure, but I happen to have been stationed in London for the past three years. Perhaps you could abuse me in a Cockney accent. It might have a *soupçon* more punch."

The response was quick, but the words came out slightly slurred and his gait was unsteady as he walked the length of the table and eyed the spread of food with seeming distaste.

"I see you've already drunk your Christmas dinner," Lainey murmured.

"And eating Christmas dinner alone must be so very comforting for you," he replied acidly. "I'm glad to see that faced with a roomful of people, you still choose to stand here by yourself."

Lainey felt her face redden. "Perhaps if my parents had kissed my hem and invited an audience every time I brushed my teeth, I, too, would have the world eating out of my hand."

* * *

Farrell lingered in front of the house as the last of her guests got into their cars. She watched Lainey climb into the back of Carol Anne and J.J. Gisondis' battered station wagon. The couple was giving Lainey a lift to the train station. Carol Anne had stopped to say goodnight to the Hornbys, a couple whose son was in little league with theirs.

Could it be true? Farrell wondered, remembering what Sugar had told her about Carol Anne earlier that week. Could she really be doing *that*?

The last cars began to pull away, people still calling to each other through their open car windows. A sense of familiarity overwhelmed Farrell. It was all so normal, the ongoing flow of their well-ordered lives.

Slowly, the undercurrent of fear that had been there all night threatened to turn into sheer terror. She shivered. John came up behind her, and she burrowed into his arms.

"We'd better get you inside," he said, kissing her briefly on the cheek.

But Farrell just stood as she was, turning her head to look up into her husband's face, his blond hair slightly windblown, his cheeks reddened by the cold. He's so solid, she thought, drinking him in, appreciating for the umpteenth time the straight line of his jaw, the ease with himself he'd had even as a college student.

Suddenly she knew she was about to make the biggest mistake of her life.

Plan your summer dream vacation with the

⑦ Signet/Onyx ⊜

BOOKS THAT TAKE YOU ANYWHERE YOU WANT TO GO Contest

GRAND PRIZE $5,000 in CASH!
3 – 1st Prizes $1,000 in CASH!
25 – 2nd Prizes $100 in CASH!

To enter:

1. Answer the following question: **WHY WAS THIS BOOK THE IDEAL SUMMER READ?**
2. Write your answer on a separate piece of paper **(in 25 words or less)**
3. Include your name and address (street, city, state, zip code)
4. Send to: **BOOKS THAT TAKE YOU ANYWHERE YOU WANT TO GO** Contest P.O. Box 844, Medford, NY 11763

Official Rules:

1. To enter, hand print your name and complete address on a piece of paper (no larger than 8-1/2" x 11") and in 25 words or less complete the following statement: "Why Was This Book The Ideal Summer Read?" Staple this form to your entry and mail to: BOOKS THAT TAKE YOU ANYWHERE YOU WANT TO GO Contest, P.O. Box 844, Medford, NY 11763. Entries must be received by December 15, 1995 to be eligible. Not responsible for late, lost, misdirected mail or printing errors.

2. Entries will be judged by Marden-Kane, Inc. an independent judging organization in conjunction with Penguin USA based upon the following criteria: Originality 35%, Content 35%, Sincerity 20%, and Clarity 10%. By entering this contest entrants accept and agree to be bound by these rules and the decision of the judges which shall be final and binding. All entries become the property of the sponsor and will not be acknowledged or returned. Each entry must be the original work of the entrant.

3. PRIZES: Grand Prize (1) $5,000.00 cash; First Prize (3) each winner receives $1,000.00 cash; Second Prize (25) each winner receives $100.00 cash. Total prize value $10,500.00.

4. Contest open to residents of the United States 18 years of age and older, except employees and the immediate families of Penguin USA, its affiliates, subsidiaries, advertising agencies, and Marden-Kane, Inc. Void in FL, VT, MD, AZ, and wherever else prohibited by law. All Federal, state, and local laws and regulations apply. Winners will be notified by mail and may be required to execute an affidavit of eligibility and release which must be completed and returned within 14 days of receipt, or an alternate winner will be selected. Taxes, if any, are the sole responsibility of the prize winners. All prizes will be awarded. Limit one prize per contestant. Winners consent to the use of their name and/or photograph or likeness for advertising/publicity purposes without additional compensation (except where prohibited).

5. For a list of winners available after January 31, 1996 include a self-addressed stamped envelope with your entry.

Be sure to read all the ideal summer books from Signet/Onyx:

INSOMNIA
Stephen King

BLESSING IN DISGUISE
Eileen Goudge

THE BURGLAR WHO TRADED TED WILLIAMS
Lawrence Block

DEADLY PURSUIT
Brian Harper

NIGHT SHALL OVERTAKE US
Kate Saunders

FIRST OFFENSE
Nancy Taylor Rosenberg

JUSTICE DENIED
Robert K. Tanenbaum

ONLY YOU
Cynthia Victor

THICKER THAN WATER
Linda Barlow and
William G. Tapply

FIRM AMBITIONS
Michael A. Kahn

Signet ⊘ Onyx⊜
Printed in the USA